Primal Power

OUT OF THE BLUE

To Maxine

Thank-you beautiful lady!

Linn FRANCES

i

For permissions, contact:
primalpowerproductions@gmail.com

Editors:

First Editor	*P. Todd*
Second Editor	*T. Smith*
Third Editor	*H. Scharfenberger*
Forth Editor	*P. Todd*
Fifth Editor	*H. Scharfenberger*
Final Editor	*P. Todd*
Graphic Designer	*Brand On Designs*
	www.brand-on-designs.com
Photography	*Rick Walls*
	www.polishedpixel.ca
Art	*Linn Frances*

First Edition August 2019

ISBN 978-1-7753760-1-9

Table of Contents

Watch for Linn Frances' next book,
"Primal Power 3 –The Face In The Waterfall"

Prologue

Previously in <u>Primal Power -The Unripe Apple,</u> Princess had walked through a wall and found herself in another world or another dimension, she was not sure. Comparatively to her new world she was very small and soon there after was asked to share a nest with a bird. The bird asked her to gather an apple, but the only apple she found was unripe and bruised.

The bird gathered other birds to take her through a water-fall where she met an otter, whom she called Rainbow Dancer. She gave her apple to The Empress, went in and out of Ol' Man Gar Cave and ended up being saved by a village of wonderful people. It was there where she met a four eared little person named Ooza.

Princess found herself having to look at her patterns before she could enter The Land of the Shimmering Bridge where her size changed and she became Thee Trusted One to Queen Chayzlazamia. Ooza had other plans and Princess began a new journey, helping the Rofonians with their battle against the humans.

In this book <u>Primal Power - Out of The Blue,</u> Princess wakes up not sure of where she is, but remembering bits and pieces of her life after she had walked through the wall. This new journey takes her on a winding road through colourful orbs, sweet burning trees, crystal wands and into a world of lost children.

Lost in the blue with a hard new friend, Princess experiences unexpected twists, turns, miracles and transformations.

Continuing the journey of <u>The Unripe Apple,</u> she gets a new understanding of this new world.. She obtains many insights about yesterday's life on the earthly plain as well as realizing that a very important aspect of life had been misunderstood.

Acknowledgements

First and foremost, I would like to thank my family, which includes my wonderful Luna, for many, many things ie: encouragement, support, patience, input, meals, editing, listening, tech support and keeping the home fires burning while I embarked on this journey.

To my friends and to my music friends, I would like to thank you for all the encouragement, advice, knowledge and inspiration because it was all instrumental in bringing this book to completion.

I would like to thank Sherry D. for her knowledge of the crystal world and her encouragement. Also, I would like to thank the many other friends, acquaintances and strangers along the way that loved my first book and wanted to know when my second one would be finished. I want you to know that your kind words have helped me more than you could possibly realize.

A special thanks goes to my close friends and family who walked with me during this journey, reading, listening, and believing in me. An extra thanks goes out to Tami, Linda, Peter, and Hillu for their editing and for being the amazing people they are. Also for reading my manuscript and expressing their kind words.

An extra special thanks goes out to Brandon, my Graphic Designer, who did a fantastic job on both my covers! He was a pleasure to work with and went above and beyond the call of duty. I am not sure anyone would be reading my books if it wasn't for his belief, research, work, and stamina to see it through.

Authors note

One day I went to a place in a meditation or maybe it was in the dream world, I wasn't sure. However, when I awoke to this world I was in awe of my experiences and wanted to write them down. To my surprise I didn't stop writing for a long, long time. This is a continuation of my journey into other worlds. A journey which helped me understand so much of what I had gone through in my life here on this Earth. To me, it is not merely fictional, but instead a spirit quest fantasy.

I am thankful for all the love and guidance from those who are in this world and those who are no longer of this world. _Primal Power – The Unripe Apple_ has already taken some people on a journey of different characters and perspectives. If _Primal Power – Out of the Blue_ does the same, then I have succeeded in giving a gift.

Presently, I have been truly blessed because my first book has also helped some people find peace with a part of their journey, thus they have given me a gift. If my second book helps someone else, I will be thankful, honoured and truly blessed.

Primal Power

OUT OF THE BLUE

LINN FRANCES

Chapter 1 - The Awakening

When I first came to this world I saw a woman so powerful she could orbit a moon and a planet above her hand. Then she spoke in a soft soothing voice and said, *'It is the continuance of time and power of persisting. It is the creative and thus the creative are often those that seek it.'* Recently, she said I was her visitor and I was her responsibility.

Now, this same woman was shining a light so bright I was not sure if she was still there. All I could see were colours, tones, and hues. There... there she is, wise and beautiful; her long, flowing wavy hair dancing with each shade.

She had taken on the role of a prism that reflected each colour as we transcended higher and higher. Looking down I could see her hand. I was small enough to be cradled in it, but I was levitating above it, my body shimmering, absorbing the tones with each new height.

Travelling through the seemingly infinite shades we reached a colour that I recognized within the rainbow spectrum of my yesterday's world. Where was she taking me? I thought she was returning my body to the forest where I had been shot.

Had she already done that? Was she taking my soul or was this part of the journey and she was taking me to a place where my soul could leave my body before she returned it to the forest in the Rofonian Nation?

Oh my, now we have become enveloped in a silver white light. There were wings upon wings, all flying as if they were waiting for the angels to come and claim them.

Transcending even higher, everything turned gold and became wondrously peaceful. Was I dead? Was I still levitating? I could no longer make out the contours of her face or her body.

She was now an illuminated golden being. She had a form, but no detail and I was now cradled, carried in a palm of golden light. I could hear music, soothing, uplifting and in perfect pitch. Where was I? Had I gone to heaven?

Then everything went purple. It wasn't a blinding purple, no, it was more like a hazy dark purple that sometimes would be clear enough for me to see the golden wings. Other times it felt as if I was staring into a pearl or maybe it was an opal shaped like a pearl. The haze would swirl around it and clear again. It was rather large and I felt myself wrapping around it or was I absorbing it? Was I becoming one with the pearl? Oh my, what was happening to me?

Everything went silent and then I could hear music again, but this time it sounded similar to a guitar. Something had changed, it was different. Where was I?? I could feel my eyelashes fluttering, finally my eyes opened.

"She has awakened!"

The music stopped and there was my human friend Peter, with his trusting blue eyes and straight blond hair, looking both excited and relieved. There was my other human friend Gorph, smiling an almost goofy smile that seemed fitting with his white and black hair.

Of course, there was my Ooza, my wonderful little four eared friend in the princely garments that Queen Chayzlazamia had tailored for him. His hair stood straight up and his lips were almost in a pout with his hands placed one on top of the other resting upon his chest.

Peter took my hand and I had to ask, "Where am I?"

"You were shot, Princess, you're in a hospital," said Ooza with an expression of distress as if it had just happened.

"But the lady with the golden brown hair, she took me to heaven. I could hear the angels and then I was in the palm of a light-being. I don't understand," and then I closed my eyes.

Voices! I could hear voices and then I couldn't. I would hear them again and sometimes I could hear music. My eyes opened again. This time I looked around the room; it seemed to be made of different coloured stones.

"This isn't a hospital," I stated, trying to figure out where I was. "I thought I had heard Ooza's voice telling me I had been shot and I was in a hospital."

Peter was speechless for a moment before he said, "Ooza told you that two days ago. You were in a hospital then and you still are. You're at The Rofonia Naroso Hospital."

"But, but the walls... the stones?"

"Yes, it's the Rofonians' way. They are to help you heal."

My brain still felt slow and I asked, "How did I get here?"

"I'm not really sure and we can talk about that later," he said, "What's important now is how you are feeling."

"I'm fine. I'm sorry."

"Sorry?" Peter questioned. "What are you sorry for?"

"I... I... I don't know. I... I... didn't mean to worry anyone."

"You're awake and that's all that matters. You have nothing to be sorry for. Can I get you anything?"

"No, thank-you, I'm... I... just want to know how I got here."

"Okay, I'll tell you what I know. On the day the Rofonians were throwing pine cones at the clones...," he started, but then he stopped and asked, "Do you remember that?"

I searched until I could see that day in my mind's eye. I was standing on a road beside Rainbow Dancer, my giant otter.

"I think so. Rainbow Dancer? He's okay isn't he?" I answered with a slight movement of my head.

Peter smiled, "He's okay, he wasn't hurt. He's gone for a swim, do you want me to go get him?"

"No, no, tell me about that day, the last thing I remember was standing in the middle of the road."

"Good, yes, you were standing on the road when you got shot," Peter said softly. "Ooza came to get me and told me you had been shot and asked me to find a human doctor. I wanted to take you with me, down the mountain to the hospital. I got in my truck and went to the road in the forest where you were. I stopped and I looked at you. Something was happening. It was really weird and I cannot describe it, it was just... weird."

"Try," I said gently.

He shook his head as if he was trying to shake his memory into a logical place. "A man in a purple robe was standing beside you, but the truth of it is, the whole thing seemed kind of surreal," Peter said slowly. "The robed man said to me, '*You are on a mission.*' '*Mission?*' I questioned. Then I told him I was supposed to be going to town to find a doctor. The robed man merely said, '*Yes. Go now. Trust yourself. Trust your mission*'. So I went to my truck and when I turned around, the man in the purple robe was no longer there, neither were you.

Princess, like I said, it was weird. I must have really been traumatized by you being shot and just thought I saw him." Peter shook his head, focused on me again and continued, "It must have been just a weird state of mind. I... I... I am... I'm just so glad you are awake and talking to me now."

Tears rolled down Peter's cheeks.

"Peter, I think the message was to trust yourself and trust you were helping," Ooza said, speaking English and rolling his R's and then in Rofonian, he continued, "Shimmering you were, Princess. Disappeared you did several times. Reminded me of Queen Chayzlazamia, only disappear I never saw her do. Turning into a shimmering angel, that is what I thought. Know I didn't, if I would ever see you again." Ooza didn't continue in his language, but instead he stretched his bottom lip as if in agony and in English, he finished, "It was scary, Princess. I was very, very scared."

"Yeah," Peter said with a nod and then nodded again, "Yeah, I must have just been really scared and so I went into town..."

"Town?" I interjected, trying desperately to bring myself out of my sleepy haze, "Yes, right, the black and white city."

Everyone stared at me for a moment and then Gorph smiled and gave me the thumbs up before he said, "Yeah, the black and white city." He tapped his thumb on the side of his head and finished with, "Just like my hair."

With concerned smiles, everyone simply stared at me.

"Please continue telling me what happened," I said, squeezing Peter's hand.

4

"Well when I picked up my neighbour (a retired surgeon and who was a friend of my grandfather's) I must have seemed desperate and in shock. The whole time I was convincing him to come with me I wondered if you'd even be there. The robed man's words kept going over in my head, '*Trust your mission*'.

Anyway, while I was getting the doctor, Gorph got a hold of his buddy who drove an ambulance. They brought a stretcher, but when we arrived back on the mountain you weren't there.

My first thought was that you disappeared, but that was ridiculous. Somehow the Rofonians, whose heads don't even reach your knees brought you to their hospital. We don't know how that happened and no one would tell us. When we arrived at the hospital we saw a lady, a human, I think, but I have never seen anyone who looked like her. She had long, golden brown hair and she was with you when we arrived."

"That must have been her, but I thought she was taking me to heaven," I whispered.

"Oh Princess, we are in heaven," Ooza said, raising his hands above his head and looking up. "We are here with my people. This is our heaven and I am a Rofonian."

That's right, he came through the portal with me and just recently learned that there were people who were like him.

Ooza patted his chest with both of his hands and continued, "Being Rofonian warms my heart, but I wouldn't be here if it wasn't for you. I am so glad you are awake. Ooza was really scared and my people... they looked scared and looked even more scared when they saw the ambulance. I have seen lots of humans and ambulances, but not them," added Ooza.

Then in his language, he said, "That lady, a goddess or an angel she was. Important, you must be, Princess." He spoke in English again, "I asked Scota where the lady came from and Scota said the same thing about her as she said about you."

"What was that?" I asked.

"A request for her was given and apparently, she arrived."

"Huh," I said, at least I think that was all I said, for it was taking every bit of strength to concentrate.

Peter continued, "I guess Scota knew her. I didn't know they knew any other humans, but I didn't know about you either. Anyway, she and my neighbour operated on you."

My mind was swirling with information and memories. I didn't know whether Scota had met the golden-haired woman before. However, I did know I was on another planet when I had met her. At least I think so. I knew that Ooza and I left the Land of the Shimmering Bridge and arrived here. I don't think I ever told Peter who I was or where I was from. No, I couldn't have, because then he would have known I had only arrived with Ooza shortly before he and I met.

Gorph and I met Raziel, not at the same time, however we both knew him, but Peter wouldn't have known who the purple robed man was. Nor would he have known that Raziel could appear wherever he was needed. The woman with the golden hair brought my body back as she said she would and then she appeared as a doctor and brought my life back and now....

Ooza interrupted my thoughts, "I knew you would be all right Princess," he said as he wiggled his head, stretched his neck, and puckered his lips, "as soon as I saw that golden haired doctor, I just knew."

"Me too, as soon as I saw her, I knew I was I going to be okay, one way or the other." My voice felt very weak and I closed my eyes.

The rest of the week was spent sleeping. I would wake up sometimes alone and stare at all the beautiful stones. Other times people were there holding my hand, encouraging me to eat a little food. Sometimes Peter, Gorph, or both were playing their guitar-like instruments.

Chapter 2 - Supporting News

When I was awake enough they informed me it was Samuel Evans who shot me. The Rofonians had him in custody. The humans wanted him back. Peter had driven into the black and white city and talked to a Judge. Apparently Peter asked the Judge if a Rofonian went to the black and white city and shot someone, would that Rofonian be allowed to come back to the Rofonian Nation before they knew if it was murder or not?

The Judge saw Peter's point of view and the decision allowing Samuel to stay on the Rofonians' mountain was made. It would be revisited once they knew if I was going to live or die.

Gorph told me about his concert. I was sad I had missed it, but thankful I was alive. Hearing and being a support to Gorph was important to me and I hoped he knew that. It thrilled me greatly when Gorph played me his new song.

Let me tell you a story
of a nation of people
who live on our planet
a planet that was once
their own
a planet that was once
their own

You can run through the valley
without a care in the world
Which is fine to do when all is right
but sometimes you just got to
stop
turn around and say
hey that's wrong
and sing your song

We believe in justice
We believe in fairness
We believe in doing what's right
So just
Stop
Turn around

Let me continue a story
of a nation of people
who registered a plan
for their land
on a planet that was once
their own
on a planet that was once
their own

(chorus)

Let me finish my story
of a nation of people
who are not asking much
but just to live on their land
on a planet that was once
their own
on a planet that was once
their own

Gorph's song triggered me to what had been happening before I had been shot. The Rofonians could be in huge trouble!

"I hope the concert created some support," he said as he put his guitar down. "I told them about how a greedy company was trying to destroy their land. Gave a speech about how wonderful the Rofonians were. People cheered. That's a good sign." Raising his finger in the air, he danced away saying, "I'll be right back."

A few minutes later Gorph brought in a wheelchair and stated, "You're gonna need it if you want to go to court."

Court, they're going to take me to court? My mind went back to the conversation I heard while staring into the turquoise (I don't know how else to describe it because at that time it was all I could see). I remember the High Priestess saying that I wasn't from this world so I wouldn't be able to be sworn in.

Gorph seemed confused. "Thought chu'd be happy," he said. "If you're not feeling well enough you don't have to go."

"No, it's not that. I just don't think I'm supposed to be there."

"Why not?"

"Will I have to talk? Will I have to be sworn in?" I asked.

"Nope. I've spoken to both Raziel and Ooza." He rocked his body and wagged his finger. "This time you get to observe."

"Raziel? Raziel said I could go and observe?" I questioned.

"That's right," he said with a nod.

"I've always been curious about how you and Raziel met, I bet that's a story and a half," I said with a smile.

Gorph seemed to be going through various emotions as he rocked back and forth, then said, "That it is. That it is." He pointed his finger in the air like an old professor questioning a student. "But what I want to know is how you know?"

His question confused me so I asked, "How I know Raziel?" Gorph nodded so I continued, "Umm, well," I thought back to the cabin he created and said, "I just met him on my journey."

"But how'd you know I met him on my journey?" Gorph said, pointing to his chest with both of his index fingers.

"Right before Raziel and I parted our ways, he looked into the future for me. He said things like 'purple stones will keep me straight' and the last thing he said about the future was 'Gorph, music' and that he had known you a long time ago."

"Huh, so that's all you know about me."

"Yeah," I said smiling and nodding at him, "Odd, when I met you, I was questioning myself whether or not I had veered off course, but obviously I hadn't."

"And that was the last thing he said about your future?"

"Yeah, it was," I said with a bit of sadness, "guess from here on in, I will have to trust that I'm being looked after."

Gorph just laughed, "That you are, Princess, that you are."

On the day of court Gorph and Peter both had trucks and the Rofonians and I travelled with them down the mountain. At the top of the hill we noticed a building outlined in black, with a white front. The big black letters stated, 'The Courthouse'.

Gorph and Peter pulled their trucks up to the bottom of the stairs. It was a very busy place for a courthouse as there had to be at least a hundred humans standing outside.

It had stairs ascending to two black doors and beside the stairs was a ramp. It looked like a small road with switch-backs. Gorph and Peter went to the back of Peter's truck to grab a set of stairs, built especially for the Rofonians to get down from the truck with dignity and ease. The risers of the courthouse steps were too high for them to climb and remain dignified, thus it was going to be a fair trek up the ramp.

As we started our trek humans approached, all wearing T-shirts with printing on the front that said, '*We support Rofonia Naroso*' and Gorph's band label on the back.

Finally reaching the doors, we entered with Peter leading the way carrying a large briefcase. Twenty, approximately two foot tall, straight backed with hair going upwards, pointed eared Rofonians, all walking side by side, followed behind. In in the rear was Gorph pushing my chair and to our surprise, be-hind us, were the humans parading their shirts.

Chapter 3 - Deciding Fate

Walking into court (not unlike the courtrooms of my yesterday's world) Peter laid on the bench, what appeared to be, a briefcase, but it was actually hinged together black mirerasen. The Rofonians' had tables and houses made of the same metal.

Two Rofonians unfolded it until it formed a long rectangular shape with a top, a bottom, and two sides at either end. Attaching braces where it was hinged they placed a long narrow piece in front. As the final step, they unfolded stairs for the rest to climb to the new tiered black bench. Now they could sit high enough to see the Judge and the Judge could see them.

Sitting at the front table was Gerald and a few of his clones. They were from the company trying to mine the Rofonians' land. Beside them was a woman whom I assumed was their lawyer. All were suited in proper court attire. Oddly, Peter, Gorph, an unknown fellow, and I were the only other humans without support T-shirts on.

The Judge arrived. The humans stood and the Rofonians stood on their mirerasen riser. We were told to sit. The Judge then asked who was representing the Rofonia Naroso Nation.

Peter stood and gave a slight bow, "I am Peter Coplanden. I look after the watchtower on the Rofonia Nation."

The Judge asked him to clarify whether it was The Rofonia Nation or Rofonia Naroso.

Peter responded with, "Naroso in English means nation."

The Judge questioned, "So it is one or the other, not both?"

"Yes, that is correct."

The Judge then went back to his original question. Peter informed him the Rofonians would be representing themselves. The Judge seemed disappointed and told us that it was proper procedure in his courtroom to have representation.

A man, who was wearing one of Gorph's support shirts, stood up and introduced himself as James Lawsmon. He told the Judge he was a member of the bar and could represent the

Rofonians if His Honour would feel more comfortable.

The Judge responded with, "Proper representation is important in my Court and as you should know, so is proper attire."

The Judge remained patient while Ooza translated to Scota. She merely studied James Lawsmon for a few moments and then she nodded.

"This court will be adjourned until this afternoon. I am trusting that will allow enough time to become familiar with this case and attain proper attire?"

It was agreed and Court was adjourned until afternoon, so Ooza, Scota, Peter and I could bring our lawyer up to speed

"We appreciate what you are doing, but there are also some concerns about you representing them," I stated.

"I know this Judge. He's a stickler for procedure and he was not happy that his courtroom was filled with people wearing shirts with logos trying to influence his decision. He resents a layman without representation, but that being said he is usually fair. I am assuming you have your case all laid out?"

"And your bill? The Rofonians do not want to be indebted and will reward you with a gift, but we do not deal with human currency," Ooza said after speaking with Scota.

"That is the least of my worries," he said with a smile. He had a surprisingly kind smile for a lawyer. "Right now, I know very little about a case that is being heard in couple of hours."

James Lawsmon listened intently to Peter and Ooza before he spoke, "You seem to have the case in order, I'm impressed. My duty is to please the Judge by being the one who calls people to the stand. I'll do my best to prevent their lawyer from tricking or harassing anyone and if I find something irrelevant to the case, I'll call it, if the Judge doesn't."

That afternoon Court was back in session. Several supporters returned, but in outfits the Judge would approve of.

The company stated that humans live here now and should have the right to mine wherever they wish. All mineral rights should belong to the humans. They had the audacity to include that when they went up the mountain to check on their mining sites they were assaulted upon the road before reaching their destination. A human had been kidnapped and they were requesting a Court Order to have him released.

Rotopa was called to the stand and Ooza began to translate. The Judge could not hear Ooza so they moved him to a chair beside Rotopa where he could speak into the same microphone.

Our lawyer established that Rotopa had worked for thirty years reading maps and laying out roads. He recently verified all the stakes were there according to their registered Plan.

The unknown human, whom I had noticed in the morning, was called to the stand. He was from the humans' Registry Office (Peter had asked him to appear in court). He verified the land title had mineral rights and it had been officially registered on the date stamped upon both the Plan and the Title.

I passed a note to the lawyer and he called Fodulza (my Ooza) to the stand. The Judge leaned in towards him and was very kind. Maybe a little extra kindness was extended because not only did Ooza have an honest face and an innocence about him, he could also speak fluent English. Truth be told I did not know the reason, but the Judge seemed to be more engaged when he spoke to my Ooza.

With rolling R's Ooza said, "My grandfather signed the deal with the intention the land would always belong to the Rofonia Nation. One of my friends told me if a registered Plan was deemed invalid that could open up all the Plans in the humans' Registry Office to be invalidated. Is that true?" he asked.

"It is a point that I will definitely take it into consideration," the Judge said seriously and gave a nod.

James Lawsmon asked Ooza, "Did the Rofonians assault the humans when they went up the mountain?"

Ooza looked down and merely replied, "Sort of."

"Sort of," James Lawsmon repeated before asking, "What did you... sort of... assault them with?"

Fodulza bowed his head and with protruded lips answered, "Pine cones." He looked into the Judge's eyes and repeated, "We threw pine cones at them."

"Pine cones," repeated the Judge sounding amused.

Astutely James Lawsmon asked, "And what did the humans fight back with?"

The Judge's face dropped when Ooza sucked in his bottom lip before he said, "Guns." The Judge seemed to have both sadness and anger as Ooza continued with wide teary eyes, "They shot my friend and she is still not all better."

"Is the human who has allegedly been kidnapped the same person who shot your friend?" asked James Lawsmon.

"Yes."

"And was permission to keep him on the Rofonia Nation for the time being acquired through a judge from this city's court?" James Lawsmon asked.

Ooza looked at Peter.

Peter stood up and said, "Yes, Your Honour, I spoke to the Judge myself." He held up a piece of paper and was beckoned towards the bench. He walked up to the front, handed it to a person, who in turn handed it to the Judge.

Peter sat down and James Lawsmon addressed the Judge, "Your Honour, I would like to call one more witness."

The Judge agreed and Ooza lowered his head respectfully towards him, climbed down, and went back to his seat. My heart skipped a beat or two, oh my, I hope it is not me for I'm not from this world and.... Thankfully, he called Peter.

Peter introduced himself as the great grandson of the man who made the original deal. He showed the Judge some of his great grandfather's notes, showing the intent was to insure the Rofonians owned both the land and the mineral rights forever.

The company lawyer for the clones began her argument by saying that no human was alive to vouch for what actually happened. Therefore the original agreement should be null and void. Then she had the audacity to say this was a human court and the land agreement was not entered upon with two humans which also should automatically deem it invalid. The registry is a human registry and is there to protect the people - not little creatures. She ended the argument by asking for the Court to order the release of Samuel Evans.

James Lawsmon gave his final rebuttal reminding the Court a tentative agreement was already in place for the Rofonians to hold Samuel Evans. He also said that, according to the plaintiff's argument, if someone is taller or shorter than you or speaks a different language then they are not people. He asked if that was a precedent the court would want to set?

He ended his argument by saying the Rofonians had a plan stamped by the city's Registry and then repeated what Ooza had said about invalidating previous registered plans.

The Judge said Samuel Evans had committed a crime. He was not a Judge of criminal law therefore he could not make a decision either way on that particular matter.

The Judge also said he usually takes time to rule, but this case was straightforward. He addressed the plaintiffs and told them not to waste the Court's time again. He also told them that before they want to mine again to do their homework and find out who owns the land and who owns the mineral rights.

They also were prohibited from entering the Rofonia Naroso Territory for any reason and received a very hefty trespassing fine. They were ordered to extend a formal apology on behalf of the humans to the people of the Rofonia Nation.

Once we were outside the courthouse we heard humans singing,

...sometimes you just got to
stop
turn around and say
hey that's wrong
and sing your song...

Humans approached the Rofonians, but with a language barrier and the fact that they had probably never seen people that small, the exchange was awkward. They did look into each others eyes and saw kindness and that was a start - a start to finding common ground, hopefully a new beginning filled with respect and kindness.

Chapter 4 - *Reflections*

Once back up the mountain I was invited to attend celebrations, but instead I retreated to my room where I could allow tears to run down my face.

The raining tears were releasing all the sadness and stress from both this experience and the one I had in yesterday's world. Like every trauma in my life, I had to look at it, learn from it and release it so I would not repeat the same mistakes.

My previous experiences had left me with a lot of fear. Fear changes energy, which can change the outcome of a situation. I had done my best to keep that energy out of this equation.

As a child I believed what was reported in the media and factual books was the truth, but soon found out the difference. Yes, I guess in my naivety I held on to the belief that my country's court system was still built on fairness and justice.

I would like to think that the case I was involved with, in yesterday's world was isolated, however, talking to others, some working within the justice system, I discovered that, sadly, my experience seemed to be within the norm. Being innocent, truthful, in the right legally and morally doesn't seem to matter. Instead, too often it seems to be who can outsmart the other. If the world parented their children like that...?!?

If I do ever get to go back to Earth, I needed to dispel my naivety and find awareness within my innocence. Wouldn't that be nice. Wouldn't it be wonderful to live in a world where arrogance, greed, and revenge were deeply frowned upon.

Each step I took in life was preparation for the next. I guess as long as I continued persevering in what is right then I would be within the laws of the universe. Those were the laws that I wanted to live by and they were the ones that should be altering and shaping me. Was that why I had travelled through a portal to this new world? On that thought, I turned my focus towards the present. The Rofonians were respected while we were in court and perhaps that means this part of my journey is over.

Finding one of the gorgeous outfits Queen Chayzlazamia had given me, I got dressed, pleased I was finally able to stand on my feet at least for a few short moments. It is when one loses the use of one's body that one learns to appreciate the smaller things in life.

Peter knocked on my door asking to escort me to the celebrations. The timing was perfect for he did not have to wait.

We left the building, veered down a stone pathway, and came to a beautiful clearing. The trees were twinkling with lights, illuminating the outskirts of the glade. Had we entered a faerie land? It felt like one.

A blue tassin stage with black mirerasen surrounding the front bottom predominately stood to one side. The blue tassin floor was lit from underneath and gave the illusion that those on stage were dancing upon a calm blue sea.

When the music ended, Scota stood on stage and gave a speech concluding what we had just experienced. Ooza gave Peter and Gorph's band a translated written copy so they too could be part of this amazing experience. Ooza had even taken the time to write it down the way we would speak English and the speech read:

"Today, peace and security came to this world. Lands were united in harmony. Success has come on many levels. Experiences we recently have gone through were not only about the land. Rofonian and human eyes linked with love, correlated with justice, and therefore produced great harmony.

Each time that a great harmony is achieved it is the dawning of a new day. So tonight we are celebrating the *Great Harmony Sunrise* because motion and power has awakened, it has in turn created a movement in time.

We must remain in touch with the time that is dawning, for it is now more important than ever to always be aware of our integrity. We must learn from our differences but like every union, it is of utmost importance that we remain true to our nature. True greatness is not impaired by temptation, instead remains secure in a position that exerts a light-giving influence without effort.

So tonight let us move within that light and secure it deep within ourselves. Let the music begin."

The music and dancing resumed and Peter spun me around as I held onto one wheel, spinning my chair in half circles. Members of the Rofonia Nation had rides while Peter pushed the chair. Gorph's band played and he sang his new song and some of his other creations. The Rofonians also played their music. It had a chitty chitty chit tit tit in its background and all I could do was smile when I heard it. A good time was had by all and when it was over Peter brought me back to my room.

"Look Peter, I can stand," I said rising to say thank-you, but tiredness must have set in for I fell into his arms. There was a moment of connection between us. In my world, I believe it would be called chemistry. That slight breathlessness and desire soon turned to awkwardness as I plopped ungracefully back in my chair. I squeezed his hand, stared into his kind eyes, and thanked him for a wonderful evening.

The next day I went to a meeting. Ooza was there and I had to remember to call him Fodulza. Scota, Peter, and a Rofonian lady whom I didn't know, were attending the meeting as well. To my surprise, Gorph had also been asked to join. I was pleased my body was strong enough to stand and I placed myself upon a chair, this time, fairly gracefully.

"Feeling a little bit stronger today?" Peter asked with a sparkle in his eye.

"Yes, I am," I said, trying to ignore the flushed feeling in my cheeks. I looked at Scota and continued, "I'm so thankful for all you have done. You have gone above and beyond."

"Above and beyond, you have for us," Scota said with a nod, one hand upon her heart and the other arm in the air.

"Please remember we all do not speak the same language," Peter said with a hopeful look.

"There are some things you that just don't need to know," I responded from across the table with a teasing look. Grinning slightly, I bit my bottom lip.

Fodulza shrugged his shoulders and with his hands in the air he looked at Peter and me. He turned his palms towards the table, slowly brought them down and spoke in English, "Scota has called this meeting today to talk about Samuel Evans."

"Samuel Evans, at present in Idocrasia," Fodulza said, translating Scota's words.

Peter reached down and brought out a contraption. It looked as if it was a set of headphones with lots of wires attached.

"The court case might have brought us a gift. I found these when I was going through the old boxes. Siand Fodulza and my Great Grandfather must have used these for meetings, as they were in a box labelled 'Listening Devices for Rofonians' Meetings. Scota, do you know anything about them?"

Ooza translated what Peter had said and everyone looked very confused except for Scota who just looked curious. She excused herself from the meeting and came back shortly. With her was the bearded gentleman whom I had talked to on the first day the three of us met the Rofonians. The gentleman studied the contraption for a bit and proceeded to assemble it.

There were three antennas - one was placed behind one of Fodulza's pointed ears and two went behind the ears that looked similar to ours. Wires extended from the side feeding into, what appeared to be, hearing aids. Taking a wire, Gorph and Peter sat on either side of Fodulza and put on the hearing aids. Immediately thereafter, there was no language barrier.

"Meeting easier will be, thank-you," Scota said. "Gorph, welcome. Desire an even counsel, I did. Kindosa this is, teacher she is. Behaving with kindness, love, respect, expert she is. Children main focus. Guns, injuries, burst of uncontrolled anger happens not among our Nation. Preesons," she said, trying to pronounce the word 'prisons' that Peter had told her about, "here, not of need. Idocrasia we have."

"Idocrasia? Idocrasia will help? Isn't that a stone? I do not understand," Ooza Fodulza interjected.

"Stone it is made," answered Scota.

"He is in stone?" asked Ooza Fodulza as he brought his arms up and somehow tightened his bottom lip while straightening it at the same time as he squeezed in his top one. It was definitely a face that I had never seen before.

The bearded gentleman indicated he would like to be a part of this meeting and wear an ear-peice. He spoke and gestured more slowly than the others but the translation of words seemed more eloquent.

"Introductions are in order, I believe. Know who you all are, I do. I am Rotopa's father. Highly, Rotopa has spoken of you. David, your great grandfather, many cycles ago I met."

He turned his attention towards Ooza Fodulza and informed him his grandfather, Siand Fodulza had been a close friend.

He continued, "Idocrasia a room, made of stone it is. Over the cycles of time, the 'why' has been lost. Idocrasia found only in small amounts on this mountain. Plentiful on other.

Told it was, Siand Coltra, a wayward soul he was, full of much angst. Whether banished or fled he did, unknown it is. Lived on other mountain he did. When returned, changed he had. Siand Coltra revealed his higher-self to him talked.

Told he was this stone, a gift to our Naroso. Releases feelings of imprisonment trapped within. Anger dissolved when close to Idocrasia. Secure in himself he became. Talked about negativity that surrounded him he had. Lurked within he said it did. Due to his past lives he said. Time with stone all that gone it was. Mission became the stone bringing it to us. Carved rooms he did for wayward souls."

"There. Explained it is," Scota stated. "Samuel Evans food, water, and music he has. Similar he may be to Siand Coltra. When heart and mind disconnect, time is needed. Respectful he is to us. Too agitated mind still is to be any good.

Fodulza, a book he found with human words, teachings were good. Samuel Evans received book. Calmer he is now. Time has been long. Importance of court took priority. Princess's injury another priority. Told he was not, whether you, Princess, will live or die. Meeting called today to decide fate.

Samuel Evans sent to preeson in the human land? Samuel Evans stays here? The injury was yours," Scota focused on my eyes, " what is your request?"

Me, having the power to decide someone's fate?!? A power to play God?!? This wasn't who I was. I was on a journey. A strange one consisting of being different sizes, in different worlds, being shot, shimmering, disappearing, and now...! I should be thankful I was on a council and not alone.

I probably looked rather dumbfounded as I thought about a society where there wasn't a need for prisons. That didn't seem possible. Didn't they have wrongdoings? Were they simply born innately good? Was this Idocrasia such a miraculous stone that all anger was gone from an entire society? I must obtain more information before giving an opinion.

"If anyone transgresses against your rules, your laws, are they merely put in Idocrasia? Is that what you do to prevent it from happening again?" I asked Scota when I finally spoke.

To my surprise it was Kindosa who answered, "Children, when young, attend Respecia," she said in a soothing voice.

"Love, kindness, respect, sharing, it teaches," she continued after studying my eyes for a moment. "Enriching wonders of mind, body and spirit it does. Older children waver they can. Talking upon initial waver, where we start. Kindness in talk. Help with understanding. Inappropriate are actions, not them. If action repeats itself deeper is the look. Maybe time spent in Idocrasia. Respect both ways always forefront. Children smart, good at giving excuses. Excuses heard with understanding. Rudeness no excuse, disrespectful it is. Wavering adults at times ask for Idocrasia. Looking within, important."

Gorph seemed very interested in the concept of Respecia. He did his body rock and expressed himself almost as if he was thinking out loud. "Human world... huh... things just escalate and rudeness... excuses... yeah, just part of life."

"Humans not grow? Humans, trapped, not free? Respecia, part of life. Opinions vary always. Ways of doing always different. Education of respect important," responded Scota.

Chapter 5 - Respecia

"Differences humans have, differences Rofonians have, given must be respect," interjected Rotopa's father. "Our Respecia human's not have? Remember, whom or what we let in our world our choice. Cannot be impaired by temptations to teach humans our ways. Area of who we are must remain secure."

"Your question, answered?" Kindosa asked, looking at me.

"I would like to hear more."

Kindosa continued explaining, "Most important education for children it is. Backup to beginning is where we go. See where things went wrong. Children taught how situation should be dealt with, they are. Beginning shows why rudeness. Always someone there when needed, but whole day sometimes in Idocrasia wanted. Staring they do at stone's coloured flecks. Three of these rooms we have. Lack of respect often happen with three. Yellow one room, blue another, green one also."

She studied me and then continued, "Said before, backup to beginning of problem. Listen we do. Help understanding, children need. Need voice to come into their own. An answer often, they have. Stand up themselves with love kindness, they learn. Graduates from Respecia taught to teach. Mission it becomes to reteach, help those not to waver. Disrespect never reaches point of harming another."

Disrespect never reaches a point of harming another!?! I'm sure my eyes widened, for I could not imagine a world like that. The more I knew about these people, the better I felt about leaving Ooza here.

In yesterday's world I didn't believe children should sit in a corner by themselves, but I did believe in timeout chairs and was quite surprised how effective they were. The children knew that was where they had to sit if they showed disrespect, however they would sit in the room with me and a timer set so they only had to be silent for a short while.

Afterwards we would talk about what went wrong; where it

went wrong; and we then would work together to find a solution. Soon they had the tools and the skills. Once they had those they tended to work things out themselves.

Sometimes I wondered if their motive, of working it out themselves, was because they didn't want to be sitting in a timeout chair talking to me. My children or the children I taught rarely disrespected each other, at least in my presence, but my way was not the way my neighbours raised their children. To have a whole nation of people raised and following similar important values was, to me, remarkable.

"Okay, I'm confused," I said, "Isn't a day a long time for a child to be sitting alone in a room?"

"Yes, a day long time. Alone, they are not." Kindosa answered, "Make sure we do, issues are resolved. Know they do, there is someone to talk to when ready they are - be that a short period or long. Rare is it, young child has a long time. Stubborn, some are. Most young learn fast, go not to Idocrasia. Usually, older ones testing boundaries. Wavering, stubborn to point talking, working not, Idocrasia only then, but rarely, full day. Necessary sometimes. Area of life off course, redirection sometimes needed. Taught they are, skills of respect."

"How do you find out what area is off course?" I asked.

"Communication. Request to be in Idocrasia sometimes asked for - time alone, think, regroup."

"That's the start of your school, learning kindness, love, and respect? Is this your way of life?" asked Gorph. "Never mind, that's not my question, my question is: Have all the parents also gone through Respecia? That is my question."

"Grandfather did not," answered Scota. "Nation different he from. Tones in our voice different. Respecia, attended for me, more than once. Idocrasia, attended also. Smoothness of voice not part of nature, stubbornness is. Here differences honoured. Respect, yes, a way of life."

"What is schooling like after Respecia, you know, what do they learn?" Gorph asked, raising his hand as if in a classroom.

"Learn what good at, they do," answered Kindosa seeming

surprised by the question. "Different areas of skills and work, are shown. Basics, introduction to new options for a portion of day learned. Choose they do,what field the rest of the day would like. Investigate they do. Classroom sometimes needed. Sometimes learn they do from adults elsewhere. If chore it becomes, encouragement there is. If remain unhappy, redirect we do to another area of interest. Important it is everyone happy. Need they do to respect themselves. Doing what they do best and what they like is how they learn. Take pride they do, in who they are and what they do."

Then Scota interjected, "Knowing our ways, important. Getting back to topic important also. Topic is Samuel Evans. Your request?" she asked, looking at me.

"My request? Do you mean what I would like to have happen to Samuel Evans?" I asked.

Scota gave a quick nod, "What done with him, would you like?"

How do I answer that? Staring at her in shock for a moment I finally found the words, "Knowing more about who you are as a Nation and how you handle things has been important. Thank-you for taking the time to educate me. However, I have never dealt with someone who has attempted murder."

Thinking back to my yesterday's world, I had once talked to someone who said had he contemplated murder. The person I was thinking about was usually full of love, kindness, and respect, but felt he had been pushed too far. It wasn't a love/hate relationship that resulted in that dark, ugly energy; it was someone who kept giving him hate, affecting his life year after year. He wanted the person to go away, but the person would not. Something he had to go through, I guess.

Then one day he realized holding onto that much hate was exhausting, only hurting him and the people he loved. Determined not to let it affect him anymore, he told it to leave and with sheer willpower to find himself again, most of it went away. After that, the hateful person no longer had power over him, but the shame that he went that far still lingered.

Shame, an emotion I know oh, so well. It's like a speck of salt, I need it in my diet or I will die. Both salt and shame bring out the flavour, but also allows for the transformation of energy. At the same time, too much is harmful to the body as well as to the mind.

Realizing that everyone was staring at me I asked, "Was Samuel angry or scared? What could cause someone to pull a trigger or take a life? I'm just wondering what he's feeling?"

"Anger? Samuel Evans was angry at you? Princess, why?" asked Fodulza.

"Because she was in his way," Peter said with a bit of a shrug, "also he must have been scared. There she stood, appearing to have the power to stop five trucks, fling guns out of hands, and stop people in their tracks. That would have been very disconcerting to a human."

"It seemed more like greed to me," interjected Gorph with a matter of fact tone that sounded unforgiving.

It was interesting, Gorph was the person who was angry and Peter seemed to be defending Samuel. I hope Gorph's anger doesn't impede his judgment, because it is important we look deeper. Although, Peter's defence of someone who had done such a horrendous crime against me, felt hurtful. At the same time I was glad he was looking deeper and trying to gain understanding, but it still hurt. I must rise above, stay focused, and try to understand Peter's reaction towards Samuel.

"Peter and Gorph, you both knew Samuel when he was younger. What was he like?" I asked.

Gorph spoke first and said very bluntly and coldly, "What does that matter? He shot you! He should go back to his city and be put in prison for a long time."

"Seeking severe punishment and wanting revenge can be similar to the hate that makes someone pull a trigger. We have to be careful not to go there. As much as I am tempted, I'm also determined not to allow what Samuel did to me to change my heart," I said softly, but strongly. Gorph looked hurt, but I still held hope that he would see my reasoning.

Chapter 6 - The Mean Musician

Kindosa spoke in her sweet soft voice, "Justice, punishment there must be, if punishment, too violent, too hard, or too long, more hate comes forth, more violence. Too weak, too soft, too short, reason there is not, to commit crime again."

"Do your prisons in the city take what Kindosa just said into consideration? What are they like?" I asked Peter and Gorph.

"I think they try," Gorph answered gently. I was happy he answered and had not taken my previous comment personally.

"If he's convicted of attempted murder," Gorph continued, "and actually goes to prison he'll probably be in there for a long time. Chances are he'll come out hateful. There's access to learning from books, but he could also choose to learn how to use the laws and legal system to his advantage. There's often abuse and a possible education coming from the people who are also in prison. Yep and that'll just teach him how to be a better criminal and a better con artist."

"As Gorph said 'if he's convicted'... Sam could get off on a technicality and get no punishment at all," Peter concluded.

Scota seemed appalled by such a thought. "Law not clear, penalties not certain. Humans, how can they," Scota paused as if searching for the right word, "respect laws."

Kindosa jumped in, "Clarity, consistency of law, important, instills respect. Learning strengthens that, without clarity lost it is, without it, society lost. Consequences, certain, must be. Focus be teaching respect."

Gorph spoke up, "That is so much easier said than done. How do you know if the person can be taught? What if that person is deaf to the punishment, obstinate, and can't be."

"Teach you do, reteach you do. Respect for life, part of nature it becomes. Most important education it is," Kindosa repeated as if defending her lot in life. "Function in field of mathematics good can not be if basics not have. Become good, function in society can not if the basics to treat others not have.

How to respect, how to become emotionally healthy vital it is. As an educator, basics there are, back to it I always have to go to. If I don't, failed I have. Continuing forward no point."

There was silence, I think everyone just needed to process all that had been said. What was said did make sense, for what was the point of becoming brilliant in your field of study if you were not happy in your life? Too many gifted humans had been lost or broken by depression. Sometimes that was from their separation of mind, body, and spirit resulting in their gifts and lives going unnoticed. Other times it was worse for their gifts were being used to the detriment of others.

It was Fodulza who broke the silence. "Nobody answered Princess's original question," he said, bringing his arms out and his head back, allowing the connected dangling wires to jiggle.

"What was my question?" I asked. Hopefully I was not looking as stupid as I felt at that moment.

"What was the Samuel man like when he was younger?" asked Fodulza with his hands moving as if he was cradling a baby. "For Rainbow Dancer now has stripes on his face and Princess wanted to know if Samuel's stripes were always there." He drew the stripes upon his cheeks with his fingers.

That was an interesting way of putting it. When I first met Fodulza, he was Ooza and Rainbow Dancer was a giant otter without stripes upon his face. He not only remembered I had asked that question before we talked about the prison system, but he also caught my question and why I wanted the answer.

"Fodulza," Peter said nicely, "I will answer your question, but first I need to remind you that we are attached by wires, so you probably should not move around so much."

"Ooza," Fodulza started and then he stopped, the rounded fingertips of one hand aligned with the other as if he needed to meditate for a moment. He separated his hands and stared upon them. With protruded lips he rolled his eyes and said, "Fodulza finds it hard to not move."

It was a nice moment and a needed distraction as smiles crossed everyone's faces, except Scota's. All the smiling faces looked at her and finally she too smiled, sort of. Fodulza relaxed and began playing with his fingertips. With exaggerated stiffness he brought his arm up, flipped his hand over, and tried not to move his head. "And the answer is...??"

"Sam," Peter said, pointing in the air, "grew up next door to me so we spent a lot of time together. Most of the time he was nice, but other times his teasing seemed a bit on the cruel side. Cruel teasing was not something I was brought up with. If I did it, I received a talking to, but Sam's father would just laugh. Sam and I had many a good time. He enjoyed spending time at my house more than he did at his own. Looking back on it, I think he liked himself better at my place. He was nice everytime he was there. Sometimes I wondered if he was cruel because it made his father laugh. I know he studied business because that is what his father wanted."

"So he likes to please, he was just trying to please the wrong person,"interjected Fodulza.

"You are being much too lenient on him, Peter. I'm not surprised, you always have been. I don't understand you Peter, or you Princess. How can you be so forgiving? He shot you! I don't think I could be kind to him after that," Gorph interjected.

"Look, I'm just thankful I'm alive. It's his anger, his pain, his cruelty, not mine. I'm not going to give Sam the satisfaction of holding onto those emotions for him. I've done that in the past and I end up being the one who hurts the most. I truly hope there's a way for him to heal. But if there isn't, I hope he gets locked away, not because I want him punished, but so he will never do this to anyone ever again."

"That's what I'm worried about. He'll do it again if we're too easy." Gorph said. "Peter, Sam was mean, always making you feel like you were messed up and couldn't do anything right. You said he wanted to please his father. He hated his father!"

"Maybe he hated his father because he was going against his nature by trying to please him," I said, wanting to believe in that little boy that Peter knew growing up.

"You two, you are both too nice for your own good. Samuel

Evans is cruel, rude, and his actions could have killed you. I don't think he has a conscience," Gorph retorted.

"If you felt that way why did you keep him in your band?" Peter asked with a look of hurt on his face.

"He was a mean musician, pardon the pun." Both Scota and Kindosa looked confused, so Gorph continued, "He had a lot of skill and he kept us focused. His ideas on promoting us were really tight. I probably wouldn't be where I am today if it was not for him," Gorph said honestly while looking a little shameful. "I guess I merely tolerated his rudeness, told my band to ignore him and not give him the power to demean them."

Scota pointed her finger at Gorph and said, "Tolerated cruelty you did. An advantage to you it was? Action like that, believe in we do not. Respecia, start immediately it would. Behaviour in you and Samuel Evans need to change. Has cruelty always been in words?" she questioned.

"Words?" I asked a bit confused.

"Words similar, different than actions," Kindosa answered, constraining the movement of her hands; the connecting wires must be very hard on them as they gestured so much.

Kindosa continued her explanation, "Noticing humans often gesture not when they speak. Energies inside must not use either or Samuel upset would not have been. Less connected words and actions must feel for you than us."

Neither Gorph nor Peter remembered him being physically harmful, or at least not until the fateful day. The day I had not yet healed from and exhaustion was reflected in my voice when I asked, "Can we change his behaviour at this stage in his life? None of us have ever dealt with attempted murder. How would we know if he could be saved or not? Do you, as a Nation that functions so amazingly, really want that responsibility?"

Everyone merely stared at me for a moment and then Scota spoke, "Overwhelmed you seem to be."

"This part of my journey has been quite overwhelming," I said with a weakness within my words.

"Meeting adjourned. Lots to digest," announced Scota.

Chapter 7 - If You Wish

Previously on my journey, I had been Thee Trusted One to Queen Chayzlazamia and that felt beyond my expertise, but to decide someone else's fate, felt overwhelming.

Peter wheeled me through the long curved hallway and the artwork we passed so often, tugged at my creative side. It was very well done and it represented much love, kindness, and sharing. When I saw it for the first time it touched something inside of me. Now, it had a much deeper meaning as it was not one person's perspective, but an entire Nation's.

Whether it was what the artwork represented or an accumulation of emotions tugging at my heart, I didn't know; I just knew I didn't have a creative outlet. That was my vehicle to move my emotions to a different place. What was I to do?

"Should we get Rainbow Dancer and go for a drive?" Peter asked. "There is a place not far from the watchtower. I could probably wheel you there. I go there when I'm overwhelmed by humans," he said as if he had read my mind. He leaned over so I could see his smile before he finished with, "Humans are quite overwhelming, you know, even when you are one."

Soon I was being wheeled down a path that was beside the watchtower with Rainbow Dancer leading the way.

"Wow," was all I could say, for the path had led us to a large crystal that sat upon a base of striped orange and blue stone. The large crystal on the top was almost clear, much like a quartz. It was very tall and towered well over Peter.

"I call it my divine temple. It's very powerful. Helps you sort out what's going on within your mind. When I come here I seem to receive an abundance of love, healing and wisdom. There's a place where I sit and I think I can get your wheelchair there. It's like an alcove and you can look at the crystal on three sides. Would you like to just sit there alone for a while? I'll just take Rainbow Dancer up the path a bit where there's a bank that leads down to a stream."

"That sounds amazing."

Peter wheeled me into the alcove and I stared into the awe inspiring crystal. It looked like a clear quartz with smokey white waves intricately embedded inside its wands and peaks. It was predominately high above my head and as I looked up every vein in my body seemed to vibrate.

"You going to be okay?" he questioned.

"Yeah, as odd as I feel I think this is just what I need."

Peter and Rainbow Dancer left. Resting my chin upon my hands I stared deep into the crystal. The words of the previous meeting ran through my mind. So did the day the Rofonians threw pine cones and Samuel shot me. A haunting feeling of falling and shimmering caused a shiver deep inside my core.

"You are here for a reason."

Looking around, I saw that no one was there. Was I hearing things? Was that high pitched, childlike voice just inside my head? Was I going crazy? It must have been inside my head. During some of the more traumatic times in my life I had thought that I heard voices of encouragement and wisdom, although no human was actually there. Had my experience with Samuel Evens triggered me to be so overwhelmed?

My thoughts went to my yesterday's world where I had been beaten, choked, and raped and how, at that time, I often felt frozen in fear. There was a time where all I had gone through prevented me from moving ahead. I finally started being able to do that and now I have to deal with Samuel Evans?

In yesterday's world it was myself I had a hard time forgiving. Even though I was aware of who had done what to me I did not harbour ill will or anger towards them. However, they had succeeded in giving me their anger and their pain. So I hadn't let it go, instead I directed that negative energy towards myself, holding onto shame that ultimately belonged to them.

The action of accepting that it happened was helping stop it from holding me back, allowing me to finally move forward. Now I need to release the shame and accept that their actions were horrendous, not mine.

Even though I have understanding towards Samuel's actions, it didn't excuse him. I guess there has to be a balance between understanding and not accepting the action, and also between accepting it happened, and not allowing it to happen again.

Oh my, I feel like something is moving?!? Turning around I realized I was surrounded by crystal and there was no longer an opening. Am I asleep? Had I fallen asleep?!? Am I dreaming? Then again this new world was so different that I'm probably awake. Could a crystal this size have moved by itself! What is happening? Will I be trapped inside a crystal forever?

"Come with me."

It was that high pitched childlike voice again! I looked around, but no one was there.

"I'm up here," said the voice.

There sitting upon the ledge of the crystal was a very tiny faerie like creature and as I looked at her she flew down.

"Are you a faerie?"

"If that is what you wish to call me then that is what I am. It is not what I call myself."

"What do you call yourself?"

"My name is Lumoona," she said as she flew close to the crystal and as she did she drew a circle. She put numbers inside of it. "I don't know what I drew, what do you think it is?"

"It looks like a clock."

"You wish it to be a clock, then that is what it is. Okay, say it is a clock. What does a clock do?"

"Well, there's usually arms coming out from the center and they move, pointing to a number that tells you what time it is."

She drew two arms with hands pointing. Then she drew arms and legs on the numbers and the center hands stopped pointing and seemed to come alive. They began waving at the numbers. Then some of the numbers just walked off the clock.

"The clock is for you. The time is changing, and you are in a transition. Now, do you wish to come with me?"

I looked at my wheelchair and merely said, "ahh...."

"Oh you can't come with me like that," she said with a smile that puffed out her cheeks. She slapped her hand on her forehead, and shook her head. She took her hand off her forehead, quickly brought out her arm and faced her palm towards me.

W-w-what is happening to me? Am I having a seizure? Oh my, I am small again, only this time I'm really, really small.

Something moved on my back, I looked over my shoulder and said with astonishment, "I have wings. Am I a faerie?"

"If that is what you wish then that is what you are."

Threads began stretching lengthwise above my chair. They were attached to each side of the crystal and reminded me of a loom. Lumoona took a thread and began to weave in and out, going forward, but always going back, sometimes underneath, sometimes on top. So I followed.

We weaved in and out and in and out of these lengthwise threads until finally we flew above them. We sat upon a crystal ledge, staring down at the amazing, but unfinished, tapestry.

"It is your life."

"What? Huh, it looks like a loom with a partially finished tapestry, it doesn't look like my life," I said and then began studying it. "Did you call it my life because I seem to get over my emotions and then I slip between the cracks or the threads when I think about the horrors of my past?"

"If that is how you wish to think about it, then that is what it is. Remember it is your life and your life was interwoven with each event. Each time we weaved in and out it is like the shuttle of a loom making the fabric of your life stronger and more durable. Why did some of the numbers of the clock leave? Did they walk out of your circle?"

"Yeah. What does that mean? Does that mean the numbers don't like me anymore?"

Oh was that a stupid thing to say. She'll probably tell me that 'if that is what I wish it to be then that is what it is'. But this time she didn't say a word and we merely sat there looking at each other. She had long curly hair and big brown eyes. She shut and opened them like the shutter of an old camera, probably hoping I would see the whole picture, but I didn't.

"It's the insincere ones, those who don't respect your time," she said.

It was much like how I felt - just when I was thinking I was doing okay, something or someone would pull me under.

Every time I was pulled underneath it seemed to be because I had, again, believed in the sincerity of someone; only to come to the realization they were full of conceit, selfishness, greed, or jealousy. They seemed to want something or maybe they simply desired to take something from me. I was not sure and they were never honest enough to let me know.

I would look at both sides and see, in my attempt to stick up for myself, I might have inadvertently done something to hurt them. At times I had more compassion for them than myself thus I would allow it to happen again. Like a clock beginning at number one and going around only to do it again.

"Yeah," I said, "I often believe everyone thinks like me and wants to learn from everything they have gone through. That they all have the same goal - to be a better person, to be more full of love. However, often it's not the truth, for material wealth, greed, self-gain, self-pity, or revenge can often be someone's goal. I just don't think that way. I guess that's what makes them insincere and not respecting me.

Is it my past energy dammed up inside of me that makes me judge another or am I finally seeing the truth? Are you showing me this truth so I can be wise enough to see the truth of what is behind the words and actions of Samuel Evans?"

"If that is what you wish it to be..."

"It's not a wish. It's a question," I interjected as politely as I could muster within my frustration, then letting my breath relax me I continued, "I'm just trying to figure out what you are showing me."

Lumoona looked up out of the corner of her eye and stared at the peaks of the crystal. Looking back at me she asked, "The clock, is it from another world?"

"Yes," I said, realizing I hadn't seen a clock since I had walked through the wall. "It's what they use to tell time and every day the hands hit the same numbers. So what your saying is, if I want things not to just go round and round then I have to let go of the insincere people and no longer have them part of my circle? If I ever get back to the world I came from, I should fill my circle with people who truly care about me?"

"If that is your wish then that is what it is."

"Fine, but that's dealing with the past and the future. Samuel Evans, he is here in the now, in this world and I don't know what to do and I don't even know how to feel."

Lumoona tilted her head from side to side as if she had heard a strange sound. She put the back of her hand to her mouth and stared into the crystal. With her teeth gently pressing upon her knuckle, she shrugged, smiled, and widened her eyes all at the same time. It was as if her smile overtook her whole body. She reached up and grabbed what looked like soft cloth and began frantically wiping the crystal.

After a few moments Lumoona stopped wiping the crystal and stared at it.

"There!" she said. "Look!"

It looked like the smooth side of a clear quartz to me. I think my expression must have been one of perplexity because she pointed at the wiped surface.

"No, re-e-eally look."

Lumoona flew closer, put her nose to the area and then flew back. Okay, maybe I needed to look closer. Flying close, I too, put my nose to the crystal.

"What do you see? What do you see?" she asked excitedly

"I see a... a baby in a basket sitting on a beach," I answered.

"What else?"

"Oh, there is Samuel Evans. He's sitting on a rock, eating food, and looking at an ocean."

"Where are you?" she asked.

"I'm right here looking into the crystal. Can't you see me?"

"Nooo, can you see you?" she questioned.

Staring into the crystal I could only see the baby and Samuel Evans eating his food.

Chapter 8 - Crystal Currents

Widening my search, I scanned the ocean and there was Samuel! He wasn't sitting on the beach anymore, he was very far out in the ocean! There I was, no longer a small faerie! I was human again. Sam and I were swimming.

Again Lumoona asked, "Now, do you see you?"

"I am far out in the ocean swimming with Samuel Evans."

"If that is what you wish that is what will be."

It's not what I wish, it's what I'm seeing, I wanted to say, but the next thing I knew, there I was, in the ocean swimming beside Samuel. I was no longer watching and I didn't feel that was fair, because it wasn't what I wished for, but all I could do was swim - swim and swim for what seemed to be forever.

There were strong currents, but Sam and I kept swimming. We swam through obstacle after obstacle trying to avoid the strong waters that were pushing us towards the sharp jagged rocks. After a while the rocks that we came upon were smooth.

The whole time I was swimming, somehow I just knew we had to get through the ocean to get back to the baby that was still sitting in a basket on the beach. As we neared the beach we could hear the baby crying. I looked over and I couldn't see Samuel anymore, but the baby's cry was even more distraught. My body hurt, my heart hurt, but I still had to keep swimming.

"I don't have the strength to make it," I cried aloud.

"You do. You will. You'll make it. Follow me," and there flying just above the water was Lumoona. "You're on the home stretch now."

"It doesn't feel like it. It's too hard. It's too overwhelming. I don't think I have the strength."

"You do. You can do this."

"But the baby doesn't even know. He doesn't even know how hard I am trying. He doesn't even know how much I hurt. He doesn't even know I'm here!"

"A baby knows. You are almost there, soon your feet will

be on the ground."

Finally they touched the ground and I saw the baby, he was about a year old. I walked up to the baby and I hugged him. As I did the baby began to grow. Smiling at him I watched the child grow and grow and to my surprise he turned into Samuel Evans. Sam was smiling and he was strong, happy and kind.

My vision blurred and the next thing I knew I had my nose pressed into a wall of clear crystal.

"You are back. I knew you would make it." Lumoona said from above me.

"What in the world was that all about?" I asked.

"You wished to know about a Samuel Evans, did you not see a Samuel Evans?"

"I saw and I swam, but I don't think I understood."

"You saw him and a baby didn't you?"

"Yes, but at the end the baby turned into Samuel Evans and was sitting on a rock, eating. Were they one in the same?"

"If you wish that to be then that is what it is." Oh, is she frustrating, but she seems to tell me when I'm wrong so I will take that as a yes, and then she asked, "What was he doing?"

"Sitting on a rock, eating."

"No, I know he was sitting there, but what are you supposed to learn from it?"

My mouth opened, but nothing came forth. Lumoona made a type of tsk sound, squinted her eyes, let out a heavy sigh and asked, "What is food?"

"What is food! Well, it feeds you. It nourishes you. So Samuel is getting nourished or does it mean he needs nourishment to grow?" I asked. I realized the answer had already been shown to me so I simply rephrased my question, "If he gets proper nourishment he will grow."

"If that is what you wish. Where is Samuel now?"

"He is in a room surrounded by rock." I answered, but I thought I should clarify so I continued, "A room made of a type of stone. Huh, there he was sitting on a rock. The beach was made of small rocks. Everything was rock except the ocean.

Does he just need the energy of the Idocrasia and perhaps the nourishment of Respecia to grow?"

"If that is what you wish then that is what it will be."

Trying to ignored her frustrating answer I continued with my analogy, "When we were swimming in the ocean, it was as if we were swimming through a vast amount of emotions. There were lots of them as there were currents and jagged rocks. As we got closer to the beach the rocks became smooth. After some time our feet were on the ground and I hugged the baby and he grew up strong, happy, and kind. So with the proper nourishment, Sam will be okay. He will be happy and kind."

"If that is what you wish then that is what it will be."

"I don't agree with that," I rebuked with a roll of my eyes. "I can wish all I want, but ultimately it is up to Sam."

Lumoona grinned from ear to ear before she said, "You were swimming too and you asked the question."

Staring at the crystal I did my best not to sarcastically repeat her frustrating repetition of words back to her. Taking deep breaths I finally was able to quiet my thoughts.

After a while I said, "I need to swim through my emotions; be able see Sam as a child, a child who was kind when he was within a kind and respectful environment. Plus, if I am able to forgive him for shooting me, he has the potential to grow and to be happy, kind and respectful again. I'll be able to forgive him. At least I think that's what the hug meant.

You also showed me that I have too many emotions right now to be of any help, but I will be able to swim through them, be full of love and end up with my feet on the ground."

"If that is what you wish then that is what it is."

"Please stop saying that, because at this point I only find it distracting. I am doing my best to get all the insight from what you showed me. For example, I swam through the currents and I did not get swept away or drown in my emotions."

"It's okay to swim through your emotions and take the time to heal, but you have to keep moving forward," she said as she made giant leaps to different layers of the crystal.

"Yes, I need to keep moving forward. Perhaps adopting the attitude I was here for a reason will give me the strength to forgive Sam, but being shot by someone is a hard thing to forget."

Lumoona flew towards me and a ball appeared in her hand. "Forgiveness does not mean forgetting and poof it's gone!" she said as the ball disappeared.

"Nor does it mean just turn the other cheek and get slapped again, as I've heard so many times before," I retorted.

"Nooo, no it doesn't" she said with a smile. "Forgiveness means not taking it on as yours and not holding onto energies of hate or hurt. If the cheek that got slapped holds onto the energy, then you hold the slap, not them. Turn the other cheek to look at it in a different way and transform that energy into not wishing any harm. First you shall find the growth and maybe someday you will find the love."

Lumoona flew towards the crystal wall, snapped her fingers and once again it was a three-sided alcove with an opening to the pathway. She snapped her fingers again and I was sitting in my wheelchair. She waved good-bye and I was about to wave and say thank-you when I felt something on my arm. It was Rainbow Dancer. I turned and looked up to where she had been, but Lumoona was nowhere to be seen.

"Oh there you are," Peter said as he rounded the corner. "I must have walked right past you, but Rainbow Dancer found you." He shrugged his shoulders and made a funny expression before he finished with, "Odd."

"Did you two have a nice time?" I asked Rainbow Dancer and he nodded.

"It still amazes me how well he understands you," Peter said as he began to back my chair out. "Do you feel any better?"

"Yes, I do."

We were out the alcove when Peter asked, "So my divine temple was a good idea?"

"Yes," I said with a smile. "I was able to swim through a lot of my emotions. Let's just say, I found a new perspective."

"Yeah, me too. Kindosa's words made me look at the whole planet differently. She spoke with such kindness and softness, yet she had strength in her convictions." He stopped, stood in front of me, cleared his throat, softened his voice and moving his hands, he said, *'Clarity, consistency of law, important, instills respect. Learning strengthens that, without clarity lost it is, without it, society lost. Consequences, certain, must be. Focus be teaching respect.'*

"Wow, I think you quoted that verbatim," I said with a bit of a laugh. "That is definitely a skill."

"When I hear something that resonates with me, it's like hearing a good song, I remember the words," he said with a modest shrug and took his place behind my wheelchair.

With a tilt of my head I became serious. "I wish the human world was one where everyone resonated to words and songs that promoted kindness and respect. If everyone had that as their common goal it would be much easier to rid the world of selfish, ulterior motives and life would be easier. Also it would be a lot easier to be able to be a judge or a teacher."

"If judges and teachers had clarity and consistency, life would be a lot easier," Peter said thoughtfully.

"Well, maybe it will be enough to help Samuel," I said soberly with a shrug of my shoulders.

"Perhaps," Peter said thoughtfully. "Thinking of Sam as a child has already changed my perspective. My parents always had consequences for inappropriate behaviour, but they enforced them in a way that promoted growth. As a child, if I learned and grew from my actions, I was forgiven, because it's all part of growing up. But if Sam does stay, they will have a whole new challenge. The Rofonians start teaching soon after the child is born. Samuel isn't a child, he's an adult who would have to be willing to be a child in order to be able to change."

"Yeah," I agreed, "and we have to keep that in perspective, because sometimes when a damaged person is put in the position where there is love, kindness and respect, often they still aren't happy and end up going back to their old ways."

Chapter 9 - *Being the Bug*

Reflecting for a moment on what I had said about people going back to their old ways, I continued, "I guess it's as if those people are seeking what was once familiar. Their hurts, pains, childhood teachings, or their egos don't seem to let them unshackle the chains within. Those chains tie them to their dark place. It is as if the thought that they deserve to be punished is too ingrained. A part of them knows that's not the way it should be, but they stay trapped and haunted nonetheless."

"You're not talking about yourself are you?" He didn't give me time to answer and with a gentle soothing voice he said, "I hope you realize once the chains are broken and your focus remains on moving forward, life can be quite awesome."

"In my case, I agree, and I'm thankful for all the kindness and love I've found, but I don't have ulterior motives," I stated. Deciding I needed to rant, I continued, "Don't get me wrong, I'm far from perfect and I don't always address issues with the love and respect that I would like to. I have been told I can be quite pointed when I am hurt, but the only motive I have is growth, so that all the stupid patterns can stop being on repeat."

There was frustration in my voice when I said, "I don't need my life to go around and around like the hands on a clock or be around those who need to play head games and find it amusing so that they can cover up their guilt or whatever? It's like they can't leave their ulterior motives or drama behind them. It's like they want to make others pay for their misconstrued way of looking at things. I think some of them put a spin on their hurt and guilt so they don't have to look at themselves. Some just enjoy manipulating others. I guess they're like a child wanting attention. Actually, I don't know what their motivation is and what it will take to get them to truly learn." I stopped and for a few seconds I was quiet after my emotional rant. I sat straight in my chair, put my hand on my chest, and quoted Scota, "*Think like them, I will not.*"

My rant had slipped past being shot and gone deep into my yesterday's world, I guess, because emotionally I still felt raw.

Peter let out a heavy sigh before he spoke and in a gentle tone he said, "Like some of those clones you met, they play games at other people's expense for the fun of it. They look at it as entertainment so they can watch the drama unfold from their words. I know, because I have been the brunt of that too."

I don't think he understood there was so much more to my rant than Samuel Evans and the clones.

In my frustration I retorted back."Well, those are the ones who are the creepy worms."

"Creepy worms?"

"Yes, ugly translucent creatures who have truly lost their way. Chances are it will take a lot of life experiences to change them and some will completely miss what their life as a human was all about," I said, feeling like judgment had crept in.

It was not my place to judge whether someone has missed what their life was about or whether or not they had lost their way. However, I was done with them affecting my life with their stuff and wished that they would grow and choose to take responsibly for words and actions. I had my own lessons to take responsibility for and I was now choosing to open my eyes and see things from a wider perspective.

"I truly hope Sam hasn't fallen to that level. He was a nice kid, at least when he hung around at our house. There's a big difference in sending a wayward person to Respecia, you know, one who wants to learn how to do it right, than it is to send someone who really doesn't care." Peter paused before he continued, "I guess I'm hoping after all that has happened that Sam finally, sincerely, does care."

There was silence between us and a great amount of trepidation was stirring inside me. I felt I had once again fallen between those threads. Lumoona had helped me get above it all, but Peter's and my conversation had left me revisiting my past and I must find my back to the now.

When I first arrived at the Rofonian Nation, they had given

me my own private room and constructed a bed for me at the Tarnana. I felt honoured to be staying in this huge building with high ceilings and mosaic art donned hallways where the leaders of the Rofonian Nation both lived and carried out their important business. There was no longer a need for me to be in the hospital and I was pleased to be back there.

Peter was able to stand straight as he wheeled me down the hall towards the meeting room. The meeting had been adjourned because Scota felt that I was too overwhelmed. I wondered if anyone would still be there so I could find out when the discussion of Samuel Evans' fate was to be resumed.

It seemed as though the only way there would be hope for Samuel Evans was... if when the bullet hit me, something went through his heart and stirred his emotions. It often takes a huge tragedy to awaken that which is higher than oneself, however would the tragedy inflicted on me be enough?

If what Lumoona had shown was true and not just a wish, I also would need to swim through my emotions to find forgiveness. Seeing myself achieving that state was definitely a goal I wanted to work towards, but I wasn't there yet.

The meeting room was empty so we left and as we headed back to my room, Scota saw us and asked, "Clarity, did you find? Responsibility issue, ready now to look at?"

I was tired and hungry and I merely looked at her. Then out of my mouth came the ramblings of my mind, "This is too big of a responsibility. I feel that, well, my being shot has put your Nation in a precarious situation. I wish it had never happened. I do not want to be involved with deciding someone's fate."

Tears started to stream down my face. "There are so many good, kind people. People who have met with misfortune and would love to have a chance to be in a world like yours. I was not like Peter, who met Sam when he was nice. The Samuel I met was someone who was rude and cruel and yet, he might be the one who gets that chance to live in your amazing world. Is that fair to those who have worked so hard on themselves? His heart is not good and kind, at least not what I have seen."

"You think, not torn up inside he is? Why? You think, all bad he is? Why?" she asked gently.

My mind flashed to what Lumoona had shown me and then to the conversation I had with Peter about the people who played games at other people's expense. In my experience those people rarely changed.

Feeling confused, I let more ramblings pour forth, "Gorph seems to think Samuel Evans doesn't have a conscience, and if that's the case, he won't have shame," I answered with a sniff. "He was so rude, fixated on hurting your entire Nation. He was horribly disdainful to Peter, mocking him and taunting him. He doesn't seem like a good person. What if he is able to influence your Nation and able to change all your wonderful accomplishments that are ingrained in your society?"

Scota looked hurt or insulted, but then she smiled and gently said, "Saying was yours, 'our wonderful accomplishments'," she nodded slowly, tilting her head towards her shoulder before looking straight into my eyes, "ingrained." Her voice changed to her business tone and she continued, "Final decision not yours to make. Responsibility not yours to take. Entirely ours, his, and the in charge humans. Decision we make, determined by his words, his actions, not yours."

"Oh?" I said in surprise.

"All done, are we?" she questioned.

My head nodded with embarrassment.

"Body of yours needs food. Afterwards we meet. The message, as to when, delivered will be," she said and walked away.

I had been fretting about nothing and now I have made a fool out of myself. It was the feeling of always wanting to do everything right, which was a wonderful trait to have, however it was also the trait that had held me back with the fear of making a mistake. It had influenced me to take responsibility for things that were not my fault. Learning that Samuel's fate was not my decision and it wouldn't be determined by anything I said or did, took a great weight off of my shoulders.

"Things do happen for a reason and I must remember that,"

I said to Peter after I had some water and a few bites of food.

"You know, there is a saying I once heard, '*Sometimes you are the bug and sometimes you are the windshield*.' I was the bug, the casualty, and Samuel, he was the windshield, for he was hard. Now he has to look at his smeared windshield and figure out a way to clean it, so he can look ahead with clarity. He's gonna have to wash and scrub the splattered grime that his hardness caused, just to be able to see."

It wasn't long before the meeting commenced; wires were put in place; and of course, the topic was Samuel Evans.

Gorph was rocking back and forth which was affecting the wires and we all felt we should hear from him first as he seemed rather anxious. He stopped his rocking and tugged on his ear (the one that didn't have the wire attached to Fodulza). He took his finger and his thumb, held onto his lips, and stared at the center of the table. Everyone sat patiently waiting.

"After a lot of soul searching," he began in a shameful tone, "I'm angry. Angry at myself. Sam was a friend. A friend I could have helped, instead I just tolerated him. I encouraged everyone else to tolerate him. Peter said Sam was different at Peter's parents place. Why, because his parents didn't tolerate disrespect. But!" he said abruptly as he clapped his hands together and holding them tightly he rocked them back and forth.

"That was then, this is now. Is it too late? I don't know. Last time Sam and I talked, it was three years ago. Three years ago almost to the day he pulled that trigger. Then, he was a bit condescending, but not horribly. I'm really angry at him." Gorph turned and looked into my eyes for a moment. "I'm really angry that he hurt you. The Sam I knew... well, I honestly don't think he would have done that three years ago."

Silence surrounded us until I gently, but firmly slapped my fingers on the table and nodded. "I need to see him," I stated.

"No, Princess!" Fodulza said, reminding me of the Ooza I had first met. His lips were puckered and fear was in his eyes.

Scota spoke firmly, "Fodulza, yours not to decide. Yours not to influence"

"Ooza is just....," I began gently, looking at Peter and Gorph, "sorry, Fodulza. I have known him as Ooza and we have been friends for a long time. You are correct Scota, the decision is not his to influence. I believe he is saying that he is concerned and worried for my well-being. Fodulza, that is how you need to express your feelings. You need to find the words."

He took a deep breath. "Yes, I have a lot to learn. Princess, I am concerned this man will hurt you again."

"Go with her, I could. With me you could come. Stop him from causing her harm, we both could," Kindosa suggested.

"No," said Fodulza, "sorry, I mean, I am not only worried about that. I am worried about his words, about how he will use them. Princess takes responsibility for her actions and I am concerned he will make it seem to be all her fault."

"Humans do that? Responsibility not theirs? Fault others?" questioned Scota.

"Yes," I answered, "they do that quite well."

Gorph must have been processing what Fodulza had said.

"He's right," Gorph said with a nod and raised his arm as if he was screwing in a light bulb, "Sam could somehow," staring at his hand he continued, "make you feel guilty."

"Understanding not what you said," expressed Kindosa.

"What don't you understand," I asked innocently.

"Not you...," Kindosa turned her attention towards Gorph, "Gorph said, Samuel Evans make her feel, to work on what has been spoiled. Concern, why is that?"

"That is not what I said. I said, somehow Samuel Evans could make her feel guilty." Gorph started rocking back and forth again and his earpiece fell off.

"Samuel, you think, make her feel, to work on what has been spoiled?" Scota asked. "Correct, sense it does not make."

Gorph said, "Felos wospoyla, Scota, what does that word mean?"

"Earpiece not in, understand him not," Scota responded.

Chapter 10 - Only Wospoyla

"He would like to know the direct translation for the word," I took my earpiece out and said, "felos wospoyla."

"Work on what has been spoiled, word means," answered Scota looking rather befuddled.

"You can understand both languages, humour me and keep your earpiece off for a second," Gorph said looking at me. "Say the words, 'feel guilty,' in their language for me."

"Felos wospoyla," I said slowly, "huh, I thought it meant guilty. What's the word for guilty?"

"Some of our words do not correspond directly with other languages. That is the closest translation," answered Fodulza.

"A word, translated not correctly?" Scotia asked.

"In our language if someone is at fault they are guilty - they have done something wrong. In the Rofonian language if someone is at fault they are to work on what has been spoiled," I said in English with my earpiece still off.

"I like felos wospoyla, it make more sense," Gorph said rocking thoughtfully back and forth. He nodded and smiled before we both put our earpieces back in.

"I guess I could have used the word, 'shame'," Fodulza said, "but that wouldn't have made sense either because shame is similar, but different. Gorph felt shame for what Sam had done, but he did not feel he was the one at fault, because he had not pulled the trigger. I can feel shame but not be guil... not be at fault. However, I can be at fault, but not feel shame. Does that make sense to everyone?"

"Nope, not really," Gorph shook his head and sat back in his chair. He put his left foot on his right knee and began to nod his head. Suddenly he pointed his finger to the ceiling, "I'll clarify, because I was agreeing with Fodulza here, that Sam could somehow turn it around and make it all Princess's fault."

"Fodulza," I began, "I think what you said helped me. It is why I have to go visit him. I know he is at fault for pulling the trigger. I need to find out if he feels shame for doing so."

"Visit Samuel, arrangement we make," Scota said with a nod. "Discussion, to continue not needed. Determined by visit, much will be. Visit when sun shines."

The sun shone on the next day and I was told I should wear my indigo robe and be sitting in my wheelchair; Peter and Gorph would be there to push me, but would not be entering the room where Sam was being held. Fodulza and Kindosa would ride in the howdah on Rainbow Dancer's back. Due to the protective ward they would remain unseen by Samuel Evans. They would be able to hold him back with the energy from their rounded fingers if it was necessary.

Handcuffs and prison wardens were part of human world, not this one. Then again humans couldn't make people sit upon their buttocks by merely pointing their fingers.

We went down marbled streets between the rows of golden houses until we came to a path that led through the trees. It was peaceful there. There were flowers scattered all around and benches to sit upon. A human size bench, looking as if it had been a recent addition, sat under a tree beside a large rock.

In the middle of this sanctuary stood a building made of stone. It reflected different hues depending on the light. It seemed to be brown, but as I looked closer I realized there were yellow and green flecks within. Thinking I had seen all the colours, the sunlight shifted slightly and I realized there was also red and blue colours within the stone.

"That's the door she has to go through?" Gorph asked pointing at a short narrow door. "Don't think it'll be wide enough."

No one had taken into consideration my wheelchair would be unable to accompany me. Laying in a hospital bed in yesterday's world determined to move my legs had given me a gift for I knew I had an ability to reach deep into my willpower. This time I was not going to be a victim and I was not going to give in even if it took every bit of strength I had.

Giving thanks for yesterday's experiences, as horrible as

they were at the time, they gave me the tools I needed. Yes, I was going forward. Taking a deep breath I carefully stood up. Good, my feet were withstanding my weight. Crouching rather awkwardly I got through the opening.

"Are you going to be alright?" Peter voiced with concern.

"Yes," I said with a swallow, "I will be fine, you two can wait out there. I will see you soon."

Inside there were more doors and thankfully the Rofonians' love for high ceilings allowed me to stand. My hair touching the ceiling reminded me I had to stay above my emotions by staying in the now. I began wondering how they carved the stone and what it must have taken to make it smooth and shape it into a building with several rooms. A project that probably took many cycles, as Rotopa's father would say.

If there were seams piecing the Idocrasia together, they had been crafted so well, no one would ever be able to tell, not even by touching. Yes, touching and thinking about the stone was easing my anxiety. I was thankful for that.

Realizing that Kindosa had spoken I said, "Sorry, I must have been deep in thought. Did you say something?"

"In there," whispered Kindosa tilting her head to the right.

Balancing myself by holding on to the wall, slowly, ever so slowly I walked into Sam's room.

Whoa, I felt lightheaded. Was it the powerful energy of being inside such an amazing stone building or was it because this was the first time I had walked anywhere since I had been shot? I didn't know.

The room was yellow, I think it had brown flecks, and there was Sam. I was standing in front of him. Then I was laying on the floor with Samuel staring down at me, jaw agape!?! I could see that, but I couldn't see part of my arm!

Was I shimmering again! What had happened?!? Shimmering in front of the Rofonians was one thing, but in front of a human? Why was this happening? What did this mean? Falling shouldn't have killed me. I shouldn't be dying.

Chapter 11 - A Shimmer of the Past

Was I destined to shimmer because I had been anointed in The Land of the Shimmering Bridge? Was I dead or turning into Woroyalty? Was that my destiny? Or did I merely exist to be the bug in Samuel Evan's destiny? I didn't want his fate on my hands. Did I get my wish?!? Huh, where was I now?!?

Queen Chayzlazamia was sitting next to me. Had they taken me back to the bridge because I wasn't supposed to leave via a portal and still needed to work on my patterns?

Queen Chayzlazamia was sitting in her comfortable position with her legs tucked into the side of her body. We weren't sitting on a bowfront or on shimmering furniture. No, we were levitating and everything was shimmering, but it was not the silver-white shimmer like in the Land of the Shimmering Bridge. This time, the two of us were shimmering yellows and browns with flecks of blues and greens. She was smiling at me. Smiling, yes, better that, than a frown or a look of worry.

"Where am I?" I asked

"In between time," she answered in her breathy tone.

"In between time?" I questioned.

"Yes, it is stretched for our needs - borrowed for us to visit."

"Needs?" I questioned.

"Okay," she said looking rather sheepish, reminding me of Chayma (the girl I met before she became the shimmering Queen). "I wanted to visit with you and I have been granted some stolen moments. A lot has happened since you were shot. The Priestess, the Empress, Raziel and some of the others have had frequent gatherings at the Shimmering Palace. I have been very fortunate as I have been able to attend some of the meetings. You have caused quite a stir among the higher powers."

"I have?" I said, still not understanding what was going on.

"Sadly though, I am not allowed to tell you very much. However, much of their conversations seemed to be about you. In those conversations they spoke about an unripe apple. It is my curiosity, that makes me ask, what do you know about it?"

"Not much...," I shrugged as I answered, "I was asked to gather one. It was unripe and bruised. I was quite embarrassed when the Empress said it was for her. She took my apple and told me not to mention it to anyone. A woman named Zelka who lived in Ol' Man Gar Cave seemed to know about it. She stomped her foot and screamed because Rainbow Dancer was not going to give it to her. The Camflages knew about it and wanted it. That's all I know. What do you know?"

"I know that the bruises are healing, but they are very deep and the High Priestess is not sure whether they will be able to heal before it is time for the apple to ripen. All of them seem to be concerned about it, but will not answer any of my questions. I was hoping you would."

"Sorry, I don't know anything. Is that what you came to talk to me about? Do I get to find out how you are?"

"I have uncovered information about my mother and my Auntie. You remember, I was quite confused and blamed her for my mother's death, thinking that she may have been the one who pushed my mother into the water. I had also wondered whether she had been working with the Camflages."

"What have you found out?"

"My Auntie had nothing to do with my mother's death and nor did my mother commit suicide," she answered.

"Why did she walk into the water?"

"Her entire being was filled with so much love and compassion, that she tamed a water dragon!"

Queen Chayzlazamia beamed with pride as she told her story, "My mother became connected to her true self! She has moved on since, travelling throughout a place they call Earth; giving strength to others so they also will be able to connect to their true selves. Apparently, those who live upon Earth also have the ability to accomplish such a feat if they truly desire to. It was my mother's destiny and destinies always come forth. However, they come forth upon the completion of breaking many patterns and no one knows when or how long it will take.

Timing for it is unforeseen and no one expected it to happen during her reign as Queen, at least not when she was so young."

"Earth?!" I gasped, knowing I'd never told her where I had come from. "She went to Earth to work with humans?"

"Yes, what is it that you know about Earth humans?"

"I used to think I knew a lot, but now, I really think I know very little," I said with a tinge of regret in my voice, "I do know humans are often stuck within their patterns. Some are born with many hard, sometime gut wrenching, obstacles to overcome. Wow, to be able to connect to their true destiny and make such a huge leap while still on Earth!"

"The High Priestess said my mother is like the Great Spirit-Hawk bringing messages to all who will listen. The hardest part of completing her destiny was leaving her two children."

I understood. I had walked through a wall and had left my family and friends behind, "hmm," I expressed aloud. "Yeah, I guess connecting to one's true destiny sometimes requires leaving certain friends and family members behind."

"In my mother's case it meant leaving all behind. If behind is the correct word for she never really left us and her love was always with me. In my experience of working with patterns there are those who physically had their mother in their life, but still didn't feel loved, so I was very fortunate."

"You really have an amazing destiny helping people break patterns. I bet your mother attained a deep understanding of how hard it is to leave," I said closing my eyes for a second, for I truly understood.

"At that same time she knew she had to. Leaving her children was the most unselfish action she could have made. She knew mothers allow a new soul to come through, a separate, independent person who is destined to follow their own path."

"To walk your true path," I said with a sigh. "There seems to be so much to learn before reaching that point. Your mother must have been a truly awakened soul."

"She must have been," Queen Chayzlazamia said with a nod

of pride. "She was able to connect with the electrically charged dynamic force of the water dragon. She had to not allow herself to connect with fear, but instead face it with compassion and courage. That in itself must have left within her a feeling of being connected to all that is alive and at the same time a feeling of being one within, of being whole and so very wise."

"Yes, like her daughter," I said smiling at her.

"Like me?!" and with a slight bow said, "I am far from that."

"I don't think so for I remember when your Auntie died. At first you were trapped within your emotions, but when Kyrone was trying to usurp your throne you did not allow yourself to stay in your emotions, nor connect with fear, but instead you faced your destiny with compassion and courage."

"I am glad you remember it that way. All I remember was that I was so confused back then, but I now know that Auntie was not expecting to be, nor was she trained to be, Queen. Really she was only the Keeper of the Bridge. She had been anointed as that, until I was old enough. Being called a Queen made her feel uncomfortable, but she felt that the people of The Shimmering Bridge needed the consistency of having a Queen so she did not correct them."

"She introduced herself to me as the Keeper of the Bridge."

"She did?" Queen Chayzlazamia said incredulously.

"She said many called her their Queen, but she was the Keeper of the Bridge."

"She did keep order. Not in the same way my mother did, but in her own way. I did not realize that, as I was too caught up in my own emotions." Queen Chayzlazamia looked at me for a moment and thoughtfully she said, "Ahh, but often feelings are hurt and decisions are made without an attempt to try to dissolve a misunderstanding or see the bigger picture.

After my mother left, The Empress came and gave Auntie another crown. She also made my mother's Shimmering Shamanic crown into a ribbon laced with a silver and gold anointing oil. I am so glad she sent me you, for I needed to have a Trusted One. I had to put that ribbon on my head the night Auntie shimmered away. I might not have become Queen if it wasn't for you. In fact, if it was not for your wisdom, there might not be a Land of the Shimmering Bridge. I had to come. I had to say thank-you!"

A sound came out of me, at least I think so as I looked into her eyes. "I think, I needed to hear that today. You called me Thee Trusted One. I remember saying I was trustworthy, but I didn't think I was Thee Trusted One. I didn't want the responsibility of being that to the future Queen, but I guess I did okay. When I first arrived here at the Rofonia Nation I didn't want the responsibility of guiding them through a lawsuit, but at least I had some experience, but now.... I guess you probably know I am supposed to be talking to the man who shot me."

"Yes," she answered.

"I didn't feel I had the wisdom when I was Thee Trusted One nor do I feel I have the wisdom to talk to the man who shot me. I know I am the one who wanted to see him, but I don't know if I should be the one trusted to report back what this man says. I merely wanted to see if he had shame for what he did. I thought I was strong enough to do this but then I became scared, worried my emotions would get in the way. Now I'm with you and I feel confused and I don't understand, don't get me wrong, I am glad I am with you, but...."

"When you were in the Land of the Shimmering Bridge, you told the truth and never embellished. You remained centered. You listened, but kept your own council and always tried to do your best. You were inspiring, encouraging, and kind."

"Wow, thank-you, but I certainly didn't feel I was all those things. You're right about one thing, I did try to do my best."

"You did not get caught up in the drama. Remember, this is Samuel Evan's world and the Rofonians'." She crinkled her nose and with a reassuring tone said, "By the way, when you do your best, it always works out."

"I must remind myself, I'm a wanderer in a strange land, and I must be non-assuming. If you have been sent here, then the benevolent forces of the cosmos must be looking after me. I think Thee Trusted One needs to trust."

We sat there staring into each other's eyes and then I said, "Thank-you for everything, for every stolen moment I have spent in your presence. Thank-you for letting me know what happened to your mother and your Auntie. Finding out what actually happened must have made you feel more peaceful."

"Peaceful! That is an understatement, for it has given me an amazing gift as it has allowed forgiveness to ring through my soul. As soon as the forgiveness happened there was a freedom and an awakening within my being. With that new growth came new insights and I began to embrace my true path. Now I know my destiny."

She smiled and she looked older, no, wiser. "When I leave the Land of the Shimmering Bridge, I will become the Angel of Life Experiences. I will travel into other worlds much like my mother. Maybe I too will be destined to go to Earth. It seems like such an interesting place."

After taking a deep breath I responded with, "Yes, Earth is definitely an interesting place. You know, most of the time one never finds out how they have changed someone's life. Thank-you for letting me know how I changed yours for the better as you certainly have changed mine for the better also."

"You being shot was horrific. Samuel Evans will be a better person in this lifetime because of you and you will be a better person in spite of him. There is a difference and since that happened you have already made a difference," she deducted. "You shimmered and came to the Shimmering Palace, and in doing so, you brought an assembly of the higher powers. You brought them together. Those who are working for love are congregating at my Shimmering Palace, because you believe and were brave and followed your destiny. So, thank-you!"

"Thank me? I don't think I did all that, but I think I needed to hear your encouraging words today," I said truthfully.

"Our stolen moments are coming to an end and now we get to observe."

"Observe?" I questioned.

Chapter 12 - The Enlightened Fly

"Yes, you falling has brought Samuel back to that horrible moment of when he shot you. Just watch," she said. Queen Chayzlazamia moved her hands and as she did, she smoothed the shimmering colours until they were no longer there, at least not below us as we now had clear vision.

We were in the Idocrasia room levitating inside a shimmering bubble. There on the floor, to my disbelief, was my body. Standing over it, looking mortified and frozen in movement was Samuel Evans. He plopped down on the floor. I did not know whether Fodulza or Kindosa sat him there or if he did it on his own. Nonetheless there he was, horror and pain were constricting his face and body in ways that made me feel compassion beyond anything I'd ever expected to feel for him.

"What have I done?! What have I done?! How could I have ever done such a horrible thing?! Oh God how could I have done this?! Oh God, help me! No, no," he yelled, "help her, help her! Do not worry about me, help her, God, help her!!"

A ray of light shone down. It was as if the ceiling had opened allowing bright sunlight to pour through, but Samuel seemed too caught up in his grief to notice.

"That's Azrael, she comes to those who are grieving, releasing the old, and bringing new beginnings. She helps people face their fears," Queen Chayzlazamia whispered as I watched the rounded yellow tube of brightness become more defined.

The brightness faded. There stood Azrael; she had brown hair with curls that circled her narrow face. Levitating above her head was a halo. Above the halo was a white orb.

Colossal, almost translucent wings captured my attention. They were somewhere between what I would imagine butterfly and angel wings combined would look like. Soft luminescent pinks and blues emanated through them.

She stood towering over Sam. He appeared to notice a light on the floor and slowly, as if he was letting his eyes adjust to the brightness, he looked up. First focusing on the bottom of her pinkish, silver-white dress, his eyes continued following up the gown ever so gradually until he stared into her face.

"Are you the Angel of Death?" he asked through his tears. "Then take me, not her. She did nothing wrong." Sniffing, he pleaded, "Please, take me. It doesn't matter what happens to me; the only thing that matters is that she's okay. I did this. I pulled the trigger. It was my greed," he sobbed, "my horrible greed. My stupid desire to prove to everyone I was better than them. Please, just make her okay. Please, please, please."

Placing his head on the floor at her feet, his body throbbing, the light ascended and disappeared through the ceiling.

"Wow, was that ever enlightening! I feel like a fly on the wall. He has no idea I am seeing this," I whispered in sheer awe. "It was the last thing I expected for I thought of Samuel Evans as hard - hard like a windshield. It never dawned on me that he would be so traumatized over hurting me. I thought he felt that I was a mere bug that was simply in his way."

Queen Chayzlazamia took my hand, "You have to go now, but I felt you deserved to see his heart. You have had so much disappointment in your life. The higher powers wanted you to see that being shot was not going to be without reason."

"Yeah, the reasons aren't always clear at the time, are they?"

"Very rarely," she said with a smile. "Farewell my friend and my love will be with you through all your journeys."

The next thing I knew, my eyes were blinking. In between the blinks I could see Samuel.

"The angel didn't take you?" he cried out with relief when he saw my eyes blinking, "The angel didn't take you, I am so glad, the angel didn't take you."

"Angel," I said weakly, feeling disoriented as the memory of Queen Chayzlazamia and Azrael was still blurred.

His hair looked tousled, not perfectly placed as I had seen it before. He looked quite different as the once clean-shaven face now had a scraggly beard. His clothes looked like something Peter would wear and I wondered if Peter had actually donated them. We both looked at each other, stunned, not knowing what to say next. I was trying to take in the now and process the stolen moments at the same time. Samuel was probably thinking he had sounded crazy rambling on about angels.

I was starting to prop myself up on my elbows when he said, "I would help you but, I... I... I am frozen for some reason."

"That's okay," I said kindly as I shifted to a sitting position. "How are you?" I asked with concern in my voice.

"How am I?" he responded angrily. "How am I? I shot you! I...! Shot...! You...! Do you understand?" he screamed as if I was too stupid to realize that fact. Pounding his chest with two fingers, he repeated, "I... shot... you!"

At that moment I realized if I hadn't seen his heart, I might not have understood his emotions. His eyes were tear-less and the anger in his voice sounded as if it was directed at me, as if I was stupid and didn't know that I had been shot. It wasn't his ego telling me that he had shot me, but instead his shame that he was the one who had actually pulled the trigger.

It seemed he simply couldn't comprehend my kindness. I believe he expected anger, for that probably would have been his reaction. I think he would have been happier if I had wanted revenge because he would have understood.

Cringing as a result of his tirade I quietly said, "You don't understand how I could ask you, how you are?"

"No, I don't! You should be angry. Be angry!" he yelled. "Hit me, beat me and tell me how horrible I am."

"Why do you want me to yell at you or beat you?" I asked.

He looked at me for a second and spoke in a calmer tone, "Because... then I could be mad at you and somehow justify my actions." Grabbing his hair he clenched his fists at the top of his head. "Now I have to be even more angry at myself!"

Nodding and feeling strong enough to cross my legs and fold my arms across my chest, I said, "So if I'm angry at you, even though you do deserve it, you'd redirect your anger at yourself towards me." I paused giving him time to process and then continued, "If I'm not angry at you, you are angry at me,

58

because you think that is the emotion I should have right now?"

To my surprise he responded with, "So you are angry at me. You think I deserve to be beaten."

Feeling frustrated I wanted to be logical, but I reminded myself that when one is in a state of fear and hate, logic can be heard as a weapon. He hated himself, but in some warped way, he may have hate towards me. In his skewed way to justify his actions he could even go to the point of thinking that if I hadn't stopped him from coming up the mountain and doing what he intended to do, he wouldn't have shot me? No, he merely would have continued intimidating the Rofonians.

In my yesterday's world I had been beaten severely for stating logic in the midst of skewed emotions and in this world I was shot for saying nothing. Taking a deep breath, I reminded myself I didn't know if he was even thinking that way. That thought made me realize saying anything more was probably futile. However, it was my moment with him and he couldn't do anything to hurt me. So with that same calmness I had earlier in the meeting room, I released my arms into my lap.

Straightening my back, I said strongly, "If I'm angry at you and want revenge, I have given in to the same hate and fear you had when you pulled that trigger." I put my arms straight and strong on the floor, "I don't want it." Using my arms, I stood, "And I don't want to be here. This is your anger, not mine."

Wanting to remain composed as I walked out I was thankful the door was open. I was also thankful I wasn't overweight or overly tall. It's odd what goes through one's mind sometimes. When Rainbow Dancer, with Kindosa and Ooza in the howdah, came out to the hall they found me leaning against the wall, taking in the energy from the Idocrasia.

"Princess, are you okay?" Ooza asked.

Gathering strength, I pushed the door shut and answered with a new confidence, "Yes, I think I'm where I'm supposed to be at this moment in time. I have seen what I needed to see and I have heard what I needed to hear, we can go back now."

We made our way back to the Tarnana. Ooza and Kindosa

talked about seeing a real live angel and he told Kindosa all about the time he met a shimmering angel Queen.

The attention was on me when we arrived, wanting me to rest, but I wanted a meeting, and a meeting was what I got. Fodulza and Kindosa talked about Azrael and Samuel's angst. Fodulza wasn't impressed with his anger and wondered if he had learned anything after having such a spiritual experience.

"Learned, had he not? Express himself, did he know how? Right words to say, right way to express, finding not always easy," Kindosa offered, looking compassionately at Fodulza.

"If I hadn't seen Samuel's heart, I would've given up on him and suggested he be sent back to deal with the human criminal system. Often it takes something profound to change someone who blames and manipulates others," I said astutely. "Seldom, without a traumatic event or a loss, do humans take a long look at themselves and desire to be on a different path. This definitely rates as a traumatic event for Samuel."

"If the fruit to the core, rotten is not, a seed anew begins there is," Kindosa surmised. "An angel seen by all, enchanted flies on wall, we were. Alone he was. When alone, was his inner seed, not shown?"

"I think so, I was distracted when Samuel thought she was the Angel of Death," Fodulza added with a bit of a pout. "I thought she was planning to take Princess away!"

"The angel was Azrael. She often comes to those who are grieving, releasing the old, and bringing in new beginnings. She helps those who need to face their fears," I informed them.

"If she is helping those who are grieving she could be like an Angel of Death," Gorph interjected.

"Maybe, but I thought of her as the angel who would come after a death or a tragedy, more like an angel of release, bringing about change," I added.

"Could've come to help you move on," Gorph suggested.

"But the eyes of Princess were closed when angel came." Everyone turned and looked at me before Fodulza asked, "How did you know the angel's name?"

60

I looked at Fodulza. "Queen Chayzlazamia told me," I said. "The shimmering angel Queen, was there? I didn't see her. Maybe I felt her because I talked about her on the way home."

"She and I had a stolen moment," I smiled, glancing at Peter who was looking at us as if we were from another planet.

"Gifts from an angel for all, then," stated Scota.

It appeared too much for Peter to take in and he wanted to steer the conversation back to a logical place - something he could comprehend. "Can we bring the topic back to Sam as he is the one who is guil... he is one who is at fault."

"What has been spoiled by fault made good through work. Take time it will. Know that, he will have to. Prepared to do the work. Come from him it must," Rotopa's father cautioned.

"The cause is no longer. Not here, at least," added Kindosa.

"I'm not sure I understand," I said hoping I would receive a better explanation.

"His upbringing, lifestyle the cause. In his life no longer. Thinking anew. Dealing with situations is new. Underway it can get, series of relapses likely less," answered Kindosa.

"Is what you're saying is, that one needs to be away from all friends, all family if they want to start anew and truly want to change?" Gorph asked, waving his finger back and forth.

"No, saying I am, is at the start, away they need to be from the cause. Difference there is," answered Kindosa.

Peter then interjected, "I think what she means is, some friends and family are good influences and others do and say things that keep you stuck in a dysfunctional place. Samuel's father certainly seems to keep him stuck."

"New seed hard to grow if soil not fertile," Scota added. "Hard for wounded to help. Wounded you are. Shot you were. Our priority you. Strong, capable also you are. Later see him."

I didn't feel strong or capable. This was out of my league. Did Scota want me to see him again? Why? Both her and Lumoona had indicated they didn't think I could help him. Samuel gets to release his old ways, maybe it was also a time for me to be away from everyone and release mine.

61

Chapter 13 - A Question And A Half

Scota indicated that a new seed was hard to grow if the soil was not fertile. Was changing one's patterns as easy as planting a new seed in fertile soil? Wouldn't it also mean keeping the right conditions after the seed starts to grow? A lot of plants get ripe and die, but was it really a death or a new phase of life? Some plants are nourishing and some don't seem to have a purpose. Some keep growing and have the potential of taking over. I think I'd prefer to be a beautiful, nourishing, yes, a non-invasive type that has a purpose.

"Princess, Scota said you are strong and capable, but do you feel strong and capable?" Fodulza asked, his voice bringing me back to the meeting.

His words were just being processed when Gorph spoke with a nod as if he was affirming his own statement, "This is too hard on her. I don't think she should see him again. She's still wounded, I don't think she wants that."

"What does Princess want?" asked Fodulza.

Well, that was a question and a half. What did I really want? I knew more about what I didn't want. I didn't want to be shot again. I didn't want to be haunted by the horrors of yesterday's world or have anxiety about events that hadn't even happened and perhaps never would.

I remember learning that my fears can be brought on by my own thoughts and words. Learning how to think and talk positively was something I needed to work on. It's like the universe doesn't hear the word 'not'. I shall cancel the thoughts of getting shot, being haunted, and experiencing that anxiety.

However, if the Rofonians choose not to reteach Samuel then he would have to go through that legal system and I would not only have to stay here, I would have to find a way to be part of this world. I think I want to move on, but I am not sure how, because both the thought of being involved in the reteaching process and the anxiety of testifying was too overwhelming for me, at least at this time. I guess Gorph and Scota were right, I was still wounded.

Finally finding my voice I said, "I would like to know what would be required to reteach Samuel. How would it be handled, because he has not been brought up the same way as you have brought up your Nation."

We talked for a long time. The Rofonians had the Idocrasia room and only one human to focus on and reteach. The consequences for his actions would require soul searching on both sides. Respect for himself would be taught first. He would be taught how to communicate his feelings.

They would be using sacred geometry, allowing him to absorb the symbols to help reprogram the conditions embedded in his mind. It was not, in their opinion, merely the conscious mind that had been affected by his childhood teachings, but it had also seeped into the subconscious.

It was decided after a time of rest, I would go back to see Samuel Evans. I was informed that Sam's actions at the time of my second visit would decide his fate.

Being wheeled once again through the marble streets and rows of golden houses, I wondered if I should have waited until I was strong enough to walk the distance. It didn't make sense to me why I had anxiety about still being in a wheelchair, maybe it was only because I was tired of having people feel like they needed to wait on me. Independence had been taken away from me. It was something I valued as it enriched me with a feeling of being capable of looking after myself.

It was easy to be resentful as I felt Samuel Evans was the one who had put me in this situation. Adapting to the demands of the time meant accepting they existed and also knowing that my actions leading up to the situation came from a place of love and that a lot of good had already transpired from it.

I was helping the Rofonians stand up for themselves in a way that should have harmed no one. Knowing that I was coming from a good place, at the time it happened, meant that more good was going to come out of this. Oh my, trusting that was another thing I needed to work on. Yes, look at what I have... look at it with a grateful heart and make the best of it.

Taking a deep breath I began feeling grateful for all the love and support I had been receiving. A smile crossed my face; I'm simply going to enjoy the attention of being waited on while it lasts. Soon I was going to have to face Samuel Evans.

Arriving at the sanctuary outside of the Idocrasia building, I asked to stop for awhile. I was intrigued by the flowers. They were quite different from those I had seen in yesterday's world.

Vibrant coloured birds were singing their songs. One of them perched on the bench in front of me and stopped singing. I stared into the small black eyes that accentuated a green and blue striped head. The pure white feathers on its body with its green and blue striped wings made the bird look very exquisite.

With a high-pitched trill, the bird sang. It wasn't annoying, but instead it was as if a soprano was singing a beautiful song.

> *When ulterior motives are not part,*
> *innocence rings true.*
> *Kindness and compassion*
> *are yours to impart,*
> *innocence in what is right.*
> *Love will bring it to you.*
> *It will sing you into the light.*

Yes, just what I had thought earlier, that my actions came from a place of love and innocence. Looking into the bird's eyes I knew there was more to it. I got it, my conversation with Samuel will have to come from that same place. Then the little bird flew away and I looked over at Peter who was staring into a flower, seemingly oblivious to the bird's song of wisdom.

"I think I have the strength to see Samuel now," I said.

To my surprise, I stood up without pain and walked to the door with Rainbow Dancer following me.

"Please do not restrain him," I said to Ooza and Kindosa,

"unless you absolutely have to, but I don't think you will."

When we walked in, Samuel stood up. It wasn't an aggress-ive stance, but more of a polite one. He smiled sheepishly, seeming very pleased to see me.

His face became sad, at least that was how it appeared. He looked at the floor and then back up at me and said, "I am sorry I was angry. I was angry at myself. You had passed-out and had just woken up and there I was, with no compassion for you. You shouldn't have come back. Don't get me wrong," he stood there shaking his head, "I'm... I'm... not very good at... I'm a mess, I'm... I'm so sorry."

"I know you're sorry or I wouldn't have come back," I said. "May I call you Sam or do you prefer Samuel?"

Maybe, bringing the conversation around to something nor-mal, he would move away from his emotional state and see things from a different perspective. That wasn't why I said it, it simply came out of my mouth, however Sam appeared to have gained more composure.

"Sam," he said. "I think I like Sam. My friends called me that when I was younger, I think I liked myself better then."

I looked over at the bed and the chair in the corner. Before I knew what I was going to say, I found myself asking, "I'd like to sit on the bed and let you have the chair, if that's okay?"

"Ah, ah, of course," he answered.

Rainbow Dancer laid down near the end of the bed staring at the chair as Sam sat down. I began propping up the pillows and curled up on the bed, leaning against the wall.

"The first time I met you I thought you were some weird, blind girl that Peter was dating. That land deal, if I could have pulled it off, was my ticket up the corporate ladder, stupid, huh?" Sam said, "Did the trial even happen?"

"Yeah, it did," I answered.

"Did the company lose?" he said tilting his head.

"Yep, they did," I said.

He just shrugged, "Figured they would, once I saw you and Peter. I figured a good lawyer would look at the mineral rights and they wouldn't have much of a chance."

"You knew the Rofonians had mineral rights and a registered plan before we even showed up!" I said, shocked he would have continued to move forward with that knowledge.

"Yep, what an arrogant asshole I am," he said looking rather disgusted. Then he sighed, looked down, and shook his head.

"Your actions then were that of an arrogant asshole," I said bluntly, emphasizing the 'were', "but I think your actions later went beyond that."

He put his hand on his forehead and resignedly said, "I don't even know why I shot you. I guess I was feeling desperate. I think it was just a challenge to me. Nothing felt real. It's like... I had been living in a game... in a world of winning and losing... at all costs. I don't even know who you are... yet I shot you." Sam shrugged and shook his head, "I don't even know who I am anymore." Sam buried his head in his hands.

What was I supposed to say to that? I didn't know, so I just sat there watching his body quiver. Thee Trusted One, the Princess, that didn't say anything. Part of me wanted to scream that he had shot me because... because nothing felt real to him!!

Then there was my compassionate side desiring to tell him there was so much more to life than greed - so much more to life than winning and losing. Life wasn't a game, unless that's the way he wanted to look at it, for as soon as he was caught in that energy he was a mere pawn. He had been nothing but a pawn in a chess game that spirals downward until he no longer knew who he was. He just pointed a gun at me, pulled the trigger not even knowing why?!? Was it that energy that pulled him downward, to blame or had it ultimately been his choice to walk away before he lost himself?

Chapter 14 - Goodbye Samuel Evans

I thought of yesterday's world and how lucky I had been when at a very impressionable age a wise man said to me, *'To look up or look down is your choice and I know that you will always look up'.* Was that what he needed to hear or was Sam caught up in too much self pity and confusion to hear anything?

Sam, to my surprise, raised his head and asked, "You going to be okay, or have I damaged you for the rest of your life?"

"I'll be okay," I answered, "once you've made your choice."

Sam stared at me as if he was checking to see if I was serious. He sort of smiled and from deep within his chest came a repeated, 'huh, huh'. His whole upper body moved up and down. He stopped and bit into his bottom lip so hard it looked painful. He shook his head and started the 'huh, huh,' again. His head went back and he broke into laughter.

When he stopped laughing, he looked around the room and said, "Look where I am and you need to know what choice I'm going to make? I don't think I have choices."

"You always have the choice of how you want to look at things," I said innocently.

Sam smiled, an odd sort of smile and took a deep breath, "Yes, I guess, I do have that choice and that is probably the only choice I have," he said, waving his finger in the air.

"Well, Sam," I said with a sigh, "actually the Rofonians are giving you a choice as to what you want to do."

Time slows when you observe closely for I swear I watched every muscle in his face relax before he soberly asked, "What are my choices?"

"Well, you can go back to the human city and stand trial for attempted murder."

"They are going to let me do that?"

"If you want to. It would be a gamble. You may get off with minimal punishment or you could go to prison. I guess that would depend on your lawyer and the Judge."

"You said I had choices, what is my other choice?" he asked.

"The Rofonians want to know if you'd like to stay here."

"Here? Locked in this room forever? That's a no-brainer."

"This would probably be your bedroom for a while, but not permanently. They would reteach you how to think and act."

"Reteach me? Or brainwash me?"

My face froze for a moment as I looked at him and I thought about my mistrust when I first arrived and I said, "Sam, do you remember playing at Peter's house when you were younger?"

Sam wrinkled his forehead and answered slowly, "Yeah."

"Do you remember how respectful they all were? How Peter's family talked nicely to each other? How they did their best not to hurt each other?"

"Yeah, I thought they were weird, but..., humph, at the same time I liked it. It was peaceful. His house felt safe."

"That's what the Rofonians are going to do. They are going to bring you to a level of respect and kindness. They are going to reteach you so you can own that level of thinking and that way of living will become yours. That's why Peter loves them so much, because that's who they are." He looked me as if he was in shock, so I concluded, "I think you would have been a different person if you had been brought up in Peter's house."

"I think... you're probably right," Sam said slowly. "I would be a very different person."

"Well, if you choose to stay, you will have a chance to be that different person and have that happiness and support. Do you want that chance or do you want to chance going to prison? Do you want to chance staying locked in a state of mind where life doesn't feel real and you're just living in a game, in a world of winning and losing. You get to choose."

"Why would they do that for me? I don't understand. I tried to swindle them and I shot you." Sam put his hands on each side of his head and shook his head back and forth saying, "I really screwed up. I really screwed up."

"Yeah, you did," I said with a raised voice. "You were like a screw trying to attach two pieces of wood together. You hit

68

your target, but the sharp end of the screw came up and out the side. You weren't paying attention to your life, your project was ruined and now you have even more to fix."

Sam looked confused. "That's one way of putting it," he said with a weird smile. Quickly he regained his serious tone and asked, "Why would the Rofonians not just want me in prison... out of their lives forever? Why are they being nice?"

"It's partly to do with you, your regrets..., your shame."

"Shame is an understatement."

"That's what I mean, you're taking responsibility, you're looking within. Also, it's partly to do with Peter. He doesn't believe the jerk you portray is truly who you are. He liked you when you were younger."

"Peter boy, I have put that man down so many times and he still believes I am a good person. Wow, that is so...."

"Idealistic, yeah maybe so, or maybe it's time you proved him right," I said, annoyed at his condescending attitude towards Peter and then in a stern motherly voice I continued, "Sam, you're getting a second chance, not a free ride. It's going to be a lot of hard work. To start with, you're going to have to take a leap of faith and show that you really want this chance. You will have to sign a confession and if the Rofonians feel you're not making progress, then arrangements will be made with the Court that you go directly to prison. You won't stand trial. You will have plead guilty to attempted murder and thus you will receive a prison sentence."

Sam became very serious. I had hit him with a stark reality.

My tone softened as I continued, "If you do the work and you can be retaught, you will never have to see the inside of a prison. You'll have physical exercises and be taught new skills. Mentally you will have to learn how to communicate and be respectful to others as well as yourself. That means not using your intelligence to irritate or hurt another. In addition, you will be required to learn and speak a new language. Emotionally you will have to take responsibility for both the hurts you have caused and also the hurts you have held onto. Spiritually you will be taught how to release them in a healthy way."

Sam looked at me nodding and we stared in each other's eyes before I said, "I know you saw, what you called, an angel and that means a higher power and guidance is there for you. That guidance is there because you started looking towards love and it believes in you." Again, I looked deep into his eyes. "The simplest concept may be the hardest, because you need to balance your love for others with love for yourself. I am not talking about self-serving arrogance that comes from a place of greed. I'm talking about a kindness that comes from inside and comes from working without any ulterior motive. However, the first step is learning how to be respectful."

Sam wrinkled his forehead and nodded for a long time. "Yeah," he said softly, "yeah," he said in a sort of normal tone. "Yeah," he said loud and strong. "I'll sign that confession, because even if I got to go back to my life, it wouldn't be the same." Shaking his head he spoke almost under his breath, "I'm not the same. I don't think I'll ever be the same."

"This is the Rofonians' offer, not mine," I said handing him the contract. "The chances of me ever speaking to you again, are very slim."

It was not my lot in life to educate him. It was my work to forgive him to the point where I could send love to his journey. I was still healing, but also, I was turning my cheek, looking in the direction of goodness. I could wish him well, but I was not at the point where I ever wanted to cross paths with him again.

He truly seemed to want to change, however, I had seen good intentions until temptation rose its ugly head. I had also seen enough manipulation in life and at this point I wasn't ready to have total trust.

Sam just nodded as he scanned the terms of the contract and then he looked up from the paper and said, "So what you are saying is I can change the packaging all I want, but the whole product is faulty and needs to be taken apart and put back together again. Until the product's rebuilt and repackaged, you're not using it, or buying it, or having anything to do with it."

"Kinda. I am sure there are some good parts worth saving."

"Here I figured you to be weak." I couldn't tell if he was kidding or not. "I don't deserve your kindness, nor Peter's, nor the Rofonia Naroso, or whatever you call them. I treat nice people like shat and those who are the nicest, I treat them the worst. I'm arrogant and I look at kindness as a weakness."

Was he just putting himself down? Was he just playing me? Or was he starting to understand how much strength it took for me to be there, be real and to be kind?

I didn't know so I said, "Sam, in some ways you're like the drunk who got lost in a bottle and hit rock bottom. The only thing now, is to do the work. Work hard on yourself and don't go back there again. Change your drink to love and kindness. You can beat yourself up for your mistakes until you become mad and bitter and want to blame someone else, simply because you can't blame yourself anymore. You can go back to your old habits of thinking that you're so smart and everyone else is weak because they try to see the good in you. You can connive and twist the truth and figure a way around everything. In the end the only loser is you.

My suggestion is you work towards bettering yourself. If this experience changes you into a better person, well," I stared at him for a moment and then smiled slightly and finished in a peaceful strong voice, "that's what would make me smile, that is what would heal my soul and help me forgive."

Looking up again, he said, "You already have forgiven me on some level, because you are wishing me good thoughts."

I no longer knew what to think. I shrugged my shoulders and merely said, "Do you still want to sign it?"

Sam nodded. He signed the piece of paper confessing to what he had done. He was aware of the human court system. He knew there was a good possibility a lawyer could get the charges dropped and he would never have to see the inside of a prison, but that wasn't what he wanted anymore. Sam had made his choice.

"Goodbye Samuel Evans."

Chapter 15 - Raw And Blistered

"Did Sam sign it?" Peter asked.

"Yep," I said with a nod and a sober face. "I can see why you believe in him, Peter, and Gorph, I can see why you don't."

"Meditation you mind if together we did?" Kindosa asked as her and Ooza slid down off Rainbow Dancer's back.

Everyone agreed and sat in a circle. *"Eyes they close,"* she began and Ooza repeated her, but in English.

Stand inside a tube of light, imagine.
Light coming from love it is.
Top of your head, feel it coming
Deep breath take
Love energy let it fill lungs.
Through entire being it flows.
Stomach muscles tighten
Hurts and resentments let light flush out.
Good and nourishing recycle them into.
Lessons need to learn, love bringing
Seed growing strong and beautiful.
Nourishment for soul each breath a gift.
The top of your head love coming it is.
Warming your heart it is.
Travelling down it is
Reaches bottoms of your feet it does.
Into ground it goes.
At peace you feel.
Walk forward, you're ready
Firmly on ground your feet
Love energy now connected

Open your eyes when ready," Kindosa finished.

Everyone still had their eyes closed with the exception of Rainbow Dancer and myself. Beams of sunlight descended from the sky. They surrounded each one of us, illuminating so brightly it was difficult to see form or even who was standing within the light. When everyone opened their eyes, the most amazing thing happened! Placing my hands on the arms on the sides of my wheelchair I stood up strong and straight.

"I feel like walking!" I announced.

"Mmmm," expressed Gorph as he rocked back and forth. "You look strong, but are you sure."

"Yeah, I am ready to give it a try."

Peter had stood up at that same time I had and moving close he nodded slightly and suggested, "Alright then Princess, how about you take my arm and Gorph can push the chair."

"No go on that one, I'm not pushing the chair," Gorph said to Peter. There was only a very brief moment of my ego inflating before it deflated for Gorph finished with, "I get the chair."

He promptly plopped himself into it and wheeled along the path. Ooza Fodulza and Kindosa shrugged their shoulders.

"Rainbow Dancer, I think I would like to view this from higher up," Ooza said with a bit of giggle.

Soon he and Kindosa were back in the howdah. There was great joy and laughter on the way back to the Tarnana. When we arrived, we all had a good chuckle as Gorph touched his tricep muscle on his arm with one hand and stared at his other.

"I have a whole new respect for people in wheelchairs," Gorph animated. He stared at his hands, rubbed his buttocks, and finished, "That wasn't easy. Can you imagine if I had to pick myself up using only my arms to move my entire body? You'd have to be pretty buff and tough to handle that life."

Peter looked at me and said, "I think Gorph figured out what people who man their own wheelchairs have to go through."

"Yeah, holy shat, the amazing amount of strength and willpower they must have. Look," he said, holding out his hands.

Not only were Gorph's arms tired and sore, but his palms were raw and blistered. Peter and I both stopped smiling and nodded at the reality of the situation.

"Let's go down the mountain, out on the town... celebrate.

We can grab some grub while we're there. Well, that's my vote," Gorph said getting out of the wheelchair.

Smiling I said, "I don't have money for that and I don't think I have the energy yet for a night out on the town," feeling that my muscles had already had quite a workout.

"What about just grub? We'll buy," Gorph said with his head tilted to one side looking at me, but I just sighed.

"We will buy?" Peter asked. "You speaking for me now?"

"A man can try can't he? Tell you what, I'll buy for her, but I ain't buying for you... unless, of course, you want me to."

Peter snickered, "Just giving you a hard time." Turning towards me he said, "How about this, it's still fairly early, you go have a nap. I'll take the contract, his confession or whatever it is, to Scota. If you feel like it, get dressed, and we will go to town, but only if you feel like it. If there is enough time we will go out for dinner, if not, we will just go to my place or..."

"Or I will bring you supper in bed, whatever my Princess needs," Ooza interjected, tilting his head in a bow.

"Yes, my Princess, whatever you need," Peter said, smiling at the voice from the howdah. He looked at Gorph and said teasingly, "We can catch some grub tomorrow and then we can see what we can do to get this contract signed and sealed by the courts. How does that sound?"

"You're all so thoughtful," I said shaking my head and smiling, "and considerate. I simply want you to know that I both notice it and appreciate it."

"We are almost at Tarnana and walking the rest of the way would be nice. Rainbow Dancer, do you mind?" Ooza asked.

Rainbow Dancer stopped and both Ooza and Kindosa descended from the howdah.

"Wow, you're so smart," Gorph said as he took the time to look into Rainbow Dancer's eyes and pet him.

"Thank-you, Ooza Fodulza, whatever you call yourself," Peter said with a hand on his chest and a bit of a bow. "The two names are a bit confusing for me, but with that being said it is a lot easier to talk to someone I can see, so thank-you."

"You are welcome Peter Coplanden," he said as his arm rose into the air and with a slight bow he continued, "I have been Ooza most of my life. It is difficult for me too as I also need to get used to being called Fodulza. The oddness of this is that when I was in the human world, I used to be a bit sad, for most of them had two or three names and I had only ever had one."

Gorph put his hand on his heart. "What's your story, Ooza."

"That is a story, Gorph, I do not wish to tell," Ooza said looking up at Gorph before finishing, "at least not today."

"Yeah I can respect that. There's many a story in my life," he turned down one side of his mouth, shook his head, "I don't wish to tell." Then he said, "At least not today. Hey, why don't you come to the Como and celebrate. I promise Fodulza, I'll not ask any questions about... the life of Ooza." He put his arm out as if Ooza's life was a stage production.

Ooza looked at me, I simply bit my lip and swallowed so he answered Gorph, "Ooza has not had many nice experiences in the human world. Ooza is now Fodulza and Fodulza is loved, respected, treated with kindness, and has a purpose. Ooza likes it here and does not wish to go back to the human world."

"Well, I don't know what happened to you in the past, but you have us now and we wouldn't let any human ever hurt you again. By the way, we are not all that bad, there were a lot of humans supporting you in court," Gorph said seriously.

"Yes, thank-you, Gorph, the support from you and your friends was amazing. In my eyes, you will always be an honourary Rofonian. Maybe someday, I will venture out into the human world with you, but right now I desire the waterfalls of kindness to cleanse Ooza's heart." Ooza had put his hands over his heart and looked down, but when he finished he glanced up at Gorph and took a bow.

To this point Kindosa had simply been listening, however in her kind voice she added, "Knowing you both better, liking you both more, for me it is. An asset both you will be, reteaching Samuel Evans."

Chapter 16 - The Beginning of Gorph

We did end up going into town later that afternoon, but by the time we arrived at the bottom of the mountain it was getting late, so we stopped at The Como, where we had originally met Gorph. We talked about how it went with Sam that morning.

"I guess I always knew that he had a conscience, but I was so miffed at him for the way he turned out. It was like he was spiralling into shathood," Gorph said.

We both laughed, but Peter responded with, "Well I knew he was spiralling downward, but I've never heard it called that."

Gorph waved his arms in and out as he explained, "You know, he was spiralling and it was to a rather stinky place. The little shats he'd hang with, brought out his worst. Yep, it was those neighbourhood shats." His palms faced each other as if he was measuring his fish story and stated, "And thus he was spiralling into shathood." Then he began to eerily sing,

One should never, ever, go there,
Cause you can spiral,
down, down, down into shathood,
and you'll never ever know,
if you'll ever ever leeeave."

We were laughing when Gorph put down his glass with a loud clunk on the table. "Where are you from Princess?"

There was silence while Peter and Gorph just looked at me waiting for an answer. An answer I didn't know how to give, so I smiled and said teasingly, "I'm not from this world Gorph."

"Well, I could have told you that, there is nobody like you in this world, but ser..." he started before I interrupted.

"Is Gorph your real name?"

"That is what they call me. Is Princess your real name?"

"That is what they call me," I said with a smile and a shrug.

"His real name is Elbridge Gorphanastiski and on his first

76

day of school the teacher called for, 'Elbridge Gorph... Gorph... Gorphan... Gorph'. The whole class broke out laughing, hence Gorph was born and Elbridge Gorphanastiski was lost forever," Peter told the story with exaggeration in his voice.

"Hey," said Gorph, looking surprisingly annoyed.

"I promise not to resurrect Elbridge Gorph...an...ass...kay," I said botching his last name, "Gorph suits you just fine."

"And Princess suits her, don't you think?" Peter interjected.

"That it does," Gorph said sipping his drink, "that it does."

"Gorph, where have you been?" came a voice off to the side and soon our table became bigger as more and more people joined us. After a while Peter and I decided to go to his place.

Gorph just said, "Ya, the 'rents are around the corner. I got a sofa, but don't forget about me."

"Never," I said with a smile and we headed into the city.

When we got back to Peter's place he asked me if I had seen anything except this city and the city in the Rofonia Naroso.

"No," I said, "just the road between here and there."

"You hadn't seen this city 'til I brought you here, had you?"

"No, you're right, I hadn't," I said honestly.

"You really aren't from this world are you?"

As I sat in the beautiful energy of Peter's house I looked into his eyes, still unsure of how much I wanted to tell him, I shook my head. Telling him the truth would take a huge leap of trust.

"I'm not much of a city person so I'm not a good person to show you around here, but I do know the surrounding area quite well. So would you like to go on a road trip with me?" he said looking hopeful. "The countryside is quite beautiful."

"A road trip? What exactly is your definition of a road trip?" I said slowly.

"A couple of weeks touring around, hiking, and seeing the amazing natural wilderness that surrounds the two cities."

"A couple of weeks?" I said with a gulp.

"Yes, but only as friends, just two friends going on a trip. I promise I will not do anything to make you feel uncomfortable. We'll take the family camping gear. There's plenty of room for two beds. There's a divider. You can have your own sleeping quarters. I'll look after everything, you just get to come along."

It did sound intriguing and Peter had something about him that I knew I could trust. He was a straight-shooter, something Sam had only accomplished with a gun. Peter's idea of straight shooting would be of a gentleman and that meant a lot to me.

"What about the tower, don't you have to look after that?"

"Well, I've solved that one," Peter answered with exaggerated pride. "I've been training Gorph while you were healing and sleeping a lot." His tone changed and he became serious when he asked, "Do you know what we realized?"

I shook my head.

"The Watchtower had always been programmed to miss the Rofonian city. The new technology I put in was done incorrectly. I just didn't realize how precise the new program was and how much it took in." Peter shook his head in shame. "I hadn't exposed it on purpose, I just didn't know. Gorph's a lot better with stuff like that and I needed his help to figure out how to integrate what Great Grandfather promised and managed to attain with his old technology, into the new technology. It's working now and the Rofonians' City is now camouflaged." Peter gave me a thumbs up.

"But isn't Gorph busy with his band?" I asked.

"Coincidentally a band member is having a baby and they wouldn't be gigging for a bit and he's really happy to have a job. You know, Kindosa asked him to attend a few classes in Respecia so the children can get used to a human."

"Really," I said with a bit of a laugh, "I wonder what they will think of Gorph's mannerisms and... sense of humour."

"Well, he gestures a lot with his hands, he should fit in."

"That he should, that he should." I said in a deep voice rocking back and forth then ended with, "He's wonderful isn't he?"

"That he is, that he is," Peter responded with a chuckle, "and 'shathood', who would come up with such a word." Peter's tone changed as he said, "Wonder where Sam will end up once he's cleansed from his all 'shathood' experiences."

"Who knows, he might do something amazing. I believe something good always comes out of a bad situation. Maybe it happens that way because I believe it so strongly," I responded. "Maybe it is what it is, and something good always happens. It started with Sam's greed, but we've all learned a lot. You and I met. I reconnected with Gorph. He wrote a hit song. We found out that there are many good "humans" in this world. I could go on and on," he said and then he brought it back to the pending question. "So how about that road trip, Princess?"

"Oh Peter, it's complicated," I said thinking about my shimmering problem and the fact I had flown by crane, been small and invisible, swam inside of crystals, not to mention defying time and dimensions. I really didn't know what was going to happen next, so I sat there in my thoughts and stared at him.

"Help me understand," he gently said. "I know you live in another world. I think you trust me, so please help me understand. It might do you some good to talk."

"That's going to be something I'll have to sleep on. We won't be leaving tomorrow as we have to go to the courthouse and deal with the... you know, the thing that Sam signed." I nodded and stood up. "Maybe, onadremaso my gentle friend."

"Onadremaso my Princess, tosolsin."

"Until the sun shines," I said smiling.

"I used to think onadremaso tosolsin meant good night, but it so much better now - may your dreams be filled with love and insight, until the sun shines," he said. Then as if he was looking past me, he shook his head. "This experience has enriched my life." His focus changed, he studied my eyes for a moment and smiled. "It amazes me on how good you are with other languages. How fluent you are at speaking Rofonian."

I wanted to tell him that I'm really not very good with other languages. I was given a gift when I entered this world. I just hear everything in English and then out of my mouth I seem to speak and I am understood. I don't need to remember anything, it just happens, but I didn't say anything, I just headed to bed with a glance upward and a silent 'thank-you'.

Chapter 17 - Coincidences

Morning tea on Peter's deck was lovely. The garden was very beautiful, but I might have liked it a bit too much because we didn't get away to the courthouse until late morning. We needed to ask questions as to how to proceed from here, now that Sam had made his choice, and had signed a confession. By the time we arrived we were told the person who might be able to answer our question was on a lunch break.

"We didn't really have breakfast. Can I buy you something to eat?" I merely shrugged my shoulders and Peter continued, "There's a little hidden away restaurant not far from here."

It was decided we would get a bite to eat and return later. We walked between a couple of black and white buildings and through a black door with no sign. Inside was a restaurant and once we were there we noticed the Judge. Not any judge, but the one who had ruled over our court case.

Was this a coincidence? 'An *occurrence that occupies the same portion of space at the same time as another, without an apparent causal connection'*. If something or someone caused this connection to happen, it certainly wasn't apparent to us.

As we walked by, Peter established eye contact and gave the Judge a slight nod.

The Judge raised his finger and said, "Mr. Cope..."

Peter interjected, "Coplanden Sir, Peter Coplanden."

"We were just talking about the Rofonians' case," he said with a nod towards his colleague.

Peter nodded slightly and said, "I don't imagine you have too many cases like that one, Sir."

The Judge smiled, "Not with such unique defendants, no. Did the one who was shot live?"

Peter didn't bring me into the conversation at all, instead he established it was now attempted murder. Presenting our desire to have the contract honoured by the courts he asked what steps were needed. The Judge's colleague, coincidentally was a criminal judge and was able to fit us in that afternoon. Only one more trip to the courthouse, then to Sam's family home and Sam would no longer be our responsibility.

After lunch, we met the criminal Judge in his chambers. All went well as no precedent had ever been set and all parties including the defendant were in agreement. The paperwork would be done, his decision filed and all would be in order.

We drove back across town and I waited in the truck while Peter went to see Sam's family to let them know their son would probably be away for quite awhile. Something told me the son who left would not be the same when he returned.

"Are we going to go up the mountain and let Scota know?" I asked Peter once he returned.

"No, I don't think it's necessary. Fodulza and Scota are expecting us to be a couple of days. However, we should let Gorph know. Do you want to head to the Como now or later?"

"Tell me something, you have the technology in place to be able to see a city way up on a mountain, don't you have any phones?" I asked ignoring his question.

"Phones?" Peter asked.

With a sigh, I rephrased the question, "Do you not have a way to communicate with someone who is at a distance?"

"Princess, like I said before, you sure are an enigma. Yeah, we have the Borg. Have you not heard of the Borg before?"

I guess I should be careful of how I answer that question, for the only time I had heard of the Borg was on the show Star Trek in yesterday's world. On that show it was described as *'a vast collection of cybernetic organisms linked together in a Collective with the purpose of assimilating or destroying all life in the universe'* -'Resistance is futile' was the Borg's slogan. So I merely looked at Peter innocently and shook my head.

"Well, that's actually refreshing. I don't have much to do with it either, but how do I describe it? I think I would need to be a cybernetic scientist to give you an actual description of what it is and I am nowhere near that, but it is how we communicate from a distance," he said as if he had heard my thoughts.

I must have looked confused and he continued.

"Some of my pictures and geological findings are there as it seems to be the only way that humans know how to communicate. However, I guess my great grandfather and the Rofonians still have a lot of influence on my family and I'm still dancing to my own beat. Fear of turning into clone, I guess. I merely submit stuff in black and white to the black and white city who pays me for my submissions and for manning the watchtower. Probably stuff ends up being absorbed by the Borg, but as long as I don't, all is good."

"What do you mean absorbed by the Borg?" I asked with a bit of fear in my eyes.

"Well," he said with a look of curiosity as if he wasn't sure where to begin, "Well the Borg is the name of the cyber-network set up for means of communicating anything and everything. I guess, to put it quite simply, the Borg would be considered a collection of interconnected networks that provide a variety of information and communication facilities. However, it seems to have a life of it's own and sadly it seems to be destroying people's ability to think for themselves."

I merely nodded and we drove the rest of the way absorbed, not by an interconnected network, just our own thoughts.

Could this be another coincidence? Was this black and white city's Borg the same as yesterday's world's internet? Was it an occurrence that occupied the same portion of space at the same time as another? I mean these people were from Earth originally and they did have a lot of similarities plus yesterday's world's internet appeared to be having a life of its own.

We drove up out of the city and stopped at the Como where we found Gorph on stage. The music was wonderful and inspiring. After a while he stopped playing and joined us. He told us he had been asked to gig there for a couple of days.

Gorph made a fist and put his thumb in the air for a few seconds and he said, "Yep, really stoked you two aren't headed back up the mountain. Good you're staying in the house, even if it's only for couple of days. It's a talking place you know, kind of magical. Yep," he said rocking back and forth, "got some really mind exploding nooks and crannies. Like it, but couldn't stay there too long, got to have the Borg, you know."

"I have a connection to the Borg," Peter defended.

Tilting his head back, Gorph laughed, looked at me and using his fingers as if he was connecting the dots, he explained, "Yeah, if he connects four or five different things and works on an ancient zapper, he can connect, even submit things." With his hand in the air, his finger pointed upward wagging back and forth beside his head, he finished with, "I rest my case."

Peter smiled, "She hardly even knows what the Borg is. You're presenting your case to the wrong person."

"Holy Shat," Gorph stopped in mid expression and stared at me before continuing, "Princess is that true?" All I could do was give him an innocent shrug and all he could do was shake his head and mumble, "Holy shat, holy shat."

"I was trying to explain to her earlier that it seems to be destroying people's ability to think. In my opinion this thing seems to be turning people into clones and has become a money making, greed machine. You know it makes me wonder if it wasn't part of the reason Sam turned out the way he did... not even thinking before he shot her."

"Yeah, yep, ya could have a bit point there, but not really," Gorph said rubbing his black and white hair. He brought his hand down and shook his finger, "I mean I use it and I don't think I'm goin' to be shooting anybody so...mmm."

"What do you use it for," I asked.

"Music," Gorph answered.

If only I could be a little more open about who I was and where I was from, because I would let them know that on Earth some cities being banning people from using their internet while walking across a road. Other's were wrapping their street posts in foam because too many people were absorbed by it and getting injured walking into them. While still other cities were embedding a set of street lights in the sidewalk so people would be more apt to notice them. It was definitely shutting off people's brains, but to what point? I wasn't sure.

My reference point was yesterday's world and not this one, so I simply said, "Maybe that's the difference, you're using it to be creative and maybe Sam was more absorbed in it and perhaps using it all the time, maybe for his entertainment, or maybe for him it was just about money making and greed."

"Good try Princess, but I'm using it to make money," Gorph said with a shrug and stretching his arm a little farther towards Peter he ended with, "The Copy does too. He uses it to submit things that he gets paid for and I sell music and advertise gigs."

"Yes, but I use a shovel to dig up rocks and I report my findings for educational purposes and yes, I do get paid for it. You submit your music and you get paid for it. Her point is that you and I use it as a tool and I don't sleep with my shovel."

Gorph waved his arm up in the air and said, "Ahhhh."

I laughed, "You sleep with your guitar at times, don't you?"

"Um, yeah, guilty."

Peter put two fingers and his thumb on his forehead and simply shook his head.

"Ahhh," Gorph said and then made a clicking noise before he finished, "I getcha, we do make money off it and it makes money off us, but it's not our life and our life is not all about it or the money." He looked at me and smiled. "By the way, I don't go to bathroom, eat, or drive while playing my guitar, but I do sometimes fall asleep creating a new tune," he said using his fingers to play an invisible guitar and rocking to the tune in his head, "cause music's my sanity."

"I read somewhere that music can open new pathways in people's brains," I replied.

"Yeah, a pathway that leads me right to my soul," he said without looking at me and still bopping to his own beat.

Stretching his arm out, he stood and with his index finger keeping time to the tune in his head, he pointed at a girl and danced off towards her. Peter and I smiled. Peter tilted his head towards the door and we walked out waving good-bye.

Chapter 18 - Orbs of the Obsmoon

Stretching after a wonderful sleep I touched the smooth headboard of a translucent crystal bed. Where am I? Oh right, this was the spare room in Peter's house. Yes, now I remember. Sauntering out of the room I passed the carved rose coloured sofas and made my way into the kitchen. There was no sign of Peter, so I found myself a piece of bread and brewed some tea.

Noticing that a door beside the kitchen was ajar, I smiled, as a door had a 'jamb' and could be 'ajar' and I was carrying my tea, actually looking for a jar of jam behind an ajar door. To my surprise, the door didn't lead me to a pantry, instead it led me into a room made of rainbow-banded black stone.

The morning sun shone through the window accentuating the hues. There were greens, blues, reds, mauves, and sometimes a golden colour glistened. A milky white crystal vein was interwoven within the stone, but as the sun shone upon it, a vibrant blue tone overtook the white. In the far corner, the black stone extended out into a rounded seat with a big cushion on top. Entranced by the energy of the room, I found myself walking to the cushion and curling up with my cup of tea.

Suddenly the sun disappeared and all was dark with the exception of twinkling colourful stars. A marbled white and blue light spanned the darkness. Soon it turned into a solid bridge that seemed to be beckoning. What if my time here in the land of the Rofonians and the humans was over? What if this bridge was a portal to another land? I wasn't sure I wanted to leave this planet for I had just started enjoying Peter's company.

Oh my, what was happening? I was being pulled across the bridge with no control over my body. The bridge was made of light, but light beams are not solid and I was no longer being pulled, instead I was simply standing on a light beam!?!

There, in front of me was a round silver-white orb with eight golden lights. The golden lights seemed as if they had electricity pulsating from them giving the illusion of lightning bolts. At the end of each bolt of lightning appeared a shiny round mauve orb with a red one following.

I was just getting used to the pattern when two glowing squares shone through, intersecting each of the red ones. Two more orbs appeared after the red, one was green and the other blue. They were smaller than the first two with the blue being the smallest orb of all.

Was I going to travel to another planet or was I brought here to stand upon a bridge of light and stare into this phenomenon? What if the squares were a door and I was supposed to enter them? Breathing deeply, I realized, once again I had no choice. Oh, here I go, for I was being moved forward over the blue bridge. Slowly I travelled through the squares and... ohhhhh, I was being sucked into the center orb.

The next thing I knew, I was standing in the middle of the silver-white orb. Beams of electricity began shooting out of me. Deep wounds of yesterday's world pained my insides. Flashes of trauma filtered through my mind:

Girl after girl
slap after slap
face
brick wall
slap after slap

no one to tell
no one who'd believe

Boy after boy
again and again
others
sung them on
again and again

no one to tell
no one who'd believe

86

thump after thump
over and over
head
wall pain
over and over

no one to tell
no one who'd believe

flash after flash
pain after pain
stop
go away
flashes of pain

love is in my well
yes I will trust
I will believe

It stopped as suddenly as it started, like they were in mid-frame then turned into a gross mass. It was as if someone had melted a bunch of negatives from old photographs - pictures that no longer wanted to be looked upon. The negatives turned hard and there were colours mixed within. Although they were mainly black and brown, there were also oranges, blues, and reds - they weren't pretty. The mass looked like something that should have had a foul smell. It appeared burnt, charred, or melted together into a hard grotesque mess.

The lightning bolts appeared again and penetrated the gross ugly mass, breaking it up like an explosion. I was standing in the midst watching tiny particles shoot out from the mass through the same light that was rendering it inert.

Ohh, my body was in pain and feeling weird. I lowered my chin and looked down at it. Oh my, what was happening to me!?!? I no longer have skin!?!? Looking at the masses that were caught within my muscles, my bones, and my organs I watched the lightning break them up and like eight vacuums they sucked the dirt away. Whoa, an abrupt suction was yanking me backwards and my leg felt like it was burning!

"Hi, you okay?" I heard Peter's voice say, "Sorry, normally I wouldn't invade anyone's space while they're in this room, but your teacup is tipping."

I just looked at him and then I looked at my body. I was fully clothed!! I was back in my own skin!!! I had no idea what to say, for I didn't want him to think I was crazy. Did this sort of thing happen to him or did it just happen to me because I was from another world? Slowly I adjusted my teacup.

Peter's hand was in front of me, so I took it. He didn't ask any questions, nor did he say anything. He merely led me back through the kitchen towards the country side of his house - the side not seen from the road. Through the window I could see it was a bright, sunny, beautiful day, but the sky was white. What had happened to the beautiful indigo sky?

I was disoriented and had no idea whether I was in the now, another dimension, or in the future, but I did know that I wasn't in the past. We walked through a sunny room that had squares of the Idocrasia stone embedded in the wall. Tears were welling in my eyes as we arrived outside onto a deck. Peter sat me down in a chair and told me he would be back shortly.

I thought about the trauma that had flashed through my mind and then I thought about the blobs. Was all the pain I held onto beginning to manifest within my body? Was what happened a rebirth - a release? Tears began flowing and I cried and cried. The next thing I knew, Peter was handing me tissues and a fresh cup of tea. The deck overlooked a beautiful garden, a garden I had not seen through my tears.

Finding my voice, I softly said, "You live in a sanctuary. I can't believe that we're even in the city."

"It wasn't a city when the land was bought. If I sold it I would be rich, but what good would that do? If I was rich, I'd want to buy it so I could live here," he told me. "You found my obsmoon room. It's an amazing room to go and meditate in. Lately, my meditations have given me a great interest in learning more about sacred geometry." Peter stopped for a moment and then said slowly, "It also can bring negative emotions into the light to release them, but it's usually a peaceful place to be. Honest." He studied me before he asked, "Are you okay?"

I nodded.

"You sure?" Peter asked, not convinced by my nod.

"I have had a lot of horrible, horrific things happen to me in the past. I guess...," I said with a sigh, remembering the masses breaking and the particles leaving, "I guess it was just my tears releasing some of those emotions. I think, maybe all that happened was just a very deep cleansing." I was quiet for a moment before I stated, "It's weird for I want to go into your obsmoon room again, but at the same time, I don't want to."

"If it's cleansing, why wouldn't you want to go there again?"

"I'm scared I might go in the room and not come back out."

"The room's made of obsidianna. It protects you from losing yourself. It's even laced with moonta - the milky white, blueish stone," he clarified. "That's why Great Grandfather embedded the moonta in the wall, so light and protection would always be in that room. You never have to worry, because no matter how deep the meditation, you'll always come back. Although, most people come out of the room refreshed, happy, and a little wiser, not full of tears."

"I guess I had a lot of emotions that needed to be released and let go," I defended, wondering if the room was that powerful or was something else happening to me?

Was the fear of it pulling me to another world actually real? I was going to have to trust and believe it was a powerful meditation room and not a portal to another world. Taking a deep breath, I affirmed if I go back in there I would have to believe I was safe, protected by the moonta and would be back.

"Can I go off topic?" Peter said tilting his head to the side.

Sniffing, "I think I would welcome it."

Chapter 19 - What If?

"Have you given any thought to the road trip? I don't want to put any pressure on you. The only thing I have to do is pick up the official documents from the Judge. Oh, and take Gorph back up the mountain, then I'm free to go. I'd love to have you join me, but you're welcome to stay here, or I can take you back up the mountain when I take Gorph. I just thought it would be nice if I could show you some of the countryside. However the mere thought of going seems to make you sad."

"I'm not sad Peter, I'm just worried about you," I told him.

"Worried about me? Why?"

"It's like this, I'm from another world. There are things that could happen to me. Things I can't explain and I don't know how you would be able to deal with them if they did happen."

"Like what?" he asked as I shrugged. "How do you know if I could deal with them or not, if you won't give me a chance?"

Peter seemed to simply want to show me his world. Looking into his eyes I could see he didn't have any other motive and for me to have this much trust was profound.

"Okay," I said, "I will try to explain." I bit my bottom lip and looked at him and he patiently stared back. "As I said, I am from another world and I don't just mean a state of mind. I am actually from another world. There is a chance I could go on this trip and not come back. What if that happened? Time moves in a different way for me. One moment I'm in one place and... a moment later I'm somewhere else. I have even had conversations with animals. Haven't I, Rainbow Dancer?"

Rainbow Dancer nodded.

"Seriously, what did you say to him to make him nod?"

"You heard me," I defended.

"That you have had conversations with animals, then I think you were speaking oughtleopar," he speculated.

"I said 'haven't I Rainbow Dancer' in English," I responded.

"No, you mumble when you talk to him."

"I do?"

"Did you ask him if he thinks you should go?"

"No, but that's a good idea. Rainbow Dancer do you think we should go on this trip?"

Rainbow Dancer nodded.

"He just nodded again. Did you actually ask him? He nodded," Peter teased, "he thinks you should go, doesn't he?"

So I asked him if he had the same fears I did about going?

"Release fears. Time for humans different. Time stood still last time," was the answer I received.

Was he telling me I no longer was human or was he merely referring to the '*stolen moments*' as Queen Chayzlazamia would call them? I rephrased my question, "But what if I don't come back and you and I actually move on?"

"Let Peter choose."

That was all Rainbow Dancer said, so I looked at Peter and asked, "What if I just disappeared out in the wilderness?"

"I would never stop looking for you," he said.

"Yes, you'd look everywhere. You'd feel responsible and I could have moved into another dimension and you would be still be searching. If you called the authorities to help you search, they'd think you were crazy, for I don't even exist, at least not in this world."

"Well, you are here and I know you're not a figment of my imagination. We do have court records verifying you exist."

"Not really, I didn't say anything in court. I just observed."

Peter paused and then said, "But we talked to the Judge."

"Did we? Again, I only observed. You did the talking."

"What about earlier with the lawyer?"

"I was merely an interpreter. I didn't sign anything. Sorry Peter, you will not find proof that I'm from this world."

"So who did Sam shoot then?"

"For all they know, Sam could have shot someone from the Rofonia Nation."

"But Fodulza said..."

"All he said, was they had guns and they shot his friend."

91

"If you are an illusion then you're everyone's illusion." he said poking my arm gently. "See, you really are here."

"I am here. I'm not saying I'm an illusion. I'm only saying, all isn't what it seems and I often don't understand what is happening." Sighing, I continued, "Put it this way, I didn't grow up on this planet, neither did my parents or my grandparents."

"They are here somewhere, right? Like you, they do exist."

"Yes, they just don't exist on this planet."

"Gorph knows you exist. You and he have a mutual friend. There is a connection from your past and I know Gorph grew up on this planet," Peter protested.

"Yes, he does know someone I know, but even he thinks I'm from another world. He may not want to admit it to himself. We both know Raziel. Raziel isn't from this world, so I don't think Gorph would be surprised to find out that I too, am not from here. Oddly, I don't think he would be shocked if suddenly I disappeared. In fact, I think he kind of expects it."

Peter stared intensely into my eyes, looked away, and said, "So what you're saying is that Sam probably wouldn't have gone to jail, because he didn't shoot anyone."

"No, he did shoot me. Like I said I do exist. I'm just not from this planet, but you're right, he might not have gone to jail because my existence here would be hard to explain."

"I am sorry, but I'm finding this hard to comprehend," Peter said holding his palms towards me.

"I understand your reaction, because if I hadn't experienced it myself, I would have a hard time comprehending it as well. However, I can't go with you unless you're at peace with who I really am. You would also have to be at peace if I disappeared. You think about what I have said and you decide whether you want to take me on a road trip or not."

His eyes were fixed on me, but he didn't say a word. After a bit, he stood, his eyes still on me, nodded and walked inside.

Sitting outside I told myself I had to believe and trust. Then I went into the kitchen, poured myself a glass of water and wandered into the obsmoon room once more. I knew cleansing one's soul was important and having such a powerful room to do it in was a gift that I may not get again.

The room was dark and I could hardly see where I had once sat. Letting my eyes adjust I placed my glass of water on the floor and climbed upon the rounded cushion. It was as if the weight of my body triggered a change and the room once again looked like a starry night lit with the colours of the obsidianna. This time it was the blue amid the milky-white moonta spanning across the room that created the bridge.

Sitting still, staring at the beautiful bridge, I observed a large mauve orb with a golden center. It seemed to have small streaks of light coming from it. I felt a pull or a twinge in my abdomen. It wasn't as bad as I had experienced in yesterday's world. At one time the pain was so intense that it would drop me to the floor. This pain, however, was intense enough that I closed my eyes for a second. Upon opening them I noticed a small red orb beside the larger mauve one. That was interesting because red was the colour of the base chakra.

Captivated by the golden center of the mauve orb, my chest began to pain. Was I having a heart attack? No I couldn't be, I I am protected, right? This must be all within my mind.

Yesterday's world flashed in front of me, a time when I had laid there with an indescribable weakness, unable to move or speak, not knowing if I would live or die, but still able to hear. The words I heard hurt then, scarred my heart much worse than the thought that I might be dying.

That incident wasn't in the pictures that were burnt earlier when I was here in the obsmoon room. Maybe it wasn't ready to be released and burnt. Perhaps I needed to feel it again to really understand where the hurt in my heart was coming from. How much hurt can a heart endure, before it manifests itself into the physical body.

Wincing, I began concentrating on my breath and filling my heart full of love. Still in pain I looking back up to the large mauve coloured ball and the small red one. I saw that opposite the red, was a small green orb, the same colour as my heart chakra. Staring into the soft green orb I realized my chest was not paining anymore, it had stopped, leaving only a slight ache in my head. Rubbing my eyes I saw another orb - this one was indigo. It took its position beside the red one as if the smaller orbs were forming a ring around the mauve one.

Feeling a pang within my diaphragm, I watched a yellow orb appear directly opposite the indigo. The pain again disappeared, but my throat had tightened as a blue orb shone between the indigo and the green.

My throat felt okay again, but my stomach started to ache. An orange ball had appeared and took its place between the red and the yellow. Now there were six orbs symmetrically positioned around the larger mauve one. Golden stars twinkled in between the six colourful orbs and my body was finally at peace.

Not again! The first pang was in my stomach and a large orange ball took its place farther out. Was it making another outer ring? A blue orb appeared on the opposite side. Each time before the coloured orbs appeared, my body felt pain and once they were positioned in the outer ring, the pain went away.

There were now another six orbs, symmetrically positioned around the mauve one. Between each one there was a twinkling golden star. Slowly, a circle of light seemed to be joining each star and each orb of the outer ring.

Oh no, it was happening again, the pain was more intense and the orbs were much larger. It started with my diaphragm this time and soon there were another six orbs.

A circle of light came into view appearing to be a double helix. The helix travelled around each rainbow colour, or should I say chakra colour, joining the larger outer ring of orbs. Rays of mauve and golden light flooded out of the center pulsating through the newly formed circle.

My eyes were closing. I felt empty and exhausted. Blinking I tried to keep them open, because the golden light in the center of the mauve was moving. It seemed to be coming closer and closer!! Still blinking, I realized that it had legs and arms and taken the form of some sort of a golden light-being!

The being walked over to me, picked me up and carried me across the bridge. We walked into the middle of the mauve orb. Rainbow colours swirled around us until a dizziness overtook me. Was I going to pass-out?

Suddenly, all I could see was an indigo orb coming straight towards us. There was no time to duck as this orb was going to hit my forehead just above my eyes. What?!? It didn't hurt. There was no pain, instead my head felt clear and aware.

The blue orbs turned into one that was coming closer and closer, the golden being had disappeared and I found myself now standing alone. I stood strong, well, almost. I did hold my breath until the blue orb collided with my throat. I could hear someone singing as the greens combined into one and entered my heart. The singing changed to a hum. The yellows joined together and went into my diaphragm, then the orange into my stomach, and the red finally settled in my abdomen.

Was this what Peter called a meditation? In the types of meditations I had encountered, my body stayed in the same place. I should be on the cushion, but I wasn't. I was standing in the center of the room upon an arched blue and white lit bridge! If the bridge was only an illusion, then I was levitating in midair! Once again I had to remind myself to trust.

Carefully walking down the arched light beam I picked up my water and drank. I smiled, feeling nothing but sheer happiness. Happiness like I had never experienced before. It was as if I had taken my shadow side and integrated it into my body. It was like my ego dissolved into nothingness. I felt aligned, optimistic, and engaged in this existence.

The only thing that mattered to me was that I was truthful, loving, and kind. The past felt at peace. The future felt exciting. The now felt intriguing. Wouldn't it be nice if life always felt like that. I traced my hand along the obsidianna and as I walked out, I glanced back at the bridge that was now fading. I was a soul on an truly amazing journey through time!

Chapter 20 - DNA

I was hungry and it had been a long time since I had cooked myself a meal. It took me a while to find food, at least some that I recognized and would know how to cook. There were many fruits and vegetables I had never seen before. Soon Peter joined in and we managed to cook a nice meal.

"Well, another twenty minutes," Peter announced. "Should we go out on the deck while we wait?" He didn't wait for an answer, instead we proceeded outside. "You seem different, lighter, more at peace. This time your experience in the obsmoon room must have been better."

"Yeah, it was, but I won't lie, this was very, very weird."

"If you tell me more about it, perhaps I can help you. Maybe I can explain something."

Doing the best I could, I explained the physical pain, the orbs, the colours and the double helix, but I didn't tell him about levitating nor about the light-being. It seemed, I don't know... kind of personal or maybe just too weird and I needed more time to process what had happened.

"My mother was good at explaining the strange symbols one sees in a meditation. I think she would tell you the colours and the pain were cleansing each chakra, one at a time. The double helix interests me," he said thoughtfully. He paused for a long time before he said, "We're all connected through our ancestors and we are all born with DNA right?"

I nodded.

"I've often wondered if we could heal past the point of what our DNA indicates? And if we could do that, then would we be able to change what science believes our genes dictate?" he asked tilting his head towards me.

"Are you saying you think it's possible to change DNA?"

"Well, they've discovered that trauma and stress can change a person's DNA, so why couldn't deep healing also change it? Definitely a thought to entertain." Peter looked at me over his

96

shrugging shoulders as if he was asking me what I thought.

"Hmm, yeah, that it is," I said with a smile as my response made me think of Gorph. "Though wouldn't we have to stop defining ourselves by who our parents and grandparents are and instead see ourselves as a separate entity?"

Looking a bit amused, he stood, pointed at himself and said, "Right now, this entity has to check on the food."

We were about ready to sit down for supper when I asked Peter if he thought we should be picking up Gorph after we finished eating. No sooner had the words left my lips, when we heard a knock on the door and Gorph was standing there.

Peter and I managed to make supper stretch into another serving. Afterwards, the boys sat and played music as I sketched a picture for Peter to always remember me by. He would always know that I did (in some form of reality), exist in his world, at least for a time.

The next morning when I arose, Peter was busy packing the truck and didn't seem to need my help. The obsmoon room... do I dare go in there once more? Had it become addictive, or was it my desire to grow spiritually - to release and heal old patterns? Maybe change my DNA? Science had impressed upon me that the heart disease and cancers of my ancestors are probably mine also, but maybe it doesn't have to be that way at all. Perhaps this was my journey of healing, and changing.

Standing at the door I remembered the orbs and the lights breaking the hardened masses that yesterday's trauma had caused. Those memories, that were burned into my mind, no longer served me. It wasn't like I was holding onto them intentionally, for most of the time I didn't have a choice. I wonder if now that they were broken into small particles would I be able to finally realize their true purpose? They were not there to destroy me. They were there to help me understand something - something profound and on a universal level.

We are all part of the universe and the universe was full of orbs. They all seemed to stand alone, have their own purpose, but at the same time they all seemed somewhat interconnected.

Perseverance in what was right was what I tried to keep in perspective throughout all of my travels. Maybe it was about having the perseverance to heal my body and my soul. The woman with the golden brown hair was levitating orbs and at that time, I saw them as the Earth and the moon. Whether they were or weren't was irrelevant. What mattered was that she was levitating orbs. What did she say? *'It is the continuance of time and power of persisting. It is the creative and thus the creative are often those that seek it.'*

The power of persisting, hmmm... do I dare go past this doorway and into this obsmoon room again?

Braving myself I walked into the room towards the cushion and made myself comfortable. A blue and white bridge instantly appeared, much like a prism casting rainbow colours from the morning sun, and glowed in front of me. A ridge of gold graced the edges and above it was a small yellow dot.

I realized that three very small silver-white dots surrounded the yellow. One was at the top and two were off the sides close to the bottom. A humming began. No, it was more like a chant. I couldn't make out what was being chanted even though it repeated itself several times. Each time it repeated it became an octave higher. When it hit a note that I felt could have broken glass, there was a cracking sound and then a swishing noise that sounded more like river rapids.

A red light shot out from the yellow dot creating a fire-like glow of red and orange. Now near the yellow dot was a bright orange orb. Then, the orange one became surrounded by six silver-white orbs.

A inverted triangle appeared in the middle. A silver-white orb with three small orbs surrounding it appeared on the triangle. Soon there were six of these clusters hanging like grapes at equal intervals along the triangle's edges.

An upward pointing larger triangle began to form and as it did, it intersected with the angles of the smaller one. Huge blue and pearly white orbs glowed at each point of these equilateral triangles. A glowing fire-like light flickered upon the inside edges of these orbs and a large inverted triangle encompassed everything with the exception of three blue orbs.

Then an outer ring encircled it all and it glowed brighter and brighter. The more it glowed the closer I moved towards it. Oh my, what was happening to my skin, my body, my form? I had become nothing except a yellow energy of light! I was getting smaller and smaller! Within a blink of an eye, I was hurtling at warp speed into the small yellow dot in the middle!

Now, I was on the other side of the yellow dot! Whether I was on the other side of the bridge I wasn't sure because now everything was mottled in greens and purples. In the midst of the mottle there were two glowing light-beings. I was now one of them for I was no longer small, in fact I seemed quite large! The three of us all looked sort of human as we seemed to have a head, a torso, arms and legs, but at the same time we were glowing. We were yellow light! No one spoke, but I could hear someone's voice talking. Whether it was male or female, I could not tell.

"Surrender, be light, be like water, go with the flow. Darkness dispelled. Energy cleared. Go forth with love. All the peace earned will not come forth immediately, but trust it will take form."

The colours faded. The light-beings vanished and the triangles and the orbs disappeared with them. I was back in my body, sliding down the bridge of light and gently hit the floor.

Walking out of obsmoon room I felt different, perhaps a bit out of sorts. Had I tried to heal too fast or too soon? It was amazing, however I think it might take a long time for me to process all that had happened. On second thought, maybe the only thing I need to do is to trust the voice that I had heard.

I saw Gorph walking out of the bedroom and Peter was coming in from outside. I was back into the normality of their lives. It was as if all that had happened had been done in another dimension and life, as they knew it, still continued on.

Chapter 21 - It's Fushie

The night before, Gorph had been drinking a fruity quaff, he called a fushie. The drink was tasty and I found myself sipping them slowly throughout the evening.

"Eww, am I fushie this morning. We got fushied last night," Gorph said walking into the kitchen scratching his head.

"Fushied? The truth is you're the one who got fushied. I remember the evening - no side effects," I retorted softly.

"I just drank tea, so I'm not fushie at all. Seems you're the only one. Hey if it's any consolation, we laughed a great deal, played some great tunes and you had a ton of fun," Peter told Gorph as he gathered some items to take out to his truck.

"Can I be of any help?" I asked again.

"Nope, I'm good," he answered. "Both tea and coffee are on. Go sit by the garden Princess, I got this."

"Okay," I said, not sure what to think as there seemed to be a little coolness in his voice, although I really wasn't sure.

Could it be because he thought I was crazy? Maybe it was only because he was concentrating on what he needed for his trip and I'm simply being too sensitive.

The morning sun was taking its place in the sky as I sat looking at the garden. All would be revealed when the time was right and I needed to go with the flow. Right now my flow was enjoying the beautiful peaceful environment and fresh air.

Gorph came outside and stood looking at the garden for a bit before he asked, "Where's Peter? What's he up to?"

"He's packing the truck for his trip," I said.

"What are you gonna do Princess?" he asked while talking through a yawn. "Are you going to go with him or are you going to go home now? Do you even have a home? Or is your home with the Rofonians?"

Staring at the garden, I merely glanced at him and gently said, "Gorph, I have no idea what I'm going to do. All I know is that I'm exactly where I'm supposed to be at this particular moment in time and that's enjoying the garden. I have no idea what the future is going to bring."

Gorph stood there and scratched his head, did a back bend that turned into a stretching yawn and said, "Well, okay then. At this particular moment in time, I'm going to go get coffee."

He walked away doing a tired morning shuffle. Shortly thereafter, he returned with his coffee and sat down.

We sat in silence until Peter came around the corner. He had finished packing and was ready to head up the mountain. He told me the Como was close to the midway mark and they served a good breakfast

"Yep, we're on Peter time," Gorph commented.

Peter didn't get annoyed, instead he spoke softly, "Would you rather eat here, Gorph, cause I'm okay with that too."

"I'm good, I'm good. A Como breakfast sounds good," he said still sounding groggy and this time with a sleepy thump of his feet he headed inside.

"You okay with going for a Como breakfast or are you hungry now? Do you want to make something here?" Peter asked.

"I'm fine," I replied, smiling at Peter's thoughtfulness. "I think Gorph's just a little fushie. I guess he will be fine too, but giving him a snack and a good strong glass of water might help his mood."

"Ya, you're probably right. I'll grab him something." Shaking his head Peter mumbled, "Someday I hope he learns."

"You don't drink that fushie type stuff," I tilted my head and finished with, "ever?"

"No," he said teasingly as he tilted his head towards me. He looked out at the garden for a few moments, as if the blossoms and the colours were absorbing his thoughts, before he continued, "Never saw the sense in it. I like me, so why do I want to alter who I am? Especially with something that makes my body and mind feel horrible in the morning. Even if it didn't, it seems silly to play with something that's... addictive."

Peter seemed reflective for a while before he said, "You

know, I think I observed a lot when I was a child. My family never drank much, so maybe it was just because it wasn't normal, but I would watch the older neighbours that drank. They all seemed to have weird mood swings... or changes in their personalities, plus their memory seemed compromised."

"Their stories were interesting up to a point," Peter rolled his eyes as he continued, "until you heard them ten times. In retrospect those people really weren't that old. I just know I didn't like watching other people being annoyed or laughing at them. They laughed too, but it wasn't a synergy, it was more like they were being laughed at. I always wondered what they would have been like if they didn't drink."

Peter leaned back and stretched before he finished with, "So I decided when I was quite young it was lots more fun being sober. Plus I remember that I had fun." He smiled, "You don't seem fushie, nor did you seem fushie last night. Do you just know your limit or do people from your world simply have a tolerance for the stuff or do they even have fushies?"

"They have something quite similar and it has ruined many a life. They just don't realize that the drinking road has a very slippery slope. It's a small part of my life. I don't like getting drunk, or fushied as you guys call it. I don't see the sense in it. I do enjoy having a drink or two, but in moderation, I had fun last night and you sure looked like you did."

I smiled at him as I thought to myself this kind, gentle man was somebody I could be in a relationship with. Too bad they didn't make more of them in my world. Too bad my journey was probably going to take me in a different direction.

"I did have fun," he said as he rose from his chair. "I'll put together a snack for the road. That should hold you two until we get to the Como. You ready to go?"

"Ya, just need to have a pee," I said, finding it interesting how uninhibited I felt around him.

"O... kay," he said, separating the syllables.

I don't think he was used to someone being that informative. Following him inside I nonchalantly said, "I heard somewhere,

102

it's an old soul who announces when they have to pee."

"Ooo... kay," he said in response to my statement, but I caught his smile as he was looking into the cupboard.

Once on the road, there was not much conversation and then out of the silence came Peter's voice. "You know maybe it's simply because old souls are just more in tune with nature - more real about who they really are."

My mouth opened and I looked at him for a second, in disbelief that he was actually thinking about that statement. I laughed and Peter merely smiled.

"Did I miss something?" Gorph said, opening one eye.

My face went a bit red, "No, not really."

"K then, going back to sleep."

We drove to the courthouse and Gorph and I waited in the truck while Peter picked up the papers that were now signed by the Judge. Was this part of my life over?

"Did everything go as planned with the Judge?" I asked.

"I don't know, it's addressed to the Rofonia Naroso, so it's not mine to open."

We drove out of the city in silence until we were almost at the Como. The silence was broken by a loud snore from the back seat thus we decided to head up the mountain instead of stopping.

After awhile Peter asked, "If you did come with me and I came back alone, what would I tell everyone?"

That thought hadn't occurred to me, what would he say? That I just disappeared? That I flew away in the beak of a bird? Or that I shrunk and hopped on the back of Rainbow Dancer and vanished into his fur never to be seen again? I thought about the Empress and the children's words while they were singing for her, '*You are the mother of all that is good; you are the mother that helps us feel understood*'.

"You could tell them I went to see my mother."

Straightening my back, I shifted and put my unshod foot on the dash of his truck. Peter looked over with raised eyebrows, though I wasn't sure whether it was my action or my words that caused the look.

After a time of silence, he said, "Your mother? How could you go to visit her? She's not in this world, is she?"

"No, she's not, but I have to find her, it is my destiny," I said quietly, thinking about the Empress.

Being on a journey to find 'the mother of all that was good', The Empress of love, was a pretty nice destination to have.

Peter was quiet for awhile and then asked, "Will you be able to send me a sign when you're safe?"

"I, I don't know," I said honestly. "I truly don't know. You might have to be very still and quiet, trusting your instincts. I'll do my best."

Peter looked very, very sad.

"Hey," I said, gently touching his knee, "I haven't left yet," I whispered. "If we go on this trip Peter, we cannot lose ourselves. We have to stay true to our own journey, our own path, and we cannot imagine things to be different. We have to be careful not to have unreal fantasies of a possible future to-gether, because that would only lead to humiliation. I want you to really think about this. I know you want to give me a gift by showing me the beautiful places you've been. I too want to give you a gift of sharing a wonderful time together, but if I am only going to bring sadness then we should part today."

The mood seemed to change and there was silence once more and I wondered whether Peter still wanted me to go with him. The road had turned to a winding mountainous path and took a great deal concentration which might be a reason why he hadn't spoken. Being able to honour another person's jour-ney was something one should do, however, it did often bring sadness. The clouds moved across the sky and the thunder rumbled across the mountains. Peter's face was very serious.

Listening to the thunder as we rounded the corners of the treacherous mountain road I did my best to release my fear.

Chapter 22 - Changing Time

"I was told once that thunder can release fear," I said gently, hoping the conversation would calm Peter's serious face.

"The thunder here releases the rain and it often comes down hard, making this mountain road almost impossible to get up."

The pressure applied to the gas peddle increased with his worry and the truck was no longer travelling up the narrow road at a comfortable speed. Lightning flashed, emphasizing his now fear driven energy.

"Peter, the rain is not here yet. Good rarely comes out of energy that is forced, especially from a state of fear. My vote is we drive at a more comfortable speed and enjoy the drive while it's still dry." Then I just blurted out, "*Slow down time to go with the flow and ask for perfect timing wherever you go.*"

"Well Princess, I know you're amazing, but I don't think you can stop a storm."

"No, I can't, but I have seen time slow down and I have also seen it speed up. Anxious energy often makes it speed up and can bring about negative results. When you're at peace and truly trust, don't you find more often than not, things work out better? I don't know how it works, it just does. When you make yourself dependent upon the harmonious and benevolent forces...," suddenly I smiled and shrugged my shoulders, "magical, wonderful things happen... like the rain waits for us."

"Well, perhaps your other world is more magical."

"Says the man with the obsmoon room," I retorted. "If you drive your truck at a normal speed without anxiety there's a much better chance we'll make it up the mountain before the storm," I repeated, trying not to feel or show fear as we sped around the corners of the narrow mountain road. "I realize these roads could be treacherous when wet, but going fast up this road puts us in danger also."

"Yeah, I suppose you are right and I'm obviously making you nervous. I will slow down."

"And be at peace with your decision?" I asked.

Peter smiled, "I'll try."

The thunder rumbled again and Gorph broke into song. Soon Peter joined in and I just hummed with my fingers snapping to the beat. Sometimes within my hum I could hear this deep rumbling hum that was also keeping a beat. I looked back at a smiling Gorph who tilted his head toward Rainbow Dancer. Rainbow Dancer could sing!

As we all sung our way up the mountain, the rain began to softly fall. Shortly thereafter, the watchtower was within our sights.

Buckets of pelting rain greeted us as we were getting out of the truck. Peter looked up, then at me, and we began to laugh. Running into the dwelling by the watchtower 'thank-you, thank-you, thank-you' poured from my mouth.

"You were right Princess, the rain held off. Did you really slow down time? Are you like Raziel?" Gorph asked as he was taking off his wet shoes.

How was I supposed to answer that, for I certainly didn't feel I was powerful enough to slow down time. Whether someone listened when I asked or whether the weather merely did as it was going to do, I'll never know. However, I'd like to believe someone listened. Maybe it was about connecting to the right energy. How would Raziel answer that question?

On that thought I said, "We were exactly where we were supposed to be when the rain started."

"Can't argue with that," Peter said, opening his guitar case, "You might as well settle in, because there's a good chance you won't get to the Tarnana tonight. I don't want my heavy truck ruining the Rofonians' road."

All was wonderful, the three of us were safe from the storm, the music was playing and Rainbow Dancer was singing along. Suddenly Rainbow Dancer stopped singing and ran to the door.

"Well, you won't mind getting wet," I said opening the door.

To my surprise there stood Ooza and Rotopa.

"How did you know we were back?" I asked.

Peter sort of answered the question for Ooza, "They always know. Don't ask me how, but they just always know."

"Please tell us what happened while you were at the courthouse. Did everything go okay?" Ooza asked, anxiously.

Peter let them know that the criminal Judge had signed the papers while I smiled, being thankful for our good fortune.

"Sam really, really wants to change," Ooza said rolling his R's, "and I am going to go to Respecia with you, Gorph, because I have never attended it before." He brought his hands to the sides of his face and as if there were imaginary strings attached to them he pulled his lips to a smile. "Besides Gorph, you will need me there to interpret for you."

"How long does this Respecia course take anyways. Tell me what am I looking at... months? Weeks?" Gorph asked.

Ooza turned and asked Rotopa.

"Making of road depends on soil, rock, weather. Respecia depends on progress, perseverance, growth. Time measured by your cycle, not ours."

Gorph looked as if he didn't know what to say.

"No worries Gorph, we will progress quickly and we will have fun," Ooza said with a reassuring smile and turned towards me and asked, "Princess, do you want to attend Respecia with Gorph and me?"

I could learn so much from the Rofonians. Then again, how much would I see and learn if I went on a trip with Peter? That was, if he still wanted me to go with him. Most of my journey felt like I was merely reacting to what was happening. All the more reason for me wonder if this was going to be a choice for me to make or was Peter going to make it for me?

My thoughts went to Raziel. He had told me not to linger in one place too long and then my eyes met Peter's. It was as if he knew that I wasn't ready to answer Ooza's question. Unexpectedly, Peter broke into song and once again, the music played. Ooza wanted me to dance so we did; soon Rotopa joined in and the crevices of time were filled with great joy.

The music stopped and Peter began tapping the front of his

guitar as if he was catching a beat for another song.

"Princess has a choice to make because I have invited her on a road trip," he blurted out.

Ooza's lips formed a small circle as he looked at me, then Peter, and back again two or three times. Ooza, what was that about? I wanted to ask, but instead I just looked at Peter.

"Are you sure you want my company?"

"Ab-so-lute-ly!"

It had only poured for a short time and by the end of the evening, Rotopa went out and accessed the situation. He believed the roads could handle the truck. We were both quiet as Peter drove me back to the Tarnana.

He was different from the other men I had met. There seemed to be a seriousness of purpose about him. He also appeared to be reliable and his aura was usually so peaceful and quiet that when he spoke, people listened. It was as if he was truly happy within himself.

To spend some time with a peaceful human might be what I need. What about Respecia? Was I sent here to learn more about a society that had no need for prisons? A society that seemed to have respect for each other - from those in power all the way down to those who were learning. One that gave second chances because they believed all problems came from a lack of respect which often resulted in an abuse of power. Now, an opportunity to learn more about these people was being presented, handed to me on a silver platter.

"You know you don't have to make up your mind, at least not at this moment," Peter observed as if he had been reading my thoughts. "The roads will be muddy so we won't be able to leave first thing in the morning. Sleep on it."

"That's a good idea," and with a nod and a bit of a smile I exited his truck, "Onadremaso."

"Tosolsin."

Chapter 23 - Fearful

Ooza and I met inside the Tarnana and talked far into the night. He told me his father was getting healthier. He said his mother thought the reason his father was doing so well was not only due to Ooza's return, but also because of his forgiveness. Scota had told him to be aware as sometimes people seem to get better before they transioflo. She didn't know which way his father would go, she just wanted him to be prepared.

"Transioflo?" I questioned for the word had no translation.

Ooza became quiet, rubbing the tips of his fingers, and then his hands joined together with the palms facing each other. His hands rose up above him until his arms were straight in the air, adjacent to his ears as if he was doing a yoga tree pose with straight legs. After a few seconds he opened his hands allowing his palms to face the ceiling. He didn't say a word.

"Is it like a soul going up to the heavens?" I surmised.

Ooza's face looked up towards his hands, his arms even closer to his ears, and smiling he said, " Father would be changing. He would be flying to new places, having new plans, and finding a new purpose. Mother says he would always be there for me, even after he is gone." Ooza brought this arms down and curled his hands towards his heart, "But I would like him to stay," he finished with a pout.

"But you would still have your mother," I said gently.

Ooza's face lit up. "She is wonderful, she is the most wonderful lady and she is my mother! Who would have thought Ooza would have such a wonderful mother. She brought me into this world. She listens to anything and everything I want to tell her. She gently tells me what will be expected from me as Fodulza, but she lets me be Ooza when I am with her."

He continued referring to himself by his name, "Fodulza's duties are beset with responsibilities. Fodulza has to balance keeping order in meetings, giving advice and at the same time being reserved on his opinion, at least until he understands more about the Rofonia Naroso. Fodulza's place in this world is much better than ever imagined. However, I have been Ooza for a long time." Ooza's hands were in front of his face and with protruding lips his eyes pleaded for understanding.

Oh my, what was I supposed to say, "Ooza, you are still Ooza and you are also Fodulza. Fodulza's a side of you that you have always had. When I met you, you were wise, respectful, kind, intelligent and always thinking of others. It's like being a new parent, one day you're silly and carefree and the next you're responsible for someone else," I said. I thought it was a good analogy, but then I found myself slowly saying, "You... just... became... a... parent... to a... whole nation."

"Oh Princess, that makes me...."

"Fearful?" I interjected.

"Yes." Ooza nodded as he put his top lip over his bottom one and looked as if he was trying to smile through his fear.

"Your journey happened for a reason," I said, probably needing to hear the words myself. "It gave you compassion and understanding on a deep level. You wouldn't have known what it felt like to be really hurt or how to forgive that. You would've been here living among those who were respectful."

"That was a lesson Ooza could have done without."

"Yeah, many times I feel that way too, but it was my life and I've gained so much insight and wisdom from travelling that road and you have too. Who knows where your road is going to take you. Who knows why the Rofonia Naroso needs your deep wisdom and your ability to see the bigger picture. When I met you, you were dancing through the woods, making up a song to help me find Bonnie. You should pat yourself on the back, because you were able to dance even though you felt so alone and had previously been so traumatized."

I didn't stop there, "Ooza, you've already learned there's a time to be serious and there's a time to dance and have fun. There's a time for Fodulza and there will be times for Ooza..." Shrugging my shoulders I smiled at him. "...like when you danced tonight. Soon Fodulza will be singing and dancing through the hallways, only this time he'll not be alone, he'll have the wisdom of his journey and the respect of his kin."

"Do you think Respecia will teach me how to respect the Ooza who had his clothes ripped and his body beaten until it was black and blue?" How do I answer that, but he continued, "I cannot ask my mother that, because she would not understand and it would hurt her heart." His hands made a heart shape and with a pout he stared deep into that heart.

After a few moments I answered, "You're right, your mother would probably want to help, but wouldn't know how. I think Respecia will teach of love, kindness, and respect as well as how to take responsibility for your life path. I also think it will teach you that you have already accomplished that."

Ooza's eyes widened so I softened my voice and continued, "But the hardest part will be, that most here won't know or understand why the inside of you sometimes screams, 'What did I do to deserve it?' or why sometimes you jolt awake at night in sheer terror. Just remember there are some things in life you are absolutely not responsible for in any way, shape, or form. They were part of a yesterday's world and some day maybe you will meet someone or some people who will benefit from your deep compassion and understanding. I know I certainly have."

Tears began to roll down my face and when I found my voice I finished with, "Ooza, you have no idea how amazing you are or how brave you are. You have taught me so much and I can't express how much you've enriched my journey."

"Oh Princess, it is Ooza that is so thankful he met you. Your compassion and wisdom has given me so much. I would never even have had the thought to leave the village, if I had not met you. Ooza always knew he was supposed to be with a princess. I bet you did not know you were supposed to be with an Ooza."

Somewhere between a smile and tears I listened as he kept his R's rolling, "You left because you had things you had to do and you also needed to arrive at the Land of The Shimmering Bridge by yourself. I had to come through the portal so we would know where it was. If Ooza hadn't been beaten then, maybe Queen Chayzlazamia would not have realized how mean the Camflages actually were. Maybe we needed to do all the things that lead us here. Maybe you are right, maybe the beatings that happened were not because I did something wrong. Are you going to leave with Peter Coplanden?"

I looked at him for a moment before I answered, "I haven't made up my mind yet."

Ooza made another heart with his hands, only this time he brought it close to his chest, and leaned his chin upon his knuckles when he asked, "Do you love him?"

"We would be travelling as friends if I go," I answered gently, but firmly.

Ooza lifted his chest, swung his arm out, "I think you should go and then maybe you could fall in love and stay here forever." A smile beamed across his face.

I told him what I had told Peter; that I might not come back. I told him about the dilemma I was having with the two offers. Maybe I was not persevering enough as I wanted to do the right thing. Maybe the right thing was staying here and attending Respecia and learning all I could while I had the chance.

Ooza was quiet for a while but when he spoke, his words were full of wisdom. "My mother told me to observe and keep quiet counsel, because if I didn't, people would flock to me to hear my stories. It is not my responsibility to entertain, instead it is my responsibility to listen, interpret and advise. Princess, you are our hero. You were very instrumental in saving our Naroso. You are like royalty and you will be worshipped and flocked to - Rofonians would hold onto your words. You would know inside if you are ready for that. If you are not, then go with Peter. See everything you can see. Learn everything you can learn."

He paused for a moment before he said, "If you are meant to learn more from us, then you will be back. If not, then Princess," he lowered his head with great sadness. Tears formed in his eyes and he stood straight as if he needed his back straight to give him strength before he could continued, "your journey will have taken you where you are meant to go."

Ooza stopped, blinked, and tears began flowing down his cheeks. "I will always remember you, honour you, and hold you in my heart." Ooza sniffed and then swallowed, "Thank-you for teaching me to read. An... and seeing all the good traits that you saw in me and for bringing me to where I needed to be." His face became taut, his neck muscles squeezed inward, and only his lips moved as he again said, "Thank-you."

He looked at me for a moment, gave me a hug, turned, and ran out of the room without looking back.

Ooza didn't come back and I was left pondering his words. I could stay here and be treated like a celebrity or royalty. Who would've thought that Ooza could handle being in such a responsible position and doing so much better than I felt I could? It wasn't that I felt I was better or wiser than Ooza. It was simply that when I met him, I didn't see him as an advisor for a Nation. I don't think I would want that responsibility, at least not right now. I think I would loose touch with myself.

To go beyond my own cognizance and take on a lofty position, one I was not ready for, could lead to a downfall. Hmmm, I believe I just made my decision and it came from a place of strength. This time I was not fleeing, instead I was being true to myself, true to my journey, and thankful I was able to choose what I felt I needed and wanted at this time.

Chapter 24 - Sweet Burning

There were tears in my eyes as I said my good-byes, for I didn't know if I was coming back or not. I don't think that the Rofonians knew that, although who knows, maybe they did.

Peter, Rainbow Dancer, and I headed out on our road trip. Perhaps I should call it our off-road trip as we were travelling on roads I wouldn't have rated as such. Every corner seemed treacherous. They wove around mountainsides with barely enough room for us to get through. Mirerasen platforms spanned across the small waterways and wooden bridges were over the larger rivers and streams.

Holding on to my stomach and trying hard to remember to breathe we approached a larger wooden bridge with deep crevices on either side and a river far below. The hopows wouldn't have an issue crossing it, but for us it was rickety and narrow, barely fitting the tires of Peter's large truck.

Once across, there were more narrow corners as we curved around the mountainside. Just as I was relieved and happy we didn't meet another vehicle (as I didn't want to see what would've happened if we had) we approached another corner.

Looking down the side of the mountain there were huge drop-offs with trees, rocks, flowers, and waterfalls. I didn't re-cognize many of the trees. They were in full bloom and it was a spectacular view, but oh my, not while driving on these roads.

Changing my focus to the beautiful amazing flowers gracing the other side of the road eased my stomach for a moment. Then my attention was focused, my back was straight, and my hands were busy gripping the inside of the truck as I was hold-ing onto the hope the road did not give away.

We made it and hours later, trees scraped the truck for we had driven off, what Peter called, a road and onto a beaten path. We drove on the path through dense wilderness and finally we arrived at a clearing.

We stopped and Peter went to the back of the truck and

brought out what sort of looked like a golden box, but no, it wasn't a box. It was layered sheets of mirerasen, similar to what they had brought into the courtroom, only it was much larger. Unfolding a part of it, Peter inserted a long pole into a metal ring in the center. Holding onto one end, he asked me to hold the other end firmly, because at the count of three, we were going to lift it onto our shoulders.

"My parents were able to do this when I was a kid so we should be able to," Peter informed me. "I haven't had to set it up since then. Look, if it starts to hurt you, I want you to stop."

I knew he was talking about my bullet wound, but it wasn't too bad lifting the pole up to my shoulder. It was surprisingly light. The square mirerasen pieces dangled from the metal ring and remained joined together looking like a golden box suspended from a pole. While holding the pole on my shoulder I watched Peter reach for another pole which was leaning against a nearby tree. This one had two prongs at the end.

Peter placed his pole between the two prongs. He pushed until the two pronged pole brought the one he had on his shoulder up to the same height. He propped it into the ground away from the mirerasen, leaving his body free to move.

Grabbing another two pronged pole, he walked around the box and did the same to the one I was holding. The two prong poles leaned at a slant and held up the golden mirerasen. We slowly pushed the poles towards the center and now the box dangled above our heads.

He pulled out a pin from the bottom and the mirerasen fell. Gasping, I stood there looking at a house with windows and doors. It was mostly made of the golden material with the exception of the windows. They were somewhat similar to the plexiglass I would see in my world and I didn't ask what it was. Oh my, they even opened.

Peter removed the poles and put them in the back of his truck, flipped his palm up and said, "Shall we?"

We opened the door and went inside. There were two rooms and even a floor!

"Where would you like to sleep, Princess? This front part is the kitchen and through that door is a bedroom."

Shrugging my shoulders and with a look of amazement I said, "Wow, in my world I have gone camping in a tent made of a cloth like material, but this is...."

"All thanks go to the Rofonians. My dad, grandfather and Siand Fodulza modified one of their houses so we would be able to use it for camping. We actually erected this tent similar to the way they erect their houses. Apparently, there is a group of Rofonians who are trained to use the energy from their fingers to raise the poles. Afterwards, they add more to their houses, but we just have the basic model."

Peter set up a kitchen, made me a fire outside, cooked supper, and I was catered to with kindness and smiles. He had even thought to pack some art supplies for me. He made his bed in the kitchen and I slept in the bedroom.

The next morning I woke up to the smell of freshly made coffee. "Thought you only drank tea?"

"Depends on my mood," he said seriously. "There's something about camp coffee that puts hair on your chest."

Looking back at him I asked, "Do you think I could perhaps have my coffee without the hair growing ingredient?"

Soon we were donned in comfortable clothes and with a backpack upon Peter's back, the two of us headed through the woods. Following some sort of a path, we ducked, weaved, and held back branches, until we saw large trees. They appeared similar to weeping willows with white flowering branches trailing on the ground. Parting the branches of one, we made our way to the middle.

The high branches curved over us creating a ceiling with flowered curved walls, long and fuzzy leaves, and of course a trunk in the middle. The trunk looked like a huge hairy leg with the hairs going upwards instead of down. My curiosity got the best of me and I gently patted the hairs on the trunk. They were soft, like the down of a duckling.

White delicate flowers speckled the green wall giving me a

feeling of being surrounded by Hawaiian leis. The glistening sun shone through the green, illuminating the tiny hairs on the leaves. Walking seven or eight steps inside this mystical tree dome, with soft pink sand below and a flowered ceiling well above our heads, I felt like I had entered the realm of dreams.

"I feel like a faerie or a gnome."

"A faerie or a gnome?" Peter questioned.

Oh right, he wasn't from yesterday's world. There every country in the world had reported of sightings of them, but very few were confirmed. Many people thought of them as myths, but others held onto their beliefs with the realization they would have to keep quiet or be deemed weird or crazy.

"Never mind. It's just that going through these trees is really fun and it... feels magical. That's all I was trying to say. It smells like something sweet is burning," I said wiggling my nose, thinking of the smell of burning sugar.

"They smell like conwallow trees to me," Peter said with a bit of a laugh. "But you're right, it is a similar smell. By the way, do you often burn sweet things?"

I just smiled and shook my head as Peter parted the branches of one tree and almost immediately parted the branches of the next. It was the same as the first one and again we took about seven or eight steps underneath the dome as we walked under tree after tree.

The smell was not really pleasing, but then again nor was it overpowering. It didn't matter because I was just inundated with the beauty of my surroundings. At every tree, Peter would look around, study it, reach up, untie a tattered piece of cloth, and from his pocket pull out another one and tie it on.

"What's with the ties?" I asked.

"They are my markers and I don't want the tree to have to grow around them, so I replace them every year."

The light seemed to be growing brighter and brighter. I felt like I was in a magical movie that was becoming more mystical by the minute. The past was gone, the future hadn't happened and I was in the now, taking in the beauty of the moment.

117

Chapter 25 - Stoned Colourful Energy

Venturing through the conwallow trees would have satisfied my desire for a new experience, but the afternoon was only starting. Coming out to a clearing, we viewed a wide circle surrounded by trees. In the middle of the glade, pillars with pointed tops extended upwards. My jaw dropped as each of these pillars reflected the sun and I could see a wide spectrum of colours, far exceeding the colours of the rainbow in yesterday's world.

The reflected colours were creating squares with straight and zigzagged lines and sometimes only lines or dots. There were also arcs, and teardrop shapes and they all seemed to be dancing an invitation to something new, beyond anything I had ever known.

"There are forty-four stones in total," explained Peter as we were walking down the grassy bank towards the colours. "There are pink rosaleen crystal wands in the middle. I know a little about the energy of the crystals if you are interested."

"Very! I would love to learn, if you're willing to teach me."

"Okay. First I will explain the positioning of the stones and then I will tell you what I know about them. The grass that you see around them does not grow any higher than it is and never needs to be mowed. There are three pink rosaleen crystal wands in the middle. Eight citrinia crystal wands surround them. They are yellowish orange or depending on the light of the day they can also be golden brown with a reddish tint. Sixteen blue indicolitia crystal wands surround the citrinia. The outer ring has seventeen purple amathasite wands.

"Wow, they're amazing!"

"I think they have been strategically placed as each one is a different height. There is only one straight line starting from the middle with the stones following it perfectly."

"So it's as if whoever strategically put them here started from the middle and lined up each stone in a straight line and then continued with each circle," I surmised.

"I never thought of it that way, anyway, if you follow that line from the middle out, the rosaleen wand is three feet high, and the citrinia, indicolitia, and amathasite are six feet high."

My brain was trying to comprehend this as we walked closer to the crystal labyrinth.

"So the straight line has three sixes plus a three?"

"Yes, but we are talking about their height," Peter answered.

"Yeah, their height adds up to twenty-one. In numerology that is equivalent to the energy of three."

"How do you get three out of twenty-one?"

"Two comes from the twenty, plus the one, thus it equals three. Three, just like the three rosaleens in the center and three stands for the trinity- mind, body, and spirit."

Peter glanced over at me. "Interesting," he said. "The three rosaleen crystal wands also are different heights. One stone is one foot, the second is two feet, and the third stands three feet."

"So, that would be one foot forward into new beginnings, two feet would be the balancing of masculine and feminine, and then the three would be harmonizing into the trinity," I said, " and that adds up to six which is guidance and truth. What colour did you say they were?" I asked.

He gave me an odd look. "The inner circle? They're pink."

"Pink crystals in my world would be opening your heart, bringing in love, being in the receptive."

"Hmm." Smiling, he said, "Well, the Rofonians agree with that for they say rosaleen heals the heart and heals trauma."

"Trauma, like getting shot?" I said with a smile.

"Yes, that would be considered trauma," he said in a teasing tone, "and the Rofonians actually brought rosaleen into your room after you had been shot."

"I didn't know that. I just knew I healed very fast. Now I'm really curious. Please tell me more about the rosaleen crystal."

"Rosaleen pulls out negative energy and replaces it with empathy and acceptance. It can also help with your circulatory system, kidneys, lungs, and even your memory. It's an amazing stone," Peter said as he sat down upon the bank. "The next circle is citrinia. The Rofonians told Fodulza it is known for zapping negative energy and because it does such a good job, it brings you protection. Similar to the moonta, it protects you during a meditation. It's a beautiful stone for you."

"I'm not sure I like that. The crystals are beautiful, at least from here. Don't get me wrong, but what I'm hearing is, you think I have a lot of negative energy that needs to be zapped?"

"Nooo, that's not what I meant. Citrinia enhances creativity and it's a beautiful stone for an artist. It's known for making someone less sensitive to criticism, because it helps the brain process people's comments on a more positive note."

"Okay," I said with laughter, "I can accept that. Maybe it would be a good stone for me."

We smiled at each other for a few moments before Peter continued, "It also brings joy because it releases fear and anger at a very deep level. The eight crystal wands in that circle are four, five, and six feet tall."

"Adding up to fifteen which is six in numerology. Four representing balance, five representing change, and then six again. This is exciting. Please tell me about the next row."

Peter didn't answer right away. We sat staring at the colours dancing through stones and around them. Even from a distance the energy was capturing my mind, my body, and my spirit.

"The next row has sixteen and is blue." There was a quietness in his voice when he spoke.

"It kind of looks indigo from here," I said softly, after a time of staring.

"That is because the outer one is a purple crystal with indigo woven throughout it."

"Are the blue stones like the Tarnana?" I asked.

"No, they're more transparent than blue tassin. They are called indicolitia. They help with one's meditation promoting vision and spiritual awareness; gently dissolving sadness and bringing peace. The indicolitia wands start six feet high and then go to up to seven, eight, and nine feet."

"Seven is a rebirth number and eight stands for...," my brain couldn't remember and flashed the number on its side. "I think it's like a meditation, the awareness of an infinite universe. Nine is triple trinity and usually means things are coming to a completion. At least I think, don't quote me on all this Peter, I'm trying to remember something from a world that seems to be farther and farther away for me."

Peter stared into my eyes for a time then softly said, "The outer row has six, seven, eight, nine and ten for heights. There are seventeen wands of amathasite. They're extremely protective and have a high spiritual vibration. They block negativity whether emotional or environmental. Due to the high spiritual vibration, the visions in your meditations can be very powerful. They can open a door to another reality, but that door has already been opened for you, hasn't it Princess."

Noticing his worried look, I asked, "Do you go to different realities when you're here?"

"I always go somewhere, but I always return to the rosaleen in the middle. I'm calmer, clearer, and I think, a bit wiser."

Nodding at his answer, I said, "You know the crystals here are different but very similar, both in name and look, to the crystals in my world."

"I don't know about the crystals in your world, however I do know that these crystals can be very, very powerful. You will be protected by the space and you will come back, because the wands are set up for that to happen. I have given you as much information as I possibly can. I want you to be prepared. Now that you know it could take you to another reality, do you still want to go?"

"If it opens doors to other realities and it brings you back to where you belong, it could possibly take me to where I belong. I could actually disappear as it could open a door for me to go back into yesterday's world. Are you going to be okay with that? Do you still want me to visit the crystals with you?"

Peter stared deeply into my eyes for a long time before he said, "Princess, if you disappear here, I will know you didn't get lost or fall. The Rofonians must know you appeared out of nowhere and Gorph, well if you are right, he will understand, but it's up to you. Do you want to take that chance?"

"I came here for reasons that I don't understand, but I'm glad I came. I have learned so much. If I do disappear from your world please always remember you have brought me joy. You have enriched my life and no matter where I am, you will be in my heart." I stared at the crystals for what seemed to be a long time, but it was probably just a short time and then with a nod I whispered, "I'm ready."

"Would you like to take my hand?"

Slowly, I clasped Peter's held out hand and we walked in a dreamlike silence towards the mystical magical labyrinth. Watching the colours shimmering from the maze, I became aware that energy was pulsating through my body. Each step I took, the pulsating became stronger and stronger. Entranced by this amazing structure, I was surprised when I noticed Peter's hand felt warm and familiar.

Time seemed as if it was in slow motion, life felt surreal, and with each inhale reaching deeper, and each exhale feeling longer we walked hand in hand towards the enchanted crystals.

Arriving at the labyrinth, I paused, touching every surface I could as we wove in and around the massive crystallized wands. They were magnificent. The stones were smooth and each one felt unique to my touch. Some felt warm, some felt cool, and others felt like they were rhythmically connecting deep within my soul.

Reaching the middle of the maze, Peter took off his backpack and sat down beside the two foot, pink rosaleen crystal wand. Facing the center he took out a candle and a carved brownish stone candle holder. It had a rim around it, similar to a dish.

Again reaching in his backpack, he pulled out a container and poured what looked like water into the rim. The center of the holder was made of mirerasen where he placed an indigo candle. This created the illusion that the candle was submerged within the liquid.

Rainbow Dancer had laid beside the one foot crystal wand, and I had sat down by the three foot one. We were out in the fresh air within a labyrinth of stone and there was metal and water in the candle holder, so when Peter lit the candle we had all the five elements.

We sat there, underneath the indigo sky in the middle of a spectacular labyrinth. Everything was bright until a white fluffy cloud scudded across the sky in front of the sun. Something very strange was happening, for I no longer was there and neither was Peter, but we were still together.

We were clad in white clothing, walking hand in hand over what seemed to be sparkling silver water. The two of us walked upon the top of the water and went to the edge. I know that sounds strange, but it was as if the water was an ocean floating in the air encased in the fluffy white clouds.

Looking farther out we could see another sparkling silver ocean, appearing as if it too was encased in fluffy white clouds and lower than the one in which we stood. When we turned around to look the other way we saw another cluster of clouds looking like it also was encasing an ocean with another one on top of that. It was as if our feet were floating on stairs containing oceans with clouds for risers. Where were we? Had we entered the heavens?

"We have travelled together before, haven't we Peter?" my voice almost echoed as we turned and faced each other.

"Yes, our souls are connected in ways we might never be able to comprehend."

He brushed the hair from my face and kissed me gently on the forehead. His strong arms went around me forming a warm familiar embrace. We looked deep into each others eyes. He placed his lips on mine and kissed me passionately.

A new sensation swirled through awakening parts of my body. It was as if he had woken up what had been lying dormant for a long time. Reeling from the kiss, with my heart still beating loudly, I rested my head upon his shoulder. My mind...my body...felt light, weightless, and the only part of me that felt as if it still existed was the strong beat of my heart.

Opening my eyes, I realized the sky was changing as now it had small white fluffy clouds. Something was different. Oh my, the clouds weren't scudding across the sky?!? Were they descending towards us? No! We were ascending towards them! I looked down and saw the sparkling silver ocean moving farther and farther away! Holding each other tightly, we rose into the clouds and then we flew with them. Now we were scudding across the sky.

Arcing its glory, a beautiful rainbow appeared in the sky. Oh my, I think we're going to go through it! We moved closer and closer, but as we neared the orange and yellow, we rose even higher until we reached the top.

Landing as if the rainbow was solid like our sparkling ocean, we sat on the top of it. Looking down at where we had come from, even that had changed. It was as if the stairs had extended and the clouds containing their silver oceans were even more spectacular.

Off to the right, we saw two purple mountains with greenery and jutting rocks. The mountains seemed to be levitating slightly above an ocean and around their bases, a golden rope formed an infinity symbol.

Leaving the bow within the firmament, our bodies began to move again and once more we were flying, scudding like the clouds. This time we headed directly towards the side of one of the mountains!! My heart was beating so strongly I could hear it. Closer and closer, with no means of control, we flew!

"I think we're gonna to hit the mountain!!" Peter yelled.

"No, Peter, we'll make it. We have come this far. We're not going to crash now. We will make it over the mountain," I whispered with unwavering strength in my voice. Instead of staring at the mountain, we changed our focus and gazed into each others eyes. If we were going to crash into the infinite mountain at least there would be kindness, respect and love in our final moments.

Chapter 26 - I Wonder

The next thing I knew, I was sitting in the middle of the labyrinth staring into Peter's eyes. What had happened?

My breaths were short and irregular, similar to what they would be after a fright or shock. Rainbow Dancer rested his head upon my lap. Peter knelt beside me and held my hand.

"You okay?" There was concern in Peter's voice.

"Yeah," my head bounced in short quick nods, but I did nod.

"You went somewhere, didn't you?"

The quick short nods were still happening. Then with a whispering breathy tone I asked, "Did you?"

He smiled, "I always do, every time I come here. It is an amazing place, isn't it?"

With another series of quick short nods I rubbed my eyes and with my palms together in front of my nose, rested my chin upon my thumbs. Was it real? Had Peter really been there? Had we actually travelled together? Are our souls connected, or had it happened because it was simply something I desired? If it was really a soul connection it would explain the familiarity and instant trust between us.

Does he remember what happened up on the ocean steps or was it just my experience? The kiss, oh no, don't think about the kiss! I could feel the heat rising to my cheeks. Had he experienced the kiss too? Did he know? My cheeks reddened even more and I placed my face in my hands.

Removing my hands, I said in a soft, quiet voice, "It is. It definitely is an amazing place." Then I buried my face in Rainbow Dancer's fur.

"Are you ready to start the trek back?" Peter questioned gently, like he was still unsure if I was okay.

"Okay," I answered, sounding timid and shy.

Weaving in and out of the crystals, I touched their smooth surfaces and stared into them. I would get close to where Peter was, but every time he looked, I would quickly appear as if I was entranced within a magical crystal wand. Catching up to him in the glade, I remained quiet and soon I was concentrating on climbing the bank.

"You okay?" Peter asked again as we reached the top.

"Yeah," I said, nodding without looking at him.

Looking around at all the white flowers that were gracing the distant drooping branches of the conwallow trees, I realized they surrounded the mystical maze. Were they strategically placed there as well? Maybe they were part of the reason this location was chosen? Perhaps the placement was just a natural phenomenon? Maybe the sweet burning smell was akin to the smell of a smudge before you entered a sacred space?

The majority of hikers probably wouldn't travel underneath tree after tree and thus never find the amazing hidden energies of the crystals pillars. Maybe the sweet burning smell repelled those who did not belong? Could the flowering conwallow trees be a result of the energy transmitted from the labyrinth? Questions I will probably never have answers to. If I want to look at life through a child's eyes of wonder I would have to accept some things are truly mystical.

"Have you ever seen anyone else when you have travelled this way?" I asked with a mere quick glance towards him.

"No, although the road is always kept up."

Visions of the terrifying ride curving around the mountain crest prompted me to say, "I guess, if you call that kept up."

"For the Rofonian hopows, it is actually quite a wide road. We are still on their land, you know."

"Do they know you come here?"

"Siand Fodulza knew we camped on the mountain, but I had not discovered the labyrinth's existence until after he passed. Because of the language barrier I've not spoken of it. I would, however, love to find out if they know the history behind it."

"Well, the communication between you and Rofonians has entered a whole new level."

"It certainly has," Peter said looking into my eyes then he added, "way beyond my imagination, but it wouldn't have happened if it wasn't for you. You do know that, don't you?"

"Actually Peter, it would not have happened without Ooza. I think you and Ooza will become good friends. I bet you he would love to go on a camping trip with you."

Walking in thoughtful silence, we eventually reached the once distant conwallow trees. Touching the softness of the leaves I examined the flowers that grew almost evenly on each bowing branch. The petals looked so fragile I dared not touch them. Their purple centres gave me a feeling of rebirth. I did not say it out loud for I didn't think I could explain why, if asked. I was surprised they smelled so sweet and calming.

A tree that gave the odour of burning sugar had calming sweet smelling flowers? Sniffing, I realized that a charred smoky smell was coming from the hairy trunk, so perhaps it was the combination of both. I stayed closer to the flowers as we travelled through the seemingly magical, domed house of leis and soon thereafter, we left the conwallow trees.

We found our way through the bushes until we finally saw our golden home. The adventure left me with so many feelings. Tiredness set in and I laid down for a nap.

When I awoke, there was an aroma of supper cooking and tea was brewed. Peter and I talked about the crystals and what the different numbers meant. The inner two rows, one of eight and one of three added up to eleven - a master number, but my memory of what that meant was condensed at best.

"I know it stands for higher expression," I told Peter as I smiled at Rainbow Dancer.

"What do you mean by higher expression?"

"Well, I think it's being above the petty stuff, having a more lofty outlook on life. Understanding there is a spiritual side to things and life is not about possessions, payback, or power over anything or anyone. It's about empowering others to be happy on their journey so they can be the best they can be, whether that is with or without you. It's about being full of goodness and expressing who you truly are, and being happy that others are doing the same for themselves."

"That sounds logical to me," Peter said sipping his tea.

"I also think it would mean the power to express yourself creatively and balanced, but I guess if you're expressing who you really are, you're kind of doing that, aren't you?"

Peter just nodded and said, "The outer two rows, one of sixteen and the other of seventeen add up to thirty-three."

"That's double trinity," I blurted out.

"Double trinity? Two minds, two bodies, and two spirits?"

I giggled and said, "I think it means..., well, it's one thing to be aware of your mind, body, and spirit, but once you're truly in tune with it, you become a spiritual teacher."

"Is that what you are, Princess?"

Laughing, I said, "I wish. At this point it is only a dream to be in tune with myself. If I was truly there, then all would be attainable." Shaking my head and shrugging my shoulders I continued, "Truth be told I don't know if it would, because I have yet to achieve it and have a long way to go."

"But it would be quite an accomplishment, wouldn't it," Peter said thoughtfully. Silence lingered before he asked, "The whole thing adds up to forty-four, is that a master number?"

"Yes it is, but I am not sure what it means. Maybe it's about mastering the balance of masculine and feminine within your spiritual expression. I don't know where that came from. I think it is because I am combining thirty three and eleven. Wow, someone or something put a lot of thought into making that labyrinth. It cannot be a coincidence that the stones were arranged like they were. It's got to mean something way more than we can even comprehend."

We couldn't figure out what the different heights meant, but we thought it was uncanny how both the crystals and the numbers had so many meanings. No wonder it had so much power that I felt energy pulsating through me even from a distance. Someone or something knew more than we could ever imagine.

What happened when we were inside the circle of crystal wands? What did my walk on the tiered oceans with Peter mean? Did we go over the mountain or did we smash into it or were we meant to go inside it? Did it too have a much deeper meaning, like the numbers and arrangement of stones? What was it supposed to be showing us?

The oceans were silver and silver represents truth. The clouds were white and white, like the snow, represents purity. Often, water in meditations and dreams represents emotion. Emotions that I had felt intensely while we were there.

"Peter," I said, seemly bringing him out of deep thought, "Do you think we went to a higher plane of existence during our meditation? Do you think we went to a place where there was so much purity and truth to our emotions that they no longer had power over us?"

Peter only answered my question with a question, "Do you think your emotions have power over you?"

"Yeah, sometimes," I said, thinking my emotions certainly weren't suppressed inside the passion of Peter's kiss. The thought of the kiss made me retreat to my inner thoughts and with a bit of redness in my cheeks, I finished with, "I guess I'm just questioning everything - maybe I'm just thinking too much. How long before the food is ready?"

"Its ready now," Peter answered.

We ate in silence and I thought maybe the kiss didn't over-whelm us or maybe it did and we were just distracted by the flight? Maybe the kiss did overwhelm us and caused us to take flight? That is, if he was really there during the kiss.

Were the two of us actually sitting upon the arc? Rainbows represent transformation - a lesson learned. Maybe I have graduated to another level. Seeing a mountain in the distance usually meant new and enlightening experiences, but this whole journey has been that. Another way to look at it was, by combining my masculine and feminine energy had I created the illusion of passion. Maybe Peter really wasn't there and it was simply about the integration of the masculine and feminine within myself.

I looked over at Peter and I wanted to kiss him. However, I think on this plane of existence and in this emotional state, I could be overwhelmed. I could let my emotions rise and probably create a tidal wave. Would he too have that reaction?

Would we be able to keep still within and not let it overpower us, or would we give into the power and experience the joy? Would we find that one or both of us had the ability to walk on water or fly to new heights? Perhaps, but we could also get caught in that tidal wave and find it too powerful to even swim through. If any of that happened then how would I be able to leave to find the Empress?

Peter had started clearing the dishes from our supper and I arose from my seat, gathering the remaining ones. Following him into our camp kitchen, I watched Peter set down the dishes, not realizing how close I was standing. Turning around, he almost knocked the dishes out of my hands. Peter fumbled to save the dishes, but I stood there, I just stood there. I didn't know why.

It was probably very rude, but I just stood there in front of him, not moving out of his way. My heart was beating loudly. Could he hear my heart? That's silly, he wouldn't be able to hear my heart beat. I sighed as he put his warm hands on my forearms. Standing there staring into each others eyes, I swore time stood still. I really couldn't tell how long we stood there. The kiss! The passionate kiss I had already decided I was not ready for, could be a split second away!

"It's all right, we didn't break anything," Peter said seeming oblivious to the passion that had risen within me. Did he not feel any passion towards me or did he just know that neither one of us should go there? Had he made a promise to remain friends or was it a promise not to do anything that I didn't want him to do?

"Yeah, you're right, nothing got broken," including our hearts I wanted to finished with, but instead I sighed and said, "I was just startled, that's all."

"Why don't you go sit by the fire. I'll finish up here and I'll brew us a pot of calming tea."

Chapter 27 - Goosebumps

The next morning, the camp kitchen wasn't there and neither was Peter's bedroll. Wandering outside, I found Peter sitting in front of a fire. Coffee was still hot and breakfast was ready.

He was being mysterious about where we were headed. I began asking him questions and he would only answer with yes or no. Even though it was frustrating at times it did cause lots of laughs, although all I managed to establish was that a cave and a body of water was involved in our new adventure.

After our breakfast Peter gave me a disc with a hole in the middle and went to one side of the golden house and I went to the other. He put a pole in the top ring of the house and then we propped it up with the pronged sticks and the golden abode raised another inch or two. Still holding the pole, on the count of three, we pushed the pronged sticks, clearing them away. The mirerasen folded enough that we were able to lower each side of the pole to shoulder height and slide the discs onto it.

He asked me to tilt my pole up as he lowered his. The disc prevented the golden mirerasen from sliding towards him and my side folded some more. He then tilted his side up high and the mirerasen once again looked like a golden box. Soon thereafter we were packed and travelling the curving roads, stopping at various places, taking in the beautiful scenery.

"The next stop," Peter announced, while holding his finger up, "there will be a hike, water, and rocks involved."

Soon we could hear the roar of waterfalls. Rainbow Dancer was excited, but also seemed sad. The sound must have reminded him of his home and his kin.

"How are you doing Rainbow Dancer?" I asked.

He nodded, looking at me with a love so unconditional that humans rarely are able to attain it.

Rainbow Dancer sniffed down the path first; a path probably used by the animals heading down to the base of the waterfall.

A large rock basin, looking like a bathtub, jutted out, filling up with water and overflowing to the final tier of the cascade. Reaching the bottom, we sat by the pool watching the now trickling water pour over the many coloured rocks. They were wet and polished, glistening in the sun as light shimmered brightly between the trees.

Rainbow Dancer danced under the waterfall, reminding me of when we first met and how the water reflected the colours of a rainbow as he danced. I told Peter about being in a basket all alone in this world, floating down a river. How I was able to obtain a paddle from the base of a basket and was doing my best to get to shore before being taken over by the roaring falls.

Arriving at the part of how my oughtleopar saved me and took me to his cave Peter stared deep into my eyes. I wondered if he was thinking that it must have been a pretty big basket, but to tell him I was once the size of the Rofonians might be more than he could comprehend, so I merely told him Rainbow Dancer got named because he was dancing under the waterfall.

Little orange and red birds flew by, singing their songs, perching on the branches nearby. We changed our focus and became quiet and still. The songs sang of new beginnings full of goodness, love, and to trust that out of the darkness would come the light.

The birds landed on the red flowers that trellised the sides of the sparkling, dripping cascade. The center of the flowers re-minded me of a rose, but the outside had extended, thin petals similar to the Rofonians' fingers. They were long and narrow with rounded ends that ballooned as if they were full of nectar.

My long hair flowed and wisps whispered around my face. I was donned in a brown dress with hints of orange and red swirling together, woven within the fabric. There was a feeling of beauty, sensuality, and belonging resonating and I felt like a magical being. Probably because my journey was no longer fraught with the horrors of yesterday's world.

Peter was dressed in shorts or maybe they were a swim trunk, I wasn't quite sure. They didn't have a hem and they weren't frayed, instead a jagged fringe of the material hung an inch or so from where the hemline would be. His hair was tousled by the wind, looking sexy - breathtakingly sexy and feelings that I probably should curb were arousing within.

It was a hot day and spontaneously I scooped up water in my hand and splashed him. He retaliated and the next thing we knew we were in the water splashing and laughing. By the time we were done my dress was clinging to my curves. A cool breeze had drifted in, chilling my skin through my wet dress, leaving me feeling self-conscious. Folding my arms across my breasts, I felt Peter put his arms around me.

"You must be cold," he said softly as he pulled me close.

Shivering, I could hear my heart beating. Even though his arms were around me, my arms were still folded across my breasts. He then loosened his grasp and backed away slightly. My arms dropped down as I expected us to embrace, but instead Peter stayed there, his hands upon my bare arms lightly tickling. Oh my, it felt too nice. His fingers moved, tracing my biceps all the way down to my wrists.

It occurred to me to turn and run, but I didn't think I could. Goosebumps appeared upon my arms. As if they were Braille, Peter studied each one intently with his fingertips moving in a circular motion. I felt my breasts going up with each quivering inhalation and down with each trembling exhalation. It was the goosebumps that he was studying, yes, because he was a geologist, of course he would study things like that.

Raindrops fell, big ones, splashing as they landed, but Peter didn't stop. He seemed to be completely immersed. All I could do was watch, feel, and breathe. The big raindrops became more plentiful. Peter began caressing my skin with the palms of his hands. His eyes focused on mine. He brought his hand to my cheek, lightly wiped the wetness away and brushed the hair off my face. His head tilted towards me just as a raindrop splashed upon his nose and splattered into his eyes.

"We should probably go," I whispered.

Kissing upon the sparkling silver ocean was quivering on my lips, but I had no idea whether that one was real or not.

However, if this one was anywhere near the intensity of that one, the feelings might be too powerful to pull away.

"We should," Peter's voice whispered within his nod.

"Yes, we should." Although I don't think my voice sounded very convincing.

"We should leave before these roads get washed out," he said, not moving and still staring into my eyes.

My face reflected the danger in that statement. The narrow roads were scary enough for my liking and now, a possibility of them being washed out!?! Oh my, reality.

"Yes, when you put it that way, we have to leave." My voice was soft, but at the same time it was strong and definite.

Unlocking our moment, we trekked back up the hill to the truck. Soon we were on our way with Peter driving cautiously over the slippery, winding roads. The pelting rain and the windshield wipers going back and forth were the only sounds heard for a long time. At least it seemed like a long time before we finally reached a straight stretch.

"We need to talk about what happened between us," Peter announced.

My body was still feeling the energy of the moment by the waterfall and I truly wanted to cherish the magic that had happened between us. The time was beautiful, special, and spontaneous. A moment that could be ruined by analyzing, so I just bit my lip. What was I supposed to say?

My heartbeat sped up for we had come to a.... bridge and that was an overstatement. The road was narrow enough, but the bridge was narrower and seemed partially washed away. Stopping the truck, Peter got out to inspect the situation. Dilapidated wood and a mirerasen platform spanned across a deep crevice for approximately the length of two trucks. However, the bridge didn't look wide enough for one.

"What are you thinking?" I asked.

"Well, it'll be tight. The bridge seems solid, but if I'm off by an inch we're...." Peter didn't finish his sentence.

I knew it would be like driving onto those weird tracks that one drives on when a vehicle goes into a service bay to be repaired. Only there wasn't a ridge on the sides and if the rotting wood gave away even a tad more, we were headed down into the river!

If we miss, it could be death! I squeezed my eyes shut hoping when I opened them, there would be a solid platform to cross, but that didn't happen. Calling upon my God of Love for protection, I took a deep breath and visualized the truck on the other side. I had to believe we were going to be okay, but that didn't happen either, because Peter was backing up the truck to get a better angle.

He put it into forward and inched towards the bridge. Our tires hit the bridge with a loud crackling sound! My side of the truck lowered! I could not look down! I had to keep imagining us on the other side, safe and truly appreciating the solid ground of the narrow winding roads.

Holding my breath, we went over a bump! The front of the truck was on the other side and the back of the truck lowered! I could feel the tires skidding on the wet ground! Finally, the back tires hit the solid ground. We had made it! We were safe!

"Thank-you!" we said in unison, glancing upward.

Peter stopped the truck and we both went to look at how much damage we had done to the bridge. Creaking and crackling sounds could still be heard. A piece of wood became loose and fell down below into the roaring river below.

"Whoa, wow!" Peter said as he hugged me. "Thank-you, thank-you, thank-you!"

"Who do you thank?" I asked.

"I'm not sure," he said with a shrug, "I just always say thank-you. I don't know about the different forces out there, but one I say thank-you to, keeps me safe. I think that's the last bridge we have to cross. We'll have to go back a different way, or... a... do something." I could hear the frustration in his voice. "Right now we are safe and that's all that matters. The other good thing is I've met Rotopa and I finally have a way of communicating, so I can let him know about the bridge."

Chapter 28 - The Demi Sexual

Back in the truck there was silence once again and after awhile the trauma of crossing the bridge was far behind us.

"I am demi-sexual." Peter said unexpectedly. He didn't look at me, he just stared straight ahead.

"Demi," I said slowly before I added, "sexual?"

"Yes," was all he said, still staring straight ahead.

I didn't want to share what was going through my mind.

"Some men and some women," he continued, "can separate their physical, emotional, logical, and spiritual. I can't, nor do I want to. It doesn't feel like a choice. It feels like it's... part of who I am."

There was silence for a moment before I spoke. "So what you're saying is when you make love, you truly make love. To some people sex is a physical or emotional attraction, but you have to be attracted to someone on all the levels."

He shifted in his seat and didn't answer right away. "Yes, when I make love, it isn't just because of a physical desire, it is much more than that. I need to be in love on all levels. It is your usage of the word 'attracted' that has me puzzled."

The sparkling silver ocean, the kiss, the flying... he was right, this was much more than just an attraction so I said, "You're right, attractions come and go. I guess I used the wrong word."

Silence surrounded us as I was deep in thought, because I really didn't know how I felt about sex. Was I born demi-sexual or was I just damaged goods who had never met someone I trusted until I met Peter? But was Peter strong enough to handle all of me? He was from another world, thus it might be a good thing that I will probably be leaving as that would prevent me from hurting him.

My mind fell back to the dark crevices of yesterday's world. I was still within the bounds of elementary school when I experienced those scratchy whiskered faces and smells of alcohol mixed with the stench of sweat. Yes, that had gravely affected how I felt about the subject.

My younger years had been confusing, with many bullies and negative, continuous name-calling both at school and in the community. Arrogant males who thought they should get everything they wanted in life. It didn't matter if they crossed boundaries or if they took pleasure from another person's pain because there were no consequences for those men or those boys, for most of them came from the families with money - families that, in their minds, did no wrong.

I was a soul with a body not a body with a soul; forgive them for they know not what they do; was what I would tell myself over and over. Often it was what gave me the strength to move forward. Closing my eyes, I once again saw the lightning bolts breaking all the blobs.

Yes, changes happened in that obsmoon room and I needed to let it all settle in, so I could truly find the strength from the pain. This time, the thoughts of yesterday's world weren't hurting my body nor affecting me in ways that often shut me down. I did feel a bit vulnerable, but they didn't take over my emotions. I didn't have to feel the horrors or see them flash in front of me. I was able to keep my thoughts logical and clear.

Maybe there were still some lingering emotions, but I can imagine them as the dust from those burnt negatives leaving, moving farther and farther away. Feeling strength as I took in deep breaths I stared out the side window. Yes, right now I was in the truck with Peter and I have a question to ask myself. 'Was being demi-sexual an innate part of who I was?'

Well, honestly life had not given me the choice to find that out, because I had wasted so much time carrying with me those memories and fears. I had lugged them around like I was holding the handles of a rickshaw and they were the passengers in the back. All of it tired me out before I could ever get far enough to figure out who I really was and how I really felt.

Those people of yesterday's world who did those despicable things were the ones who were messed up. Logically knowing that and totally feeling it, were previously two different things, but not anymore.

Smiling at the power of loving myself, my spine straightened and just like the dust I had blown away, I was also letting go of that rickshaw. Yes, because if I was going to carry passengers, they would have to be deserving of being carried. I wasn't sure where I was going, but I knew it wasn't backwards.

It felt like a new energy touched my hair and soon it seemed to tickle the back of my neck. I'm reclaiming my energy and my strength because I didn't deserve that, no one does. They were the ones who were wrong and it wasn't my fault!

It would take a while before I was ready to be with someone at this point in my life. Yes, this time there would definitely have to be a very strong mental, spiritual, and emotional connection... the physical, well that would be a bonus. But if both people were demi-sexual, they would need to know each other for a time, be able to communicate, and know that they are truly compatible on all levels before they could be physical with each other. Hmmmm.

Whether I was demi-sexual at birth, I will never know. Really, the why didn't matter and Peter had just given me a term for how I felt. A term that required very little explanation. I shrugged my shoulders and I could hear myself saying, 'Sorry, I'm demi-sexual and that's just who I am'. I really like this new way of thinking.

Not ready to share my thoughts I simply said to Peter, "We have something very, very, special and we shouldn't complicate it by adding something physical to it. Thanks for expressing who you are and thanks for being clear." How much time had passed before I actually said that, I wasn't sure, and it probably seemed out of the blue.

"I thought I was clear before we went on this trip," he said.

I wanted to say that I wasn't the one who pulled him close and tickled his arms! Nor was I the one who announced that I was demi-sexual!

"Yes, your original intent was clear, but now it is so much

clearer, thank-you," I retorted with a cold chill.

"You sound a little bit upset."

Was he being condescending or merely oblivious? I was sure glad we hadn't gone even a little bit further physically as my emotional bells were ringing. Part of me wanted to ring those bells loudly in Peter's ears, letting him know that he was treating me as if I had come onto him. Another part of me wanted to withdraw into a place and let those bells keep ringing.

'A weak person gets agitated and plunges ahead when faced with obstacles, but you're strong," I heard a woman whisper. *"Calmness is often the medicine that makes things go well, for disagreements often become silenced if we do not gratify them with injured retorts."* Where did that come from and who had whispered in my mind? *"The sun will shine for you, but only when you're ready and only when the sky becomes clear."*

The sun will shine for me when I was ready? The voice was right, I had let my injured thoughts of yesterday's world bring me back to the energy of being injured. It was as if the thoughts of that time carried a powerful hidden energy and if I stay within that energy I could end up on an emotional roller coaster and perhaps never find what I was looking for.

Someone who is demi-sexual has to honour who they are and come from a place of strength. Yes, and that strength also carries a powerful hidden energy. Energies lurk on many levels, ohh it was going to take a while to understand it all.

However we are in the now and Peter may merely have been confirming it in his mind as well as mine that we started this trip as friends and we needed to keep it there. Thus I shouldn't be upset at him for confirming our original intent.

Okay, we had a moment and now we needed to back up. Sometimes backing up allows communication to come from a different position and go forward from a better place. However, I don't need to back up as far as those horrors in the past anymore but I do need to back up a little.

Softly I replied, "I think my mind went to places that I don't want to share, but I will say, I think I am demi-sexual too. I just hadn't heard it called that." I bit my lip and looked at him for a moment before I continued, "Also, I was a little upset because it sounded like you were upset at me for what happened by the waterfall."

"No Princess, I was upset at me, not you. The only thing you are at fault for... is being too darn beautiful - inside and out."

I don't know why it happened, but I'm glad he didn't notice the tear running down my cheek, and in a very gentle voice I said, "Thank-you. Everything really is a lot clearer now."

Allowing the windshield wipers to mesmerize my mind, we drove in silence. After a while the rain began to subside, the curves in the road straightened and we were descending downhill towards bushes. Were we at the end of the road?

Off to the left through the bushes, a rainbow had appeared over a body of water. Was the end of the rainbow on the other side of the trees? I wanted to run through the bushes just to see if it actually was, although I didn't say it out loud. There was really no other place to go and Peter veered his truck off the road and into the bushes towards the coloured arc. Was I going to get my wish?

Peter didn't say a word as he got out of the truck and headed towards the back of it. Maybe I would feel a bit better if I put my indigo robe over my dress. It was mostly dry, but I still felt damp, cold, and maybe a little vulnerable. So I got out of the cab robed and still a bit timid, but at the same time I was excited to run towards the rainbow.

Peter pulled out the golden box and laid it down on the ground. He then went back and unloaded the long rods. Well, I guess we're not checking out the rainbow as we're setting up camp instead. Part of me wanted to say something, but I thought about the unstable weather and as much as I didn't want to admit it, Peter was doing the logical thing.

Chapter 29 - The Hunter

Camp was set up in record time. Peter told me there was a very beautiful beach on the other side of the trees and asked me if I would like to see it. We didn't run through the bushes, but instead we walked down a path. We didn't find the rainbow, but we did find something I had never seen before.

The beach was blue and my unshod feet cast a printed mould with each step into the finely crushed blue stone. Looking out at the turquoise ocean we saw waves cresting far above our heads as the two of us began exploring the exposed beach, finding stones, shells, and bits of coral.

As each treasure was found I ran over to Peter who named and told a formation story about each one. He explained the levels of the sand and earth underneath the ocean and how on this planet the third level was blue. The blue was located deep beneath, but somehow the bay seemed to bring it up to the surface, making this area very unique. Larger rocks surrounded the inlet, some black, some deep blue, and many were indigo, much like the sky.

Gazing out upon the ocean, Peter spontaneously took my hand and led me off to the right. There was an opening in the rock and crouching down, we ventured into the cave smiling at each other and giggling like little children.

Examining the inside, I found most of the rock smooth. Near the top was a roughness and a jaggedness causing me to think the ocean didn't reach it very often. The cave didn't go very far and at the end was a large black rock. Reaching up to the right Peter was able to move the black rock. He wiggled it and manoeuvred it until it rolled slightly.

Peter, in all likelihood, had already inspected most of the rocks and knew the one at the end of the cave would move. Still, somehow, he managed to give me the feeling of newness as if he too, was seeing things for the first time.

Peering through a crack, he stayed there as if studying what he saw on the other side. Curiosity was getting the best of me and like a little child I wanted to say, 'let me see, let me see'. He didn't let me peek through the crack, instead I watched as he worked the rock back and forth until it rolled completely away, exposing what seemed to be a different world.

There wasn't any blue sand, nor the same magical feeling. It was quite beautiful though, just different - an ecru sandy beach with the ocean lapping in. It was no longer the turquoise surfer heaven, instead it was deep blue with mediocre waves and rocky banks that framed the beach under the indigo sky.

The closest bank looked climbable and the one farther away was steep and stretched skyward. Carefully we made our way out onto the ledge that overlooked the ecru beach.

Peter began rolling the rock back into place so I asked if he wanted help.

"I would, but there is no room for the two of us to stand on the ledge," he said.

"It's like you are hiding it and it's our very own secret little cave," I said teasingly.

To my surprise Peter's answered in a serious tone. "I am hiding it. We are in human territory now. Often I will see people sitting along this beach or going for a walk. It's still a very remote area so there's only a small sector of people who come here. With the weather the way it is today we probably won't see anybody, but I still...."

"So the other beach and the cave we just left belongs to the Rofonians and this beach belongs to the humans?" I interjected.

"Yes."

"And that's why the road ended because we're at the border. But our truck is on the Rofonian side and we can't go back over that bridge. There is no other road, is there?" I didn't give him a chance to answer, instead I continued, "There's a lot of thick bushes, a beach and a cave. How are we going to get back?"

"Well, my brain is still working on that dilemma. I'm doing my best to keep my mind clear and trust that I will come up with a solution. You, Rainbow Dancer and I are either going to be walking into that watchtower or walking into my house un-harmed, just trust that, Princess."

Peter was right, focusing on the end result was what we needed to do. A solution would come easier to a clear mind than one cluttered with worry.

Peter braced himself as he walked. The ledge descended for quite awhile before inclining slightly downward towards the land. Steadying myself on the rock bank which abutted the Ro-fonian side, I looked at the water and the beach. I knew oceans; this ledge would be covered by water if the tide was in.

Finally, we came to an area where we could climb down. We angled towards the edge of the beach and walked for awhile before coming to a climbable bank of rocks. The bank lasted for a short stretch before turning into a steep, towering embankment that loomed well above the water level.

The Rofonians' bay seemed to be farther out into the ocean and the tide was already there so it was going to have to be a short visit on the humans' beach. That would be my surmise if the tides on this planet were the same as my yesterday's world.

"I'd like to climb those rocks right there and just sit by my-self for a few moments," I said gauging the ocean.

"Is everything alright?"

"Yes," I gave a smile of reassurance. "I'm used to being alone. Would like a bit of my own space, but nothing's wrong."

"I'll continue walking then. You won't have very long be-cause the tide is coming in. We'll have more time tomorrow. We can come back when the tide starts to recede."

A slight shiver went through me. Why did I feel there was not going to be any time for the beach tomorrow? Was I even going to see this beach again? My eyes went to the looming embankment. The water next to those steep rocks could get very high, trapping someone there and the force of the water could lift someone up and slap them hard against the rocks. We weren't even planning to go that far today, so why the strange thoughts? Why the shiver?

"Are the tides high here?" I asked.

"They're high enough to do damage. Don't worry, I won't go too far." He sounded almost condescending, but I think it was more of an attempt to tease and reassure.

My sensitivity meter was still quite high. Our earlier demi-sexual conversation had brought yesterday's world too close for comfort. Hopefully, time by myself would bring about a new perspective and allow that new energy to settle in.

Climbing rocks in a robe was not an easy feat. Should I take it off? Oh, but then I would have to carry it and I was not going to leave it, even on an unoccupied beach.

The rock bank didn't ascend too far and wasn't too steep. Climbing carefully I stopped at a spot where I had a nice view. If a six foot man stood on the beach, I would probably be a bit above his head.

Oh how wonderful, there's a lovely little hollow with a bit of land jutting out above me. A perfect place to sit; I wasn't too far up and thus should be able to get down easily. With a bit of encouragement, Rainbow Dancer joined me. It was as if we were sitting in our own little cave, staring out unto the ocean.

Rocks, similar to these, were my sanctuary when I was younger - those private little spots where I could hardly be seen by anyone. Places no one would look to find me and I could sit in peace with my pen and paper and write poetry or sketch. Places like this one helped me stay sane, although it was amazing I actually got through it all unscathed. No, it was far from that, for those childhood experiences had left a lot of scars.

Scars so deep that even when those horrible times didn't come to my conscious thoughts, they often reared their ugly heads in nightmares. Nightmares that jolted me awake and kept me from wanting to go to bed at night. It was those hidden energies that seemed to overpower me at times.

It sounds so simple just to blow the dust away and let go of the rickshaw. Even though I know its not always going to be easy, if I get a whiff of those energies, I will now fill myself with love, keep blowing that dust away, and keep imagining the rickshaw rolling farther and farther away. Who knows, maybe someday that love energy will be able to completely overpower the other ones.

Love overpowered when Ooza needed my compassion after finding him beaten inside the box when I was in the Land of the Shimmering Bridge. It was Queen Chayzlazamia who said to Ooza that no one should ever have been treated in that horrifying manner. She was correct, no one should ever have been treated like that. However, it happened and going through what we did, as well as coming out the other side, changed us and made us who we are.

Most of the time Ooza and I could simply look into each other's eyes and see that deep understanding. An understanding, so profound, it was indescribable. Without that, Ooza may not have made it to the place he belonged and the Rofonians may have lost their four eared ones forever.

When I had to help the Rofonians with the lawsuit, I had to change my perspective from being the victim to being a person who had attained wisdom from her journey. My experiences, as hard as they were at the time, made me who I am today.

"...and I'm not so bad, am I Rainbow Dancer," I whispered, patting his fur.

Hidden in our little alcove of rocks we watched the tide coming closer. I leaned forward to see if I could see Peter.

Whispering again, I said, "I don't see him. Hopefully he's on his way back soon, cause that tide waits for no..."

Suddenly, I was interrupted by small voices above my head.

Slinking back into my alcove I heard a boy's voice say, "We should go back and just say we are sorry."

"No, our mother died trying to get us out of there, so we are going to succeed," said a girl's determined voice.

"He's coming!!"

"Come on, down here," the girl's voice whispered and soon thereafter they were sliding down the embankment close to where I was sitting. There were three of them, looking as if they could be from the Rofonian Nation.

With barely seconds to think they passed us, using the rocks

145

as slides and soon were on the beach. Then a human passed us holding a shotgun. Placing it on the rocks, he climbed down a bit. He grabbed the gun, and did it all over again.

He looked like he should be hunting rabbits, but I knew it was not rabbits he was hunting. He didn't see me sitting there and my first thought was to grab his shotgun, but I was too far away. Although it probably wouldn't have been a smart thing to do as his hands were really never too far away from the gun. What was I to do? I can't let this happen.

Once the man was on the beach, Rainbow Dancer jumped up and followed him. Oh, my Rainbow Dancer, do you even know what that is? It's a shotgun! Please don't get shot!

Hiking up my robe, I proceeded to climb down the rocks. Oh no, I lost my grip! I was starting to slide! Thankfully, the man didn't turn around. My knee and my shin throbbed with pain as I hit the sandy beach. The rocks were now marred with my blood and skin, but I had no time for pain for I was too busy following and watching Rainbow Dancer.

The man was now walking between the looming wall of rocks and the ocean. Rainbow Dancer had almost caught up, but he didn't attack him, he simply ran pass. Where were the children? I couldn't see them anymore. Where was Peter, maybe the children had caught up to him. Maybe Rainbow Dancer was going to stand in between, but Rainbow Dancer didn't go get Peter, instead he ran over to the edge of the steep rock embankment and simply sat like a sitting duck!

I continued running as fast as I could, but the man had already caught up to my oughtleopar. He stood in front of him. Propping his gun deep into his shoulder joint he pointed it right at my Rainbow Dancer!

"Hey buddy, what the hell are you doing?" Peter appeared, yelling from farther up the beach. "That's my pet you're about to shoot!"

Chapter 30 - Trepidation

Turning his gun on Peter, the man walked farther down the beach towards him. If I was him I would have been keeping an eye on Rainbow Dancer, but oddly, Rainbow Dancer didn't stand up and attack the man or stand in between them, he just sat and watched. At this point the man's back was towards me and I wasn't far behind.

Finally, I caught up to Rainbow Dancer. The man had Peter still held at gunpoint a short distance down the beach! Rainbow Dancer stood up when he saw me and exposed the three that were being hunted, just long enough for me to see. Slow down time to go with the flow, ask for perfect timing and perfect protection wherever we go and with a quick nod of my head, I went over to Rainbow Dancer and patted him.

"Climb up into the compartment on his back, no human can see you there. Sit quiet and trust," I whispered, hoping the ocean would mask my words and the mystical look of my robe would ease the children's minds.

Turning, a sudden gust of the wind whipped my face with my hair. The wind had picked up and the ocean was no longer lapping, instead white crests were topping each wave. The tide was coming in fast and furious. Between the now raging ocean and the steep embankment was the man's back with his gun still pointing right at Peter!

Peter was not who the man with the gun was after so I thought Peter's gentle mannerisms would have disarmed him by now. How long was this man going to let Peter talk before he did something stupid? The hunter exuded angry energy and determination when he passed me earlier and that combination of emotions seemed a recipe for disaster in my eyes. Oh my, I was going to have to do something, but what?

My eyes were widening as each wave shaved the beach and the steep rock was now predominately looming. The roar of the ocean concealed my approach. Everything began feeling surreal - like I was acting in a movie. Instinctively my arm went into my sleeve and pulled out my almost forgotten shimmering sword. Then my arm reached up and my shimmering sword extended itself to the side of his throat!

"Drop... your... gun!" Well, that just came out of my mouth.

"She's killed before. She will not have a problem doing it again," Peter said surprisingly very convincingly.

The gun dropped. Peter picked it up. Oh my, Peter had never handled a shotgun before! His shoulder would probably break if he had to pull the trigger and if this man shared the same observation we were in trouble.

Of course he hadn't handled a gun, he studied rocks and plants, loved nature, and that's what I loved about him. He did not have to prove his masculinity by being rough and mean like some of the boys that handled guns. At one point, I knew that type, more than I cared to, but at this moment I was thankful I had felt the need to show them, I could use a gun too and hit a bullseye just as well as they could.

Oh my, now I will have to take on the masculine, the role of the protector! It was a side of me that most of the time I suppressed. What was I supposed to do next?

My sword moved slightly from the man's neck. Still holding it there, I carefully moved in front of him. Lowering it I did my best to emit an energy proclaiming I knew how to wield it, even though I didn't, but the man didn't know that.

"Look, I'm just a guy looking for my kids. I thought he was hiding them," defended the hunter with his hands in the air.

Looking confused Peter asked with some compassion, "Your kids? And where do you think I would be hiding them?"

"Should I check his pockets, maybe they're hiding in there?" I asked sarcastically.

I was so out of my comfort zone. Even wanting someone to feel stupid was out of character for me, but a man who had lost his children in a place that had an element of danger would tug at anyone's heartstrings. I didn't want him tugging at Peter's.

"Do you always hunt for your children with a shotgun?" I

said with my voice stern and my eyes glaring in disgust. I did not give him a chance to answer as the surf was breaking close to the embankment and the water was now above our ankles. "Turn around! Start walking!"

Wading through the water I followed him, pointing my sword. Peter was behind me with the gun. Thankfully we did not have to go too far before we would be at the bank where I had been sitting. We passed the place where Rainbow Dancer had been, but he was nowhere to be seen and there was no choice but to find a place where we could climb to safety.

All our lives were now in danger. My shin and knee were throbbing. I still had my robe on so climbing the rocks would be even more of a challenge and I wasn't about to put the sword back in my sleeve. No siree, I wasn't ready to underestimate the man's ability to try to overpower us.

Watching a wave wash my blood stain off the rock made me realize adrenaline was probably muting some of my pain and we were not out of danger yet.

The man began to climb. Where was my Rainbow Dancer? Was his cargo safe? I must see them all safe within my mind, although right now I need to concentrate on the task at hand. The man's head turned. Was he going to try to kick the sword out of my hand?

"Unless you want this sword through your foot, I suggest you keep moving!" I yelled in an authoritative voice.

Needing both hands to climb and hoping he wouldn't turn around again, I finally slipped the sword into my sleeve. What if he stepped on my fingers? Cancel that thought. Just believe. Believe that we were being protected.

Arriving at the hollow Rainbow Dancer and I had sat in earlier, I lingered for a moment, then silently indicated for Peter to follow. We ducked into the spot unnoticed.

"Where did you two go?" the man yelled from above.

We could see the tip of his head leaning over the cliff, but he would have to climb back down to be able to see us. I took the gun from Peter, cocked it and lodged it deep into the soft tissue of my shoulder, ready to shoot.

Peter picked up a rock. He threw it in such a way that it went up and over, landing in the bushes close to where the man was. We could only hear the loud crash of the ocean, but Peter threw another one anyway.

Had we scared him off or maybe he would think his 'so called' kids were hiding in the bushes? Sitting in silence, not knowing where the man was and not wanting to give away our location, Peter and I watched the water rise higher and higher over the rocks we had just climbed.

After a while Peter whispered, "Where is Rainbow Dancer?"

"I don't know, I have been watching for him, but I haven't seen him yet."

"We can't go back the way we came. It's underwater. If we stay here, he could bring others with more guns," Peter said.

"What are we going to do? Are we trapped?"

"It will be at least two to three hours before we will be able to go back the way we came. If he hadn't delayed us, we would have made it, but you're right, we're trapped."

"What if we climb. Couldn't we go though the bushes?"

"The horthor bushes are between us and the truck. They are full of huge poisonous thorns. I guess we could use your sword and cut into them, but we would be taking a big chance."

"I wish I knew if Rainbow Dancer was safe," I said scanning the ocean. "What if he tried to go by land? He could have run into the horthor bushes and he could be poisoned."

"You know, worrying over something you have no control over or do not know, is a waste of energy." There was a gentleness in Peter's voice, "Rainbow Dancer is an animal and one that likes water, so my bet is that he went back the way we came. His instincts probably kicked in and he probably went back before the tide was this high."

He's right, I thought, "But we blocked the cave!"

"We did, and if he tried to go around there is an undertow and those waves are coming in pretty fast."

"Oh, that eases my mind!"

"Sorry," Peter said looking a little abashed. "There's always a light at the end of the tunnel. Rainbow Dancer is strong and he's a good swimmer. He'll be okay."

Rainbow Dancer knew water currents. He had been quite efficient at working his way through the white water near the otters' cave, avoiding the dangerous falls. I have to believe in him, but what about his passengers - where would they go? How would they handle this situation?

Peter was staring out to the ocean and I concentrated on remembering the feeling of shutting down the cabin for Raziel.

Focusing on the rock blocking the cave with the intent to move it, I brought my arm up and down. I thought of Raziel. I thought of the Empress. I thought about the women with the golden hair and of my God of Love and I felt strong and magical so I stayed within that magical moment.

Having no idea whether I succeeded or not I heard Peter say, "I think the tide has turned."

We studied the rocks and saw that the water was not coming up any higher. In fact we could see some wet areas that new waves were not covering. Our hopes rose and then quickly deflated as we watched another wave crashing, breaking, and covering that wet area.

"Or maybe not," Peter finished, sounding dejected.

"Or maybe that one was simply a lone wave. Let's give it a moment," I said, trying to reassure him.

Watching intently, no other waves came quite that high and a smile beamed across my face.

"Can you swim, Peter?"

"I swim like dog," he said, sticking out his tongue and moving his hands as if they were the paws of a dog.

"Oh," I said, a bit disappointed. I was a swimmer and often swam in the ocean. I swear I was swimming before I walked.

"I told you, there's an undertow. There is no way that we're swimming around those rocks." His lips tightened and he shook his head.

"You told me a short time ago that there is always a light at the end of a tunnel. Well, I just saw the light at the beginning of one," I said, emoting a bit. Peter looked confused so I continued, "The rock must have been moved. I'm sure I saw a small glimmer of light."

Peter peered at the cave, "I think I did too and that is odd, because the cave is dark and we shouldn't be able to see light though it. Rainbow Dancer couldn't have moved it, could he? Nooo, the sun must be reflecting on something."

Smiling I said, "Never underestimate my Rainbow Dancer. You and I had to crouch when we went though the rock, right?"

"Yes."

"If I went now I might be able to reach the ledge."

"Even if you walked the shoreline, you would still need to swim to get to the ledge. Look," Peter said, pointing at the rock bank separating the two nations. "Those waves would knock you right off that ledge. There is nothing to hold on to."

"Then I will just have to climb down and swim straight from here to the opening."

"It's too dangerous, Princess and it's a long way."

"I am a very good swimmer, Peter."

"But if you got swept out to sea you could be pulled into the undertow," he said shaking his head. "The tide will be low in a couple of hours and I'm sure Rainbow Dancer is fine. If the man was coming back he would be here by now."

My thoughts went to Rainbow Dancer and the children on his back. "I can't wait. I need to know where Rainbow Dancer is, besides it will be dark in a couple of hours. You stay hidden and wait for the tide. I'll be back once I know if he's safe."

Peter pressed his lips together and shook his head.

"Listen, I am going to go whether you like it or not. I will be okay," I said gently, but firmly. "But before I go, I want you to know how to properly use a shot gun, because if you have to let off a warning shot, I don't want you to break your shoulder."

I showed Peter how to shoot a shotgun, where to lodge it, how to brace himself, and where the safety was. Pulling out the pouch I had gotten from Rainbow Dancer's cave I reached in, took out the string, and put my pouch back. Taking off my robe I stood in my brown dress with the interwoven orange and red. I folded my robe until it was a small strip of material with the arms hanging out.

With my back to Peter I took my dress off, exposing my underwear and bare back. Pushing the dress inside one a sleeve I then used the arms of the robe as ties and placed the material across my breasts. Taking the string, I secured it. I didn't want to lose it, nor did I want it to puff out once it was in the water.

"There, I have a bathing suit," I said, proud of my accomplishment. Peter just stared at me with his mouth open.

"That's miraculous, you... just put a dress in your sleeve. Where did it go? How did you do that? Where did the sword come from and where did it go? Was that in your sleeve too? Is this magic? Are you a magician or something?"

Turning to him, I put my hand on his cheek and gently said, "Some things are called magic and others are called miracles. All I can tell you is there are many, many things I do not understand. All the amazing, wonderful things that happen to me, I consider miraculous and sometimes magical. If it comes forth out of goodness, out of truth, and out of love, then I credit it to being looked after. I will be safe, I promise."

Touching my lips with his, I softly kissed him, not a passionate kiss, but more one of fondness. I climbed down the rocks, slid into the water, and swam towards the end of the sloping ledge. I knew the receding tide would naturally bring me closer to the hole in the rock. If I started angling towards it now, I could miss it and be swept into the undertow.

Swimming a hundred lengths of the university pool in yesterday's world used to be a mere warm up exercise. However, I was out of practice and knew this wasn't going to be easy. It was very astute of Peter not to join me, for swimming in the ocean was certainly not like swimming in a pool, but I had swam in the ocean and thankfully my father had taught me about currents and how to swim in them.

Making sure the waves didn't get in my mouth as the saltwater could make me sick, I quickly studied each wave until it broke. Swimming hard and fast, it took every bit of my strength to remain on course. Strategically moving with the ebbing tide, I swam underwater to avoid the crashing waves.

The sea swelled in unexpected places and the saltwater, regardless of my efforts, filled my mouth. Spitting was my only option, but water still made its way down to my stomach. I felt ill, but my life as well as the lives of others depended on me to keep going. Wave after wave, stroke after stroke, tired and sore, I finally was within reach of the ledge!

Saltwater blurred my eyes. Where was that opening!? It was not there anymore! I was going to grab the side of it and brace myself! It's gone!

The opening in the rock we had come through was higher than the ledge and during my swim the tide had lowered. This doesn't make sense, the opening should be mostly exposed. I was so sure, so how could this be possible? I know I saw a light coming from the tunnel. Peter thought he saw it too. Maybe it was only a reflection of something else and just wishful thinking.

If the rock was still covering the hole, where was Rainbow Dancer? Could he have gone around into the undertow? Was he okay? Panic started in my stomach and was working its way to my throat. Being aware of the danger can bring about success only if I go forward with caution and circumspection. I knew that, I had given myself the same advice at the waterfall when I first met Rainbow Dancer. He saved my life and now he may be in danger, but I am in immediate danger. Focus!!

The cave was definitely not exposed. If I was not careful, a wave could take me and slam me hard into the protruding rock ledge. Oh no, the receding tide was pushing me towards the undertow and I needed to grab onto something, pronto!

Chapter 31 - Life or Death

There! A piece of rock was jutting out. If I could catch hold of it, I could brace myself and have time to think. That was if it wasn't too slippery and if it held my weight. Oh my, I was being pulled by the ocean and I was going to go past it. Angle! Swim! Ouch! My already injured shins slammed hard against the ledge and I was being pushed out again.

Suddenly, I was being jerked back just as a wave filled my mouth with water. Spitting out what I could, I held my breath and went under. My eyes stung as I opened them trying to see. Oh no, my foot was caught between the rocks!!

The ledge seemed narrower. I must be a fair distance past the opening. I have to catch a moment between waves, I need air. All I could do was use my hands and guide myself under the water until I could get a good grip. Maybe I could position my head directly above the rock that was holding my foot.

Air please! In yesterday's world I could swim underwater the full length of an Olympic standard pool. I can do this; I can do this; I can hold my breath. How long was my foot going to hold me here? Was I going to have enough room to reach the ledge and get my head above water? I need to be thankful right now that the angels were keeping me alive and aware.

There, finally I was able to grab a rock, then another, and another. I inched myself up until my nose was above water.

A wave was coming towards me, so I took a deep breath and held it. Water covered my head. I still had a grip! The tide was going out and my head should be exposed soon, I hope. At least I was somewhat safe. Again, I was able to get air before the next wave crashed upon my head.

A flash of yesterday's world went through my mind when my canoe was pulled into the whitewater. I lifted my child up so he could take a breath and hold it as wave after wave hit. At that time I simply believed we would be safe. It didn't enter my mind that we wouldn't be.

In this world I can't let any fear based thoughts enter my mind either. Holding the rock I took another gulp of air and I held it in as another wave crashed down.

Just like in yesterday's world when I was in the canoe, I knew if the canoe stayed upright and we kept moving ahead that the danger would soon be over. This too will soon be over. The waves in this world seemed to be becoming smaller and I was able to take another gulp of air.

In yesterday's world, miraculously, the canoe stayed upright and kept moving out of the rapids. I have no idea how it happened as the canoe was two inches below the water level.

I must believe not being able to move was my miracle. My foot being caught must be a blessing. Being pushed into the undertow could be my demise. I am safe and the tide receding.

Finally, my head was completely above water and the waves now were even smaller, only hitting the back of my neck. Relieved, but knowing I was still in danger, I studied the rock.

The tide was higher when I had first seen the light and I was at a distance, maybe I had seen the light coming in from the top. Yes, the rock was still covering the opening, but it was not touching the rocks behind. It had fallen off the rimmed edge that had allowed us to push it out of the way and it was now down on the ledge we had walked upon. Would there be room to get through the back or through the top? Had there been enough room for Rainbow Dancer?

The ledge was finally exposed enough for me to be able to stand on it, but I still couldn't move my foot! Looking at the rock wall, I realized I could move my hand onto one stone and get a secure grip with other. Trying to wiggle my foot, I held on. There, I could move it, but barely. Oh, if only I could move it little bit more? Thankfully the cold salt water was probably preventing it from swelling. Finally, it came loose!

Carefully, clawing my way bit by bit, I was able to get on the ledge. Climbing to the top of the rock to see if I could get through the opening didn't seem like a viable option as it was too wet and slippery. Would I be able to get through from the back? I had to believe there was room, there just had to be!

Thank-you, thank-you, thank-you for getting me this far. I was bruised and tired, but it didn't matter as I was safe for the moment. Inching myself around the rock I saw a bit of light coming from the back. I leaned, pushed, and finally the rock moved a little! Thank-you, a little was all I needed and I held my stomach in and inched my way through to the other side.

Swimming and partially walking through the water that was trapped in the cave, I made my way to the blue beach. Where was Rainbow Dancer? My voice called to him, but to no avail. Calling and at the same time, fumbling and fiddling with the string, I was able to once again wear my indigo robe.

In yesterday's world when my family pet, a beautiful long-haired collie-shepherd cross went missing, I would call and call. Dispirited, I would wander home only to find him curled up asleep by my front door. Our little golden camping house was already set up. Maybe, just maybe, Rainbow Dancer would be there - curled up by the front door.

Dusk was setting in and had dimmed the bay. The land, leaves, grass, and trees were all a blur. Queen Chayzlazamia's ring! It had brought light to the tunnel when we arrived on this planet, perhaps it would give me enough light to find the path. Rubbing it and twisting it, the ring began to glow.

Searching, I saw a bit of an opening. Was it the path? What if there was more than one path? I should have paid attention. Oh I'm so stupid, why didn't I take notice of where the path was? Why was I being so hard on myself? I wasn't expecting to be alone in the dark trying find my way back.

Old patterns die hard. Again I was placing blame upon my-self. Whenever things went wrong toxic thoughts often wafted through my mind. Why do I do that? The chastising thoughts, the blame, the worry, and the pain, I was tired, sore and losing my positive outlook. Have I not learned anything? I was being looked after. I have love and all the benevolent forces that saved me. Right now, I needed to be thankful and trusting.

Limping through the opening in the trees I made my way

down the path, thankful for the bit of light I had. It seemed so much longer than the path I had been on earlier this afternoon. It was still light then and my hand was held in excitement for what Peter and I were going to see. Now time was different, not only was it darker, I was injured and unsure about where I was going. So of course it would seem longer, time is man made and often changes with the circumstances.

This wasn't an area used by many people so chances were high there was only one path. What was I seeing? It looked like an opening ahead. Where there was an opening, there was usually more light. A gleam of gold shone in the distance, I was on the right path!

The moon had risen above the trees and even though my legs were still throbbing, the rest of my time travelling the path felt shorter. 'Thank-you', I said aloud as I arrived at the golden abode. Finding my way to the door, a heaviness returned, for Rainbow Dancer was still nowhere in sight.

Where could he be? Panic rose throughout my being. Find the light! There were lanterns inside so I burst through the door. It was pitch black inside with the exception of the soft glow emanating from my ring which meant I could see a couple of feet in front of me. Something or someone was here! My breath went in, but it didn't come out. My eyes were trying hard to adjust to the light when soft fur touched my hand.

"Rainbow Dancer, you're all right!" I said leaning down giving him a hug. "Have you taken good care of the passengers? Are they all right?" Using my ring, I peered inside the howdah. "They are not in there. Did something bad happen?"

Sighing, I blinked my eyes in an attempt to keep the tears from surfacing when, 'find the light' went through my brain again. Making my way to the kitchen area, I found a lantern and took it outside. Matches, I was going to need matches.

Trying to find them might not be an easy feat. Finding my hand automatically going into my sleeve I pulled out the pouch. The matches were in the same bag as the string. Thank-you! Thank-you for this amazing cloak that Raziel gave me for the bag with the matches was dry!

Soon the lantern stopped flaming and simmered down to a gentle light. Taking it inside, I shone it around, but saw nothing or should I say no one. Where were they? The door was shut to the room where I kept my bedroll. Approaching with consideration, for I did not want to burst through in case they were scared and hiding, I decided to announce myself.

"If you are in there, it is just me. The one that helped you earlier," I said with my voice full of kindness. "I am going to open the door now."

When I opened the door, two girls were curled up and peeking out from the bedroll that they were holding. It was as if the bedroll was going to help protect them from whatever or whomever entered their space.

The boy stood in front. He wasn't holding out his fingers like the Rofonians' would if they were protecting someone, but he did give the impression he would defend the girls to his death if that was what was required. It gave me a gentle smile as it was as it should be, I only wished I had a brother who would have done that for me.

Staying in the doorway, I went down upon one knee and softly said, "You are safe here. It's all going to be okay. I would love to get you food and give you reassurance."

I paused on that word, wondering if they understood me and I continued, "when I say reassurance, I mean, I would take more time to explain what's happening, but... but okay, I will just tell you this much. I know many people your size and they are my friends. Right now, my other friend, the one who was down on the beach with me could be in trouble. I might need Rainbow Dancer's help."

Again, I paused. How would they know Rainbow Dancer's name? I finished by pointing and saying, "His help. I'll be back as soon as I can."

So far I had been able to speak all languages and be understood, but six small eyes stared back at me and not a word was spoken. "I am going to hang the lantern up here so you will be able to see."

Backing out the door, I stopped and hung the lantern up high on the hook. It was high for them, certainly not for me as the ceiling was just inches from the top of my head. The place glowed with brightness and I wondered whether they would be more comfortable in the dark as it is easier to hide. Oh well, no time to worry as I needed to find Peter and something inside me said it was urgent. Oh no, I might need the light.

"Oh, oh, I'm so sorry. I changed my mind. I... I... I need to take the light with me."

Taking the light of the hook, I noticed Rainbow Dancer had already left. Watching as he bounded towards the path I followed, limping as quickly as I could. This time there was more light and I was grateful for that.

The moon had now found its place high in the sky and it was reflecting ripples across the water. Hobbling over the blue sand I crouched down to go through the cave. Rainbow Dancer had already squeezed past the rock that separated the territories and by the time I did, he was already sitting on the ledge.

It seemed to look different, probably because I couldn't see the rock bank were I had left Peter - it was too far away. The roar of the ocean had subsided, but it still looked like there was water beneath the ledge. Hoping the sound of my voice would travel, I yelled out Peter's name, but received no response.

If he was still on the rocks would he be able to see my light? Was he even still there? The knot in the pit of my stomach grew tighter. It started when I felt that sense of urgency to find the lantern, but now the pain was almost overwhelming.

"Rainbow Dancer, Peter was over there on the rocks. You know, where you and I were sitting, but my eyes are not keen enough to see that far in the dark," I said leaning down to give him a hug.

He shook his head and looked rather annoyed. He sat there stiffly as if, he was concentrating deeply and didn't want me to interrupt. Changing his gaze, Rainbow Dancer stopped looking outward and began looking down to the right.

Abruptly, he stood, made his way over the rocks, and disappeared into darkness. I tried to shine the light where he had been looking, but I couldn't see a thing. What was that? Was Rainbow Dancer swimming in the ocean below the ledge? Was he swimming towards where I had left Peter? It didn't look like it. Since the light was so close to me, following his movements in the dark water wasn't easy. Oh no, I couldn't see him anymore.

Concentrating, finally I saw him, he had turned around and was heading back, but not directly towards me as he seemed to be heading towards the shore. Inching my way, I eventually came to where the water was the same height as the ledge. I could barely see him. He looked different. He seemed darker and bigger. Why would he look bigger?

Ohhh, he had Peter! Peter was not moving and was flopped over Rainbow Dancer's back. Quickly, I looked for a place where I could put down the lantern and have two free hands.

Leaning over to grab Peter I heard Rainbow Dancer speak for the first time, at least the first time I didn't have my forehead next to his, "The rock! Move the rock!"

Awkwardly, but as quickly as possible I made my way across the ledge, leaned my body on the rock and pushed. Oh good, it moved and I was able to make the opening wider. Stay logical. Trust, because going into my compassionate emotional side could cause me to panic. I couldn't allow that to happen. Peter had to be okay. He had to come through this.

Rainbow Dancer had made it up onto ledge when I yelled, "Peter!" hoping he would stir. There was nothing. He just lay motionless on Rainbow Dancer's back. Rainbow Dancer travelled across the ledge and Peter was now close enough to touch. "Peter!" I yelled again, but again, nothing.

Was he alive? How was I going to get him off of Rainbow Dancer's back without hurting him? He had to be okay. Rainbow Dancer didn't stop, he just kept on going into the cave. Grabbing the lantern, I followed and he continued on through until he arrived on the wet blue beach. Finally, he stopped.

It was as if my instincts took over and I wasn't in control anymore. I put down the lantern and somehow got below Peter's body. Using my back, I flipped him down upon the beach. He landed on his back with a splat upon the wet sand. If he had a broken neck or anything like that, I could have killed him! Why I reacted like that, I had no idea.

The shock must have caused him to go into convulsions. Immediately I rolled him onto his side and he coughed and sputtered until he could finally ask where he was.

I began to cry and cry. Oh my, was I being selfish by crying? I should be thinking about Peter right now or the children in the golden abode, but I couldn't help it, the tears just flowed.

"Are you okay?" came Peter's frail voice.

"You almost drowned! Peter, I almost lost you. How did it happen? I thought you were waiting until the tide went out."

"Ahh, I don't know," he mumbled, rubbing his temples.

Was this still grogginess from his trauma or had he hit his head? Sniffing, I wiped my tears and looked at him through my glossy eyes.

With help he sat up and between coughs he said, "It was getting dark. I thought the tide had gone out enough and I would be able to walk. I tried to stay close to the rocks. I found the ledge and thought I was being careful but I guess I lost my footing and fell. I did try to swim. I think I swim like a rock. Thank-you for saving me."

"You owe your life to Rainbow Dancer, not me. I merely brought the light to the ledge, but it was Rainbow Dancer who saw you. He jumped in the water and he brought you back."

"I need to get out of these wet clothes," Peter stated with determination as he tried to stand up.

"Yes," I said, "and you need a cup of tea." It was then I exclaimed, "But I have something that I need to tell you."

"Can't it wait?" His voice sounded frustrated as he stood up saying, "My head is not all here yet."

"Not really. We have company," I blurted out.

Chapter 32 - The Lost Children

"Huh!?" Peter said while spasmodically rubbing his ears that were probably full of water.

Did he actually hear me say that we have company?

After a while he said, "Company?"

"Three children," I said timidly as we began walking. "One of the girls is probably Ooza's age and... and... a teenage boy and a little girl."

Walking on the wet, slanted, crushed stone beach, my feet sank with every step. Now, with an awkward conversation, Peter trying to get his land legs back, and me trying to ignore my pain, the trek was even more difficult.

"The path is this way." I guided as he seemed to be weaving in the wrong direction. We stopped at the beginning of the path and he looked at me and stared into my eyes.

"So the man was right. He had lost his children. We have to take them back," he firmly stated.

"It's not that simple. We can't take the children back." My voice probably sounded frustrated. Maybe it was panic at the thought of returning them to that horrible man. Nonetheless, my voice was not as soothing as it should have been.

"It is that simple. You cannot keep another person's children no matter what you think about their father." Peter's voice was annoyed as I think he had his fill of turmoil for the day. "We WILL be taking them back!" he yelled over his shoulder as we headed down the path.

Had the children heard him yell? If they had, they would probably leave. I knew I would if I was in their position. We were still quite a distance from them, but I had lived by water and I knew when the tide recedes the sound travels far into the quietness of the night. Immediately I imagined a sound barrier between them and us and hoped it not only worked, but it had come down quickly enough to muffle his words.

My tired arm was holding the light high so Peter could see

where he was going and I was finding it difficult to remain composed and reverent. Fear and trembling had travelled deep within and instincts have a hard time coming forward when in a state of fear. I need my instincts so I have to find a way to become calm. I just have to.

Even the words 'have to' seem to be creating a block within, so I must find another way to talk myself through this. Breathe in calm, breathe out fear, breathe in calm, concentrate, breathe in deep, breathe out, okay, again. Alright, now I was feeling a little bit better, but was I ready to calm Peter's emotions?

Once he met the children I felt his attitude would change. He had been traumatized too, but I wasn't sure I would be able to handle his reaction if I tried to explain. Peter's body was exuding angry energy and we were within hearing distance of those who were already so full of fear and mistrust. I didn't want to take the chance that they would retreat even further.

Hopefully the children would be there and Peter would be feeling better. Yes, dry clothes, a hot drink and the awareness that we survived. The children survived. We were alive. There were many things to be thankful for. I simply needed to bring Peter back to being that wonderful, gentle man whom I had first met - the Peter whom I felt the children also, would instantly trust.

Yes, I could do this if I only could muster up enough concentration to get through this excruciating pain. I began to hum, for I knew that singing often worked as a painkiller.

We were almost off the narrow path and maybe I could get him to stop long enough to see reason and how important it was for him not to be angry when he walks through the door.

Arriving at the field where we could see the golden house, Peter didn't stop. He seemed angry and on a mission. I yelled for him to please wait, but he only continued walking. Stubbornness had overtaken him. It felt like in his mind I was wrong, he was right and it didn't seem to matter to him that he didn't know the whole story.

He probably thought the man was looking for his children,

so therefore, had a right to hold him at gunpoint. Actually, I had no idea what he was thinking and I had no right to assume, but obviously his thinking wasn't logical. I knew he had gone through so much today and perhaps was not himself. Then again, I hadn't known him that long and maybe this was just a side I had never seen.

Limping as fast as I could, I watched him go into the golden abode, come back out and light the other lantern. By the time I arrived it was beaming brightly, showing me that the door to where I kept my bedroll was open!

Peter was still oozing frustration when he turned towards me and, in what sounded like an angry tone, he said, "There are no children in here!"

"There has to be. They have to be here." Anxiety was in my voice for I knew we might be their only chance at freedom and maybe even survival.

Peter stood in the doorway and I was panicking. Even though I was doing my best not to be swayed by his emotional state I had to see for myself, but neither Peter nor his tension moved out of my way.

How do I handle this correctly? As a child, Peter's actions and raised voice could have had me completely frozen in a state of fear. Now, I only felt disrespected and dismissed. We both have had enough trauma for one day and this was not about me. Closing my eyes I pressed my lips together.

"Can I look?" I said through my teeth, trying not to sound as upset as I felt.

He glared at me, walked through the door, and said, "See!"

Logically it didn't make sense that I didn't believe him and had to see for myself. Still I looked around the empty room even though I knew there wasn't any place to hide. I felt ashamed, however that feeling only lasted for a split second.

Looking into his glaring eyes I spoke in a strong, but gentle voice, "I realize you have gone through a lot of trauma today. We all have, but right now I have to find the children."

"No, you don't... have to," he said rudely. "They found their way here. They can find their way back."

My jaw dropped in disbelief. I didn't care how much I trusted Peter when I first looked into his eyes. Right now, they were not the same eyes and there was nothing or no one that was going to stop me.

"They didn't find their way here. Rainbow Dancer brought them," I blurted out, probably more animated than it should have been. I simply stood there looking at him, I think I was hoping for some understanding.

"Rainbow Dancer brought them?" he said slowly. "And you knew this. Did you know this when we met the man?"

Previously I couldn't tell whether he was angry at me or the situation, but now, it definitely seemed directed towards me and I felt it, but I no longer had anymore strength.

"Yes," I said, but my voice was weak, my eyes were wide and I backed up a step or two.

To my surprise my hand slowly moved to my sleeve. I said in a strained voice, "I realize you feel out of your element and out of control, but that doesn't give you the right to disrespect what I feel is the best thing to do. So get rid of that ego of yours and stop projecting your macho insecurities on me."

Peter must have noticed that I had backed up a step or two. "Whoa, whoa, I am not small brained like those macho guys and I wasn't going hurt you," he said, his eyes softening as he held his palms towards me. "I could never do that. Oh my God, I'm such a jerk. Oh my God, I am sorry. I'm so sorry. Look, I'm... I'm not mad, I just have had a hard time thinking this through. I'm... I'm just tired and frustrated."

Realizing I had been holding my breath, I said, "Peter" as my breath let go, "I appreciate the apology and I realize you're frustrated. What I'm saying is, your frustration is your own and stop projecting it on me. The day has been hard enough and it's not over yet. I have to focus. I have to go look for them."

"Then I will come with you."

"No," I said bluntly, hoping my voice carried some softness and I made sure it did as I continued, "you need to get out of those wet clothes and have a hot drink. You need to look after you right now and find that wise, gentle Peter whom I first met, because I might need your help later." I walked past him and went out the door, shutting it behind me.

Focus on the now and not on Peter's shat, but the now made me realize the heavy lantern handle, that had earlier indented into my palm, was causing me to wince. In fact, there weren't too many parts of my brain or my body that didn't hurt. Sighing deeply, I put the lantern in my other hand and walked away from the golden house.

What do I do now? I don't even know their names, so how do I call out to them? Which direction should I go?

"Please come back!" My voice had entered the quiet of the night. It was so insanely quiet. It was the type of silence many people never get to experience. "I can help you!"

Chances are they would have gone into hiding and even if one of them had a bit of trust for me, the others would have convinced them that Peter was mean. Once you have been around malevolence it seems wired into your psychological mind. I knew that all too well. I knew it would take a safe refuge as well as a lot of releasing and reprogramming themselves to change those patterns and adapt to new conditions.

"Please come back!" I pleaded as I limped towards the road. "There is a city and those who live there are not human or mean. They're your size. They look like you and this city is too far for you to walk. The city is far from the humans' city. They don't trust humans either, but they do trust Peter. They will treat you with respect. You will need our help to get there, the city's too far away and we have means to get you there. Please come back! I promise you will be taken to people who are like you. Oh please, please come back!"

The road was so silent and empty I could hear myself hobble. It seemed like an extremely long trek with no one answering my pleas. I turned and went back to our little house.

Opening the door, Rainbow Dancer greeted me and Peter was sitting in a chair. My stomach, once filled with saltwater, now was empty with hunger. I needed to find food, pronto.

I looked at Rainbow Dancer. "Why didn't I take you with me! You would have found them," I exclaimed.

"Did you find them?" Peter said opening his eyes.

"No," I said in a voice that sounded close to tears.

"Where did you look?"

"Up the road and then I turned back thinking I should go down by the beach, but I am so hungry."

"I'll find you something to eat," Peter said as he stood up.

My eyes studied him. The hot drink and bit of sleep must have been what he needed as his energy felt so much better and his eyes were once again, kind and loving.

"I'm sorry, I was frustrated... wasn't thinking," he said softly.

"You probably had a wee case of water on the brain," I said weakly, trying to bring in a bit of humour, but Peter merely nodded so I continued, "I'm sorry too. I should have told you when we were on the rock bank, but I was too scared that the man with the gun would hear. And... and... I didn't expect the rest. It was a very traumatic day." We stood looking awkwardly at each other for a few moments.

To my surprise he took me in his arms and he held me. It actually was quite wonderful and I could feel love, strength and soon felt myself coming back to my center.

"I have to go look again," I said pulling away. "I thought I would go down to the beach. The rock is off the rim and down on the ledge. I didn't have a chance to cover the hole once Rainbow Dancer carried you through because you became my priority. Now I don't know what to do."

"It needs to go back," he said.

"But what if they have gone through it and they need to come back?" I asked

"Or what if they are still here and their father, you know, the man with the gun, comes through it?" Peter asked.

I wanted to say that he wasn't their real father, but I merely responded with a long sigh.

"If they went through the hole then they have probably gone

back to him," Peter said gently, interrupting the sigh.

"Yeah, you're right. I'll go put the rock back, but it will show a tiny sliver of light from the top. They are small enough, they will be able to get through and it probably won't even be noticed by anyone else," I said, starting to leave.

"You need to sit. I've rolled that rock away and manoeuvred it back onto the rimmed edge before. It's tricky to do, even in the daylight. Tonight, I promise I'll just roll it along the ledge and leave that sliver of light. Hopefully it'll only take me a few moments and I'll come back and make you something to eat, okay?" Peter said, handing me a mug of tea.

With a tired nod, I sat in the chair. Rainbow Dancer and Peter left. I should have gone with him. I should have said more and I should get myself something to eat. Ohh my leg, oohhh... I shut my eyes. After awhile I opened them, had sip of tea, and shut them again. I must have dozed off as time, for me, went quickly and the next thing I knew Peter was back.

"Did you see them?" I asked.

"No," was all he said.

"Did you call for them?" I asked.

"No."

"I hope they didn't go back that way."

"Maybe the man's not as mean as we think," Peter spoke as we looked at each other with doubt in our eyes. "I'll get you something to eat and we can look again in the morning."

"Or maybe after I have something to eat, I will feel strong enough to look again," I said taking a sip of tea with hope that the pain in my body would ease enough to make that happen.

Peter was true to his word and shortly thereafter a plate of food was set in front of me. Not wanting to upset my already queasy stomach I chewed it very slowly as I looked around.

"Peter," I said softly, still searching the area with my eyes. "Where is Rainbow Dancer? Did he go with you when you went to cover the opening of the cave?" I asked, wondering if Peter would have noticed if Rainbow Dancer went through to the human territory before he rolled the rock back?

Chapter 33 - Trusting

"I don't think so, I don't remember seeing Rainbow Dancer, but..., but...,"

"But that doesn't mean wasn't with you and he didn't go back to the human territory," I said, finishing his sentence.

"Yeah," Peter said nodding. He shrugged his shoulders and rolled his eyes up slightly and continued, "He'll be fine and we'll go look for him the moment we finished eating."

Peter was still eating and my food was barely finished when we heard a noise.

"Rainbow Dancer!" I exclaimed as I rose to open the door.

"Careful, Princess, it might be the man with the gun," Peter whispered.

"No, it's Rainbow Dancer," I said before opening the door. "You found them. He found them Peter!"

"The children? Where are they?" Peter said looking rather confused as he stared at Rainbow Dancer.

"They're in the howdah!" I retorted, forgetting he couldn't see inside. "In the... on Rainbow Dance... right, you can't see them because they're not from the human world you...?"

"But he is or he'd be able to see us," the boy said looking at Peter as an alien enemy. "I am right aren't I? Why are you telling him where we are?"

"Yes, he is a human," I said gently. I was going to continue, but the boy interrupted.

"Is he going to take us back?"

"No, he's not," my voice was soft, but my words were firm. "His family has helped your kind for generations. He is a very nice man."

"Something stabbed her when we were out in the woods." He tilted his head towards the older girl. "I think she might be dying," he said with almost no emotion.

"Oh," I swallowed, "I'm going to need more light so I can see it better. Can we go inside?"

"No, bring the light out here," he ordered.

"Peter, I'm going to need you to hold the light. Something stabbed her out in the bushes."

The lantern, shining though the doorway, wasn't positioned where I could see details. However, I could see the other little girl. She had long, very curly soft blue hair. Truthfully I was not sure if it was actually blue or if it merely looked that way because of the lighting. Her lips were parted in both fear and wonder. Her large eyes were opened wide and her cuteness pulled at my heartstrings.

"The light will be bright so hide your eyes," I whispered to her as I put my hands over my eyes and she copied the action.

"She probably got stabbed by a horthor," stated Peter as he brought the light closer so I could see better.

"How would we be able to tell?" I asked.

"It will have three rings, surrounding the wound. Usually they're purple, " Peter told me.

The older girl was very weak, but she managed to raise her shirt enough so we could see the wound. "There are three rings Peter, they're on her lower back, between her spine and side."

Peter put down the lantern and left. He quickly walked past the golden abode, stopped for a second, turned around, and went inside. Carrying with him a packing box, he headed towards the beach.

"He is going to bury her in that box. He is looking for a place to do that. He is going to let her to die," the boy stated.

Watching the fear swell in the girl's eyes, I gently, but firmly said, "No."

I knew Peter was on a mission and even though I didn't know what he was doing, I knew he wouldn't leave like that without good reason.

"He's gone to get something that will help," I reassured.

"Gone to get the other humans and that won't help us."

"No, he blocked the entrance to the human territory, so no other human can come here."

"We are not in human territory?" he said with confusion in

171

his voice.

"No, we are not," I said, anxiously looking towards where I had last seen Peter.

"...but he is human. I am not sure about you."

His statement made me smile, but I don't know why. "He'll be back soon with something to put on the wound."

"I hope he can help her," he said, still without any emotion; he was so different from Ooza.

It was hard for me to put on a brave face, for the girl looked so wan and barely conscious. Her hair was also curly and long. She was exquisitely beautiful even in her ailing state. Her little sister brought her hands down so her eyes could once again peek at me. I smiled and winked at her. Her eyes sparkled a bit and she covered her face with her hands once again.

The boy matter-of-factually stated, "She is a princess. I do not know if there are anymore like her."

He had sounded so definite and I had to ask, "And are you a Prince? Are you her brother?"

I wondered, was she really a princess? I knew that sometimes when a person was traumatized they could hold onto a fantasy to keep themselves going. I needed to be careful, so I simply looked into his eyes. He was a nice looking boy. He didn't look anything like the other two. His jaw was kind of square and his lips were thinner. He had long, straight raven black hair that didn't stand up. His ears were pointed, but the points curled at their tips.

Studying me for a moment and in a robotic tone he said, "No, I'm a stud."

My jaw dropped. He was a stud? Stud, that can't mean what I think it means, can it? "You're a stud?!?"

"Do you not know what a stud is?" he asked.

I think at that moment he was hoping I knew the answer and I was hoping I didn't.

"Eh, I know what it means for animals, but...." before I could finish, he interjected.

"I am supposed to impregnate her. The older men, they

would rather be whipped. The humans thought I would be more successful, but she convinced me to run. She was very convincing."

My head turned. I had heard something in the bushes. I was glad, for I didn't know what to do with my face. Seconds later, Peter came running up with a box of blue mud.

"What are her eyes like?" he asked quickly.

"He wants you to open your eyes," the boy told her.

Opening her tired eyes, she looked up at me. How was I supposed to answer Peter's question? I had never really looked into her eyes to know how different they actually were?

"Cloudy and turning grey," the boy answered for me.

"The blue mud will suck out some of the poison, but in her condition, it will need to be more powerful. I'll be right back," Peter stated and went back inside.

"The blue mud makes sense to me. On many occasions I placed brown mud on a bee sting; it really works and sucks out the poison," I said, trying to reassure him.

"Bee sting?" the boy asked.

Oh right, that was my yesterday's world, so much for me re-assuring him.

"Trust him, because he's going to look after you and do everything in his power to heal you and protect you," I said looking into the girl's fearful eyes. "I know it takes a lot to trust a human, but he is not like the others, I promise."

Peter brought out a bowl and a stirring utensil that seemed to have a flat block at the end then a dipped area like a spoon, and a handle. Running over to one of the trees, he removed several of the buds, or were they nuts, I wasn't sure. Cutting them open, he deposited their insides into the bowl, mashed them with the utensil, and added some of the blue mud.

"Adding tazotaka makes it more powerful. The blue mud could go on really thick so Princess, you will need to be careful as to how much you put on. It needs to be the same thickness as the width of the tip of her nose and then the wound will have to be bandaged."

"This works on humans, but we're different. What if it does not work on her or worse... kills her?" asked the boy.

"That's why it is the tip of her nose, not my nose," Peter said gently and added, "It was the Rofonians who taught me this cure."

"Rofonians? Who are the Rofonians?"

Peter appeared confused, "They aren't Rofonian?"

"I don't know. Their hair doesn't stand up, their colouring is a little bit different, and the tips of their ears are curled and not pointed, but other than that, they look very much like them."

Peter appeared thoughtful for a moment before he spoke. "This will work. The Rofonians are your size and the..."

"How do you know we are the same size? You can't see us," the boy interjected.

"Because she says you are and I trust her," Peter answered softly.

"Okay, I also trust her. What else were you going to say?"

"The ratio of tazotaka and mud was changed to work for my grandfather. I did my best to scale it back down to what I remembered the original recipe was and that's the best I can do. We can use three treatments. It's not going to cure her over night, because it takes days of drinking a special tea, brewed with several herbs. We need to get the tea in her. If a human gets stabbed with the thorn, I am assuming it would take longer for the thorn to have an effect on us, but honestly don't know about her." Peter pressed his lips together and shrugged his shoulders. "I'm doing my best."

"We need to get her to the Rofonians don't we," I said as more of a statement than a question.

Peter let out a breath, pressed his lips together again, visibly swallowed and nodded. He turned towards the house and said over his shoulder, "While you're dressing her wound, I'm going to check to see if I have any of the herbs."

When he came back he was carrying some boxes that he put in the truck.

"We are going to have to leave," Peter announced. "I have

174

some tea at my house and my house is closer."

Well, I was going to have to trust that, as it kind of made sense, because we had come down the mountain and were closer to human territory than the Rofonians' city. The humans had better roads, the bridge was washed out and I knew we could not go back the way we came.

"How are we going to get to another road?" I asked after administering the bandage.

Peter didn't answer, he was too busy retrieving the poles with the two prongs. He took them out of the back of the truck and attached them onto his front grill. He instructed Rainbow Dancer along with his three passengers and myself to get in. The boy insisted on staying in the howdah so Rainbow Dancer simply jumped into the backseat. Apparently, we didn't have time to pack because Peter got into the driver's seat.

My index fingers were pressed against my lips and my palms felt glued together as Peter turned his truck towards the horthor bushes. It was odd, for out of the corner of my eye I thought I saw Raziel. I smiled, moved my hands away from each other at the exact same time Peter, with the poles sticking out in front of the grill, drove straight into the horthor bushes. The bushes parted and opened like an ivied arched gateway!

Once we were out of danger of being stabbed, Peter stopped and got out of the truck, took the poles off, and began pushing the bushes with one of the poles.

Getting out of the truck, I asked, "What are you doing?"

"I can't leave an opening for the humans," he said quickly.

I looked back at the girl. Was Peter so conditioned not to leave a human imprint on the Rofonians' land that he couldn't see the urgency. I have certainly done some odd things when I have been panicked.

Gently I said, "It is not that important right now and I think the Rofonians would agree."

Glancing up I mouthed a thank-you as Peter returned to the driver's seat. Not only was I giving thanks for Peter listening to me, but also for getting through the horthor bushes, and for the clarity of mind in my exhausted state. Again, I thought I saw Raziel and for whatever reason, I brought my hand up and twisted it, similar to one turn of screwing a light bulb into a socket. Before turning my head back around, I saw everything looking natural as if nature had not been disturbed at all.

"Peter," I said, "the bushes moved back to their natural state and you can't even tell we went through."

"Really? Well, I guess, cause they seemed to just move out of our way, they didn't break so yeah, that makes sense, at least I think it does. I really didn't know what I was doing. I just thought the poles might help either by pushing them out of the way, or... throw them off guard, I don't know... and the truck would do the rest. I really did not expect them to just move."

"It was pretty amazing how it happened, wasn't it?"

"Yeah, it was," he said slowly, "Did you do that?"

Smiling, I said, "I don't think I'm that powerful, but thanks for thinking I am. Tell me something? You said you thought the poles would throw them off guard, what did you mean?"

"Well, the humans believe, if you go into the horthor bushes you won't come out alive. They say the bushes are possessed and that they can even swallow up a truck. Which, in some ways, is kind of good, because there are a lot of horthor bushes running along the bottom of the mountain. Some humans think that the whole mountain is polluted with them and on the bright side that keeps most of them from exploring the mountain."

"Huh, do the Rofonians believe that too?" I asked.

"I don't think so, but then again there has been a language barrier. All I was told was to memorize the recipe in case I came in contact with one. The paper I was given had what the Rofonians would take and also had the conversion on it." Peter gave a big sigh before he said, "I have to admit though I am glad to be on a road. How we were going get back with that bridge out had been weighing heavily on my mind."

"I bet and I bet it took everything you had to put those poles on and drive through those bushes."

"Yep, it sure did, but I had to believe I was driving through them for the right reasons and I had to have faith that the right thing was going to happen. How's our passenger?" he asked.

Shifting myself so I could turn around and look I heard Peter's firm voice ordering, "Never mind, look forward and natural. I think we've got company."

Not too far ahead we saw lights in the middle of the road. Peter slowed and as we got closer we saw a group of three men waving us down.

"What if they are after us?" asked the boy.

"They can't see you so just sit quietly," I ordered.

"It's either stop the truck or run them down. Well, let me do the talking," Peter said as he slowed the truck.

Two of the men came over to the window and wanted to know what we had in the truck. One shone a flashlight on Rainbow Dancer lying in the backseat and the other shone his into the box of the truck. The third man remained standing in front of us in the middle of the road.

"Haven't seen you before. You're not from around here. Where are you from and what are doing out here?"

"Live inland a bit, don't come down to the shore as much as I'd like to," Peter answered. Imitating their accent, he tilted his head towards me and with a mischievous look, he said, "Just out with the little woman, you know, showing her around."

I knew what Peter was alluding to, so I acted embarrassed. The man from the middle of the road came over. Oh no, he was the same man who had pointed the shotgun at us on the beach! A gasp came from the backseat.

Rainbow Dancer looked at the man who had pointed the shotgun at us and growled, masking the sound of the gasp.

"I know you. Where is my gun?" he said menacingly.

To my surprise I had an accent as I blurted out, "The one you pointed at our pet and then at us, 'cause we were walking on the beach."

Peter looked at one of them, shrugged his shoulders, and responded, "Just left the gun on the rock bank. I didn't want his gun, I just didn't want us to get shot."

177

Chapter 34 - Pulling Heart Strings

Thankfully that satisfied the men and we were dismissed. Also, I was thankful the boy had earlier decided not to get out of the howdah which meant the children were protected. Once again, the appreciation for the protective ward given by The Empress was profound.

For awhile we drove quietly into the night until Peter broke the silence. "The roads are maintained and pretty straight. It's going to be a long night, are you too tired to drive?"

Peter was exhausted and it might be his only chance to get some shuteye. My only concern was the truck was a bit different than what I was used to because for me, tiredness was not an issue. In yesterday's world I often had to function with very little sleep. Odd, if all the trauma I had gone through had not occurred, I might not have acquired the skill.

"Maybe I should be asking, do you know how to drive?"

"I can drive, I just haven't operated a vehicle like this."

Before long I was driving and it seemed as though everyone was asleep and then I heard the boy's voice from the howdah.

"Where exactly are you taking us?"

"Peter's house so we can get some herbal medicine. His house is located in the human territory, but because of where it is, the chances are very high that no one will see you. Although, I think it would be wise to stay in the howdah until we are inside the house."

"Are we going see the Ro... Rofonians? The ones you say we look like?" he questioned.

"Yes, Peter will get you there by mid morning. They will probably put her in a healing room and I have complete faith that she will be nursed back to health. Also, I know all of you will be safe, cherished, and treated with respect."

"Will I still be a stud?"

I smiled at that comment, but I wasn't sure why, as their whole situation was very sad and I merely answered, "No."

"Why?"

Oh my, how do I answer that, "Because... in your case it doesn't show respect for you or for the other person."

"Why?"

Oh, he is asking difficult questions. Where do I begin? A brief flash of the horrors of yesterday's world came into my mind. Then suddenly a flash of Peter and I in the truck came to the forefront and for the first time I was glad I received flashes, because this time the flashes brought wisdom. There was wisdom in both the horrors and in Peter's and my conversation about being demi-sexual.

"If we truly want to understand our purpose for being here, we need to understand things on a deeper level. There are four main elements: earth, fire, water, and air. If the soil didn't have the other elements it wouldn't be able to support the growth of plants. The planet needs all these elements to work together in harmony so everything can go well. We have a physical, mental, emotional, and spiritual side. We need them to work in harmony so everything will go well."

There was silence for a moment before he spoke, "What you are saying is, if the elements on the planet do not work together, we would have one natural disaster after another, but what does that have to do with my question? The humans say that being a stud is an honour."

We drove for a little while longer as I thought about what he had said and what I had said. "I get the feeling from you that your entire race was being controlled; either by being whipped, or by repetition. Well, that's abuse and manipulation. It's often done to make you believe and do things a certain way. Those humans who kept you didn't want you to think for yourself and thus your mental side wasn't being respected or honoured.

Most of us need guidance to know the difference between right and wrong. When you are respected and allowed to grow within, then you usually make good choices. However, if the people who are guiding you don't know the difference, then the only thing you can do is do your best to be on a path of finding love within yourself."

"I think I am starting to understand," he said slowly.

I realized then I needed to bring it back to his question so I said, "To be a stud should be a choice and if it's not your choice then you either live with your hurt or you deny your emotions. Because you were forced into it, it's no longer about respect, love, or kindness, or goodness. If being loving and kind is who you are spiritually then you would have to deny that aspect of yourself also. If the one receiving is not a willing party, then it is extremely detrimental to them. If both people make the choice on their own then it's a different matter all together."

"Now I understand. If we do not respect and realize we are like the elements and allow our physical, mental, emotional, and spiritual aspects to work in harmony then we will have one personal disaster after another," he abridged.

"Yeah, you got it. Just remember the only way to achieve growth is to go towards love, kindness and goodness because the opposite of that is... hell. You know you are amazing, because what you said was exactly the point I was trying to get across, although I think you said it so much better."

"So I did not do anything wrong because before I left, I thought about what I did not like and what most of the males there did not like about what we had to do. I listened to the others. I listened and honoured our Princess Amita. I thought about it, though, but I do not think I feel emotions. Maybe I do, because I must have felt something. I just wanted to take her to a better place, but I didn't know there was one."

"There is. It sounds like you honoured everyone including yourself. Princess Amita, so that's her name. What's yours?"

"Michael, at least that was what the humans called me."

"What did your mother call you?" I asked.

"I barely remember her. I do not even know if she is alive."

"That's sad, because mothers are to be treasured. Did Amita tell you she was a Princess?"

"The men, who are my size, told me she was a Princess. They said she had the ears of a Princess and her name, Amita,

180

was a name often given to royalty. At least back in the day when we had royalty, but that was before I was born."

"The Rofonians call one of their flowers Amita," I informed him. "By the way, they believe in respect and that is who they are. What is different about Amita's ears?"

"Underneath the top curl of her ears are teardrop holes," he continued. "I checked for myself. According to legends, the royal family embedded jewels in their ears. Only a true royal would be born with those teardrop holes. The humans made her into a slave and that dishonoured our whole race. I have no idea what the girls did as slaves. I have not been with the girls very long. The little one has never even spoken a word to me. I don't even know if she can talk, but Amita says she is her little sister. I had to help them. It felt like the right thing to do," Michael said, his voice was beginning to sound tired.

"It was the right thing to do. If it wasn't, you wouldn't have found us. We are going to help you and all your lives will be different, but a lot better from here on in."

After a while, Michael also fell asleep and I drove on into the sunrise in silence. Arriving at the city's edge, Peter woke up, and again we changed drivers.

Finally, at his house, Peter began brewing a mixture of herbs together into a tea and I checked on our guests. The little one was still sleeping. She looked so innocent and sweet, although Amita's frail, limp body tugged at my heartstrings.

Reaching in, I took her out of the howdah and laid her on the sofa so Peter would also be able to see her wound. Her eyes fluttered, but I had no idea whether or not she was even conscious enough to understand what was happening.

Waiting for the medicine to cool, we removed the blue mud. To my eyes, the wound looked different and I tried to describe to Peter what had changed. Some of the poison had drained, but Peter remained very worried. She barely stirred as I talked to her gently, letting her know we were dressing her wound.

Michael woke up and came over to the sofa to watch. He told her we were good humans and to trust we were doing everything we could to help her. His words touched me deeply.

"Thank-you," I told him softly. "As soon as the tea cools down, we will have to wake her. The tea will help."

"I'm going to make a bit of food for the drive up the mountain. Do you want to help?" Peter asked.

I looked at Michael's worried face. "It is your belief, not your worry, that is going to help her. Talk to her and let her know how wonderful life is going to be. Give her strength."

Walking to the kitchen I heard Michael saying to Amita, "Thank-you, it was your knowing and your belief that we would be better off and we are going to be. You were right, we are not supposed to be treated like those humans treated us. You knew it and you knew it was a huge risk and you took it. You chanced losing everything to find a place of respect.

I didn't believe you. I tried to talk you out of it. I was too scared of losing my shelter, but you believed strongly that we are supposed to be respected. You are so strong within. You told me that The Empress would intercede and help, but she couldn't help until we made the choice - until we took the risk. I guess I needed to see that there are good humans. The Empress must have sent them and they are taking us to a really good place. Be strong Princess Amita, we are almost there."

His words were powerful, but still had little or no emotion in them. There didn't seem to be any joy or sorrow. He was listening and knew the right words to say, but was he actually feeling them, for his voice sounded almost robotic?

Walking into the kitchen, I said to Peter, "I know your vacation was cut short, but I'm so glad we were there to help."

"This is more important than a vacation," he said softly. "And watching you wield a sword and swim all that way was amazing. Your gentleness is..." He paused as he put the food in the pan. Turning to me he placed his hands on my shoulders and looked me in the eyes before continuing, "is so beautiful and so strong." He played with my hair on the side of my face and then he told me, "I think I am falling in love with you."

Oh my, someone who saw me as beautiful and strong, but I

knew I had a weak side. It was an emotional side that was sometimes too sensitive and could become confused. It was that same side that believed in respect, kindness, and love and could no longer handle someone being cruel. I could be very strong and gentle, but if I became confused would Peter be able to handle it? Would he be able to bring me back to the strong and beautiful girl he saw or...? Oh I had a lot of emotion and part of that was stirring and manifesting into feelings for Peter.

"Oh Peter," was all I said and we had the most amazing kiss. A kiss that made me float above the clouds and stand upon silver water. A kiss that made me hear the sound of a waterfall and the wind whistling through... the tea kettle! It was what was whistling and Peter merely turned his attention towards the food. He didn't seem affected by the kiss. He just seemed deep in thought. I wondered what he was feeling as I poured the water for the tea. I preceded back to the sofa where I saw Michael still watching over Amita as she slept.

"Amita is the heart of our Nation. She is our Princess and she is not allowed to die," he said with the most emotion he had expressed thus far. It still was not a lot, but for him, it was.

"Michael," I said softly, "we're going to do everything we can. Peter is bringing healing medicine for her. Soon he will take you to a whole nation of people. They're not your nation, but there are a lot of similarities. From the stories I have heard, I think you'll find that they will know where you came from and how all of you once lived. At one time, there was great respect between your nation and theirs." With a reassuring look I finished, "I am sure there still will be. Amita will get the best of care and I have to believe she will be alright."

Michael nodded and I stood there for a few moments holding my cup of tea. I walked back into the kitchen and gave Peter a kiss on the cheek. We smiled warmly at each other for a moment before Rainbow Dancer and I wandered outside. The sun was beginning to rise and the two of us sat in Peter's garden watching a beautiful blue butterfly.

Odd, for I felt our guests were going to be okay. Michael

183

believed The Empress guided them to us, but I think she was guiding them to the Rofonians and we were merely a vehicle to get them to there. Peter was so good with them and seemed to have so much love and respect. Had I come to this world to find that? Was he the one? Had I just needed to come to another world to find what I had been looking for?

"Rainbow Dancer, do you think I am supposed to stay?"

Placing my head on Rainbow Dancer's, I heard him say, "Connect your heart to your higher self, your guides. They are yours, not mine. I need to be here right now, that's what my guides are telling me. I can not speak for yours."

"There are more like Michael and Amita, aren't there. You were given a howdah that most humans can't see and it wasn't given to you for the sole purpose of protecting me, was it?"

Rainbow Dancer shook his head.

"Everyone is on their own journey and mine just seems to be conflicted right now. There's this strong feeling of anticipation and I can't seem to shake it. If something happens and I have to leave you, thank-you for travelling with me and being such an amazing friend."

"All roads lead us to where we are supposed to be," was all Rainbow Dancer said.

"Yes," I said quietly, "I guess some of us just take longer to get there. Some of us are supposed to travel together for a lifetime, while others connect with us for a short while and are merely there to help us along the way."

Placing my forehead on his, I heard, "If you leave, do not be sad, for in my heart, you will stay. Be like the sun in midday. We will meet again. Our energies are tied with a bond of love."

Nodding my head sadly I sat back and looked around. Who knows, maybe this is just a weird feeling, maybe I will be staying. There are so many here who will always be in my heart. I love this property, the house with all the healing stones, and the beautiful garden. It's so beautiful here, so peaceful. I love all the different flowers and.... two butterflies!!?!!?

The Empress' voice rang through me. *When you see the*

butterflies will you be able to pull the string?' I thought it was because she saw me as a baby and not because I might not be ready to go. My world seemed so far away now and I had become a part of this one. If I stay, I could have a life with Peter, whom I seemed to be falling in love with. He seemed to have so much to give and was so accepting and kind, why now?

What about Princess Amita? If I leave, I'd never know if she lived or died. I wonder who she had to leave behind? She probably loved some of them, but knew she would have to leave them behind if she was going to have any chance of freedom. She had to take that risk. Amita, Michael, and the little one seemed so traumatized and yet they trusted me. Did they still need me? Probably not, they trusted Peter now and soon would be safe with the Rofonians.

Were those butterflies for me? I was trusted and loved here. I would have music, healing crystals, Ooza, Peter, Gorph and all the others, but on the other side I would have to deal with a black and white world. Sadly to say in a way it was like Earth. A place that could take someone like Sam and let him fall so far into a world of cruelty, revenge, and control of others, that he lost himself. Maybe he needed to, so he could appreciate and recognize true goodness when he found it again.

The High Priestess indicated that me being shot was random, *'unforeseen'*, I believe that is the way she described it, but in retrospect it seemed so planned. Sam would not have stayed and been able to go to Respecia if he hadn't shot me. She also said they knew Sam was going to act, but they didn't expect the other gun. Maybe The High Priestess knew that the part of him, who remembered his childhood with Peter, was strong and he was actually done with the cruelty, revenge, and control of others. Maybe the renewal was supposed to happen and the *'unforeseen'* just made it come about sooner than they expected.

It was interesting how Sam arrived at the turning point in his life and then was given a choice. He could have chosen the clones' world, but he didn't. He chose to be in a world of respect. Yes, he chose to leave his world behind.

Chapter 35 - Into the White

Kindosa was going to have her hands full teaching or reteaching those who were already scarred by a black and white world. Ooza would be there helping her along. If anyone understood what it was like to be traumatized by a human world, he did. His scars may be different, but he would understand the emotions. My scars were different, but I understood when the Rofonians thought Ooza was rude. I knew his heart and I knew he wasn't meaning to be cruel.

Ooza and I both have come a long way to get here, although I was no longer worried about him as he was finally where he belonged. I would love to stay and be able to spend time with him. I wonder, do I too, have a choice?

Oh my, I came to this world for a reason, met the birds and was told to find an apple. It was bruised and unripe and I was embarrassed when I realized it was for The Empress. Then I began a new segment of my journey with Rainbow Dancer.

The first thing we did was walk straight into the darkness of Ol' Man Gar Cave where we met Zelka. She was the first one who sought after the unripe apple. Zelka was cunning and I am sure she had her share of trauma. I don't know her story and what made her into who she was. She definitely seemed to be searching for goodness for all the wrong reasons, taking advantage of those who were kind and compassionate.

She played on their kindness to lure them into the darkness of Ol' Man Gar Cave. I thought Rainbow Dancer took me there, but it wasn't him, it was I, because originally I was the one who wanted to go into my darkness to learn. For whatever reason, I thought I would be able to help others from my horrible experiences, but the cave was void of love.

When the realization became so strong that this darkness was going to overtake Rainbow Dancer, I had the strength to ask him to leave. We found out later it was that cave and that darkness which had trapped so many others.

He almost died trying to save me, but the wonderful people of the village put their lives on the line to hide us and nurse Rainbow Dancer back to health. I knew then that I had to leave them behind and they respected my journey, because they knew it was an important one.

Is journeying onward still important? Would I be happy here with Peter and Ooza or would it merely be existing? Or worse, would I end up being injured living in a Black and White City?

Why do I feel so lost at this moment - lost between worlds, between choices, scared of making the wrong one? When I first met Ooza I felt lost and I told him I was a traveller who was a little lost. At that time, Ooza looked around with both his hands and his eyes, then rolling his R's he said, "*You are not lost - you are here.*"

Yes, I am here, sitting staring into the garden and there are only two butterflies. That seemed normal as butterflies are part of life, especially in a garden. Right? It was merely a part of life. Maybe I shouldn't be so worried that I might leaving.

Standing up, sighing at the garden, I walked back inside. The little one was awake, curled up beside her older sister. Amita was sitting, leaning against Michael. A tiny bit of colour was beginning to come back into her face but her eyes still looked somewhat cloudy and grey. Although now, when I truly looked, I could see love and wisdom making its way through her pain and weakness.

"She has a long way to go," Peter said gently. "She could relapse quickly without the correct amount of herbs. The Rofonians will know what to do and be able to give her the right dosage. We need to go as soon as she has finished drinking her tea. It should give her enough strength for the drive. Come on. Let's leave them alone for a few moments."

Peter took my hand, "Come, let's go sit outside."

To the garden? I didn't want to go outside, what if I see more butterflies?

The two of us sat in the garden and Peter asked, "If they are not Rofonians, then who are they? Where do you think they came from?"

My mind travelled back to Scota's history lesson. "Scota told me originally it wasn't just them on this planet. There were three other nations here, but the Rofonians were the only nation who had Fodulzas who understood human language. They also were the only ones who had rounded fingertips so that they could defend themselves against the humans and their guns. After the humans came they searched for the others and only found destruction," I said recapping her story for Peter.

"Did you tell them that?" he asked.

"Michael and Amita? No, it's not my history and I think the humans who did this to them are horrid. I don't want to project my..." I stopped because I couldn't find a word that described the horror that I felt. My palm faced the garden as if I was stopping traffic before I continued. "...my ...lack of forgiveness towards controlling, manipulating, barbaric...humans," I said realizing my teeth were together and only my lips had moved.

I took a breath and finished with, "So, all I told Michael was that the Rofonians will know where they came from and how they once lived. Scota says that hatred only takes you away from love and goodness. She is much wiser than I, and should be the one who tells them."

Peter merely stared at the garden as if he was processing all. I stared at the two butterflies, strangely they seemed to help dissipate the anger that I was feeling towards humans.

Oh no, there aren't just two butterflies anymore, now there are four! That was still within a normal range. Wasn't it? I love butterflies for they are so beautiful and it was hard to believe they came out of the egg without wings.

Some of them began their lives plain or not very pretty. During that stage they would eat and probably be doing their best to survive, hoping they wouldn't be stepped on or eaten. Then they wrapped themselves in a cocoon as if they were purposely shutting out the world to heal from all their trauma. While protecting themselves, they would appear as if they were remaining still, but actually they were working within. Coming back to the world beautiful, with wings and the ability to fly, it's no wonder they symbolized transformation.

Was that why I left yesterday's world? Did I move through the wall so I could close off yesterday's world? Was this new world my cocoon?

Was I like a baby who had flown into its mother's womb or a caterpillar who had spun a cocoon to be protected? Was I here so I could grow and change form? Was I like a butterfly? Was life about all the different stages a person has to go through to be able to fly? But... but I think I have actually found someone whom I believe I could fly with and I think I have found a place where I would be respected.

More and more butterflies came and I yelled, "Why now? I can't leave now!! Peter!!"

Peter jolted from his beautiful moment of watching the butterflies looked rather surprised at my panic.

"The butterflies! They are here!!" was all I said with the realization Peter knew nothing about the butterflies and what they meant.

"Eh, they are beautiful," he said, "they gather here once a year. I'm sorry, I... I... I don't understand your panic."

They came into his yard once a year! Perhaps they were not really meant for me. With a deep breath I began to relax and closed my eyes for a second when I heard the strong parting words of The Empress. *'Remember when you see the butterflies, it is time to untie the string'.*

Taking another deep breath, but this one was different, I rose from my chair and gave Peter a beautiful kiss. The type of kiss that makes time stand still. It was a kiss that reached deep into my soul and told me everything would be all right. The kiss excited me and at the same time, empowered me and gave me the strength to go on.

Tears were streaming down, blurring my vision and I knelt down in front of Rainbow Dancer. "I know you're needed here. I know I have to go on alone."

Rainbow Dancer nodded and I buried my face in his fur.

I turned back towards the butterflies, noticing they were beginning to take flight.

Wiping the tears from my cheeks I looked at Peter, and all I could say was, "It's my journey. I've come this far Peter, and I have a purpose. I don't think... I don't think I should waver from it now."

Reaching into my sleeve I pulled out the little bag The Empress had given me. Holding it in my hand I put my fingers onto the string. Gazing into Peter's eyes, remembering the kiss - it was hard to think of anything else. Was I really doing the right thing? Looking back at the remaining butterflies I remembered my promise to The Empress.

With tears still rolling down my cheeks I said, "Peter, I think I have to go and I have to go now."

I pulled the string and everything went white.

White, white like snow, but it didn't feel cold and it didn't look cold. White, white like a cloud, but it didn't seem fluffy. It was thick, similar to a dense fog, but more compact. It was all around me. Well, I was still standing and that was a good thing. I wasn't sinking and that was another plus.

Hesitantly, my hand left my side and moved through the whiteness. Stretching my arms upward, I moved my right arm slowly in a half circle and did the same with my left; nothing changed. Holding my right arm outward I brought it behind me, twisting my upper body to the right and then to the left. Yes, I could move!

Bending from the waist, I allowed my head to enter into the whiteness trying to see something... anything! There was nothing but white, so I straightened myself up, I arched backwards, gazed as far as I could, and it was the same.

The whiteness appeared to continue on forever. Moving my foot out gingerly, I took a step. I could walk, it was holding my weight, but there was only more whiteness. Had I done the right thing? I had left my Peter, my Ooza, my Rainbow Dancer, I had left them all behind. Was I supposed to?

Rainbow Dancer and Peter had the little girl, Michael and Princess Amita to take to Ooza and the Rofonians. They were on a mission. A mission I felt was going to eventually bring about enrichment, empowerment, and joy. A mission I was no longer a part of and I was going to miss seeing them grow and evolve.

Rainbow Dancer and Peter would probably have to go into a territory with humans who were cruel - humans who whipped people when they wouldn't try to impregnate another. Yes, Peter and Rainbow Dancer would have to, they would just have to find a way to help Amita's people.

Did I have to leave because I was weak? It was hard for me to be around cruel people. I had been there, done that. It was no longer part of what I desired for my life. I knew the damage it could do to a gentle soul. I knew how toxic it was being around humans who manipulated and brainwashed. The ones who disrespected and believed others were there to be used and controlled.

I knew how difficult it was to remain clear, compassionate, and forgiving around those types of people. Also, I knew how difficult it was to remain strong within the power of love and not hate myself for being manipulated or hate them for what they were doing to me or others.

Helping with a land issue and standing at a courthouse was one thing, but standing up against those who thought they could hunt other people with a gun was another. I had already been shot and maybe I was not strong enough to do it again.

Gorph showed me that not all humans on this planet attacked and belittled and that there were many good ones in his black and white world. Humans who believed everyone had the right to their boundaries. If the Rofonians desired to live within a place of goodness then no one had the right to bully their way in with cruelty and manipulation. Thankfully goodness prevailed and it did so because good people came together and said 'no' to cruelty.

Is that why I saw the butterflies? Was I being selfish? Did I not possess enough love to help those people who wanted kindness stand strong and say 'no' to cruelty?

If I had stayed, Peter and I would be instrumental both in helping those like Amita escape and fighting the injustices. The Rofonians would probably send their people down to Peter's golden tent by the ocean. They would be protected by the horthor bushes and their rounded fingers would keep those humans where they belonged. They were very capable of looking after themselves. They had Gorph and James Lawsmon, the lawyer, to help if they needed to fight the injustice in court. It wasn't my world and I would have had to pretend to be someone else.

Peter and I did that on the beach and on the road when the men stopped us - we pretended to be someone else. I did it in the Land of the Shimmering Bridge with the Camflages - not being able to think or feel. To be a spy wasn't my desire, nor to be a saviour. My desire was to be happy, free to be me, and in a safe place where I could heal and be full of love. Then maybe I would be able to be there making the changes that needed to be made.

On second thought, maybe my perspective was what needed to change. Perhaps my purpose had already been served. The Rofonians now had their Fodulza back and they had help with their court case. Now, a precedent had been set – they were not only entitled to their land and their laws, but they are also considered people within the human world. The decision made by that Judge might help stop Amita's people from being kept as slaves. Although I would probably never know, because I pulled the string and I was in the white.

White, why the white? White was supposed to be good. It was supposed to be pure, but why..., but why do I see only nothingness!?

Chapter 36 - My Rock

The Empress wasn't here, nor was Queen Chayzlazamia, nor Raziel. There was no one, nothing, but white! Have I done something wrong? I heard the Empress' voice before I left. Did I really? Did I just think I did? Now, what was I to do? I didn't seem to be in any danger. Was I in a cocoon? Did I need patience now? Did I only need to wait? Sometimes when you don't know what to do, the best thing to do is nothing.

I just want something or someone to hold on to. There was not anything here to do that - not one solid thing. Doing nothing means to stay still and that includes my brain. Please stop.

It never seems to help me when I feel sorry for myself or when I go into a of state worry or fear. Maybe, I should change my perspective. Doing that has worked in the past.

What did I have? I still had my body and it seemed to be functioning and pain-free. I shall be thankful for that. My indigo robe was still indigo. It hadn't turned white so everything wasn't white. My hair wasn't white. I had my mind, which seemed a bit confused at this moment and maybe over-thinking everything, but that didn't mean it was going to stay that way.

Suddenly I felt overwhelmingly tired. Do I lay down? Can I lay down? Maybe I'm already laying down. If I sleep, maybe there would be something in my dreams that would help. It was as if I was being enfolded in angel wings, holding me safe and secure. Nothingness took over my mind and I fell asleep.

It was deep sleep and if there had been a dream, I didn't remember it. I opened my eyes, was I dead?!? Was I blind?!? Right, I was still in the white. The nothingness was still here.

Could I make my arm disappear within this void? No, the white still moved with me. Would I be able to gather it in my hands like snow? No, but it did seem to move between my fingers and it also seemed to move through them.

Deciding to close my eyes, I concentrated on my breath. A thought came into my head. I told it go away and it did for a second, but then it came back. The few seconds of silence gave me something, a second of peace I think, thank-you for that. Thank-you, I said to my thought, you can come back later if you need to, but right now I am concentrating on my breath.

A little more peace became apparent and I wondered if it was because I had more respect for myself. Instead of an angry demand towards unwanted thoughts, I was being polite and gentle to myself. Why did I need to have my eyes closed? I couldn't see anything, maybe it just felt safer, more familiar. Opening them, I stared into the nothingness.

Whenever I felt I had nothing, I knew I had to move. It was movement that created change. Whether the movement was writing rambling thoughts or what I was thankful for (no matter how small it was); or whether it was moving a paintbrush; or going for a walk - it was movement. Since I didn't have anything to write or paint with and no one to talk to, I shall walk.

Well, at least I was moving. I was going forward, at least I thought I was. What was this whiteness? What did it mean? What do I do? Maybe I would eventually be able to walk out of it, but there was only more whiteness everywhere I looked. There had to be something. It all couldn't be nothingness.

Snow was white, sometimes appearing like bits of fluff coming down from the sky. Each snowflake was different. They had their own sacred geometry, all interwoven as if an artist had taken the time to intricately paint picture after picture. Like the Creator wanted to show the world, even though it was cold, there was still beauty.

Yes, it was a choice to see the beauty or look at snow merely as another winter day where everything was just white. It was my choice to see nothing but white emptiness or to look closer, find its beauty, and be thankful it wasn't cold. Actually the temperature here was perfect.

It hasn't been cold here and I haven't seen snow since I moved through the wall of time. It was the cold that made the plants stay deep underground, taking a rest so they could re-grow in the spring. The white snow provided the moisture for the seeds to sprout. This white didn't feel wet nor did it feel dry. I shall be thankful for that.

I need to find a way to get control of this situation. I laughed at the irony as there is nothing here for me to control... except for thoughts. Thank-you thoughts for making me laugh, however could you please be still for a moment so I can study this nothingness. Something had again changed and I became very peaceful.

After some moments of peace, a thought would enter and respectfully I would ask it to leave. The peacefulness felt so beautiful. A thought came and this time I listened because it seemed to come from a different place, it came from a place of peace. The Empress!

She was the one who asked me to pull the string, but *'be present'* was all I heard. There must be something she wanted me to see. Maybe it was about concentrating on what was right in front of me. At this moment I have no other choice except to realize that I was in this white for a reason.

Energy began moving through my body, touching and tingling my muscles, my cells, cleansing my being. It felt healing and beautiful. Slightly raising my indigo robe, I looked at my legs that had been slammed against the rocks by the ocean. The once bruised and gaping wounds were disappearing in front of my eyes!

I had called the white a nothingness. I had doubted instead of feeling thankful and trusting - wow, my apologies to The Empress. Perhaps at this time I should be looking closer and I began staring at this amazing rejuvenating white energy!

Ohh, there were designs within the white! One looked like an ammonite. Another reminded me of the seeds within a sunflower. There was one like a pine cone or was it a pineapple?

It was as if all the designs were following the Fibonacci sequence. Nature most often followed that sequence where each Fibonacci square connected to form an ever spiralling circle. Here the spirals were made of small white fibres. They were barely noticeable, but once discovered, difficult to miss.

These spirals seemed to be going through me - going through my brain, creating a trust and a love that was so profound. I felt innocent and alive! I walked and walked in awe, admiring the innate detail woven within the white.

Gazing up, the designs reminded me of the spirals existing within the galaxies. Oops, I fell! Did I trip? There was nothing here to catch my foot on, how could I have tripped? What could have made me fall? Well, one thing to be thankful for, it didn't hurt. Kneeling, I turned around to examine what I had tripped over, but everything still appeared to be white.

Searching with my hands I felt something! It was about a foot high and about two and half feet wide. It felt like a rock, but it didn't feel that way when I tripped over it. A rock would have been hard and it should have hurt, at least in the reality I came from. Especially because it had been hard enough to send me flying, or should I say falling, to my knees.

How could something be so hard to touch, but soft enough to not hurt? Maybe it had moved, sort of absorbed within the whiteness or maybe the whiteness had cushioned my fall.

Still studying it with my hands, I noticed the white was moving away. It definitely did seem to be a rock. It was grey and on top of it, little pebbles were gathered within a tiny puddle of water. It was as if I was on a beach and the tide had deposited pebbles on top of the larger rocks. Here, there was only one rock to deposit pebbles on, if that was what I was really seeing? I couldn't feel anything else and sadly I couldn't see anything else, not even a beach.

Maybe that was a good thing, as I thought of my freshly healed wounds. Yes, being slammed against rocks I could do without, although a beach would be something normal - something I could relate to. The whiteness did not cling to the rock, nor was it going through it, but I was still enveloped by it. Well, I had wanted something solid to hold on to and now I had my wish. The rock was cool and fairly smooth and at this point, I wasn't ready to leave the one solid thing I had found.

"I think I am going to call you 'my rock'," I said aloud, I felt a need to break the silence. "So I guess I'm going to have to make you my friend."

Sitting beside the rock, I caressed its surface. "Maybe I am talking to you because of loneliness. Loneliness can make a person insane, you know. Although I haven't been alone for that long, but I don't know where I am or what I am doing here. Perhaps this is simply my way of feeling like I have company and why do I have a voice box if I can't use it? I always wondered why singing aloud was accepted, but not talking... oh my, something must be wrong with a person who does such a thing," I said sarcastically. "That's the way it was, where I came from, humans always making strange rules and assumptions. There was so much judgment of others, but I'm not there anymore."

Looking around at the whispering white swirls I paused, "Acceptance, yes, living within truth and innocence, hmmm, odd, I feel rather content and happy." Gently I rested my ear upon the rock and then brought it up suddenly. "What was that? Did I hear something? My rock - was my rock actually talking to me?" Placing my head down once again upon the rock, this time not so self-absorbed, I listened intently.

"I burn and yill, pu me in yeyer," I thought I heard.

"I burn and yill, pu me in yeyer? Is that what you said?" I asked raising my ear from the rock. "You sound quite muffled."

Placing my head back down, this time I heard, "I'm brun and yiyow, pu me in yeyer."

"Is that your name? Are you Brun?"

"No, I'm brunen yiyow."

"Your name is Brunen Yiyow. Oh! I think I might have figured it out, you're not the same rock I've been talking to! You're brown and you're yellow! You're one of the pebbles!"

Peering closely at the pebbles, finally I found a yellow one. Taking the stone into my hand, it reminded me of a three-sided pyramid or a D4 die. Turning it I realized it had two brown sides and two yellow. I held it close to my left ear.

"Ye, pu me in yeyer. Yeyer me beda."

I started to put the stone near my left ear when I heard, "pu me inye wite ear."

"You want to be in my right ear?" I said shaking my head. I studied the stone and it wasn't too small, thus wouldn't go inside my ear canal, but instead it looked about the size of an earpiece. I didn't hear it say anything else so I merely shrugged my shoulders and I placed the brown and yellow stone into my right ear. Surprisingly, it was a comfortable and snug fit, "There. Can you hear me?"

"I can always hear ye, but can ye hear me clearly now?" came this soft but high-pitched voice.

Even though it was in my ear it still sounded quite far away, but I could hear the voice clearly thus answered with a yes.

"Good. Sit down."

"I am sitting down," I replied, feeling a bit confused.

"Are ye sitting on top of the rock?"

"No, should I be?"

"Yes. Temperature changing, the white is clearing away."

"Oh, okay, thank-you," I said, about to sit upon my rock and then I stopped and asked, "I won't be sitting on anyone will I?"

"It's alright, ye won't hurt anyone," it replied sweetly.

So I sat upon my rock. What would happen when the white cleared? Would I end up on a beach? The surface of the rock had a bit of water which could indicate we were in the fog, close to a tidal area. Then again, I could be on the side of a mountain after a rain. Yes, that too could explain the white. Maybe I was engulfed in some sort of cloud.

Although it didn't seem like any cloud I had seen, but that didn't mean it wasn't. Then again, I don't think I had ever taken the time to study the clouds or the fog to see if there were designs embedded within.

"What happens when the white clears away?" I asked.

"Each time is different so I don't know," answered the brown and yellow stone lodged in my ear.

Well that answer only made me more curious.

Chapter 37 - The Tears of Life

The white began to clear below me, although it was still white all around me, but even that seemed to be moving. I was looking downward at what perhaps could be sea level or land that seemed to be in the middle of a rock formation. Maybe I was on the side of a mountain. I couldn't tell.

"There is a large circle with black dots around it," I said, narrating the scene. "The white is clearing some more. Oh, I think the black dots are the tops of people's heads? They're all wearing a kind of... loincloth? Their skin is of a darker nature, well, darker than mine, but you don't know what mine looks like. Anyway, they all have black hair and brown skin. The hair looks long and straight from my view, but I am fairly high up looking down upon them.

They're a little bit off to the side of where we are and they're all standing around a very large disc. Perhaps I should say bowl, for it appears to be indented. It sort of looks like a huge satellite dish that I would see in my yesterday's world, but you don't know what that looks like. I... I hope I'm making sense."

"Ye are. Go on."

"Okay," I said. "There is an area mostly surrounded by rock and that area has the dish that they are standing around and there's a circular opening at the bottom of this dish and it looks as if all the people are staring into it. The area also has a small clearing, and then there seems to be a cave. Maybe it's not a cave. I can't really tell as it could simply be a big indent in the rocks. I wish I could tell you what it was, because now there's fire coming from it. Above the indented area there's a hole where smoke is coming out. It's as if the rocks had formed a chimney."

"Does ye know how many are staring into the circular opening?" the voice asked.

"There were, I think... eleven or twelve people standing around the dish, but they aren't anymore, because they are now moving and going towards the cave. Am I still doing okay?"

"Yes, I see it like a picture. Ye doing good. Keep going."

"They are dancing now, or doing some sort of movement, I think it's a dance. Oh, they appear to be human, I guess that's a good description if you know what a human looks like. Anyway, some of them are male and some are female. I even think some of them might be children. Two of them seem to be stoking the fire, but I can't really tell, at least not from this position.

Now they are all running back and forming a semi circle. They are closer to the dish and quite a distance away from the fiery area. They're holding hands and their mouths seem to be moving. They could be chanting or singing," I said with a sigh, "I can't tell, but their arms are stretching high into the sky."

Sitting watching, I wondered what to say next as I was not completely sure of what I was seeing. Was there some sort of a ritual happening in front of me or was I merely an invisible observer looking into another dimension? Suddenly there was an explosion. Jolting back I think I might have let out some sort of sound. The explosion must have been loud for I was quite far away from where the cave was located.

"Is everything okay?" came the voice in my ear.

"The fire exploded much like fireworks, it was different though...," I sighed before continuing, "I will try to explain it. Colours came shooting out in all directions, but it didn't last very long and when it was over everyone bowed to it. Now they're down on their hands and knees looking back and forth. I don't know what they're doing."

"Looking and listening," came the little voice in my ear.

"They are placing their heads to the ground, oh now they're leaning back, and standing once again. It was kind of cool watching them, for they were all synchronized as they curled their feet back under themselves and then stood. It looks as if they came back to their same place in the circle. They're holding hands and taking a step forward. Again they're down on their hands and knees and placing their heads to the ground. Do you think they're still looking and listening?"

"Probably."

"One person stood up and cupped his hands. Now they're all standing up,"

"Good, they think they found one."

"Found one? Found what?" I questioned.

"No worries, I tell ye later. What else is happening?"

"A person just walked up and put his ear to the other person's cupped hands. Now he's dancing. They're all dancing! They're all dancing around that person. One of them just left the dance and came back carrying a bowl. The man with the cupped hands put something in the bowl."

"That's good," was all the brown and yellow stone said.

"The dance just stopped and the bowl was put down on the ground," I narrated.

Suddenly I smiled and gave a silent thank-you. In yesterday's world a member of my family was blind and often my words were that family member's sight. I had always believed I was the one helping her and had never realized she was helping me develop my gift, until now.

On that thought I continued, "Each person in succession has taken a seat on the ground around the bowl forming a circle," I said, being the eyes for the stone in my ear. "Now a woman is going to the middle of the circle where the bowl is. She's sitting down beside the bowl. It looks like she's crying and trying to catch her tears in the bowl. Do you think she's crying? Oh, I guess you can't tell, sorry. I guess it just doesn't make sense to me why she would be crying into a bowl."

"She is crying the tears-of-life," said the little voice.

"What do you mean? Aren't all tears the same? When I cry, am I crying the tears-of-life?" I asked, for I had never heard tears called that before.

"I don't know 'cause there are many different types of tears, although they all fit into two main categories, but I don't know which type ye cry," the voice explained. "One category is called the tears-of-self and the other is called the tears-of-life."

"But I thought crying was the soap of the soul as it cleanses deep inside," I said, feeling a bit defensive over my tears.

"They can be good, but there are the tears-of-woe and those tears can be full of self-pity. Sometimes a person is just very self-absorbed, not seeing the love and not seeing any of the good, only seeing their hurt and thus crying the tears-of-woe. Then there are the tears-of-use, flowing to make someone else feel sorry for them or to manipulate a situation. There are also the tears-of-mire, crying over the same thing over and over again - usually those include blame. Anyway, all of these fit under the category of the tears-of-self."

"So you're not supposed to cry or feel sorry for yourself?"

"There's a difference." The voice seemed a little frustrated like I shouldn't be interrupting.

I reminded myself that when I truly listened I was often given the gift I was supposed to receive. "I'm sorry. I really do want to understand," I said.

"There are the tears-of-growth," the voice said. This time I thought I could hear breathing and I wondered whether the voice was actually coming from the small yellow and brown stone or was it being transmitted from somewhere else. Again I reminded myself to focus and listen to what was being said.

"The tears-of-growth truly release the hurt - they come from the desire to let go of the pain and release the deep hurt held within the core. They hold a desire to move on. There's the tears-of-change, the ones that desire to find another perspective and again, it's forward movement. Then there are the tears-of-love that come from a place of unselfish love for another soul. They all create healing, so therefore, they are the tears-of-life, at least that's how Tuppie looks at it."

"Who's Tuppie?" I asked.

"I'm Tuppie," the voice answered.

"Well Tuppie, now the person who had been crying the tears-of-life, as you call them, has moved and is standing by the blazing fire. She seems to be yelling something," I said, continuing with my narration and then paused so I could listen more closely. "I yenya na, I think that's what she yelled. Now

202

she is sitting down off to the side, cross-legged, and her palms are together against her chest."

Watching quietly I told Tuppie about the two other people who came one at a time, and went to the fire and cried, 'I yenya'. Then they sat down. A third and fourth came together and in unison they sang, 'yen, yen, yen ya, yii, yii, yen ya'. They sat in a line extending outward from the right side of the fire - all cross-legged with their palms together.

The ritual continued with one arriving, singing, sitting and then another, both singing 'I yenya'. Then two more people walked up together and performed the longer version. They sat to the left of the fire. Two more people came. When the last person arrived, she began with the 'I yen ya' and then went into the 'yen, yen, yen....' She could have sung in an opera for every part of her soul was in her voice.

When she ended with the 'yii yii yen' she held each note a little longer with the last held the longest. She raised her arms and brought her hands to her heart for a final 'ya, na'. Her arms fanned out as she ended her debut. Turning, she walked to the end of the shorter line, sat in the cross-legged position, and became still like the rest.

Everything went silent, even my mind quieted. It was the type of silence not even a cricket would dare disturb. Suddenly I jumped, for the fireworks had begun. After the explosions had subsided I seemed to have better vision. It was as if someone had handed me a pair of opera glasses as I watched a woman walk out of the fire.

"There's a woman. She appears to be dressed in blue seaweed. Don't take me wrong, it's displayed elegantly upon her body. She's beautiful, I've no idea if she is young or old as she's the type of woman who displays no age, only beauty. She is greeting the first person and extending her hand slightly above that person's head. The person clasped her hand and then stood. She seems to be doing that for everyone."

I paused and watched for a bit. "Yes, now everyone is standing very still. She is walking over to the bowl and laying down on her side. Her face is away from the bowl and she is arching her back and circling her body around the bowl. Wow, is she flexible! Her head is now touching her feet. The others are moving," I narrated as I watched them quietly proceeding back into a circle. "They now are all sitting with the encircled bowl in the middle. Oh no, she has disappeared! She's no longer there! It's like she has turned into blue smoke!"

I watched the ring of smoke rise into the air. The higher it rose, the more dense it became until it clouded my vision and consumed what had remained white. At least I still had Tuppie, but now I was in the blue! My foot tested the waters, sort of, as it wasn't a liquid, but nor was it a solid. It was blue nonetheless, and again I was unsure whether it would hold my weight.

Blue was the colour of the Earth's sky, but this was darker, a deeper blue - somewhere between cobalt and indigo. Anyways, the Earth's sky wasn't actually blue. It was the colours within the rainbow - that was probably why Earth's children had rainbow chakras. It was the Earth's atmosphere that gave it the blue hue. The blue sky had a continuance of time as it was always in motion, orbiting around the sun.

Blue was also the colour of the ocean. Due to the gravity and the pull of the moon, the ocean was always moving with currents and tides. Movement happens as each new day creates a new time with the ending of yesterday and beginning of today. Now that I understood tears, I guess it would be time that would bring joy and tears-of-life, tears-of-growth and change, tears of saying good-bye or grieving the yesterdays which are no longer.

I was no longer around those who made me feel unlovable because I didn't accept cruelty. I had chosen not to be around it and people might think of me as weak for making that choice, but I knew it came from strength. Had I cried those tears-of-life? Had I created a movement like the blue of a waterfall to bring forth the fresh, clear water from a mountaintop so I could nourish the land below? Was that what the blue was about?

Chapter 38 - Blue Puffs

Were the hard-earned tears of yesterday's waterfall what gave me the determination to stay within my journey? Had I trusted enough and let the tears-of-life work? Had I honoured other people's journeys and let them follow their paths even when I felt they were going in the wrong direction?

Putting my hand up to my ear, I wondered if my new friend had also gone into his own thoughts for he hadn't asked what had happened after the woman disappeared.

Then out of the blue my friend asked, "Are ye blue?"

His question made me smile and after a moment of gazing at myself, I answered, "No, I'm not blue, but everything else is. Blue is an expression that often means sad and I'm not blue in that way either. No, I would say... I'm curious."

My eyes studied the intricate designs, that now had fine blue hairs interwoven within, and moved like smoke curling up from a pipe, displaying images.

"What are ye curious about?"

"I guess I am curious as to why there is blue all around me and also... why I was supposed to see some sort of ritual from another world?" I asked, thinking that maybe it was like the tears-of-life and I was the student of life.

"Who knows, maybe ye were here to narrate for me."

"I don't know. I feel I need to process it."

"Okay, what did ye see?"

"I don't even know where to begin. I guess at the very beginning, that would be a good place, wouldn't it? They were looking into a huge dish. A dish represents nourishment. Maybe they were looking for nourishment."

"But there was a hole in the bottom of the dish."

"Maybe they were sending the nourishment down," I said, trying to look at it from a higher perspective.

"Let's say they were sending nourishment. What else did ye see?"

"There was fire, it was contained, thus providing warmth, light, and energy to the situation. There were twelve participating in the ritual. That must mean something. Where I come from there are twelve months in a year and twelve disciples. There is a twelve tone where twelve notes of an octave are considered equal and an entire musical composition can be made from that. There are twelve signs in the zodiac.

I think of twelve as growth and development. So now we have nourishment going down and twelve people helping with the growth and development. What do you think?"

There was a chuckle from Tuppie. "Sounds interesting, but what matters is not what I think. It's ye's journey. It's about what ye get out of it, but ye have me intrigued, what else?"

"Well, they did some sort of dance."

"Dancing's good, isn't it?"

"Usually, as it's movement and can bring joy to a situation. So does holding hands and singing. They formed a circle and a circle has no beginning and no end so it can represent wholeness. Unless your mind is going around in circles and then it's not good, but they weren't going round and round."

Again there was a chuckle, but he instructed me to continue.

"Then there was the explosion and afterwards they looked, listened, and ended up cherishing something small that came out of it. In the past, when my life seemed to have exploded around me, all I could do was find something good to cherish,no matter how small it seemed. If you look for the good in everything you go through, that is when you will start to see and experience the magic of life," I surmised.

Tuppie chuckled again before he asked, "What did ye see in the blue?"

"I saw intricate designs swirling through the blue, but to tell you the truth I don't remember them because I was trying to figure out what I had just experienced."

"What I am hearing ye say is ye missed it because ye did not stay in the present - in the moment as it was happening."

"Yeah, I guess you're right. My mind often does that, but is it not important to reflect and try to figure things out?" I asked, probably because I wanted to defend myself, but Tuppie let out a weird noise. "Are you okay? Are you crying?"

"Me not sure and now I am wondering if time to reflect was the main reason I am in this form. I think it needs to balance."

"So live in the moment most of the time, but always remember to take time to reflect and learn from what you've gone through. Is that what you're saying?"

"Or ye will be given that time, but maybe not in the form ye want it," he said with a sigh.

"In my yesterday's world there were seven days in the week and there were also stores that sold items for money. At one time the stores were not open on a day called Sunday, so everyone had a day when everything was quiet. People claimed it was for religious reasons, but to me it meant one day out of seven was there to catch up with each other and often it was a time to reflect. It was a time to look at where they had been or where they were headed. Then it changed and everything became very busy, very money oriented, and full of contraptions to entertain the mind."

"Taking those moments for understanding and guidance is important,"Tuppie stated.

"Yes, and so is taking the time to live in the present so you don't miss things when they are happening right in front of you. Speaking of the present, the whole time I've been talking to you I've also been walking. I've been moving; although I'm not sure where I'm going, but I am moving forward," I said with a bit of pride. "I hope I am going somewhere, but nothing's really changed, except my perspective. So I guess that's something."

There was a silence.

"Are you still there?" I asked Tuppie.

"I am," answered a very sad voice.

"How come you sound so sad?"

"Because ye have been walking and now I am probably far away from my home."

"Oh my gosh," I clapped my hand over my mouth, "I never

thought.... I never asked. I took you for granted and I totally disrespected you. Honestly, I didn't mean to take you on my journey, especially without you knowing that I was doing so. We must go back." I stopped in my tracks as I spoke.

"Is everything still blue?"Tuppie asked.

"Yes," I expressed with humiliation.

"So how does ye expect to find ye's way back?"

With one foot planted forward, I twisted my body and looked back. There was no way of telling which way I had come. I sighed as I told Tuppie what was happening and that yes, it would be futile to even try to go back.

"If it's consolation, the blue, which was once swirling with designs, now is sparking. An occasional spark sometimes comes close, but most of them are in the distance. It's as if at the end of a curl or whiff, a blue puff appears, lights up for moment to show off all its glory, and then disappears."

Tuppie gasped and then in a voice that sounded like it was going to cry, said, "I remember seeing those sparking puffs, only I called them sparkling snowflakes."

"Really! Do you know what they mean?"

Sounding almost bitter,Tuppie emphasized the 'ye' and said, "It means ye can fly."

"Fly! Fly? How do you know that?"

"Because I used to be able to fly,"Tuppie told me, sounding rather dejected.

"You used to fly?" I questioned with compassion in my voice. "What happened?"

"I was naive and kind and sent to Earth to help someone. I did an okay job, but I kept finding people I thought I could help. I got too involved and became tangled in other people's webs. The only way I could handle life on Earth was to put a hard shell around myself. Then I found myself alone, crying the tears-of-self. I didn't grow so I remained alone, trapped within my shell, lost and not knowing how to get me back."

"So you were on Earth. That's how come you understood my descriptions so well. By the way, your shell is the most beautiful I have ever seen. It's not just yellow. It has waves of yellowy gold that ripples through brown. You don't seem at all naive to me. You must have cried the tears-of-life 'cause you seem quite wise and you sound like you are very kind. Often it's the kind ones that people hurt."

"It was not anyone's fault. It was me who was at the mercy of their moods, their hopes, their fears, and their insecurities. I had a choice, but I didn't take it until I was too entrenched and then it felt like it was too late,"Tuppie told me.

"But when you're sweet and innocent it's hard not to be at the mercy of another, especially when it concerns matters of the heart. Did your heart become filled with revenge and try to get them back for their cruelty?" I asked.

"No, I didn't become rotten. I don't think I know how to be cruel. I just put a shell around me and wouldn't let anyone in."

"You're letting me in, you seem to be very open and honest."

"I guess I am, but it's easy, because I find you quite sweet."

My head was beginning to feel heavy, but still I managed to say, "Thanks, but you simply needed to find nice people, there are a lot of them on Earth, more than you would expect."

The sparking was still happening and I realized the sparks weren't beside me or behind me. There were only sparks in front of me and everything else was engulfed in the blue haze.

Suddenly my head felt like it filled with air, similar to becoming lightheaded, but different. It kind of felt like the air was ballooning in the crown of my head.

Then it seemed like it was leaving my body and I began to feel like I was moving upwards. My arms, my legs! They felt weightless! Had I become airborne? Was I actually flying!?! The sparkling snowflakes became brighter and brighter as I weaved in and out of them. Trying not to hit them, I flew faster and faster. With my stomach facing the ground I was soaring through the blue.

Chapter 39 - The Golden Ball

"Oh my, I am flying! I can't believe it! I am flying! Wow, what a feeling! What a rush! Oh my, we are out of the blue! The blue has cleared away!" I expressed my delight to Tuppie, for I wanted the experience to be enjoyed by both of us.

"It's fascinating below us. I see blackness and I see lights. There's some sort of path. I am going to swoop lower. Here we go, weeee! This is so much fun! I hope you're having fun too," I exclaimed as I swooped lower, soaring slightly above what looked to be black ice. "The path, it seems to be a river, at least I think it's a river. It's green with streaks of purple sunken between cliffs topped by black ice or shiny smooth black rock, I'm not sure. The riverbanks are bright with orange and yellows. The sky seems dark, but the lights of the bank seem so bright that it doesn't matter."

"Ye remind me of the excitement I used to feel. Thank-ye for being my eyes and helping me experience my life again." The bitterness in Tuppie's voice seemed to have disappeared and his mood seemed to be excited. I think he felt my joy. "What kept me alive for all those years when I sat alone in the darkness was the knowledge that true joy comes from within. There were times when the darkness overtook me, but there were also a lot of times that I would sing, or allow my mind to go to good places, good memories, always believing someday there would be a light at the end of the tunnel."

"As long as you believe, then the light will always be there and you will always find it." I don't know where those words came from, to tell you the truth, it didn't even sound like my voice. "Way up ahead it looks like the river flows around a bend. Should we follow it?"

"What else do ye see?"

"A smooth black rock, ice and then darkness, just darkness."

"Ye are actually asking me whether I think we should follow a path with beautiful colours and bright lights, or go into the darkness?" Within the high-pitched soft voice that seemed far away, I thought for a moment I heard a deep chuckle.

"Well," I squeaked in my defence, "I just wanted you to feel like.... you have a say in, what is now, our journey."

"When it's important ye must always stay on your path and never, ever, let someone lead ye into darkness."

For a second I thought of yesterday's world and how often I had let other people, or other people's circumstances, lead me into their darkness. However, sometimes it was the darkness that helped me see the contrast and ended up giving me more wisdom and appreciation of the light once I found my way back. However, his words were definitely good to live by.

"I wonder what's around the bend? It's coming up so quickly." I tilted my body to the side and followed the river. "The scenery has changed. It looks to be a landscape of soft feathers." I was in awe as I described it to Tuppie.

"It's as if every species of bird that has ever existed has donated feathers. Some of them are swirling up in the air and others are laying upon the ground. The sky's a lavender colour and the clouds are pink, purple, and green. Each one seems to have formed a picture of a person. One is a man with different tones of green and purple hair. His finger pointing upwards."

My eyes followed the pointing cloud and I realized, in the distance there was what looked like two mountains ascending upward to the sky. As I got closer, I told Tuppie they looked like angel wings with a large golden ball levitating above their crests. So I tilted my body upwards as I was going to have to fly very high to get above the ball. The closer I got, the higher I flew, but just when I was almost there, the golden ball grew and encompassed the whole sky.

"Oh my gosh, I am going to hit the golden ball!" I cried out.

Bringing my arms above my head as if I was going to dive into a pool of water, my biceps were hugging my ears protecting Tuppie from the potential impact. Gasping, I squinted my eyes wondering if my fingers were going to break.

The ball was not a solid, nor was it a liquid, nor was it a gas, but there was an impact of some sort. Oh no, it was as if the ball was moving inward! I was pressing into it, but it wasn't breaking! It was moving, swirling, and making a noise. A loud noise sounding like bees. The golden ball was splitting into bee-sized pieces! They were buzzing and circling around me!

The impact should have slowed me down, but instead I was speeding up! I was flying at warp speed! The little golden pieces were circling around me and they too, were moving at warp speed! My skin felt as if it was being ripped off of my body. It was taking every bit of strength to stay in the diving position. The original incentive had been to keep my Tuppie safe, although I was not entirely sure if I would be able to change my position even if I wanted to as my arm would probably be ripped off by the velocity.

Fear rose within me. The golden bees seemed to fuse together and once again I felt like I was pressing the ball inward, unable to puncture through it. Then everything became a blur and I was twirling around like a drill bit spinning at high speed. Did I puncture the ball or did the ball tightened up? I was being catapulted in another direction! When I come out of this... if I come out of this, I hope I will still be flying.

The next thing I knew, I heard a loud booming voice. "Yuz all right, little wee one. Yuz gonna be just fine if yuz stop movin'. Yuz landed in my hair. Yuz a bit tangled. There, I'z just gonna to put yuz on a branch of tree and yaz be just fine."

I was upon a giant's hand, a gentle giant, but a giant nonetheless. Do I let him place me on the branch? No, that might not be good, if he pressed a tad too hard I could be squished. Walking to the edge, I saw a humongous tree with ridged bark, his hand lowered and I began to walk upon a branch.

"Yaz be just fine here," he said.

Unexpectedly, he tilted his hand and I lost my footing.

Slipping down between the ridges of the bark, I yelled, "Tuppie!!!!"

The brown and yellow stone had dislodged itself from my ear and Tuppie fell, tumbling off the branch. I couldn't move!

I couldn't help him! All I could do was lie there watching what appeared to be a very pretty tiger-eye stone tumble like a thrown D4 die. Each side hitting again and again, missing the inner ridges of the gnarly bark, Tuppie tumbled and toppled across the branch, only to fall far below!

Every breath was painful as my arm was twisted underneath me and my leg was caught. I was trapped between ridges that were approximately half my height. I had to find Tuppie. I wanted to cry, but I was determined not to cry the tears-of-self.

Closing my eyes, I imagined every inhale and exhale folding in upon itself. As it did, I imagined I was becoming a bit smaller. Finally, I was able to get my leg loose and shift my position. I was able to move my body! Yes! Now I can move my arm, get a hold of the edge and climb to the top of the ridge.

"Tuppie! Tuppie! Where are you?" I yelled weakly (that was an oxymoron) but I really was doing my best to project my voice. I knew Tuppie wouldn't be able to answer me, at least not loud enough for me to hear. However, if he could hear me, maybe my voice would be somewhat of a comfort.

Oh my, I was pretty sure I had seen him fall, but a lot was happening. What if I hadn't and he had fallen upon the same fate as me and was lodged between ridges of the gnarly bark?

Tilting my head back and forth I scanned every part of the branch, checking each crevice for the brown and yellow stone as I inched myself across, finally making it to the edge. I laid on my stomach and peered down to where I thought Tuppie had rolled.

Large, vibrant green leaves were obscuring my vision and under some of the leaves were big red balls. They looked like apples. Apples!? Where was I? For a moment I stared at the apples and placing my hand upon my forehead, I closed my eyes. When I opened them I thought I saw something yellow and brown upon a leaf that lay on the ground far below.

"Tuppie!"

Oh no, he's gone! No, there he is! I found him again! I

must observe! Take note of the surroundings for I would have to be able to find Tuppie again once I arrived at the bottom of this tree. Oh my, I was high up and flying out of the tree would definitely be more efficient. Then I could set my sights on my destination and free fall into a soft landing beside the leaf.

Closing my eyes I tried to recreate the feeling I had moments before takeoff. Changing my vibrations with happy thoughts would help. Concentrating, I imagined air going to the crown of my head, but it did not feel light and neither did my body. I was probably in too much pain to fly. That was if flying was even an option here, for I seemed to be in another world. That thought brought my vibrations back down and left me with the feeling that flying was impossible.

"Tuppie!" I yelled hoping I could hear something.

I must find out if my little stone was going to be alright. Okay, what could I do? Maybe I could find a branch or a twig that would bend under my weight so I could lower myself down to another branch and eventually reach the bottom.

It was not going to be easy and I was going to have to go out on a limb. That was a cliché, but as corny as it seemed, it helped as it made me smile. A state of mind during a challenge can bring forth success or failure. Success would have to be my only thought and to call upon those who were protecting me, so I could find Tuppie.

Crawling out on a small branch until my weight took it down, I assessed my new situation and looked for another one to inch across. One by one, little by little, I descended. Glancing down to the blood dripping from my hands ripped raw from trying to hang on, I took a breath of courage and finally made it to the bottom branch. Oh no, I was still too far up.

What was I to do? There was no choice, I had to take the fall! Crawling out on a branch, I lowered myself down as far as I could, and let go. My feet hit first, then I landed on my buttocks. The impact caused me to sit for a minute, but I was fine. Now, how was I going to find the leaf that Tuppie had landed on?

Chapter 40 - Finding Tuppie

The wisdom the little stone had given me nourished my soul and had helped me to take flight. I wish I could take flight now as it is easier to see things when you are above them. I should have taken another look when I was on a lower branch.

Now that I was on the ground and not taller than the grass I felt lost in a dense forest even though I was only in an orchard. There were rotten apples, bruised apples, unripe apples and I felt like I was back at the beginning of my journey when I had first found the unripe apple. I was small then too, but not as small as I am now.

Oh my, I shouldn't be thinking about what I should have done or how small I was. I wonder if Tuppie would have called that 'thoughts-of-self', for my thoughts would probably be similar to the tears-of-self he talked about.

All right, time to switch gears and see myself finding him. Okay, what did I see when I was above it all? I must look up and gain that perspective again.

That was where I was sitting in the tree, at least I think that was where I was, when I saw Tuppie sitting on the leaf. He was beside a flat rock that had an apple sitting upon it. The rock was at the end of a tree root and now I remember, the tree had a knothole. Yes, it was similar to my life - if I observe enough, I will find my way.

Was that the tree I was looking at? I think I found it, it looked like the same knothole! Ducking under a small twig, I saw a rock and climbed upon it. Now I needed to find the root, and then the large rock with the apple on top. There it was and there was my wise Tuppie sitting on a leaf! Soon we would be reunited!

With tears of relief forming behind my eyes I was yelling, "Tuppie, you're not alone, I am here and I am coming for you!"

Turning around like a child, I went down the rock backwards and began travelling towards the tree with the knothole.

It was quite a trek, going around apples, under twigs, and climbing rocks, always keeping my destination in focus so I wouldn't get lost along the way. Finally I arrived at the rock, but I couldn't see the apple nor could I see Tuppie.

Studying the rock as it loomed in front of me like a steep smooth sided mountain, I felt overwhelmed. Once again gaining my perspective, I carefully walked in the direction where I thought Tuppie was. I peered on top of a leaf, but Tuppie was not there! Gingerly, I continued as I didn't want to disturb any foliage and chance losing him again. I looked on the top of a different leaf, but he wasn't there either. Glancing back at the rock, I could see the root of the tree and once again reorienting myself, I walked towards the tree, and peeked over at a leaf.

"Tuppie, I found you!!!" I exclaimed as I ventured onto the leaf. "We're in a giant apple orchard, but I don't know why? Oh no, you're cracked!!" I gasped. "What does that mean?" I asked, staring at his broken body. "Are you alive?"

"It eee I gee."

"Hold it, I can't hear you. I don't think I should put you in my ear. I don't want to hurt you so I'm going to lie down and hopefully then I will be able to hear what you're saying."

"I think I am dying," I heard him say. Tears rolled down my cheeks, "I have no chance of coming back. I am going to die in an apple orchard. Was I rotten? Did I give ye a stomachache? I know I put on a hard shell, but was it that hard? Was I so horrible that I'm not even going to come back?"

"No, no, no, no, you were not horrible. You said so many amazing things. I think it was my journey that brought us to an apple orchard, not yours." My voice was quivering. I didn't know what to do. How do I save a cracked talking stone?

"I'm so glad ye's here. I'm not alone. I'm not in darkness anymore. Thank-ye so much for not letting me die alone."

Ohh, ohh, I have to keep it together. His voice sounded so weak and he seemed farther away than when I had first heard him speak. Then suddenly I remembered Tuppie saying that singing kept some of the darkness away.

"Let's sing," I suggested and I thought that I might have heard a very, very faint, '*I yenya na'*, but then there was silence, so weakly I sang, "I yenya, I yenya, 'yen, yen, yen ya, yii, yii, yenya."

Hoping my singing might give him strength to sing too, I listened, but still no voice. I wrapped my fingers around the beautiful brown and yellow stone that I had grown to love so dearly. Hugging Tuppie with my fingers, I could see how beautiful he was as his bands of gold glistened in the sun.

"I yenya, I yenya, yen, yen, yen ya, yii, yii, yen ya," I continued, softly singing with tears rolling down my face. I placed my fingers upon my lips so I could swallow my pain, my guilt, and as the tears pooled into my hand I filled myself with love and began to sing again. Lifting my head I closed my eyes, and with all my soul I held my, "yii yii yen". I held Tuppie close to my heart as I raised one arm for a final, "ya, na," and held that extremely emotional note as long as I possibly could.

My eyes opened. I was not alone! There, curled around me in a back bend, was the lady with the white hair and the blue seaweed dress. Blue energy rose from her skin. It curled around us making a cylinder, or at least that was what it looked like. Gazing to the top I watched as the cylinder filled in.

It was like being inside a tin can, only it wasn't made of tin, it was made of the blue energy. Focusing on Tuppie, I noticed his shell had cracked open exposing a seed. Out of the seed sprouted a green plant. Ever so slowly and ever so gently I placed it upon the ground. Its growing roots began finding their way into the ground. The plant grew and grew.

It was as if I was watching a nature program that was speeding up time. The plant became taller and taller and the stalk grew wider and wider. I had no choice, I had to back away into the blue for its stalk overtook the cylinder. The plant grew into the sides of the cylinder and its leaves disappeared into the blue lid. All I could do was try to peer through the fog and wait. Oh my, Tuppie had grown into a plant, he's going to live again!

It wasn't long before I saw him turning yellow and wilting

like a plant would in the autumn. Tears began rolling down my cheeks again, for I had become hopeful. The seed had taken root. Would it grow again or was this just his way of dying?

Soon the stalk started to peel away and it looked like legs, brown legs. I don't think I would have reached as high as an ankle even if I could see the feet. Then the blue became even thicker. The denser it became, the more difficult it was to see.

Everything was blurred into the colour, swirling around me like a tornado! I was being scooped up in a very large hand. Not quite as large as the one that put me in the tree, but still very large. The fog was twirling away, twisting and turning until there was a huge blue cloud above and I was gazing into big kind eyes belonging to a man with long black hair.

"Tuppie???"

"Thank-ye," he said with a nod and a much deeper voice.

I travelled with a voice of wisdom, locked inside a hard shell that was tiny enough to fit in my ear, and then watched a truly amazing transformation and he was thanking me?!?

"I didn't do anything," I expressed with disbelief.

"Ye saved my life," he said.

"I didn't... I don't know why you're thanking me, I took you on my journey without your permission. I dropped you, let you fall and when you fell, you cracked. That was my fault. Now you aren't you anymore, you are somebody else, and...."

"Hush, it's okay because I do not see it that way. I was the one who put on a hard shell. Ye found me lonely upon a rock. We were listening to each other and I was finding myself while sharing ye's journey. We were both finding understanding. If my shell was not so hard, I could have walked along side of ye. We could have flown together and I could have eased ye's fear. I guess it was all part of the journey that both of us were on. I heard the man say he was putting you on a branch of one of those tall trees, but I don't remember falling."

"You fell out of my ear and tumbled onto the ground."

"Then ye didn't drop me, I fell. Ye found yeself in a tree and I was on the ground. That's why it took awhile before ye could get back to me. I thought I was going to die alone. All I could think about was how much I wanted to live. How much I loved ye and wished ye were with me. Ye never gave up. When ye found me, my hard shell had cracked. How did ye know to cry the tears-of-life and call the Seashamana?"

"I do believe I was crying the tears-of-life, but I didn't call anyone, I just sang the only song I thought you might know."

A deep chuckle came and broke into laughter that was so full of joy it almost knocked me over. The laughing ceased and he became serious and gracious when he told me he was glad I took him on my journey. He was glad because he might be still sitting alone beside a puddle he couldn't even drink from.

"How did you get there, anyhow?" I asked.

"That's a story to be told if we have time. Time is a gift not always given. I was born in this orchard. I am going to be okay. I am back where I belong - I am back to being me. What is important now is... what brought ye to this apple tree?"

"You already know what brought me here," I retorted.

Tuppie looked confused and simply said, "Go on."

With I sigh, I repeated what we both already knew, "I came to this apple tree because we were flying, and then I landed in someone's hair. The person was trying to put us in the tree and you... then you fell out of my ear at the same time I was trying to get a grip. I tried to find you. What more can I tell you?"

A deep chuckle started again and he threw his head back in joyful laughter. I felt kind of rude since I had to cover my ears because his laughter and his voice seemed extremely loud.

"When I found you, you were quite distressed over being in an apple orchard. You thought you were a rotten apple and you were going to die," I replied, not understanding his laughter.

Once again he became serious, nodded, and in a quieter voice said, "Yes, I was."

"Why?"

Softly, which was still loud for my small ears, he said, "A rotten apple doesn't sprout. It has stopped growing. I guess it's compost so it comes back in some form, but it's not the same."

Chapter 41 - The Son of The Tree of Life

"You had already cracked open and you still thought you were going to die."

"I didn't think ye would know to cry the tears-of-life. My ways and my beliefs are so different than ye's. I didn't know ye had such a deep respect for other customs. That ye would listen to someone else's song and sing it back so they could be nourished. I didn't know ye could call the Seashamana so I didn't think I would ever find my roots again."

"Yeah, that's right, you had roots that went into the ground," I said, moving towards the edge of his hands so I could see if they were still there. "And now you have feet, how come? How did you go from roots to feet? - From plant to man?"

Feeling rather confused, I continued to sit upon his cupped hands. It wasn't much different than sitting in an armchair. With my back against his fingers and my arms resting upon his thumbs, I stared into his face and watched him laugh. If I stood I wasn't even as tall as his head and certainly not as round. When he laughed my handy armchair moved up and down.

His white teeth and the whites of his eyes contrasting his darker skin was pleasing to the eye. Normally I find joyfulness quite catching, especially coming from such a kind, pleasant face as Tuppie's, only this time I didn't. Maybe it was because his laughter was so loud, but I did very much want to enjoy him, however it felt dangerous for my eardrums to listen.

Finally I said, "Do you think you could... whisper, because your voice seems so much bigger than me?"

Tuppie looked concerned and then he whispered, "Thank ye for letting me know. Yes, I can whisper to ye. I apologize for laughing at ye's question, but going from plant to man is just who and what I am. It's like I always need to be planted firmly into the ground, before my feet are able to move forward. Don't ye need to do that?"

"Eh, yeah, I guess, but not in the same way. It's more like an energy. If my energy is scattered it usually means that I am too caught up in my thoughts or my emotions, which makes it hard to move forward. If I am grounded and firm about who I am and where I am going then moving forward is easier, but, but... I don't have roots that go into the ground. You sprouted roots and roots can keep you from moving forward too, but yours didn't, you stepped outside of your roots," I said shaking my head and still feeling quite confused over what I had seen.

"There is a time to stay connected to ye's roots and there is also a time to have faith in their nourishment and move forward on your own. It's my time to move forward."

"How do you know when it's your time to move forward?"

"Only ye can answer that."

"Yeah, I guess you're right." Then I tilted my head and looked at him and said, "All this time I thought I had a talking stone in my ear, but I didn't, did I? No, I had a talking seed."

Tuppie smiled. I thought he was going to laugh, but instead he became serious as he said, "I am The-Son-of-The-Tree-of-Life. I should always produce a new seed, but my seed became lost, I had forgotten who I was and what I stood for."

"Wow, no wonder you're so wise. I have never met anyone like you," I said sitting a little taller, "I am honoured. Well Tuppie, Son-of-The-Tree-of-Life tell me, do you remember what you stand for, now that you are no longer a seed?"

Tuppie laughed and then said, "Ya, I better, 'cause I need to get it right. Let's see if I can remember how it goes."

I stand strong
through all the cycles
of change
Rooted
in goodness
nurtured by earth

I reach high
with a profound belief
in miracles
Knowing
when to grow
and when to go within

My core power
gives me inner strength
and trust
I relinquish control
over events
and other trees or beings

I weather
the storms
and rejoice the good days
I know spring
will arrive
only when it's ready

I branch out
with talents
and abilities
I produce
the buds
and manifest the leaves

My leaves
are my beauty
to shine for a season
My work
lies within my roots
finding the nourishment

I keep my core

healthy
and alive
I am grateful
to be a part of
The Tree-of-Life

"That's soo beautiful and so inspiring. I wish I could go back to my beginning to be inspired, but I don't think I'd find too much inspiration. I do think my mother would have liked to have brought her children up in a place of kindness and respect, but instead it seemed full of jealousies, judgment, and manipulation. I guess my roots aren't as profound as yours," I said without self pity, as it was merely the way it was while I was growing up, for my roots definitely lacked in that area.

"Were ye not taught about something more profound than your immediate family or yourself?"

"I guess. Well, I was brought up within the Christian religion, although I think of myself as spiritual not religious."

"Why, what is the difference?" Tuppie whispered.

"I believe spiritual teachings are everywhere. Since I left my world I learned about love from an otter. An otter that gave me so much unconditional love and joy. I learned about healing and love from a village of people and from a magician, or maybe he was more of a mystic or angel? Anyway, he could make cabins appear and disappear. I learned about love through a Shimmering Shamanic who believed her mother conquered her emotions by taming a water dragon."

I looked up to the sky for a moment before I continued, "There are Gods and Goddesses, angels, higher beings - I'm not sure which, but I know that they are all looking out for me. Then there were the Rofonians who taught about forgiveness, healing, and respect. Now you, and you have taught me so much. You see, to me, it doesn't matter where I get the teachings. In my yesterday's world there are many religions with messiahs, gurus, gods, goddesses, and with every one of those religions I hear them talk about love and forgiveness."

I must have looked perplexed when I said my last sentence for Tuppie threw his head back and laughed. This time it was a silent laugh, then he looked at me and asked, "If ye feel that way about religions then why do ye not want to be religious?"

"Because I have found religious people sometimes voice that their way is the only way. Like love is an exclusive club and if you don't believe exactly the way they do, then you're the one who is evil or your eternity will be compromised."

"That doesn't feel like love to me."

"No, it doesn't to me either. I guess that's why I call myself spiritual because I have a bit of a different perspective than most religious people."

Leaning back on his fingers I stared into his eyes, but he didn't say anything so I explained, "Christian religion believes in one God and I innately believed that was love. Then I was told about a sometimes angry, jealous God and that God was male. Those negative emotions and a gender placed upon healing and love, just confused me. Love is everywhere so a God of Love has to be a great spirit energy and an energy that has the power to be whatever gender it needs to be. I just think love is kind and giving and as long as your belief is giving love, hope, or help that... that is what is important and shouldn't be judged by another."

Tuppie just looked confused, "Don't religions have someone to guide them towards love?"

"Well, yes, I think they all do. I know the Islam religion has Mohammad, but I was brought up with the Christian religion and Jesus is its messiah."

"Is Jesus not ye's messiah?"

"Mmm, more like a friend, my mentor, someone to aspire to be like, even though it feels unreachable, still.... to be so wise, so full of love, forgiveness, and healing."

"So this Jesus of ye's, he's alive?"

This time I smiled, "Yes and no. I believe his energy and what he represents is very much alive, but no, he was hung on a cross to die when he was in human form. I remember crying

224

when I was a child, because how could there be a society that does that to someone who is merely teaching about love."

"He had a very large following?" Tuppie said, although I wasn't sure if it was a question or a statement.

"He did, but how did you jump to that conclusion?" I asked.

"At one time it was not uncommon on Earth for the people who wanted manipulation and control to murder someone for having too much influence on the masses."

"The people who followed him just believed in love. So what you are saying is those who wanted control and wanted to manipulate, killed Jesus! He died because of those people's greed and I didn't murder him and the people who believe in his teachings, who they call sinners, didn't do it either."

"Where did that come from? I didn't say ye murdered him." Tuppie moved his head back with a look of shock on his face.

"No, you didn't and I'm sorry, that's my baggage not yours and I shouldn't have projected it on you. It's just that I loved him from the moment I can remember. It was as if I was born knowing him. However, I was told that he died because of my sins. I was a child when they told me that and I felt like I had done something wrong and I was a horrible person."

I wondered whether the look I gave Tuppie, was that of a plea; a plea for him to help me let go of that guilt.

"Guilt is one of the most common forms of manipulation..." was all he said.

"Yes it is," I said quickly, not knowing if that was all he was going to say, "and he didn't believe in that, in fact he is reported to have said as he was dying, 'forgive them for they know not what they do'. People go to church for faith, hope and community so why don't they just say Jesus died at the hands of people who wanted greed, control and manipulation and it is up to us to keep his love alive. Why can't they just say we are good, kind, and loving people and let's bathe in the strength of that love, so we can pass it on."

"Ye is right, but perhaps the priests and other leaders, who lived in his time didn't know how to run a country without that control, so forgive them for they did not know. If ye is the one who is guilty of misunderstanding and ye's intent is not coming forth with ye's words, ye accepts it, takes responsibility for it and then ye is working within the-tears-of-life and ye learns anew," Tuppie said before he asked, "If he was so amazing why do ye concentrate on his death?"

Thoughts of teaching and misunderstanding swirled about, but Tuppie merely sat there patiently until my processing mind found its way back to his question. "You're right, his life was amazing, and that's why I call him my mentor," I said with a new found smile, "I guess I think of him as a wise, experienced friend who vibrated at a different level. He lived within a realm of love and believed that the love energy that is everywhere could heal all and do anything and everything. What he did in his life seemed to prove that. However, rarely in the religious sector does the focus seem to be on learning how to get their vibrations to that healing level. I just think that really should be the goal."

"Yes," Tuppie answered, "Ye's vibrations changed when we flew. Did ye's Jesus fly?"

This time it was me who laughed as I said, "He probably could've, but I don't think the people of that time were ready for that and he grew up in a completely different time than what I did. Truthfully I think many people in my yesterday's world would think I was insane if I told them that I had flown." I paused, thinking he probably did know how to fly.

"Not only was it a different time, but his life on Earth took place geographically in a completely different region than where I came from. All the people have to go by is a section in the book written about him and it was translated from another language," I said.

"The meanings of words change with each generation and hopefully each generation is growing and changing. If the words were translated from another language years ago, maybe what was written about him was saying that he died because of those people's sins, it's not much of a difference," said Tuppie.

I smiled, "Yes, one word in a sentence can change the meaning. You know another thing that I have often heard people say is that he said, 'I am the way and the life, and the only way is through me,' but that doesn't seem right either for he had confidence in who he was and what he believed in, but he did not have an ego."

"No, it does make sense. Ye said he was all about love, right?"

"Yes he lived and breathed it."

"He was love. Love is the way and the life, and the only way is through love," Tuppie reiterated. The-Son-of-The-Tree-of-Life was quiet for a moment before he said, "If ye take his *'I'* and change it to *'love'* then ye will understand his journey. According to the trees he vibrated to a love energy and he and his friends walked alone, connected to love's higher vibration, spreading that word, but not connected to any organization."

"So he wasn't about organized religion and it isn't about that, it's just about love." I looked deeply into Tuppie's eye's before I finished with, "Yeah, because he said the secret to the kingdom is within. To me that means looking within and finding my own way towards a love that can bring about healing and miracles. It's so hard sometimes though, to stay in that state of love and not get dragged down by others, but Tuppie, thankyou," I said. "Thank-you for letting me express how I feel without judging me for my opinion."

Tuppie nodded, "When ye interconnects with others, ye shares, ye points them in the direction of higher vibration love, because that is part of ye. Don't let others drag ye into their journey, ye needs to think about ye's. It's up to them to think about theirs. But if ye has made a detour, remember as long as ye is always trying to turn things around and transform them into something good, then ye follows the good, thus ye will always be looked after and that's all that matters."

Chapter 42 - Singing Leaves

Tiredness was setting in. I think the last time I slept I was in the white and I really didn't remember the last time I ate.

"Our journeys were interconnected, weren't they?" I asked Tuppie, but I didn't wait for an answer. "We were looked after when we came out of the blue. We flew and we arrived where we were supposed to... didn't we? If I am going to fly again I think I need to work on my landing skills," I said with a yawn as I curled up on one of Tuppie's thumbs and closed my eyes.

Suddenly a breeze came forth and whispered across my face. I don't know if my eyes were actually open when I saw several of the leaves on the trees opened their eyes. All I remember was thinking that I didn't know they had eyes. Little mouths appeared, and they seemed to dance and sing.

You are the rainbow
of your life
The prism of time
Fly into the night

"What was that?" I asked Tuppie, at least I think I did.

Tuppie threw his head back and laughed, "Oh, ye heard them. Welcome to my world. It is the leaves that grow and bring me wisdom. Hearing them is music to my ears. It has been a long time."

Was I dreaming a dream within a dream? I looked at Tuppie and he had lowered his chin to his chest and was looking at me out of the top of his eyes.

The breeze blew and whispered across my face again and the leaves sang,

Come alive
Be peaceful yet
full of life
You know what is right

"I only wish I knew what was right. I do try, I really do," I said in a very sleepy voice and I was sure I heard him laugh and the leaves singing:

You are the joy
bring it to life
The colours of the time
Will rise into the new
The colours of the time
Will rise into the new

Tuppie laughed again, but this time I was pretty sure I was asleep for there was a black bird with an iridescent blue head and blue wings approaching and squawking at the same time.

Then I realized his squawking wasn't really squawking, it had a beat and the sound was very beautiful, somewhere between a harmonica and a saxophone.

The next thing I knew there were little animals with colourful tails, faeries, and more birds with iridescent blue heads. The animals were making sounds like instruments and the birds were flying in the air with their squawking sounding like horns. The faeries and leaves were singing with voices that stirred emotions deep inside. It was as if they were singing to all my trauma, all my pain, as well as all the joy and miracles in my life.

A soft rain began to fall, however the sun was still shining brightly, reflecting a sparkle on each drop as a rainbow arched its glory in the sky.

You are the music
of your life
The song of your time
Be like the sun
on the morning dew

You are the flower
with a seed to nurture
Watch the strength
of your colours
bloom as they grow

You are the sparkle
The smile of your dream
The truth of the myth
The action of the mime

You are the indigo
The rainbow of your life
The sign of the prism arch
The way of the climb

Then everything disappeared except for one bird and it gave a squawking sound very much like a horn out of tune and I think, maybe, at that moment I opened my eyes, if they weren't already open.

The bird stopped squawking and it also stopped flying. It fell to the ground as if it had been shot with a bullet!!!

"Who are ye?" Tuppie eyes changed and I could no longer see his love. He seemed to be looking at me and through me at the same time when he said, not in an angry tone but instead more with concern and then his voice seemed to change. It still wasn't angry, but his tone was different. "That isn't allowed in this world and that is what ye does. Ye have to go back to your world now. Ye can't stay here. Go! Now!"

Oh my, this couldn't be happening. My mouth remained opened for a moment and then I said calmly and curtly, "Put me down. Please. Now."

His expression didn't change when he lowered his hand with me still on it and without looking at me said, "The portal between those two trees is open. Ye run now and ye will run right through it and it will take ye back where ye came from."

I looked over past the bird laying upon the grass and I could see the hazy energy coming from the portal. Apparently it was going to take me back to where I came from. Looking back at my giant Tuppie, who I loved so dearly, whom I had flown with and now had implied I was evil and had done something horrible to this bird. This was not the way I wanted to leave. This was not the way I wanted to go back to Earth. I blinked my tears away, swallowed and looked at the bird on the ground. The innocent bird that had fallen out of the sky. It seemed so... still.

I looked at the portal, climbed off his hand and began to run. I ran as fast as I could. It really wasn't that far, however, I was a little person and the blades of grass were similar in height.

The judgment, the betrayal, the feeling that I was unworthy, the abandonment, and all those emotions that were so strong in yesterday's world were in the forefront, beginning to bubble like a volcano about to erupt. My emotions were an obstacle course in my mind and so were the rocks and apples that stood between me and my destination. It took awhile, but slowly I made my way towards the portal.

"Ouch," I said as I fell with my hands stopping my face from hitting the ground.

Looking back at the tree root I had tripped over I heard him say, "It's going. It's going to close."

"Something good has to come out of this," I mumbled. Straightening my arms I put my hands strong into the ground. "Yes, something amazing is going to come out of this experience. It just has too." Still mumbling, I pushed myself up, "I have to keep going."

The bird was simply lying there looking much bigger than I was and I couldn't look at it as just an obstacle in my way. Had I done something while I was sleeping? I couldn't have, could I? Why does Tuppie, who seems so wise and so knowledgeable, think I harmed it?

Looking at the portal, back at Tuppie who I thought I could trust, I looked back at the bird and one of my conversations with Raziel popped into my mind. Yes, I need to uphold my own individuality, follow my instincts, and be true to myself. Suddenly love filled my being and I looked at my hands and I could see an energy coming off them.

Kneeling beside the majestic large bird I put one hand gently on its neck and stretched so the other would be close to it's heart. I was hoping I would feel a pulse or see its chest move up and down, but there was nothing. Focus on the bird with the intent to heal, I thought as my mind went in a trance.

I had no idea how long I stayed within this state of love, but after awhile I felt a bit of of beat. Stay with it, focus, keep your trance and trust. Aaah! The bird opened its eyes and moved its head and with a sigh, I smiled.

Gently I whispered, "It's okay, it's all going to be okay."

The bird didn't close its eyes and it lay very still for a moment before it began to move. It was humongous compared to me and when it moved, I moved. Its feathers fluttered and I had no choice but to back up. Standing, it looked at me and opened its beak, "squawa-wak" and then once again it was playing music.

Looking up I saw that the portal had disappeared into the trees. I must have gone into quite the trance, because I hadn't noticed Tuppie walk towards me, nor did I notice him sit down beside me.

"Whoa, wow that was amazing," I said standing up while staring at my hands in disbelief.

Whispering he said, "Ye's vibrations are up and ye is like ye's Jesus, ye have healing hands."

"Maybe, when I remember to be full of love, but Jesus is in a league all of his own," I said softly, still in a state of awe.

Then the bird flew away and the downdraft of it wings caused me to land on my buttocks.

"It looks like the little squawker's going to be okay," Tuppie said, putting his hand down for me to walk upon. Still in shock I walked up his fingers to his palm.

There was silence for a moment before The-Son-of-The-

Tree-of-Life whispered, "Ye is The-Daughter-of-Love."

When Queen Chayzlazamia called me Thee Trusted One, I didn't believe her, however I do remember how much those words empowered me. They encouraged me to be that trustworthy person she believed I was.

I studied his eyes for a long time, maybe because I was still in shock over all that had happened. Maybe, I was simply in a state of disbelief, or perhaps I stared because I needed to see his kindness and his friendship, I wasn't sure. All I knew was that there was confusion and betrayal circling around in my head. I wasn't ready to let empowering words instantly take those feelings away.

So I simply sat there studying his eyes while in my head I recapped everything I knew... from the bird abruptly falling out of the sky to all the confusing emotions that were going through my head as I ran.

Getting to the part where I felt my emotions were bubbling like a volcano, I spewed, "The-Daughter-of-Love!?! How can you call me that after what you thought I did to that beautiful bird? You thought I made it drop out of the sky! How can you tell me that I'm The-Daughter-of-Love after you ordered me to go back to where I had come from? You looked at me like you didn't even know me and felt I shouldn't have been here at all? You said that I had to go back. Now...," Tears welled in my eyes as I looked into his. "I don't understand."

Tuppie became more serious than I had ever seen him since he had taken his human like form and in a very gentle tone he said, "Those words were not for ye and it never dawned on me that ye would take them as yours. Those words were for the ugly energy that had come through the portal. Didn't ye see it too? I was sending it back and back it went. Ye are The-Daughter-of-Love and ye did not hurt that little squawker, ye saved it. What came through the portal hurt the bird."

He looked deep into my eyes before he continued, "What ye did for the bird is even more amazing than before. Don't ye see what ye did, ye were really hurt, but didn't turn ye anger back at me, nor did ye go through the portal. No, ye didn't do that, instead ye transformed that energy. Ye have lots of love in ye and ye let love flow through ye. Ye turned ye's cheek and went towards what was good and that is what ye is supposed to do. As ye were putting that love back in the bird I watched that ugly energy go back through the portal and the portal closed. Are ye okay, now?"

All of a sudden I felt forgiveness, forgiveness for him as well as forgiveness for me. I could feel my back straighten and I felt beautiful and strong.

"The squawker was doing it's best to bring ye vibrations to keep ye in a place of love. What came out of the portal was searching for an unripe apple, but was throwing it's ugliness at ye. Then it changed it's direction and caught the poor bird off guard."

My eyes widened as I said, "So the faeries, the birds, the leaves, and all the others were there doing their best to keep my vibrations full of love so I wouldn't be affected by the ugliness. Wow." Holding my heart I continued, "I've learned so much on my journey, but I don't understand the unripe apple."

"What does ye not understand about it?" Tuppie asked.

"Well, soon after I came to this world, I was instructed to find an apple. I don't understand much about apples, but I'm glad I didn't bring a rotten one, because it ended up being a gift for The Empress. However, it was a bit unripe and it was bruised," I said with shame. "This isn't the first time that someone or something was trying to get the unripe apple. I don't understand why it's so sought after and I'm totally confused by the importance of it. Did they want my apple because they want to turn it to rot. Are they succeeding?"

Tuppie once again threw his head back in an almost silent laughter. "So ye were my assignment? I couldn't find ye and I felt like I had failed. I guess ye had to find me. Hmmm, everything's happened the way it was supposed to happen, hmmm. Apples, it's all about the apples."

"Why do you think it is all about the apples," I asked.

"Don't eat rotten apples. Some unripe ones can be very bitter and upset your stomach. Those that are not truly ripe can have some bitterness, but also can have a lot of nourishment. Look at the wor...,"

Tuppie didn't finish, instead he turned his head and didn't look back at me. He looked rather sad and concerned. It was as if someone was telling him very sad news.

No one was there, at least not when I turned my head, but something had changed. The blue had descended from the cloud above.

Large, giant stairs formed out of the blue, inviting us to walk up. Tuppie would have to carry me or I would have to fly, for the risers of the stairs were made for someone his size. To my surprise, Tuppie placed me on the ground.

"I have to leave ye. I am so, so, sorry." He looked as if he was about to cry. "I am so sorry, I am so very sorry, but ye are The-Daughter-of-Love and ye are protected, remember that."

Wow, Daughter-of-Love! My back straightened once again and I felt taller; I think it was because I liked that thought, but to be loving enough to deserve that title. However, if I was The-Daughter-of-Love then I have many, many brothers and sisters, and I was not the youngest, nor was I the oldest. I had better get it right this time and always be thankful, because like Tuppie, I now had strong roots to be proud of and I had a lot to live up to.

"What do you mean you have to leave me and what do you mean its all about the wor...?" I asked.

Tuppie didn't answer me, instead he turned and began to walk up the stairs. The blue stairs began to fade, not unlike a cloud dissipating within the sky. Tuppie also began to fade and then he was gone.

Chapter 43 - It's Apple Applicable

Was Tuppie going to say work? Was I supposed to go back to Earth and pick apples for a living or was I supposed to look at the work apples were doing? I mean, they do nourish the body and house new seeds to grow anew. Ohhh.

I remembered being with Raziel and wondering if I was dead. The only thing I found out for sure was, I was alive in this world, but did that mean I was dead on the Earthly plane? Was I going to come back as an apple tree? Maybe I was supposed to work at finding my roots. Is that what he meant?

Tuppie was a tree in human form, a tree with roots, who had learned how to fly. Was that what I needed to know? If I became an apple tree and I worked hard enough on myself, someday, I too, would be able to fly again.

It was hard to believe Tuppie and I were flying only a short time ago. When we were soaring I felt above it all. I enjoyed having him as my companion and now.... all I could see was a giant apple orchard and I felt very alone and very small.

Tuppie must have felt very alone sitting on a rock all by himself. There were no trees and leaves there. He must have felt alone and small too. Even within the hardness of his shell, he was beautiful and interesting. When his hardness was taken away he also became joyful - cryptic, but joyful.

He did look sad when he had to leave. Maybe he didn't understand why either. I was usually the one who had to leave, maybe I should have more compassion for those I have left. What was I to do now that he's gone? I don't understand why I'm all alone again. I miss him, I miss Ooza, and I miss my Rainbow Dancer.

My mind wandered back to Zelka and Ol' Man Gar Cave when I was hidden in the howdah. Zelka seemed so nice until Rainbow Dancer wanted to leave. She told him he had the unripe apple and pleaded with him to stay. When he wouldn't, she demanded that he did and stomped her foot causing parts of the cave to collapse and we barely got out alive.

Why would Zelka care about an apple and what did that have to do about work? Zelka didn't even know I was there and I hadn't told anyone about my apple so how did she know about it? Perhaps the ugly energy that came through the portal was in the cave and wanted me not to trust the Empress to look after my apple and therefore worry. Worrying is fear and fear attracts fear. Maybe 'worry' was what Tuppie was going to say.

The Camflages wanted the unripe apple. Perhaps they thought, if they killed the seeds of my apple, (not knowing I had already given it to The Empress) I too would rot away before I was able to help save Queen Chayzlazamia's Queendom. That would have had gravely effected her world. Was 'world' more apple applicable?

The Camflages got inside people's head, twisted people's words, and played on their insecurities causing them to change their vibration. Maybe it was all about the words.

Studying a leaf I thought about the singing leaves and how they were singing empowering words. Maybe those words weren't just about raising my vibrations in the moment, but also about how kind words can help keep them raised.

Oh my, my body hurts, my head hurts; I must still be feeling the after effects of my earlier crash landing. How do I keep my vibrations raised when I feel like this? Leaning my tired body against some roots I began humming and breathing into the pain. Once again, I was thankful for the teachings from my yesterday's world, for it was practising yoga that taught me how effective it was to breath into my pain.

It was yoga and reiki that taught me how to let go of my thoughts. I was supposed to be disciplined in it at all times, well I obviously wasn't there yet. However, some of those moments where I have found it, have been very important.

Breathing deep, I thought about what Raziel would say, yes, I'm exactly where I'm supposed to be and I am the size I need to be. From here on in I will work at letting go of my worry and at listening to more empowering words.

Chapter 44 - Crystal Wrappings

Was it letting go of my thoughts what allowed me to fly? I know when I was paying attention to the sparkles, I was aware and in 'the now', when it happened.

What an amazing journey! I had flown, watched a miraculous healing and a miraculous birth happen right here in front of my eyes. I met The-Son-of-The-Tree-of-Life and that was a true honour, but now what? Perhaps if I could figure a way that I could have roots and fly at the same time, maybe I could create a cabin if I needed one! Perhaps create food, like Raziel did before I went to the Land of the Shimmering Bridge. Was that magic or was it a miracle?

When Jesus created food it was deemed a miracle, however Raziel was not Jesus. Jesus fed the masses and Raziel only fed himself and me. Still, there is no doubt in my mind miracles exist in all different shapes and sizes. Maybe Tuppie was right, it's simply about love. Was that what had led me here? Was love the reason for my journey?

As soon as I entered this world I had nothing else to rely on but my instincts and my desire to find goodness, and really, that's all I have right now. What helped me to move forward was knowing I was protected. Am I still protected now that I have pulled the string?

A breeze began to blow. This time I actually stopped thinking and listened. I could hear the rustling leaves. That sound I had heard many times before, but now I knew they could sing. Would I still be able to hear them without Tuppie? I thought that about the cabin, I was able to shut it down without Raziel, but to create it? Well, I wasn't there yet. It does not mean I never will be, it just means I am not there yet. Oh, there I go again, getting in the way, my brain needs to get out of the way. Maybe my encounter with the Camflages was for a reason. Think nothing, nothing, nothing. Was that music that I hear among the rustling of leaves? I became very still.

It's only a cycle
It's only a cycle my friend
That's why you feel so alone
but you're not
You're not alone
Stay rooted in goodness
If rooted in goodness
my friend
then you are never alone
You're never alone
So stand tall
Stand tall
Let the cycle of change
shift with the winds
blow with time
move with your world
as it shifts into
your time

Listen, listen, listen
Listen, listen to the whispering
wind

Sweep far into your new life
For your dreams are yours to hold
The turquoise blue brought
you insight
your guide is here I'm told
A million songs sing far into the night
Listen, Listen to the whispering wind

Shifts into my time?!? What does that mean? How does the
world shift into my time? I don't know how to make it shift.

The turquoise was bringing me insight? Turquoise was all I
could see after I was shot. Was that where I would find my

guide or was my guidance within that colour?

Tuppie had said he reaches high with a profound belief in miracles and knows when to grow and when to go within. Wouldn't that be nice. If I could attain that at all times then I would be able to create food and be able to fly. Wait! I did! I did that! Yes, I did, until my mind allowed fear to enter into it's realm. At least that was what I had thought, but was it really my fault I stopped flying or was it simply part of the miracle?

A miracle that made Tuppie a man and I guess, even though I don't know why I am alone, sitting in an apple orchard, I have to trust that its all part of my miraculous journey.

Maybe I was being left alone to process all the wisdom I have attained or perhaps realize that I have some within. My back straightened, I thought about Tuppie saying I was the Daughter-of-Love, I smiled and felt the kundalini energy run up and down my spine. Yes, that inner strength of love.

Tuppie also said that he relinquished control over events and other trees and beings. Looking around, I smiled, my arm went up in the air and I said aloud, "Yes, I relinquish all control over every single one of you apples."

My smile waned as I thought about how he controlled the ugliness that came through the portal, but did he? He didn't try to change it or manipulate it, he merely sent it away because that energy wasn't within the realm of love and thus it was harmful to himself and others.

Tuppie said he weathered the storms and rejoiced in the good days. Trees either went within and strengthened their core or they budded and bloomed, rejoicing in the sun and warmth of the spring. Trees knew when to grow and when to go within and humans think they're the smart ones. Was this the cycle that I needed to 'let shift with the winds'? A cycle where I needed to stand tall, go within and strengthen my core. If that was right, then I must trust that 'spring will arrive only when it's ready'.

Earlier, Tuppie had said, 'My work lies within my roots finding the nourishment', but how do you find that nourishment?

Oh my, there was so much to learn and process from his world.

I have looked at the roots of my existence and was doing my best to break those unhealthy patterns rooted within me. I have tried to get nourishment from them and not let them pull me backwards, but it hasn't been an easy feat.

Staring at the sky, a small wisp of blue floated by and I heard a voice say, "Daughter-of-Love where are your roots?"

Daughter... of... Love, I repeated slowly. Yes, *'stay rooted in goodness'*. If my roots are within the energy of love, then I shall find the nourishment that I need. That nourishment would keep *'my core healthy and alive'*. I thought about the core of the tree and I began to focus on mine.

Standing, trying to imagine I was a tree with roots in the ground, I looked up and saw the most beautiful tree. It's branches went up and then meandered towards the ground. The leaves were plentiful, seeming more like a very large bush than a tree. I wondered, was it that tree's leaves who had been singing to me? Smiling, I made my way towards it, went under it's meandering branches and touched it's huge trunk.

Suddenly, I was being surrounded by a hard translucent shell! Was I turning into a seed? The shell didn't stop. It reached down into the ground like the roots of the tree. It grew around the huge tree and was reaching way up with me inside! It went high in the sky until I could no longer see the top.

What made this happen? Was the translucent shell there to remind me of the crystals when I was with Peter and we had gone to the tiered sparkling oceans? At that time I was at peace, it was similar to a meditation, but more than that. Oh my, that's what I need. I need to be still... at peace. Easier said than done. Focus... focus... focus on my core.

Doing my best to remain still and peaceful, I felt something moving within my body! A blackish colour was rising up, up, up through the point of the crystal wand! I began to feel a light coming up from the ground and going through me. Was this what Tuppie meant by the roots finding the nourishment?

Watching, I could see that the blackness was rising and a

beautiful yellow light was coming from above. I didn't want to taint or darken the light with my pain. It wouldn't stay dark, the light would change it, right? It would, wouldn't it? That was my fear talking and maybe it wasn't my pain that was connecting with the light. I didn't feel any pain, nor did I have any flashbacks so maybe it was just an unknown energy. In the dreamworld black often represents that, so, let go of all the fear and instead be thankful for the pureness of the Love energy.

My attention was redirected, as a pointed crystal wand appeared, adjacent to the one that the tree and I were inside of, rooting itself into the ground. When I looked back up to the darkness leaving my body, I saw that it hadn't dissipated within the light, instead it had formed a string of beads.

The beads were alternating, one dark and the other gold. It turned and went into the another pointed crystal wand rooted into the ground. I watched, thinking I shouldn't try to figure it out, instead I should trust and the darkness kept beading with the light, descending far into the earth below.

Oh my, what was happening to my spine? No, it wasn't my spine that was moving. The tree I was leaning upon was moving! Standing within my crystal, I was able to get enough space between the moving tree and myself.

The trunk grew from it's base, taking its massive amount of leaves and branches with it. It grew within the crystal casing, higher than trees were supposed to grow - at least any tree I had ever known. No more branches or leaves grew as it only had the ones it had originally started with. With the leaves and branches at the top, it grew until it reached the clouds. Oh my, now another crystal was growing around me, it seemed to be protecting me from the expanding tree.

Abruptly, the crystal around the tree exploded and the top foliage of the tree broke! It was a clean cut and completely split from the tree. Why did that happen? Emotions were flooding through me. Wasn't the tree supposed to get more leaves so it could manifest its talents and abilities? Perhaps it had completed its manifestation.

Sharp debris fell and thankfully I was protected. The crystal I was inside of was morphing and becoming more oval shaped. Oh my, oh my I was moving! It was as if I was within a glass elevator and I rose through the branches high into the sky. As I moved, the inside of the tree began to bubble over with little tiny golden pieces. Much like when I hit the golden ball.

Time was not there to stare upon this magical moment, for I was falling! Thankfully, I was inside the oval crystal elevator, but I was falling too fast for my comfort! All I could see below me were reflected prisms and the next thing I knew, I was standing upon the ground between two pieces of rock.

There were indents where I must have been housed and the rock was actually a geode, looking as though the two sides should be joined. It swirled like an embryo within a sea of small sparkling diamonds and there I stood looking into the translucent geode and then looking to the base of this huge magnificent tree that reached up into the heavens.

Thank-you for my life! Thank-you for the gift! Thank-you for showing me that my life and the worlds that I have wandered through were created within eternal mystery.

Exhausted, with my hand on my heart, I walked through the orchard, pulled the sword from my sleeve and cut into a ripe part of an apple. Clear clean energy nourished my body with each bite.

After I ate, I still didn't knowing which way to go, so I sat down between an apple and a root that extended from the tree with the meandering branches. I hope I find some sort of understanding, so when I leave this place, I can take the wisdom with me. That was if I ever leave this place. For all I knew I was back on Earth and just really little.

Ooza was a little person when he lived on Earth, but I was even smaller than him. His life was very hard there, but he was a strong soul. His journey gave him skills and compassion, which will help those who will be arriving via the beach and the cave. He has probably already met Princess Amita. I hope she is alive and the horthor poison is gone from her body.

As much as I missed my Ooza and my Rainbow Dancer, I was thankful for my journey. I was a Daughter-of Love and I felt enriched by all the souls I had met along the way. Yes, this journey has come a long way in empowering me. I curled up beside an apple and fell into a deep sleep. My dreams were about Ooza, books and crying because I had to leave the village. Rainbow Dancer and I were Zelka's target and I knew, I was putting others in danger by staying. There was a flash, advising Ooza to keep his distance from Zelka. Then I was talking to Cythera and Raziel and asking them to protect him. There was Rainbow Dancer, Bonnie and there was Chomp. Then there was darkness, there was fire, and there was Zelka and she was laughing. The laughter wasn't joyful, it was mean. No, it was beyond mean, it was eerie.

Rainbow Dancer was hurt and village people were helping him heal. Ooza was in a protective bubble saying that he wanted to find his Princess. Next, he was wearing Queen Chayzlazamia's scarf and she was promising to dress him like a prince.

My disjointed dream continued with Rainbow Dancer, Ooza and I running on the side of a mountain and he was telling me he concentrated on being home and fitting in. I wanted to remember that and I began to wake up.

My eyes saw the apple orchard and I closed them again and in the dreamworld I saw Princess Amita, only she was strong and healthy with jewels in her ears. She was smiling at my Ooza. Then I was crying, sobbing, and in fetal position crying yii, yii, yen and I had no idea why or if I was doing it right. The dream ended with me holding the last note of the song and seeing the Seashamana around me.

Chapter 45 - The Tree Trunk

When I opened my eyes, I wondered if I was seeing the same portal that Tuppie had seen, but it disappeared before I could completely focus on it. The leaves were rustling off to the side and four deer and an elk walked into the orchard eating apples and nearby nettles. Would the deer or the elk eat me too? Was I really back on Earth? Oh my, I was barely taller than the apples. Have I been sent back as a small rodent or large insect?

"Psst!"

What was that noise and where did it come from?

"Psst!"

There, I saw something in the leaves beside the tree trunk. It was smaller than me with a roundish head and its eyes were like the small diamonds in the geode. Its neck was long and it had wings. It was, and even its wings were, golden and shining bright. Then it disappeared. Sort of, for it might have turned green, I wasn't sure. Had my eyes played tricks on me?

I glanced over at the huge hoof of either a deer or an elk, I had never seen one from this perspective, so I wasn't sure. I swear my eyes became quite large and I wanted to yell, 'please don't step on me!'.

"Psst," I heard again and when I turned, I saw a golden light, maybe it was a creature; again I wasn't sure. It did seem to be holding a piece of bark or was it a small door? Anyways it looked like a door and it seemed as if it was being held open, beckoning me to go inside the tree.

Taking a chance of having a deer or an elk step on me or going inside a tree with a strange looking golden creature, those were my choices. So I ran to the door. Once inside, there was a space surrounded by wood and two little golden creatures.

"What does ye want?" one of them asked.

"What do I want! You beckoned for me to come."

"Well, ye woke us up," said the other.

"Sorry, I didn't mean to," I said timidly.

"Ye didn't mean to? How could ye not mean to?"

"Truthfully, I have no idea how I woke you up. I don't even know who you are."

"We are the Wight brothers and we have not flown for a very long time," one of them said looking quite confused.

"We came from Yggdrasil," said the other, as if that was supposed to trigger something for me.

I didn't know what to say so I just said, "I'm... sorry."

For quite awhile they stared at each other, tilting their heads from side to side, and sometimes they looked upwards. It was as if telepathically they were having a conversation.

What could I have possibly done to make these bright little golden creatures think I was the one who had woken them up?

The first one turned to me and asked, "Ye really don't know who we are, do ye?"

"No, I don't and I'm sorry I woke you. I really didn't mean to disturb you," was all I could think to say.

"This is an enigma," the first Wight brother said to the other. They tilted their heads back and forth before looking at me and saying, "Ye are an enigma."

"I'm... sorry."

They seemed to be talking to each other again, although I couldn't really tell. Then the first one continued, "It is not ye's sorry that we need."

Then the other one said in a less frustrated voice, "Ye came from a place of innocence. Do not be sorry We are the ones who are confused. I guess we thought we would be wakened by somebody powerful who knew they needed us and why. We need to figure this out. What power did ye use to wake us?"

"I'm sorry, but I don't have any powers and I really honestly don't know why this happened."

Again they talked and he said, "Honesty and innocence are very powerful. I see Love within ye and Love is the most powerful of all."

Having no idea why, I broke into tears. I don't know what

kind of tears they were, maybe they were tears-of-self, but all I knew is that they just happened. "I try, I truly try," I said through my sniffles, "but I make so many mistakes. Actually, I'm not always honest and I'm not... not always innocent and I'm not always full of love. I do try to always come from that place, but sometimes I'm just not clear." I thought of my dream and Zelka's laughter. "Sometimes I'm just full of fear, but I really do only want to always come from a place of Love."

"Ye are very trusting, ye have shown ye's vulnerability. Ye do not even know who we are and yet ye are willing to scrape the bark off ye's own trunk and yell for the fungus to come and destroy ye's core," stated the first one.

Jolted from my tears, I wiped them from my face and then I nodded. "Well, sometimes I find life an enigma," I said, getting stronger as I spoke. "You just finished telling me honesty and innocence are powerful. And then you tell me, by being so, I am yelling for the fungus to come and destroy my core, so I'm confused. Honestly, I too am just trying to understand."

"Oh, now we see her bark," said the first brother.

"Her bark didn't attack and it didn't come back with blame," said the other.

"No, it merely questioned," said the first brother. "She did not take the comment to heart, crying like she had made the mistake, nor did she attack, blaming us for her tears or her emotions. She stayed within her honesty and innocence."

"She upheld her individuality and was true to herself," said the other.

"She differentiated," said the first one.

I had heard those words before. They were similar to, or the same, as the ones Raziel said. Right, follow my instincts. Did I feel any danger when I walked in here? Did I feel like I should run away as I did with Ol' Man Gar Cave? No, I felt protected and safe the moment I entered their tree fort. On that note I sat on the floor, crossed my legs, and listened as these two beings, who had just woken up, banter back and forth.

"Her bark is strong." said the other brother.

"Resilient to fungus, but not gnarly," said the first brother as he moved his head back and forth. The light in his crystal eyes varied with each movement.

"Sometimes fungi can lodge within cracks of gnarly bark."

"Many of those trees move."

When I left Raziel, soon after he told me to differentiate, Rainbow Dancer and I were on the edge of a cliff. I climbed a gnarly tree. I remember thinking before I climbed it, that it looked as if it could move in an un-tree like manner and it did. It took us down to the mudflats where the ugly transparent creepyworms chased us.

"Roots are not deep enough."

"They move up and down, but not forward."

This time I interjected and with excitement in my voice I quoted Tuppie, "*There is a time to stay connected to ye's roots and there is also a time to have faith in their nourishment and move forward.*"

"Life is like an ecosystem, it is.. all.. about.. finding.. the balance," remarked the other brother slowly, tilting his head from side to side. "Ye look like ye is from the planet Earth, but ye don't sound like ye are. Are ye?"

"Yeah, how do you know what an Earthling looks like?"

"We used to live within the ecosystem there. We gave and gave. The more we gave, the more they wanted. Again and again, we compromised ourselves. The more we did, the more they took. We showed signs of our vulnerability and we were attacked," the first brother told me.

"That's not all true," said the other, "there were a lot who were giving and receiving."

"Yes, and some were giving so they could receive."

"Yes, some did it out of fear of us not being there, instead of from love and appreciation for us being there. It is like they forgot that they are male and female and their yin and their yang has to be balanced inside."

"We have to remember we are raw energy."

"We're an energy and we spent time being still, for a reason.

Now that we are back, we will have to dance for those who come from a place of Love."

"Yes, until we do something they don't understand and then they will stop talking to us and blame us. They won't realize, we are only trying to help," said first one.

"There is a reason why a human from Earth woke us up. There has to be a strong movement towards love and working in harmony there. I suggest ye drop ye's frustration before ye go there and talk to Earth Mother. Maybe then we could find out what is really going on."

Finally, they acknowledged I was still there and the first brother asked, "So ye came from Earth?"

"Yes," I answered for the second time.

"Do ye have a life still on Earth?" he asked.

"I think so."

"Well, either ye died from ye's previous life or ye have a life still on Earth."

"Honestly, I don't know. I've been here for a while."

"She has to still have a life or she wouldn't have been able to wake us," said a female voice.

"Mother Wight! How long have ye been here?" the first brother asked, as a white figure, looking the same as them, flew down from the wall.

"I have been here the whole time listening to ye boys. Ye's ready to fly off to Earth to find out what is going on. Ye won't even come see ye's own mother first, to find out if that is the right thing to do. Do ye not think I have any wisdom? I brought ye two up didn't I? Guess I gave ye too big of an ego, because ye don't even come talk to ye's mother anymore. Ye think ye know it all."

"Mother Wight, um, um, we are sorry," they said in unison.

"Now listen here Missy," she said looking at me still sitting on the floor, "we were protected by Ancient Crystallized Wisdom. Ye would have to be innocent to do this, yes, but ye would also have to be far from naive. Ye know exactly what is going on. So what is it, girlfriend. I am tired of listening to ye's, 'I don't know what happened', drivel. Why did ye wake us up? What is it that ye are expecting from us?"

"I, I, honestly, I don't know. I don't even know anything about Ancient Crystallized Wisdom."

"Ye can't go through all ye have been through and not know. Ye would have had to have been buried in the darkness of Earth with the desire to grow to find the light and the truth. Ye would have to have roots strong and deep into Mother Earth with faith and determination to find nourishment. Ye would have had to fully understand and live the twelve gifts of the Seashamana. Ye would have to go into the blue and find its beauty and that is only part of it. So don't ye come across all naive to my boys. They may buy it, but I do not."

I didn't know what to do or say, "Eh I, I, well I have been buried in the darkness of Earth, but not in the way I think you mean and I don't think I have roots, at least not like a tree."

"Were you underneath the Earth?"

"Eh, well once when I was little I fell into a big hole and my parents had to pull me out. I fell into a basement once. Plus while I have been on this journey I have spent time going down a river which was inside a mountain, but I could always see the light. Except when I, when I," suddenly I felt quite light headed, maybe because the energy felt very strong, but I took a deep breath and continued, "fell into the basement and when I went in Ol' Man Gar Cave, but I didn't stay long there. I didn't want to be there. I just wanted, I just wanted to be in the light."

"Ye really are naive. Ye really don't know."

I merely shook my head.

"Ye were completely innocent when ye woke us up and ye have no idea why or how."

This time I nodded my head.

"We have to figure this out. Ye were not buried like a seed, but ye were kind of buried and ye sort of felt buried by darkness. When ye sort of felt buried, did ye always have the desire to grow?"

"Most of the time, yes."

"Did ye always try to find nourishment?"

"Most of the time I tried."

"Did ye always try to see the light?"

"I guess, I did always try to see at least a glimmer."

Mother Wight looked confused, "But ye roots would have had to be strong and deep into Mother Earth."

"I love Mother Earth, it amazes me how she keeps adapting, compromising, and giving."

"But ye have never had roots?"

"No, I try to imagine I do sometimes, just so I can stay grounded and receive the gifts I'm supposed to be receiving. I guess I always try to have faith and determination. I usually always try to find the nourishment."

"Ye would have had to be above it all for a long time."

"Well, I feel like I've been on this journey for a long time," I said, shrugging my shoulders.

"Alright, what about the twelve gifts of the Seashamana?"

"I do not even know what they are," I said shrugging my shoulders again.

Mother Wight started to laugh and then she repeated, "Ye don't even know what they are?"

"No, I don't think so. I've seen the Seashamana three time... well, two times for sure, the other one I was just waking up, so I guess, she could have been part of my dream, but she never spoke to me."

"Just waking up," she laughed again, "yes, just waking up. Ye have only seen her two, maybe three times. During ye stay with the Ashaman, did ye or did ye not learn the twelve gifts?"

"Is that what you call the people who stood around looking down at the big bowl?" I knew I had botched the description of them, so I didn't wait for an answer, I merely continued, "I did not really stay with any of them. I merely observed them. Does it have anything to do with tears? I learned about tears."

Mother Wight only sighed before she asked, "Do ye know the only way to truly rejoice?"

My mouth opened and "Eh," was the only sound that came out.

Chapter 46 - The Blue Yonder

Standing there, I probably looked dumbfounded, but really, what was the only way to truly rejoice? I didn't know. Then the Wight brothers in unison chanted:

"The only way to truly rejoice
And have joy
Is to always:
Learn the truth,
Hear the truth,
Observe the truth,
Accept the truth,
Honour the truth with love,
And Present the truth,
with love and respect
for yeself and others,
Always.

And always
Love and serve,
within the truth
Live, walk, and work
within the truth
And finally be
Grateful for the truth

I probably still looked rather stunned. Should I ask what the truth was? The truth seemed to vary with perspective.

"Did ye not learn the twelve gifts of the Seashamana?" Mother Wight questioned, but didn't give me time to answer before she asked, "Have ye even walked within the white?"

Finally, something I knew I had done. I responded with excitement, "Yes, I have." Oh my, I hope I didn't sound too much like a child who had succeeded in getting the correct answer.

"And ye walked within the blue?" Mother Wight asked.

"Yes."

"Ye had no fear and saw the beauty of the blue."

Was that a question, I wasn't sure, so I just said, "I think so."

"So ye were able to get out of the blue and see past it?"

"Yes."

"Were ye able to fly?"

"Yes,"

"What am I missing boys?"

"Heeding ancient crystallized wisdom while being trapped within darkness, so ye can find joy while being a seed," they said in synchronicity."

"Oh," I gasped covering my mouth with my fingers for a brief moment. "I wasn't the one who woke you up."

"Honey, were ye the one that hit the golden winged disc? Were ye or were you not?"

"Yes, but...."

"Ye were the one inside a crystal at the top of the tree?"

"Yes, but... but when I hit the golden winged disc, I had Tuppie with me."

"Tuppie?" She emphasized, although I wasn't sure if it was recognition or confusion.

"When I met him, he told me to call him Tuppie."

The Wight brothers interjected saying, "T .U. P. P. I. E. Trees Unite Protecting Purifying Into Eternity."

"Well, he didn't spell it for me and he didn't tell me it was an acronym. I... I didn't know who he was. I... I thought he was a rock until his shell cracked open and then I still didn't realize he was a seed until the Seashamana came, and.. and his roots went in the ground, but then he grew... into a... man."

"He was a crystallized seed when he was with ye?" she questioned.

"Yes," I said.

"And ye are sure he called himself...?"

"Tuppie," interjected one of the Wight brothers, "He was trying to get a message to us."

"I don't know anything about a message. I learned his name before we had even flown. Like I said, I thought he was a talking rock, but that was far from who he was," I said with a bit of shame. "Once he became a man, he said he was The-Son-of-The-Tree-of-Life."

"The-Son-of-The Tree-of-Life woke us up!" said the boys. "We have been woken up for a very, important reason."

"Where is he now?" asked Mother Wight.

"That I don't know, he walked up blue stairs into the sky and faded away. I'm assuming he is somewhere in the blue."

"Gather the troops boys. We are flying into the blue."

Standing by the door, I listened to the hum, watching many golden Wights fly upward and beyond. I felt like the teacher watching the children run out of the school and away into the blue yonder. Only I wasn't the teacher. I was the student and being a student of life meant school was rarely out.

Reeling from my crash course of experiencing some of the ancient crystallized wisdom and learning some of life's great mysteries, I wondered, would I be able to move forth, walking within the truth? Would this infinite source remain with me so I could always feel the warmth within my core?

Has my life always been about being conditioned and trained for something greater? Have the trials and tribulations I have gone through been for deeper understanding into something far beyond me? Holy, wow, little ol' me, somehow part of the divine plan?!? I would never be alone again.

Even if I was a tree growing alone in a field, I would still be branching out with my talents and abilities. I would always be The-Daughter-of-Love and Mother Earth would always be there giving me nourishment. Tuppie was The-Son-of-The-Tree-of-Life and to him getting nourishment from the Earth was innate. I guess it is for humans too, we just eat differently, although where I came from, it was often a forgotten truth.

If I was a tree, I would love to be an arbutus tree for it often grows by the ocean enjoying a beautiful view. It has beautiful green broad leaves that are sustainable year after year. It also produces red berries within every season. I guess my desire would be to produce nourishment as well as to shine with sustainable beauty all the time - not just for a season.

However, there was something wonderful about growing in the cycles of nature - about taking the time to go within so the manifestation of a new seed can sprout nourishment.

Staring at a bruised, unripe apple, I smiled, for I had given my apple to The Empress so I knew it was being engulfed in love all the way to the core. It was being nourished until it was sweet and ripe. She would make sure it never rotted.

Throughout my journey I have had to learn how to trust in the benevolent forces. Wouldn't it be nice if I could always feel that energy of love straight through to my core and always feel it running through my spine. Was that kundalini power?

Many of the apples were bruised, starting to rot and again I thought of Tuppie's words. "*Don't eat rotten apples and some unripe ones can be very bitter and can upset your stomach. Other ones that are not truly ripe can have some bitterness, but also can have a lot of nourishment. Look at the wor....*"

Thud...what was that? An apple had fallen from the tree and was rolling on the ground towards me. It was slightly bruised, ripe and looked deliciously nourishing. Thank you! Apples may be about the words, or the world, or maybe even about the worrying, but right now, for me, it was about the nourishment.

I pulled the bag out of my sleeve and brought out the jack-knife Rainbow Dancer had given me. Cutting a small piece off of the huge apple, I bit into its ripe juicy flesh. Feeling the nourishing healing energies throughout my body, I gave thanks.

My eyes followed a tree up to the sky and suddenly I broke out in joyful laughter. The sun was shining bright, however, blue clouds began to illustrate the sky. The air cooled. Should I see if the Wight's door was still open? If I need shelter, it will be open or protection from the elements would be provided in another way. There was abundance everywhere as long as I trust, believe, and pay attention to my instincts.

Watching one white snowflake as it descended from the sky

and then another, I merely saw the beauty and not the worry of the coldness coming. The apples would soon be going to seed for they weren't rotten, they were simply going through a cycle. A cycle of not giving nourishment to their two legged, four legged and winged friends. Instead giving thanks to Mother Earth as they were fertilizing the soil because soon there would be a cycle of cleansing and going within. Then a different cycle would begin where they would be seeking nourishment so they could grow anew and be able to give outwardly again.

It's sad how many people chastise themselves or are chastised for going through their cycles and not being amazing at all times. On Earth there were many healers, messiahs, prophets who the masses flocked to. How difficult it must have been to be expected to be a healer at every waking moment.

Were they meant to be healers or were they simply meant to be waking people up? Did they want to teach the people to feel love within themselves and spread that healing energy? Or did they want to be worshipped like a god and be expected to be the only ones who could heal and perform miracles?

I would like to think they were full of love and they wanted to help wake people up, so those people could also know about the magic of love and be able to feel it deep within their core.

Watching these quiet, soft, beautiful puffs fall from the sky, I felt their wet coolness as they purified and cleansed me. It was almost as if I could feel a shift in everything around me and I became acutely aware that there were birds calling out that it was time to find shelter.

There's a cold breeze coming
and we need to find
a warm place to be
Come on
Come on
Take shelter from the storm

The leaves that were left on the trees were waving in the

slight breeze.

Good night
Good night
It's time to close our eyes
Good night
Good night
Our cycle is complete

Snowflakes landed upon them as they fluttered their ending note. Twirling and dancing, the leaves left to begin their new journey, caring for and fertilizing the soil for new growth.

Come on
Come on
Take shelter from the storm
There's a cold breeze coming
and we need to find
a warm place to be

That was the song that the birds sang while I spontaneously twirled and danced along. My head was tilted towards the sky. My arms were stretched in the air, watching the birds and the leaves. Moving and twirling in a moment of joy, that's when I saw it - a sparkle and then another.

Playfully catching the sparks of energy, my head began to feel like it was filled with air. My body felt light and began moving above the rotting, bruised apples. Up to the tree tops I flew, past the few ripe apples that were still attached to the trees and then I saw it - the tiniest apple I had ever seen.

It was ripe and beautiful. Smiling, I landed and picked it from the tree before I took flight again, flying high above the trees and into the sky.

Wow, I had no idea where I was going, I was flying and that was all that mattered. The heaviness was gone, the worry was gone and I was back on my journey. A journey towards love.

Soon a familiar voice found my ears, "The snow is descending upon our wings. It is not a time to be flying out in the open. You need to go back to your nest and be safe until you know which way to go."

"I would love to go back to my nest," I said with a smile. "But I am lost and in a strange land. I do not know which way to go, I do not know where it is safe."

"You made it back and you're flying!" said my bird friend.

"I am back! I've had an amazing journey!" I felt my cheeks puff out as I smiled brightly with a new sense of awareness.

"Would you like to share my nest for the night?"

"I would love to share your nest for the night, thank-you for all your kindness."

We flew up to a nest that was neatly tucked in and sheltered from the weather.

My bird friend said with a bit of a bow, "Your apple is now ripe and it is beautiful."

"Thank-you, but it's not the same apple. The one I gathered before I left on my journey, an Empress took. It was weird, for a lot of people seemed to be after that apple, but I still don't understand why an unripe apple was so sought after."

"There are those who hunt the weak and the injured."

I was still confused and asked, "Was the apple symbolizing me - bruised and unripe?"

My bird friend merely repeated, "There are those who hunt the weak and the injured."

"Do they hunt the weak and the injured on purpose?"

"Some do and some don't know why they do it, they just do. Some change when they realize what they are doing. Some don't," my bird friend answered. "Tomorrow we shall sing. Rest now, be joyful, and sleep well."

"Thank-you, thank-you so very much," I said, nodding.

A slight bit of sadness weaved its way through. I had been excited to share my adventures, but my bird friend nuzzled his head into his chest and closed his eyes. A new day would soon arrive and sleep might be just what I needed.

Chapter 47 - The Return

The next morning was odd. My bird friend didn't say a word and simply hopped upon the edge of the nest and sang:

One of the wonders
You of longevity
Patience and perseverance,
Oh wise woman of time
You that brings guidance
You that brings perseverance
and transition of time
Let's form a dance
Let's form a dance
Time to gather
Time to dance together
We will form a dance
We will form a dance
Oh wise woman of time

"Now we wait for the white birds, right?" I asked.

My bird friend nodded.

"Thank-you for sharing your nest," I said. "Thank-you for everything. I have had amazing adventures and I have learned a lot," but before I could continue, a white bird flew towards us, sat on the edge of the nest and looked at my bird friend.

My bird friend placed my apple on its wing; similar to a penguin presenting a stone to its potential mate and said, "She has gathered."

I didn't remember gathering anything, unless I was only supposed to gather an apple. The white bird jumped into the nest. He brought his shoulders back and down and stared into my eyes and I began to feel sleepy.

The next thing I knew, I was no longer in the nest, instead I was in the air, gliding. I was flying! Or... was I only dreaming

I was flying? Everything felt surreal. Was I still in the nest? Had I fallen asleep? Is it possible to sleep-fly? In yesterday's world one could sleepwalk, but sleep-fly? If I was awake why don't I remember flying away, but if dreaming, why was I aware enough to think?

Oh my, I have become caught up in the wind. Catching my balance, I became acutely aware of the present and felt wide awake. One can wake up while sleepwalking, maybe I just woke up while sleep-flying.

Snowflakes were glistening in the sun. I felt a bit awkward, for flying was still new, nonetheless I was managing. Hearing a familiar rumbling sound, I swooped lower. It was a wagon with vegetables.

Once again I was on the back of the wagon smelling the dirt and the sweetness of the vegetables! I was on a wagon like this when I first met my bird friend, but this time I didn't hide. I had no worries, so I simply smiled and enjoyed the bumpy ride.

After a while I saw another wagon ahead of us with two people in the front. Oh no, I think we're going to hit it, but the man's donkey slowed just inches from the other wagon. We travelled like that for a bit and then the man began waving his fist saying words that I didn't understand.

His words became clearer as he yelled, "Hey, doesn't that animal go any faster?" Before the person had a chance to answer he screamed, "Get out of the way!! This is a road you know! Hurry up! Move!"

A strikingly beautiful woman in the passenger side turned around and in a loud but calm voice said, "Would you be this rude if you felt we were not moving fast enough while walking on a path? Would you be this intimidating to an older person or a young child walking through a doorway or lining up at the vegetable market? Are you always this much of a bully?"

"No," he said defensively. "That's different."

"Well, which is it? What is your truth? What is your true personality, because it is still you, whether you are in a wagon or not. By the way, up a wee bit there is a place where we can move out your way."

She faced forward again and soon they pulled over so we could pass. She smiled and waved at me. Why didn't I jump onto her wagon? I didn't know where I was going and I would feel a lot safer with her. Waving, I turned back to look at where the man was going and I saw the corner with the cobblestone path, and it was then I knew the temple was my destination.

Standing on the back of the wagon, I jumped, ready to fly onto the cobblestone pathway when something happened. I didn't know exactly what, but my body tingled, it felt strange, and the cobblestone pathway began to blur.

Oh my, was I going to pass out? Phew, I didn't. I was standing on the pathway?!? In the distance I could see the very large woman coming with her broom. She was still wearing her grey dress and the funny, almost wooden looking hat with a brim.

Now what was happening?! I wasn't passing out, I was growing taller! I was probably up the woman's knees. Pleased that I was no longer the size of an insect or of a mouse, I moved my shoulders back. Standing tall and proud, I thought of the Rofonians as I took confident steps towards her.

"It is a beautiful day," I said loudly, projecting my voice towards her.

"Yes, it is," she said looking down and then she lifted her head and smiled. "And a new day it is at that," she commented with a slight bow of her head.

The doors of the temple were large. Not quite as large as they looked the first time, but I was not as small as I was then. It was all in the perspective. My feet stopped as I stood and stared at the large looming doors. Was I ready to enter the temple?

"The doors are open, my friend. That they always are."

Out of the corner of my eye, I swear, I saw her leaning on her broom, but by the time I turned my head to acknowledge what she had said, the large woman was no longer there.

As I walked slowly to the door, I realized it was open, just slightly. Would I be able to squeeze through? No, not even if I held my breath. The doors looked very heavy and large, looming far above where I stood. I have to believe I have been led here and thus I will somehow find the self-confidence and strength to push them open.

A deep breath filled my chest. With my spine straight I approached the door and to my surprise it swung open, exposing the large room. Only this time it wasn't so empty as there were three chairs, instead of one, and also there was a table.

Pink and grey tiles reflected the colours from the stained glass windows until a glow of a golden-white light entered. Staring in awe, I wondered if it was too bright for my eyes and then I saw her. She still looked wise and beautiful with her long, flowing, golden brown hair framing her face. She sat still, cross-legged, slightly above the floor with her eyes gazing upon two round orbs levitating slightly above her hand.

An aura of light illuminated around her. Was it the brightness of her aura that had prevented me from seeing her when I entered the temple? She had not changed since I first walked through the wall and began my journey. This time, though, I was sure she was aware of my presence and for a brief moment I thought I saw her smile.

Then she began to fade. It was odd, for the brightness around her was still there, but it was like she was see-through and I could now see the two doors on the other side. They did not have knobs or handles and I stared at them as if I instinctively knew they were going to swing open and they did.

The man with no hair entered the room and exposed his bald shiny head as he bowed. His brown hooded robe was not unlike my indigo hooded robe, but he still reminded me of a monk. His hands were folded in his sleeves, he did not seem to acknowledge that I was there.

Staring into the brightness he said, "We have a visitor."

Last time I was here, I was hiding under a chair, but this time I didn't want to hide. Standing straight backed and confident I watched as the light shifted and she took form once again.

"I know," she said in her soft and soothing voice.

"Do you think our visitor has learned about the primal power?" he asked as if he hadn't really seen me.

"Ahhh, the one that is light-giving, active, and of the spirit," she said with a nod and a glance that led back down to her still orbiting world, but she hadn't really answered his question.

Primal power? I didn't learn anything about power, did I? I was introduced to ancient crystallized wisdom and to some of life's great mysteries, but power? It wasn't about power, was it? It was just an amazing journey. I mean, I learned a lot. I learned about love, about connecting, about respect, release.... Oh my, the Monk's walking towards me.

He bowed to me! Do I bow back? Instinctively I heard, 'yes,' so I did.

"Welcome, please," he said in his soft voice, "I know who you are, but I do not believe I have introduced myself. My name is Bong."

He said his name as one would if they were making a sound effect for a gong. I made a feeble attempt to copy it, "Bong?"

He crossed his arms, nodded, and with the same oddness as he had the first time, he repeated, "Bong."

I was somewhere between amused and surprised. I didn't know what to say, so I simply stood there wearing a stupid grin.

Then he distracted me by speaking in his normal soft voice and saying, "There is a chair waiting for you."

Oh my, the chairs... the chairs with the crystal balls at the bottom of the legs. When I first arrived, I was as tall as the balls, now I am much taller, but the chair was still very big. How was I supposed to sit in it? I wished I had the Rofonians' golden steps but maybe, if I reached my arms as high as they could go, I would be able to awkwardly climb onto it.

We walked across the floor in silence. I hurried because I knew how slow I had to walk when I was with the Rofonians as their legs were much shorter than mine. Wearing my indigo robe next to them, I probably looked as odd as Bong did next to my small frame. Had I looked like a monk in an indigo robe to the Rofonians?

As I neared the chair, glowing golden stairs appeared, allowing me to walk up them and sit gracefully.

"Thank-you," I said with relief.

Bong gave a slight nod, as I sat dangling my feet off the edge, like a child full of innocence and joy. He sat in the chair beside mine. We faced a wooden table etched with a landscape and figures. It appeared as if it told a story. To the right of the table was the woman with the long golden brown hair.

There was silence for a moment before she spoke, "It is the continuance of time and power of persisting, you have persisted and you are here. Is there anything you wish from me?"

Is there anything that I wish from her? Huh, I didn't know what to say. Here was a chance to ask this amazing woman anything! However, to be in her presence was overwhelming.

"Is there anything you wish from me?" Bong asked and I was thankful for his interruption.

"Tea would be lovely, thank-you," answered the woman.

"I shall go then." Bong stood up and walked across the marble floor and when he arrived at the swinging doors he turned towards us, bowed and left.

Everything was still. Was she simply waiting for me to answer her question. What was I to say? I closed my eyes and all I saw was apples. "I thought I might see The Empress. This time I have a ripe apple," I said.

"Ah, you have learned about the forbidden fruit," she said with a smile and a soft kind voice.

"Apples are forbidden?" Oh my, that was a stupid thing to say, for I knew that was not what she meant, so I asked, "Does the apple or the fruit, symbolize words?"

"In the beginning, the word," she nodded and finished with, "was misunderstood."

Chapter 48 - Eating The Apples

A door swung open, my head turned, and my jaw dropped slightly. I expected it to be Bong, but instead two children entered.

In yesterday's world I would have guessed the girl with light shining from her eyes and long curly hair would have been about seven or eight years old. She had the brightest smile and eyes I had ever seen. The boy also had long hair, only his was straight. His eyes had a shine of curiosity and his aura seemed to have a sense of purpose.

The two of them bowed and walked towards the chairs. I turned my attention back towards the woman with the golden brown hair, but she was no longer there. The children simply sat in the chairs and didn't say a word. We sat there for a few moments looking at each other.

"I am The-Child-of-Love," the girl said with a smile that made her eyes look even more bright than they were before.

I had to smile and with a bit of a bow I said, "I have recently discovered that I am The-Daughter-of-Love."

She bowed back, "Then we are sisters. Pleased to meet you and you may call me Windwillow."

I was about to express that it was a beautiful name and say hello to Windwillow, but before I could the boy said, "That is a beautiful name. Hello Windwillow."

They came in together, but they did not seem to know each other. Maybe she merely made her name up for the day and he was playing along or was he reading my mind?

"Well, everyone seems to call me Princess and you both can call me that too."

"Hello Princess. You are here because you have questions about your journey," she said astutely.

"Yes!" I answered, even though I didn't know that was the reason I was here, "Do you know about my journey?

"We know you met The-Son-of-The-Tree-of-Life," said the

265

boy, his hands pressed in a prayer position as if he was trying to contain all the excitement and awe expressed by his eyes.

"He's Breezy, The-Son-of-Love," Windwillow said, bringing her arm out. She didn't point one finger at the boy, instead she pointed with all her fingers straight and spread apart. Closing her fingers, she brought them to her heart before she asked, "What did The-Son-of-The-Tree-of-Life tell you about your journey?"

Windwillow's front teeth protruded slightly over her bottom lip and she smiled, seemingly excited to hear my answer. She wasn't the only one who was excited. I was also, because Tuppie had taught me so much and I was going to be able to share some of his teaching with someone.

Recapping some of my journey, I finished with what he said just before he walked up the blue stairs, "I've been trying to figure out whether he was going to say words, worry, work, or world? What do you think was he going to say?" I asked.

Before they could answer Bong appeared. He set the tea on the table and straightened back up. The children's eyes widened and in unison they said, "Bong," like they had hit a gong.

A vibrating golden energy illuminated, manifesting itself into what appeared to be a solid. Bong stood beside it, put his palms flat upon the lit wall, spread his arms out to the side and moved the light, exposing the inside of another room.

Inside the new room was a large, lit dish, not unlike the one I had seen when I had first picked up Tuppie.

Again there were people of all ages, but this time they were of all races and many different hair colours. There were twelve of them standing around the bowl all looking down at the bottom, until Bong took his place among them making thirteen. The children didn't move, so neither did I.

Windwillow stretched her arm out with her palm up and an orb, looking like the planet Earth, appeared on her hand. Staring into it she said, "Do you see that mother, she is worried about her child. She has forgotten about the purity of love.

She thinks worry is love. She paces in her darkness and her fear. Do you see her?"

"I'm sorry I just... I just see an orb, I don't see further than that," I answered.

"Oh," she said looking at me as if I was from another planet, but in a gentle voice she explained her reaction, "I have never met anyone who could not see inside the orbs."

"And I have met very few who could," I said with my eyes pleading for compassion. "However, right now I am following what you are saying and maybe someday I'll be able to see. Please continue."

To my surprise she didn't say anything more, nor did she continue looking into her orb, instead both she and Breezy picked up their tea and became enthralled with the people standing around the dish. I was not sure if I actually shrugged my shoulders at that moment, but I too picked up my tea and did the same.

After a couple sips of tea, Bong raised his head and said, "Bong!!"

Then in succession, the others around the dish raised their heads and the first one said, 'Bong', and the reverberating sound went around the bowl until it ended with a hum.

In unison they took two large steps backwards and three golden stairs appeared leading up to the rim of the dish.

Sipping our tea as if we were watching a movie, Breezy, Windwillow, and I sat waiting for something else to happen.

One woman, who stood on the far side of the dish, looked at the person next to her, made eye contact and did the same with the rest around the bowl. She put her hands in a namaste position and put her chin to her chest. She brought it back up again, brought her arms to her sides, her shoulders up, then back down, and with perfect posture she walked up the stairs. She sat upon the rim with the soles of her feet together and her knees off to either side of her body.

The golden stairs disappeared and everyone took two steps forward, taking their place looking down to the bottom of the bowl. I heard a faint 'bong' before she gracefully, in one sweeping motion, brought her head down, her legs out, and taking on a similar shape to a banana she lay on the inside rim.

Hearing another soft 'bong' the children stood up as she began to move feet first around the sides of the bowl.

Windwillow looked over at me, smiled, and said, "You can watch now. Go, run softly, and take her place."

My mouth dropped as I looked at her in disbelief. I looked over at the very large bowl.

"It's alright," she reassured. "Go quick so you can watch."

Timidly, I tiptoed over. The golden steps took on a different form which allowed me to walk up gracefully and look down the bowl where the lady had been looking. I was just in time to watch her take her last one and half rotations around the bowl and go feet first through the hole in the bottom. As she did, I thought I saw a spiral slide appearing in front of her and disappearing behind her.

Once she was out of sight, there was a moment of silence and again Bong raised his head and said, "Bong!!"

The one next to him raised his head and repeated it, and one by one the others around the dish, in succession, raised their heads, and reverberated the sound. By the time the reverberating 'bong' sound came to the last few people, it was only a hum. I was pleased that I only had to join in on 'the hum', because I was not sure that I could have mimicked their sound.

In unison they all seemed to take two large steps backwards again. There was room at the top of my stairs for me to do the same. Again, stairs appeared leading up to the rim of the dish. The child beside me looked at the person next to him, made eye contact, and one by one eye contact was made with the rest of the people around the bowl. The child put his hands in the namaste position, put his chin to his chest, brought it back up and walked up the stairs in perfect posture. He sat on the rim of the bowl with the soles of his feet together.

The stairs disappeared and everyone took their place looking down at the bottom of the bowl. A faint 'bong' happened and he lay on the inside rim of the dish and began circling around the dish until he descended down the hole.

The hole then turned into a purple, pinkish orb. The orb cleared and I could see what looked to be a hospital room similar to what I would see on Earth. There was a woman pacing with another woman who sometimes was standing beside her and sometimes looking like a light form. Also there was a light beside the child in the bed.

"Can you see inside the orb?" Windwillow whispered.

It was only then that I realized she was standing beside me.

Nodding I whispered, "But it all just went blurry."

"It is the mother spreading the blurriness of worry and of fear. The energy she chooses to be within, is her choice. The woman who left here has connected with the energy of a loving friend or nurse. Here, we work within the energy of love so she has to get her vibrations back up so we can do our work."

Then Windwillow smiled the cutest smile and music played, the bowl disappeared, so did the room, but not the people standing around. Music began to play and we danced and we danced. As we danced, I saw ribbons of colourful light energy streaking between their hands and sometimes they would toss it in the air or towards the ground.

We were dancing for quite awhile before the people in the room faded and I found myself once again sitting in the chairs with Breezy and Windwillow.

"Do you see that couple?" asked Breezy, holding an orb.

Everything had become serious once again, and I still could not see anything but the orb.

"I see," said Windwillow.

"I hear," Breezy added. "I hear lies, manipulation, jealousy, blame, and hate and those words don't have any nourishment."

"The shame of it is, those two people really do love each other." Tears fell like gentle rain upon Windwillow's cheeks. "There is so much work that needs to be done."

I thought about the village where I met Ooza and I realized that I hadn't heard those words there. There was nourishment, healing, music, and joy in that little village. In the Land of the Shimmering Bridge those words were only part of the Camflages' language, but not that of those who shimmered. In the Rofonia Naroso there was Respecia because those negative words were forbidden.

Breezy looked at me and said, "In my beginning, I guess I was born innocent and there wasn't forbidden fruit around, but there must have been in that couple's life. They just took too many bites and I think now those toxic words are so familiar to them that they wouldn't know what to do if they had the right nourishment."

I nodded, thinking, yeah, in the beginning.... Yeah, I guess in my beginning, I too ate that forbidden fruit. Sadly, people are still dishing it out, some even put it on a platter as they serve it.

"You are probably right. I wonder if they heard what you just said, whether they would really understand what you meant.

When I first began my journey here, I ended up in a village where I was given a bag of love. I was safe when I called upon the benevolent forces and remembered that I had Cythera's bag of love and protection. Her bag of love and protection saved my life while I was being chased by those creepyworms on the mudflats. I didn't see the Shimmering Bridge until I saw my patterns. I needed to see them first, before I could escape, because it is only my patterns that I can change."

Windwillow nodded and responded saying, "That makes sense."

I changed my focus to Windwillow. "I was that bruised apple and I am the one who should have been innocent. It is so hard being innocent and not being naive. Naivety is being gullible. I want innocence with awareness. So, I think I finally have it right or am I just stupid and keep making mistakes?"

"Living here at the temple, I'm learning, growing, changing, and becoming wiser every day, but I don't get it right all the time. Does that mean I am stupid and making mistakes?" The light in the Windwillow's eyes dimmed and her voice was grave with concern.

At that moment Bong entered the room looking confused. The children turned and said, 'Bong', and once again the room within the room appeared.

"Why would it be a mistake to learn, grow, change and become wiser ever day?" Bong asked as he walked towards the new room.

I did that. I was putting myself down, not realizing that I was projecting my conditioning.... that conditioning I thought I had awakening from, was still there. The thought pattern that 'if I don't answer it right, then I was stupid and I have made a mistake'. I just projected that onto a sweet innocent girl. It was my words that caused the light in her eyes to dim.

"I saw the light fade a bit in your eyes when you thought you had made a mistake and I am truly sorry."

"What did you learn?" Breezy asked.

About all the mistakes I had made and how I had been stuck in patterns, I was about to say, but instead I laughed at myself, smiled, and said, "I am learning, growing, changing, and becoming wiser every day."

Meanwhile Bong had opened the other room exposing the dish with only ten people around it, for neither the woman nor the child were there.

"The other two are not back yet and duty calls," Windwillow informed me.

"Remember, do not bite into anything that takes you away from love and that includes words you tell yourself," cautioned Breezy.

"Words like food," I said, thinking about Scota's wisdom and then I smiled. "Some foods are hard to swallow, but I like your idea better, just don't take the first bite."

He and Windwillow walked away to do their duty and I watched for a time. After a while I looked over at the woman who had reappeared. She was sitting motionless levitating two orbs and I smiled and bowed.

"It is your birthright to shine and feel love," she said with a slight nod.

"Wouldn't it be nice if I could give that gift to others and always remember to cherish it," I said with a radiating smile. "In the now, and in the future?"

"Ahhhh," was all she said looking at her orbiting globes.

"I think I'm ready to go back to Earth," I said with a smile and a nod.

"The choice will always be yours," she said as she levitated. "Because you are here, not to control my destiny, but instead to give love, guidance and protection." The memory of her being there after I was shot, flashed, so I finished with, "And sometimes make miracles happen, especially for those who truly desire to heal and come from a place of love. Thank-you for loving me and seeing who I truly am."

She smiled within her stillness, however she didn't disagree or agree.

"Am I supposed to stay and find the Empress?"

"Ahh, love is everywhere," she said in her soft soothing voice and the light around her became brighter.

"Am I going back to Earth? Is this why my journey has brought me back to the beginning?"

"Ah, in the beginning." Then she became still, so very still.

In awe I watched as she seemed to become more and more engulfed within the light. First glancing towards Bong, the children, and the others, I turned and looked back at her and the orbiting worlds and suddenly the whole room changed.

It was like it had got dark on this side of her and light on the other side of her. Not knowing what to do, I shifted myself into a more comfortable position where I could stare at what looked like the whole universe with all the stars and planets.

The whole universe had taken over the room. There was too much to think about, too much to digest. Suddenly my mind became still, there were only the stars, and then there was nothing. Feeling very tired, I closed my eyes, hoping when I opened them, I would be able to see.

It felt like just a blink, but when I opened them back up, the darkness was gone, there were no stars, just a large room with paintings on very high ceilings.

Paintings - some reminding me of my journey here, as they were very close to what I had experienced. Others made me look at my experiences in a different light. Some had nothing to do with me, but seemed conducive to a lot of beliefs throughout my world and beyond.

Still others reminded of my life on Earth -my 'yesterday's world'. What had happened to that life? A life that seemed so real, but now it felt as if it was the illusion. An illusion that had been lost in an unreal sense of time?

Looking across the large empty room with three chairs, I stared at the door. It was open a crack with a light shining through. Was the opening an invitation to another journey? Or was it the way to the portal taking me back to Earth?

My eyes gazed around the empty room with the marble tiles that seemed to go on forever. The stained glass windows were once again reflecting colours on the floor. Will she return again? Or is she still here, shining a light so bright that I can't see her with my naked eye?

Will she answer more of my questions or do the answers lie in a story that has been coloured with the chakras of time and there to be reflected upon? Reflected upon like the stained glass windows with the pieces that were once separated and now put together. Funny though, I can only see the whole picture when the light is shining through.

Wondering if Windwillow and Breezy were the ones who were going to sit on the rim this time, I made my way over the pink and black tiles.

Chapter 49 - A Seed In A Cave

On one of the windows I saw a village of people, dancing and playing instruments. It looked like the village where I had first met my Ooza. Something about the thought of Ooza made me smile. He had so much goodness in him, but Zelka's words made him feel like he wasn't accepted for who he was, but in Zelka's case it wasn't merely her words. No, it was her intent that was skewed and that intent came with an energy.

Ooza became messed up because he thought of her as someone who truly cared about him. He took a huge bite of the forbidden toxic fruit and digested it far into the wounds of his childhood.

Zelka was from the darkness of Ol' Man Gar Cave and only cared about herself. She seemed to like the ugliness and wanted to lure the village into that same place. She was very good at manipulation and knew how to pretend she was the victim and how to pretend she was very loving.

I remembered Ooza saying, '*she says that my singing and the way I dress makes people think I am strange or better than them. I shouldn't be this way. Do I come across arrogant? Am I hideous? I shouldn't be this way. People here are only nice to me because they feel sorry for me. Zelka says she likes me the way I am but she is just worried about how other people see me'*.

It was Zelka's earlier words, energy, and intent that made him feel like he should change, and not sing or be his happy self. She made him feel like she would be the only person who could accept him for who he was and everyone else was only pretending.

The energy and intent behind what is done and said is the most important and sometimes the hardest to see-through. Many Zelkas aren't translucent like the Creepyworms, thus often it is often hard to see what was at the core of their fruit.

As a child I grew up in a type of environment where people

274

were stuck within the pattern of controlling others. Was it merely their pattern of controlling others or did they enjoy being that way? At that time, I changed my clothes to please them and I curbed my singing and dancing and became trapped within their darkness and they still weren't happy. I wonder, was it just a case of misery loves company.

After a while they didn't have to serve me that toxic fruit anymore, because I would serve it to myself. I had to learn to sing and dance again, I had to learn to honour my child within and love myself. Have I changed enough? Have I learned enough? When I go back to Earth, will I able to stand tall through all the cycles of change?

Ooza didn't always stand tall through the cycles of change, but he always got back on his feet and he always remained rooted in goodness. Will I be able to always believe I am rooted in goodness?

Today I know I am rooted in goodness and I know that everything I went through was all part of a journey that I'm learning from. Yes, I have to trust, because I really want to see my family and friends again so I will trust and believe I can go back to Earth with a new perspective on life. Yes, I would go back and be much more about the now, because I was stronger.

To stay strong, I was going to need to find amazing people like Queen Chayzlazamia and the Rofonians. Plus, all those wonderful people I met in the village. Cythera, Bonnie, Chomp, and all the healers, yes, those who just love me for me. The ones that, without a second thought, would risk their lives to save mine. They knew what to do and they all worked together to make sure Rainbow Dancer and I were looked after and able to heal.

Looking at the stain glass pictures, I saw otters playing in a waterfall and another picture of a mother and child. Studying them some more, I saw white birds carrying a basket. I thought of Earth and the story of the stork bringing children to their families and then I thought about the cranes bringing me to the waterfall and what an experience that had been flying through

275

the mountain.

Unexpectedly, the stained glass window began to glisten and move like waves upon an ocean and then disappeared from my view. The side of the wall had different colours reflecting upon it and I was walking backwards. Or was the wall going forward? I was not sure. Suddenly, I disappeared. Where had I gone?

Oh my, I had moved through the temple wall, but I wasn't back where I started. I was with the cranes and I wasn't being carried anymore, I was flying! Yes, I was flying on my own! I must be caught in their updraft as their wings were flapping and to me it was an easy flight. We flew high above the trees towards the mountains. I don't know what I have done to deserve to fly, but wow, was it amazing.

We were close to the mountains when I had a weird feeling. Was I changing size again? Oh no, we were all going to crash into the mountain wall!! The cranes shifted and I was shifting, just not in the same way and I lost my updraft! The next thing I knew, I was inside a crane's mouth, peeking out and holding onto the edge of it.

We zigzagged in and around the massive rock banks. Wow, thank-you, it still was hard to believe how much I was being looked after.

Darkness was setting in when we arrived at an opening and in the distance I could see a beautiful waterfall. Oh no, the crane shook his head and I was no longer in its mouth. Falling, I have been here before, only I was in a basket and the cranes caught me, but they were flying past me. Caught once again in the updraft, remembering I could fly, I watched the moon peeking its light over the top of the waterfall.

Was I headed back to the village? Was that where the amazing people I need to find lived? I thought I was headed back to Earth. Abruptly the cranes dove into a pool of water. I followed, but this time I was swimming - swimming on my own! I arrived at a place where colours were still reflecting, only there was water coming down hard and furious. Was it a rain storm? Where was I? The walls around me were dark and damp. It actually reminded me of Rainbow Dancer's cave.

Had I gone back to that time? - A time before I had seen the Empress, before the unripe apple was given away; before Rainbow Dancer and I had headed on our journey? There wasn't a crane to be seen and it seemed like I was in a cave behind a waterfall. I didn't see any otters. I couldn't have travelled back in time or could I have?

My fingers edged themselves to my sleeve. Yes, I was still in my indigo robe - the robe that Raziel gave me and that was after Rainbow Dancer and I began our journey. My eyes closed for a few seconds. Listening to the water, I evened my breath. Standing against the damp cave wall I heard music. The water seemed to be humming a song.

That is when I heard the familiar voice. "Hey ye, ye in the waterfall, we should be going soon."

Well, I seemed to be the only person in the waterfall. The voice sounded deep and familiar. I felt disoriented. I peeked through the water. There was no one to be seen. Placing my hand on the rock, I stuck my head through the cascade.

Oh no, the water was blinding my eyes, I still couldn't see anything. Blinking, I realized that there was a pool of water down below. It didn't seem to be that far, but I was unsure if it was deep or if there were rocks beneath the surface.

Laying on the ledge, the water pelted my head, clouding my eyes. I inched and squirmed. Finally, I was able to bring myself out of the water where I could see. Oh my, was I back on Earth? There were flowers and ponds and steps in the background. Wooden steps like one would see in a tourist area. The water below was deep. Should I slide myself down and swim across to the other side?

Something began to move! It was a large turtle and it disappeared much like the turtle had when I was with the cranes. What was I hearing? The water was too loud. Suddenly everything went still, so very very still. I was frozen with part of my head sticking out of the waterfall! Water that was no longer moving! Even the drops at the end of my hair hadn't finished dropping! I couldn't move forward and I couldn't move backwards! My eyes could move and my chest was still going up and down. I guess at this point I shall be thankful I can breath. Voices, that was what I thought I had heard; did I hear people talking?

"I know my mission is to take her back. This journey of hers is over," said the jovial familiar voice of Tuppie.

"Not yours to say."

Was that Raziel's voice?

There was laughter. "I have been sent here as her connector. I know my mission."

Tuppie, the Son-of-The-Tree-of-Life is my connector?!?!

"Back there she is needed," said Raziel.

"Yes, I know," Tuppie said with a laugh.

"No," Raziel's voice replied.

"No!" Tuppie laughed some more before he questioned, "Why does ye say no?"

"No, not there, back to Ol' Man Gar Cave," Raziel clarified.

Ol' Man Gar Cave!?!? No, no, no, I don't need to go there. I'm never going to go back there! No, no, I'll go with Tuppie. I'll take my chances on the blue or out of the blue into the white, or jumping down a hole and coming back through fire as a seed or a rock.

Sorry Raziel, but I am not going to go into that... horrible energy of Ol' Man Gar Cave, I tried to say, but my lips couldn't move. Did they even know I was here? Did they know I was listening?

"What needs to happen will," Raziel stated. I wanted to question what he meant, but since I was only able to listen, he continued, "The village believed Zelka was innocent. Marred now with gossip, torn with insecurities and guilt, most were lured into the darkness."

Chapter 50 - The Face in the Waterfall

Oh no, not the village people! They were all so wonderful.

"I could go instead," offered Tuppie.

"Connecting is your job. Rich soil under you. Light above you," Raziel said.

"Yes, I'm merely The-Son-of-The-Tree-of-Life."

"A tree not known to them is who you are."

"They probably would need someone they trusted and ye are right, they do not know me," Tuppie said sadly.

"It is she who needs to go," Raziel stated.

"Why her?"

"Zelka thinks she has won," Raziel anwered

I don't care if she thinks she has won, I don't think I'm strong enough to go back into that ugly energy. That cave is too evil! It's my life so why can't I be part of this discussion.

"She was a good student through our travels and was able to fly for a short time, but not ready. I know that cave and I don't even know if I'm ready. Princess is much too innocent, also somewhat naive. I can't believe ye would send her there."

"She is strong. She released the Wights I hear," said Raziel.

"But she did that with power of innocence not the power of ancient wisdom. Raziel, ye is a magician, ye is an angel, ye knows about transforming energy, why don't ye travel into the ugliness of Ol' Man Gar Cave?" Tuppie pleaded.

"Noticed by Zelka I would be," Raziel answered

"Wouldn't Zelka notice her?" Tuppie asked.

"Maybe, maybe not"

"Chomp, his baby, his wife are trapped." That's Bonnie's voice, what's she doing here? "Cythera's husband is with her baby, but Cythera is trapped."

Oh no, not Chomp, not his baby, and not Cythera. I didn't know they had babies. Have I been gone that long? Stopping my thoughts I listened as her voice continued, "Cythera tried to get them out, but her anger must have come forth when she

279

tried and she has been unable to get out of the cave."

Cythera, the one who saved Rainbow Dancer and me, by making us our own little secret garden! Cythera, who gave us a bag of protection which saved our lives again! She was so amazing and powerful and she has been unable to get out?!?

"Chomp, Cythera, babies?" Tuppie questioned, "I see why you need help, but I don't understand why ye need her. There has to be someone else. She has been bruised more than most. If this Zelka sees her bruises we could lose her too. Are ye ready to take that chance?"

"My name is Bonnie and these people are very important to me and to her. If Raziel thinks she's the only one who can go there, then I trust him. We are asking for help. She will have angels on her side. She will have miracles and all the magic that comes with the light. She has to make it through."

"It is dark in there, young Bonnie, and I know that it is hard to see the light when ye are in the middle of darkness."

Yes, The-Son-of-The-Tree-of-Life because he had been a seed trapped within the darkness of a hard shell.

I heard him continue, "If she goes back to blaming herself, or if in her resistance she blames us, ye, or life for making her feel like she had to go into that ugliness again, then...."

"Support is never found within hate and blame. Her decision will need peace and strength from her core. She has that, yes." Was Raziel asking or did he know?

"Yes," confirmed Tuppie "or we couldn't have released the Wights."

"Faith, trust, she will have to have. If the choice is to go back, she will have to follow the turtle heads." He paused for a few moments and then said, "Goal to find the light must be the focus. Knowledge, she will find it,. Movement towards it, cannot cease. Apples nourish by staying within core. Wight roots hollow," Raziel said in his monotone voice.

"I don't understand," stated Tuppie

"Deep roots to crystal rise. Find flight," Raziel answered

Well that answer didn't do anything to help me understand.

"Do you think she will be able to get them all out?" asked Bonnie.

There was a pause before Raziel spoke, "No." Then there was a longer pause before he said, "To stay is theirs, not hers to decide. Leaving those behind, she will have to be within core until top is chopped"

Last time he spoke that way I didn't understand until I needed to. I was glad everyone was patient and didn't interrupt, because when his words made sense I was sure glad I had heard them.

"She will go, won't she and she will get out, won't she?" asked Bonnie.

"I cannot answer that. To go or not to go is hers to decide. No blame or judgment on her choice. Choice not ours to make. Swimming across the dragon's domain. She will leave them far behind. Turning around not an option. Behind the veil. Behind the piano keys. Options then still her choice."

With the water droplets still frozen in time, I wanted my voice to be heard, but it was still silenced. Well Raziel, I guess you have succeeded in putting me between a rock and a hard place. Cythera couldn't make it out of that cave and she was way more magical than I could ever be.

The choice was mine, right? However, I was their hope and apparently their only hope. No pressure here.

Earth! I could go back. I could swim across and leave them far behind. No judgment, no blame, yeah, just love, but could I keep that faith within the darkness. They got themselves there, probably trying to help.

It doesn't make sense. We're supposed to be kind and we're supposed to help, but often we're taken advantage of and end up getting trapped in someone's darkness. Now I was being asked to be kind, change my course and to help those lost in the darkest of dark and not get myself trapped. Oh my, I must send them love for they are already trapped.

Suddenly the water formed a film around me. It kind of felt like my head was inside a bubble with water pouring down its rounded sides.

"Why are you concentrating on forbidden words? Why are you worried?" said a voice.

"Windwillow!!! Windwillow is that you?" My lips worked! "Yes, it is me."

A light breeze slightly warped the bubble around my head and it seemed to clear the drops of water that had been pouring down its side. "Where are you, I don't see you. I do see a willow tree," I said, trying to peek out through the bubble. "Are you in there?"

"I am in the wind and I am in the willow and you are in my orb," she answered in a voice that made me think of Windwillow's bright, shiny eyes and her beautiful smile.

"But we can talk to each other, I didn't know you could do that with the orb."

"Neither did I, but remember, you won't be able to hear me if you are full of blame. It was only when you sent them love were you able to hear my voice."

"Oh Windwillow, what am I supposed to do?"

"It's your journey and I can't answer that, but I can listen."

"I am just trying to make sense of my journey so I can receive the guidance I need. I came to the conclusion that I couldn't find love in the darkness and that was why I couldn't go into Ol' Man Gar Cave. The energy was sooo horrible, when I was in there before, fear permeated straight into my bones," I told Windwillow. There was silence. "Windwillow are you there?" Again there was silence.

Oh no, has she left me? I tried to move, but I was still stuck watching the water pour down. I could still see the weeping willow. That was good, wasn't it? Weeping, weeping, willow. I got it. She can't help if I'm weeping with worry. Oh, my tears-of-self.

The villagers are the ones that are truly stuck in the darkness, but I still have a choice. Earth has its share of challenges and I have patterns to break and I am worried about those on Earth. I thought I was supposed to go back there and I felt like

I was ready. There I go again, I must send love to those on Earth and to those in the cave. Yes, I have to keep sending them love for I am The-Daughter-of-Love.

"Yes, you are The-Daughter-of-Love. Do you hear me now?" came Windwillow's voice.

"Yes, I do!"

"Trust your journey, believe in it. No one can control who you are, not when you know that you are rooted in goodness," Windwillow's voice whispered.

"The woman in the temple relinquished control over my journey, but I also know she was there to save me when I was shot and really needed help. What was it that Scota had said when she was talking about the clones? They were caught in a power-over cycle and if they continue... eventually they will be no more than hopows. They will be no more than automobiles because they believe it should be about control and that is what they will create. Then when she spoke about what the clones were doing she said, *"Defend we will. Think like them and power-over, we will not."* Is that what you mean?"

"I am not sure I know what you mean. I don't know about Scotas, hopows, or clones," Windwillow answered.

"Well," I said, trying to reword it. "If I believed my journey is being controlled and I put blame when it doesn't go exactly the way I want it then, I will create a state of being controlled and blamed. If I believe my journey is protected by Love then I will create a state of Love, but is it even possible to create a state of Love in the darkness of Ol' Man Gar Cave? I'm scared if I go there I might spiral backwards. If I go to Earth I will have The-Son-of-The-Tree-of-Life as my connector! At least I think that's what Tuppie meant. If it was, then I will find the right people and find my way towards goodness. Isn't that the way I'm supposed to turn, towards goodness and happiness? Isn't it what I am supposed to do? I don't understand."

"Believe that is where you are going. Believe in Love, no matter where you are," she answered.

"What if I get stuck in the web of their lives and never get out. What if I mess up?"

"You just don't..." was all I heard.

"Don't what?" I asked, but I couldn't hear anything else. "Don't get stuck? Don't go into Ol' Man Gar Cave? Don't go back to Earth?"

Windwillow didn't answer.

"Windwillow, please stay with me!!"

Still there was no answer, tears streamed down my face and through my tears I said, "If you can hear me, I guess I just want to say thank-you for listening."

It was then I heard her voice, "Please remember that I can hear you and please remember to feel my love."

Her voice faded with her words and... Huh, my bubble burst and there I was with the water streaming down my face once again. I could see cranes standing, guarding each side of the pool. I could see the river with the coral waving on the sides beckoning me towards the waterfall near Ol' Man Gar Cave. Oh my, it was blurring and I could see the familiar flowers and wooden stairs. Do I leave it all behind? If so, will I ever be able to come back? My vision blurred again and once more the cranes appeared.

Was I caught between worlds with my options depending on my success? What did that mean? Do I hold my breath and take a deep, deep dive into the middle of the mountain? My vision blurred and the familiar flowers were back and I thought I saw Tuppie.

Bringing myself up on my hands and knees I pondered a small dive and an easy swim.... but what about the villagers that saved Rainbow Dancer's life and my life too? They had accomplished something amazing - a community with just love and acceptance. I remember thinking I certainly didn't want to see anyone ruin it, but it looks like that has already happened.

Now they were trapped in darkness and I was in a position to help, but was I strong enough? Was I capable or would I be trapped with them, in darkness, forever....

Maybe I will end up a mere face in the waterfall, maybe I

would be a picture, tastefully positioned in a row of stained glass windows with the sun reflecting upon my tear drops of indecision within a waterfall?

Again I saw the cranes and in the background I saw Bonnie and Raziel.

I heard Raziel say, "Clarity needed, clear water, deep, deep, yes, valve must be locked."

Once again it changed, only this time there were two people walking down the wooden stairs. As they approached I could see it was a woman and a tween (at least she looked as if she'd be about that age).

"The moon's going to be full tonight. Did you know that?" I heard the girl say in her elated tone.

"No I didn't. I guess I don't really pay attention to things like that," responded the woman.

The moon is going to be full tonight? The moon was full last night, but this looks like Earth, maybe time is different here.

As the girl walked closer, she looked right at me and said, "Look, there is a lady in the waterfall."

The woman glanced at the waterfall, smiled, and responded with, "You have such a wonderful imagination."

The girl left the woman's side and walked under the willow branches. Her face peeked out through and she stared at me for a while before she said, "I see you magical lady of the water-fall, I really do see you. It doesn't matter what anyone else thinks, because I believe in you and I know, all you have to do is believe."

Watch for Linn Frances' next book,
"Primal Power 3 –The Face In The Waterfall"